Aereas swung his ornamental sword, aiming for the fiend's great neck. Just before the blade contacted the gray-pink scabrous flesh of the vrock, something massive struck Aereas and sent him spinning.

The sword whirled into the open beak of the thing and slashed through its bony cheek, widening the evil smile on one side. But it did not cut the head loose, did not even puncture the eye.

As the blade was wrenched from his hand, Aereas tumbled over and saw his attacker. Above him, the sky was not blackness, but prickly armor and a fierce, hate-filled grin of glee. A cambion. The elflike face of the warrior was a mask of blue-black steel, leering after him.

Aereas struggled to escape this thing, but it lunged toward him and clasped his neck in an iron grip.

A sudden panic swept through Aereas, a terror like nothing he had ever known. It was not the crushing force on his windpipe, nor the horror of wrestling a thing from the Abyss. It was something else, as though the cold touch of those clamping fingers not only held him now but extended their reach back through all his days and would hold him forever, irredeemable.

He thrashed, and the grin of the cambion deepened. Its teeth were like a wall of yellow pickets, its lips black and lumpy as a dog's.

The darkness in Aereas's eyes thickened, giving way to a pulpy redness. He knew it was his own burst blood vessels he saw. The world closed in until only that yellow smile remained.

The BLOOD WARS™ Trilogy
J. Robert King

Blood Hostages

Abyssal Warriors
June 1996

Planar Powers
December 1996

BLOOD
HOSTAGES

The BLOOD WARS™ Trilogy

BOOK ONE

J. Robert King

BLOOD HOSTAGES
©1996 TSR, Inc.
Cover Painting ©1995 TSR, Inc.
All Rights Reserved.

First Printing: January 1996
Printed in the United States of America.
Library of Congress Catalog Card Number: 95-62075

9 8 7 6 5 4 3 2 1

2616XXX1501

ISBN: 0-7869-0473-9

TSR, Inc.   TSR Ltd.
201 Sheridan Springs Rd.   120 Church End, Cherry Hinton
Lake Geneva WI 53147   Cambridge CB1 3LB
U.S.A.   United Kingdom

To the Editors:

Bill Larson for Heart,
Jim Lowder for Carnival,
Eric Severson for Rogues,
Patrick McGilligan for Hounds,
Barbara Young for Hostages,
and Brian Thomsen, Marlys Heeszel, Lisa Neuberger,
and Sue Weinlein . . . for patience.

PART I

THE READERS

ONE

KIDNAPPED BY
GARGOYLES

This place is a miracle, thought Aereas, his lean adolescent frame draped over the guest bed of his uncle's sprawling cabin. It was midnight and hot, and he was wide awake. He lay there in the candlelight, his thin nightshirt moving just slightly in the window's warm breeze, his brown eyes tracing out the complex cluster of rafters above.

If he knew his uncle, this jangle of rafters wasn't haphazard carpentry, but adherence to some sublime order, some undefinable purpose. He wondered suddenly if the rafters echoed the constellations: Nunieve the Watchful, Valasares the Tricksy, Jouan the Fierce. . . . Perhaps Uncle Artus had fixed the spinning, whirling heavens into the ash boughs of his guest-room ceiling.

Aereas thought on this. How many summer nights have

I lain here and not noticed those odd rafters? How many summers have I spent in this place without noticing the strangeness of it, of Uncle Artus? Aereas was seventeen now, and that made for thirteen such summers, thirteen years—an ill-omened number at best.

Artus. He'd always seemed eccentric and amazing, but this summer the man reeked of otherworldly knowledge and power. There was about him the scent of distant briny beaches, horned and many-headed monsters, vast caverns, and tumbled skies.

Of course, Artus had traveled, mostly because of the ogre wars. He'd been an airman in the griffon light cavalry, and had seen a thousand thousand places. Occasionally, now, he'd bare a scarred shoulder or a lashed back to tell the story of how he'd gotten this or that wound, and to Aereas the crisscrossed flesh seemed a map of the journeys the man had taken. Those adventures were echoed also in Artus's voice, with its strange cant, its inflections of sultry jungles and rarefied mountaintops. To look into the man's pale blue eyes was to see other lands: Artus had flown griffons into swirling cyclones, seen sunken Lockervale, visited the Six Corners of Magic, consulted with the fey . . . and lived through it all to build this cabin, a sprawling monument to his travels.

But now Aereas sensed something else about the man, something that sent a tingle of possibility through his brown hair.

Take, for instance, the cabin's foundation stones. Aereas knew that each had been handpicked by Artus, hand-scrubbed, and placed for texture, color, shape, and size. But it was only this summer that he'd found out the walls were more than walls. During thunderstorms, they channeled lightning strikes; on sunny days, they stored heat.

If Artus had harnessed the power of storm and sun, what other forces intersected in his aged, leathery hands?

The key to that genius lay on Aereas's slowly breathing,

sleep-softened chest. A journal. *The* journal—Artus's account of his travels. The book could explain it all. . . . And that, more than anything else, was why Aereas couldn't sleep.

He had known of this book from the time his mother had let slip about it, but no one, not even Artus's adopted daughter, Nina, had seen the book. . . . Not that the cousins hadn't asked to see it; not that they hadn't diligently searched the cabin to find it. They'd discovered plenty of other things—lodestones and astrolabes and miniature siege weapons and tunnels leading into living caves—but never found the book. And Artus had never given it over.

Until tonight. After an hours-long discussion of medieval tribalism and oceanic weather phenomena—a conversation that had sent Nina fleeing from the vaulted dining room—Aereas had decided to turn in. That was when, without discussion or even request, Artus had relinquished this single thin volume into Aereas's hands.

"Here's the book you've been asking about," the man had said simply, his balding head glistening in the light of the low-burning candle that had lit their discussion. With an avid attention that was both paternal and avuncular, Artus had continued. "Not even my daughter has seen this. But you're seventeen now, and it's time for you. I see more than a little of myself in you. In fact, I'd say you're the spirit and image of a young me. And if you're going to understand me—understand yourself—you'll need to understand this."

Aereas had grasped the book in one hand, running the other through his hair. "Are you sure? I'd just decided this thing didn't exist, or if it did, that I'd never see it."

Artus had nodded sagely, though his veined hand quivered slightly as he patted the book. "It is time." He then had smiled—that guileless, wise, and wide-eyed expression he had. "I imagine if your mother were still alive, even she would say it was time."

Aereas had swallowed then, deeply, studying his uncle's

short, round form as though the man were half gnome—a
notion that seemed more than possible now, as Aereas lay
on the guest bed, beneath those astronomical rafters.

"Here goes," he muttered with a sigh, then slowly
opened the book. There was no introduction to this world-
shattering work, no preface or preamble. The whole thing
started with a simple date—"E.T. 3025 (175 C.C.)."

Aereas paused. Epoch Time 3025 (175 Caonan Calendar)
was almost 500 years ago. Either this was something other
than a journal, or his uncle had secrets Aereas was not
braced for. He peered at the book again.

*E.T. 3025 (175 C.C.) Unless I've gone barmy, I'm tem-
porally dislocated. Yeah, I must be, though I'm as surprised by it as the reader must be.*

Again, Aereas paused. "I." That was the telling word. Either Artus believed he had existed five centuries ago, or he
was writing a piece of fiction. The next words confirmed it:

This isn't addle-coved fiction.

The sentence was underlined, as though the very book
could read Aereas's mind, sense his doubts. That fact was
horrifying enough to make the rest of it—the strange text,
the promise of secrets revealed, even the arrangement of
beams in the ceiling above—seem bearable by comparison.
Aereas read on:

*Of course, the temporal dislocation is unimportant
given my spacial dislocation. I'm out-of-town, at least,
and most likely out-of-touch altogether. In short, I find
myself on another world.*

Aereas had braced himself for this startling revelation,
but now gaped stupidly at the open page. *Another world.*

*It's got to be another world—not so much because of
the strange name the locals call it (Toril), but because of
the smell of it, and the weight of me on it, neither of
which is right. I gave old Sung Chiang the laugh, all right,
but maybe the last laugh's on me. Where the hell am I?*

*'Course, I'm doing my best to find out. On arrival, I
tried a quick circumference experiment, using a nearby
tower and its shadow. I learned within half an hour, as I
sat in a small café (which, by the way, has no interest in
my brass jink; thank Nunieve for gold), that Toril is a bigger world than our own world. The hourly triangulated
progress of the tower shadow across the square proves it.*

*As I already said, I first knew the place was different
by the smell. Oerth had such a scent as this, of sweet
grasses and wide-open places, and now I know that Toril
does, too.*

*And, yes, I should have known I'd end up out-of-
touch and out-of-time. You can't jump through just any
of Chiang's magic portals and hope to land right side up.
I'm lucky my little trip to Gehenna didn't put me in the
dead-book.*

This time the book nearly closed, Aereas's finger marking the strange words. A trip to *Gehenna?* The *dead-book?*

Who was this man, this Uncle Artus? Aereas was beginning to think he didn't know him at all. Was he just a
short, plump, slightly gnomish, hermitlike genius? Or was
he some archmage, some fantastical spy? Despite the
man's cabin, sprawling and organic, attuned to celestial
powers, despite the stories of griffon-riding and ogre wars,
Aereas had difficulty believing that Artus had actually
traveled to other worlds, let alone to Gehenna. That place
was supposed to be filled with volcano fire and fiends.

And what of Nina, Artus's adopted daughter—Aereas's
cousin? Was she from another world, too? She fit the part:
beautiful, proud, her olive complexion alien amidst the

ruddy stock of Artus and his forebears. She was clear eyed and volatile next to Aereas. She was mysterious, angry, fiery, ineffable. For all the cabin's wonders, she considered it a sort of prison.

Not that it had always been so. When the cottage was no more than foundation holes with cedar-frond ceilings, Nina had been happy. In those young days, she had been a feral creature, rushing past lodgepole pines to leap hartlike down craggy slopes and dive into tidal pools below. She had taken Aereas on many such runs. But as the cottage grew toward completion, with its inevitable rafters, so too did Nina. And she seemed to fear completion as though it were death.

Aereas sighed, his breath wafting over the book clutched warmly to his chest. Yes, she was a creature of mysteries in a place of mysteries, and the weight of those thousand enigmas pressed wonderfully upon Aereas. He lifted the book and again found his spot.

Good portal or bad, I'd not even be alive (albeit in this incorrect place and time) if it weren't for such a solid yugoloth guide.

Aereas shuddered. Yugoloths were powerful fiends that Aereas had only just convinced himself didn't exist. Now, with all the terrifying fury of superstitions once dismissed, those beliefs came rushing back upon him.

Being so dislocated in time and place, and having found so delightful, elegant, and inexpensive a street-corner café, I thought this the perfect spot for starting this account . . . and for rooting through my keys.

Aereas's eyes had barely passed the last letter of that last word when there was a long hiss from the rafters. No, not from the rafters, actually. From the lofted study his uncle kept in a high corner of the cottage roof. The sound had been like an intake of breath—only too long, longer by far than the breath Aereas had gasped and now held in his lungs.

What had that sound been? Imagination, spurred by thoughts of yugoloths and Gehenna?

No. There it was again. It was like the hiss of a burning log banked in the study fireplace, and the scent that wafted slowly down from the rafters was tinged with smoke.

Now there were low voices. Someone—Artus, obviously—speaking to someone else. Nina? No. The voices were too low, and though Aereas could hear none of the words, he could feel the subvocal tension of the exchange. Artus would never speak to his adopted daughter that way.

Aereas rolled his feet from the bed and lifted the candle from his nightstand. When he stood, the book remained in the warm well where his body had been.

Artus and his visitor seemed to be alerted, whether by the crackling creak of the straw mattress or Aereas's looming, nightshirted shadow leaping up toward the open ceiling of the loft. There came a hushed silence, then the telltale click of a lock, the gentle grinding of a bolt being drawn into place.

Aereas moved toward the door of his room and, with equal care, slid the latch back from it. As he silently opened the door a crack, there came a troubled rumbling from the narrow stairway beyond—from the study at its top.

"Unc?" Aereas called, his voice gagged with fear.

His inquiry was answered by an abrupt thump, followed by a clatter and a shout. Then came the urgent roar of his uncle's voice: "Blast! They've nothing to do with it!"

Aereas bolted up the twisting stairs that led through cedar-paneled darkness to his uncle's study. His candle-shadow thrashed through the passage as his bare feet slapped the oiled wood of the treads.

Another calamitous crash from the room beyond. Then, from behind Aereas, came the booming thump of Nina's door flying open into the hall.

Aereas reached the stout door that led to the study and tried the latch, though he knew it was locked. He stepped back and smashed one muscled shoulder against the wood. It thudded dully but did not give way.

"Unc!" he called out again as he struck the door a second time. The taper shuddered in the candlestick, threatening to go out.

"Get gone, boy!" shouted Artus, the sound seeming to come through gritted teeth. This command was followed by the shattering of a window. "Get Nina away. Take the horses!"

"What's going on?" cried Nina, from directly behind Aereas. She had always approached that way, swift and silent and intense. Her nightshirt flapped dangerously close to the sputtering candle as she lunged for the door and clutched the latch.

"He said to run," Aereas gasped hollowly to his cousin.

"Like hell," she replied, her brown flesh going red.

With a gesture that was both graceful and imperative, she thrust him out of the way and lifted one foot before her. The nightshirt rose up her slim leg as her heel smashed thrice into the stout door. At the third strike, the wood gave.

The door flew inward, drawing Nina and Aereas after it into a room in shambles.

The tight, triangular loft was strewn with books, some lying half in the hearth where the fire licked at them, others torn and tattered beneath the ubiquitous shelves. Artus's armillary sphere, a complex figure of brass arcs and model planets, lay toppled on the floor. Its slim rods were dented, the planets rattling against the flagstone fireplace. The desk and chair were overturned, and Artus's wineglass lay against the wall, flung somehow whole to where it had splashed its redness on a patch of plaster.

All of this Nina and Aereas saw in a moment, before their gasps told them it was not smoke they had smelled, but brimstone. Then they glimpsed the threadworn fabric of Uncle Artus's house slippers disappearing into an impossibly small cabinet. One big toe, jutting through a worn slipper sole, wriggled a final time before the feet slipped from sight.

The cabinet shuddered for an instant and was still. It was Artus's tobacco stand, a narrow octagonal pillar meant for storing long-stemmed pipes. Its cupboard, knee-high but less than a handspan in width, was where the slippers had just disappeared—a space too small for a man's feet, let alone his whole body.

A moment later, there could be no doubt where Artus had gone. The hollow echo of his voice spilled out of the stand: "Get away! Take the horses!"

Gaping, trembling, the cousins staggered toward the cabinet. Then the lifting of hairs along their necks told them they were not alone.

Spinning about, they saw a small gray gargoyle crouched in the transom above the study's door. It could have been a harmless bit of statuary except that, with needle fangs bared, the creature spread its stone wings and dropped on them.

It attacked like a hairless wolverine, a blur of fierce claws and teeth. Aereas struggled to push it away, feeling its scaly flesh beneath his fingers. Nina snatched up a book and used it to shield against the thing's barbed, lashing tail. Neither could keep at bay those fangs, gnashing in its grinning, cherubic face.

Aereas reeled back toward the door, but the thing sunk its teeth into his shoulder. He was borne to the ground by the unreal weight, the horrific strength of that tiny, repulsive being.

Nina lunged away for a moment, grabbed a flaming brand from the hearth, and swung it at the thing. Its clawed hand flung out like a tiny bear trap to seize the burning end of the log, and the beast hissed in a sibilant, abyssal voice.

The language it spoke was one neither cousin had ever heard before, but both intuitively understood it: "Think, deary. I live in Gehenna. You expect a little fire to scare me?"

That grin again, the needlelike teeth clicking together just as the creature's claws sunk into and burst the tip of the firebrand.

Aereas, despite the throbbing wound in his shoulder, reached out with his other hand and latched on to the beast's barbed tail. He immediately wished he hadn't, for the thing pierced him like a scorpion's stinger. He screamed, thrashing his pinned and helpless hand, all to the gargoyle's amusement.

Through the shouts of her cousin, Nina lunged for the creature. Her hands wrapped about its stony neck to throttle it. The flesh beneath her fingers was cold and hard, and the imp laughed as it inexorably rammed its teeth toward her. They fastened shallowly into her straining cheek, slicing through skin to meet near her own teeth. Then, in a red spray, the thing lurched back to admire its work, to swallow.

"Still aren't thinking, are we?" it asked. "Let's not underestimate our opponent."

Nina locked her elbows, struggling to keep the creature back. It could have killed them both already—that much was clear in its lightless eyes. It either didn't want them dead or was having some cat-and-mouse fun before the kill.

Nina grimaced, the teeth once again looming closer. "Is that where they took him, my father—Gehenna?"

"Why not wait and see?" asked the imp. Its tightly toothed mouth was so close to Nina's bleeding cheek that she gagged from the brimstone breath. It took another nip of her olive flesh, leaving long thin lines of blood, and said, "After all, that's where I'm taking you as well."

With that, the imp's bear-trap claws wrenched Nina's hands from its neck, and its barbed tail flipped Aereas bodily into the air, as though tossing a straw dummy. Next moment, it held one wrist of each cousin in grips like shackles.

"Do let's be going," it hissed in self-satisfaction, ignoring the futile pummeling of human hands on its head. "The high-up man hates to be kept waiting." It dragged them toward the open tobacco stand and its absurdly small doors.

"To Gehenna, then, is it?" Aereas gasped out through the lancing pain from his shoulder. "Unc's been lots of places, but I doubt Gehenna is one of them."

The imp laughed at this and gave Aereas a capricious wink. "That's right, boy. Lie back and think of Caonan. It's easier for all of us that way."

Nina glared sharply at her cousin, her expression easing when he managed a wink over his blood-mantled shoulder.

"One place he *has* been, though, is the sacred grove of Halliel!" So saying, he snatched a glass jar from the mantel and smashed it over the imp's stony brow. The watery contents of the jar sprayed out over the three of them, along with tiny, biting teeth of glass. But the small jabs of pain that Aereas and Nina felt were nothing next to the agony of the gargoyle.

"Holy water! You monsters!" it screamed, releasing its grip on them as its forehead specked and mottled and began to melt beneath the stuff.

The dancing feet and lashing tail of the beast drove Aereas and Nina back, and only splashed more of the puddled liquid on the horrific creature. As terrifying as the beast had been before, now it was worse, thrashing in its own melting flesh, languishing like a slug covered in sea salt.

Aereas and Nina clutched each other in horror while the thing writhed and dissolved away into a molten mound of dissolute flesh.

It was over. That quickly.

The room that, a moment before, had been a place of toppling furniture and fluttering books and blazing logs was now silent and still. For a long while, the only movement came from the viscid bubbling pulp of the imp.

Nina and Aereas both stared at the spot, shocked and reeling. Their repulsion at the stuff was matched only by their relief that the gargoyle no longer lived, and by a strange gratitude that some of his flesh remained; otherwise, they wouldn't have believed what had just happened.

"What was that?" asked Aereas, his eyes indicating the ruined study as well as the foul puddle.

Nina gently prized herself free of her cousin and moved toward the soupy spot. "I've seen lots of strange stuff with my dad and his travels and inventions and all. . . ." The words caught short in her throat, a sob beginning to form, though she didn't let it emerge.

Aereas moved to comfort her. "It's all right. We're safe."

She pushed away from him, refusing both his comfort and her need for it. "I'm not worried about us. I'm worried about Pa."

Aereas nodded at this, watching his cousin stagger to the tobacco cabinet and squat down beside it. "Did you see what I saw?" Nina asked.

Aereas drifted to her side. "His slippers, still on his feet, being dragged between these doors . . ."

As he said it, his initial impressions of the cabinet became all the more undeniable. The slippers themselves could not easily have been crammed into that tiny space, let alone the man wearing them. And the cabinet within was tall and narrow, just right for holding some of Uncle's more exotic ceramic pipes, but no place for stuffing a pudgy hermit. Indeed, those slender pipes yet stood, undisturbed, within the narrow space where the man had disappeared.

"How?" Nina asked simply, summing what both of them wondered.

Aereas knelt beside her and reached toward the pipes. As his fingers passed between the doors, a faint blue-green sparkle indicated that the cabinet was magical. His arm felt warm, as though autumn sunlight fell onto the back of his hand. He grasped one of the pipes.

Or did not. His fingers seemed to be within reach of the thing, but his hand closed on nothing. He withdrew his arm with a startled chuckle, blushing at his fright, and then reached back into the cabinet.

His hand kept going, fingers closing on nothing. With a mutual gasp, they both saw his arm strangely foreshortened, as though it were sunk into refracting water or seen through one of Artus's massive fish-eye lenses.

That made Aereas draw his hand out right quick. The flesh, which a moment before had seemed both puny and distant, suddenly became solid and real again. Aereas shook the pins-and-needles feeling out of his hand and laughed nervously.

"This is no typical tobacco stand," he blurted.

Despite what she had just seen, Nina thrust her own arm in, and it slid through to the shoulder. Her hand seemed dwarfed and distant through the small doorway. She recoiled, swallowing a large lump in her throat.

"A . . . magical portal?" she wondered aloud.

"I've heard of such things, but that can't be. I've seen Unc take pipes right out of there and smoke them in that chair."

"He could take pipes from a portal as easily as from anywhere else. But could it really be a magical passage . . . to another place?" Nina replied. "You're not supposed to be able to see through portals—at least that's what I thought."

"And a portal to where?" Aereas mused.

"To Gehenna," replied Nina in a tone that verged on certainty.

"Gehenna . . ."

"That's what the gargoyle said"—Nina's jaw clenched as she thought—"and knowing my dad, Gehenna is as good a bet as any."

Aereas stumbled back, bleary-eyed, and seated himself on an overturned chair. "But I . . . I . . . Before tonight, I thought Gehenna was just a concept, a metaphor, not a real place."

"I suppose I thought so, too," said Nina, a dangerous look entering her eyes. "I guess, like the imp said, we'll be finding out soon enough." She stood, brushing off hands and knees in a gesture of decision.

"Whoa, wait a moment," said Aereas, rising beside her. "What do you mean, 'we'll see'?"

Nina had been heading for the door of the study but now spun on her heel, her hair circling in a wide black halo around her intense face. "All right. *I'll* see. They took my father. I'm going to get him back." And again she spun, this time stomping through the doorway.

Aereas was close behind. "Wait a moment. We don't know anything about what lies behind that . . . that portal, if it *is* a portal!"

"So we should prepare before going through," Nina said. She curved through the last turn of the stairs and marched into her room. "Pack, I mean. Besides, we do know one thing. We know my dad is in there."

"Yeah," Aereas agreed dully. His eyes were becoming frantic as he watched Nina grab a small rucksack and begin stuffing it with garments from her clothes chest. "But we had trouble fighting a little imp," he pressed. "If Gehenna's what I think it is, we won't last a heartbeat."

"And how long will Father last?"

"Look at what you're doing!" Aereas demanded, trying to wrest her hands away from the packing. "What are you packing? Have you any idea what the weather is like in Gehenna?"

"Hot," she snapped.

"There's eternal fire and smoking brimstone, there's worms that eat flesh off living bodies and never die, there's infinite ice fields cold enough to freeze a fiend up to its belly button. . . ."

"You just described half of Caonan, too," Nina retorted wryly as she drew the bag closer and stepped over to her wardrobe. She flung open the doors and plucked up a dagger and slingshot from one of the shelves.

"A dagger and slingshot!" Aereas cried out. "What good will they be against . . . against whatever lives there?"

"You're right," Nina said distractedly. "I'd better take some salt and garlic and alum as well."

Though Aereas had thought she was joking, Nina set the weapons on her bed beside the clothes she would be changing into, then snatched up her bag and headed out of the room, down another turn of the stairs, and into the kitchen.

He caught her at the threshold to the small, well-stocked pantry off the main kitchen, and there he spun her around and said through gritted teeth, "You aren't your father, Nina. The knowledge he has about . . . about—*we don't even know what we are talking about!*—about where he went, let alone where we'd be going. Don't you see? He *understands* these things. If anybody can survive Gehenna . . ."

Nina stared at him angrily, and something fragile in her eyes seemed to break. She looked away. "He's my father," she replied simply, then pivoted and went into the pantry.

"And he's my uncle," Aereas retorted, refusing to follow her one step farther. "Don't you think I want to rescue him as much as you do?"

"If that's true, you'd better pack." When she stuck her head out, she was sorting a number of small vials into another sack. She chose one and handed it to Aereas. "Dab some of this on your shoulder and hand. It's the last of Dad's healing salve. He said not to use it unless it was an emergency, but this qualifies." Nina patted a bit of the salve on her own cheek. "And if you're so afraid of being ignorant," she continued, "you'd better get up to the study and see if you can find a travel book or something."

"By the time I'd find anything usable, let alone read and understand it, the trail would be cold."

"Then you'll have to find a book to take with you, I suppose," she replied. The fierceness in her eyes softened for a moment, and she lifted one hand to his cheek. "Oh, Aereas, what's so different about this? How many times have we gone chasing off into the wild world, half-prepared and half-cocked, and still come back in one piece?"

"That was different," Aereas said, calming now. The touch of her fingers against his cheek was smooth, warm, wonderful. "That was your backyard."

"My backyard—where I saved you from the bobcat, where we swung a hundred times over Deadman's Creek, where we put out the burning Joshua tree. My backyard was never such a safe place."

"It was never Gehenna," Aereas countered levelly.

"Don't worry. I'll be there to save you."

She suddenly was pressed up against him, her sweet soft scent filling Aereas's lungs for a moment. Then came the cool tingling of his cheek as she drew slowly away. "There's a spare rucksack in my wardrobe."

She turned and trundled out with a sackful of provisions.

✦ She's Your Cousin ✦

"She's your cousin," said Aereas's mother. She gestured with one hand, the other clamped down on her broad-brimmed hat. It flapped like a dark bird against the silver sky.

Aereas did not look at his cousin. Instead, he frowned down at his calfskin shoes. They were good shoes. He'd worn them in just right, just like his brother had showed him to do. They would make him fast.

There was a hand beneath his chin, his mother's hand, and he felt her cool blue shadow engulf him as she lifted his face.

"At least look at her, you shy boy."

Aereas didn't, not at first. He looked instead at his beaming, kind-faced uncle, also large and dark against the sky. In the shadow of the man's curved arm stood a small dark girl, eyes so deeply brown as to look black, hair the color of a broken-open black walnut shell. Her face was small, all eyes, with which she watched him as intently as he watched her.

Aereas turned into his mother's great thigh and the curtainlike floral fabric there.

She patted his head and cooed. "You two will get to being best of friends, I know."

TWO ⊕

THROUGH THE
TOBACCO STAND

Aereas packed the journal in with his clothes, which remained in the rucksack he had brought to the cabin three days before. As he slung the thing over his shoulder, he considered how comfortable linen and sackcloth would be in Gehenna, by all accounts a tropical clime.

When he returned to the ruined study, he wondered if he'd ever again see the books he had brought on this vacation—the Gothic tale *Sanctuary* and the book of Yenrsian poetry. He'd left them behind to make room for the journal and any other useful books in the study.

He began with those strewn on the floor, assuming the gargoyles would have consigned useful volumes to special destruction. This was not so. The books were mundane histories, collections of epic poems, sketchbooks, building plans, illuminated texts. . . . Each volume, after he paged through it and dismissed it, Aereas set neatly on the nearest shelf.

The room was tidier by the time Nina arrived.

"Don't worry about straightening. As long as the fires are out, we should be safe to go," she said.

He looked up to see that her nightshirt had been replaced by a leather jerkin and breeches and a pair of high leather boots—her favored attire for moving silently through the woods. Her belt and bandolier were replete with knives and weapons of all varieties, many of them abducted from the kitchen cupboards. She looked just as she had before any of their previous excursions.

"I'm looking for references," he replied. He nodded toward the utensils and turned back to the books. "By the way, we're headed for Gehenna, not the bakery."

Nina blushed slightly, sliding a rolling pin onto a side table. "Well, who would have thought holy water would come in handy against a gargoyle? I just wanted to be prepared."

"Speaking of which, have you got any more holy water?" Aereas asked, pausing in his search.

"Sorry, fresh out," Nina replied wryly. "Did you find anything useful?"

"Not much," said Aereas. "Mostly histories and such. Of course I hadn't expected there to be any books called *Gehenna on Five Guineas a Day: a Rescuer's Handbook.*"

She laughed, her voice softening. "Sorry I'm being so—I don't know—demanding. I'm asking a lot of you, and I know this isn't your battle."

"Hush," he replied gently, setting his hand on hers. "You know I'd go to Gehenna and back for you."

They both laughed now, though Nina went on to say, "You're sure you don't mind?"

He shook his head. " 'Don't mind' is not how I would have said it. But I'd mind more letting Unc—" He stopped short, realizing that what he was about to say would be unwelcome. "Besides, I do have one book that should help us out. This," he said, handing her Artus's journal. "I've not gotten past the first page yet, but if that's any indication, I think the book will have a lot to say about—"

"Where'd you get this?" she interrupted, incredulous, turning the book over in her hands. "This was . . . in here?"

"No."

"I didn't think so," she said wonderingly, then winced at what she had given away. "We always knew Dad kept a journal, but you know as well as I that—"

"Just tonight, he gave it to me." Now it was Aereas's turn to feel embarrassed.

"*Gave* it to you?"

"To read."

"He never even admitted having it."

"Well," Aereas said, his voice becoming suddenly grave, "I'm sure he wanted us both to read it. . . ." He made a snatch for the book, but Nina slipped it quickly—a little too quickly—into her pack.

"Later," she said, ending the discussion. "Now we've got to keep our heads up and eyes open. Let's go."

Aereas nodded. Shouldering their packs, they stepped solemnly to the tiny tobacco cabinet and knelt beside it.

"I don't know. I feel kind of stupid," Aereas admitted, "like I'm trying to crawl into a dollhouse."

Nina nodded. "Keep thinking of it like that. It's sure better than thinking about crawling into Gehenna."

Aereas chuckled humorlessly. "I'll go first."

"No. He's my dad," Nina said. "I'll go."

That was easier said than done. To believe she could squeeze through the tiny portal, which was barely large enough for one arm, was easier than actually doing so. It was like swallowing a pill, one-tenth the size of a piece of steak, that just didn't want to go down.

"I've never done this before," Nina said awkwardly.

"And you think I have?" asked Aereas with a laugh. "Just pretend you're trying to worm between the rafters of your dad's barn, like we used to do all those summers. . . ."

With that simple statement, a flood of memories descended on Aereas: the fort they had built in the hay with the single huge bale for a door, the sight of the sunset over Shadow Mountain from the top of the tallest oak, the fishing and swimming, the devising and deciphering of codes. . . . They'd lived a thousand lifetimes together in those faded summers.

Now they risked their single lifetimes on a tidy little tobacco stand that led who-knew-where.

"Here goes nothing," Nina said.

She edged forward, holding her breath, as though that would somehow help her slide through the impossible space. She reached into it with one hand, which plunged past the open doors as though into water. A rippling glitter shone between the doors, and beyond it, her hand again looked foreshortened, both stretched and compacted.

"There's a wood floor on the other side," she said, the tiny fingers of her tiny hand patting what appeared to be the panel at the base of the stand. "I'm going to take a look."

Aereas tensed. His hands were frozen in a grasping gesture, but he did not move to catch hold of her.

Nina slid onto her stomach, head pushing through the glimmering membrane of magic as though she were diving into a pool or—more correctly—emerging from one. The blue sorceries slid along her ebony hair, lifting it strand by strand from her face and holding it outward. Somehow, impossibly, her forehead pushed past that too-narrow gap, and her brown cheeks glowed with motes of light. Then her eyes were through, like those of a surfacing swimmer. She released the breath she had been holding and gasped in amazement.

"It's big in here . . . lots bigger."

The sound of her voice came muffled to Aereas. His hands clenched into anxious fists. "What is it? What is it? Is it the fiery mountain of Gehenna?"

"It's a closet," she replied flatly, "and it looks just like the inside of the tobacco stand."

"Just like the inside, only as big as a closet? What about the pipes?" Aereas asked.

"They aren't pipes. They're alpenhorns, a whole set of them, about as tall as I'll be when I crawl through. I'm going farther."

"Wait!" called out Aereas, though he had no idea why she should.

It was too late anyway. Already Nina's ears had slid through the portal, and she had wriggled in past her stomach. Then, in one smooth motion, the rest of her, hips and thighs and calves and feet, slipped through.

Aereas peered into the stand. There she stood, a tiny, perfect replica of herself beside the pipes—horns—piled into the far corner. She was just their height.

Aereas let out a nervous and humorless giggle, then waved stupidly at her. She seemed not to see him, nor the portal she had just passed through. Nor did she respond when he called to her, though he could hear her tiny voice.

"I can't find the portal . . . can't see you." Her words were tinged in fear. "Can you hear me? Stick your hand through if you can."

Aereas crouched beside the cabinet and complied, seeing his hand shrunken and weird in the center of the closet. Nina reached her tiny hand out and clasped Aereas's, and he let out a sigh of relief. Too soon.

She yanked, and he found himself lunging through the portal as though she were pulling him through a hedge.

The gradual emergence she had experienced rushed over him in the space of a blink. He tumbled heavily into her, and into the stack of alpenhorns leaning against the closet wall.

"What in hell's name—" Aereas began, but Nina cut him off.

"Quiet!" she exclaimed breathlessly. "No need to announce our arrival."

Aereas was too busy steadying the sliding pile of horns to answer. Once that was done, he whirled around to glimpse the portal through which he had just emerged, but saw only the dim, wood-paneled closet, his cousin, and scraps of paper receipts that littered the small room: flecks of dust as seen from outside the tobacco stand.

"We came through there?" Aereas asked, gesturing toward the closed door.

"Yes," replied Nina, her voice both amazed and fearful. "Through the closet door. The wood must be an illusion covering the portal."

"Can we get back?"

Nina shrugged and stuck her hand out. It struck hard against the door, and she shook her fingers. "Apparently not. At least not without a key."

Aereas released a long, nervous sigh. "Here we are, then. Out of the backyard. We may as well start looking for your dad."

Nina nodded quietly. "And since he's obviously not in here, there's nothing for it but to open the do—"

Her reaching hand and tentative words caught short as the door swung wide to reveal an imposing silhouette beyond.

Well, perhaps not imposing. The pudgy little man was shorter than either of them, rounder than both of them. He had a long, bulbous nose that jutted far from pointed eyes and gray, bristling brows. Even so, the crossbow trained on them, the shimmering magic of the steely quarrel, and the bright light that streamed around the figure made up for any shortfall in stature.

"Scragged, you fiends!" he snarled as the door slammed against the wall beside him. The oath devolved into a puzzled throat-clearing followed by a gasp. "Saints and proxies!" he cried in apparent contradiction of his previous opinion. Then, with uncanny speed, he lunged at them.

Nina recoiled beside the alpenhorns, but Aereas was still yammering and fumbling with his knife when the little man seized his wrist and hauled him out into the blinding light.

It was the second time that day Aereas had been hauled through that same space, though this time he passed through the doorway rather than the door. He ended up in neither a closet nor his uncle's study, but rather in a tight, bright space.

Next moment, his hand was batted away from his knife, and he was borne, prone, to the floor.

"I don't know what kind of hellish pit this is—" Aereas gasped beneath the pinning knee.

"It's been a long while, Artus," interrupted the powerful little man, "but've you gone barmy? Don't you remember old Boffo?"

Aereas did not, nor was he "barmy," nor was he Artus. He had started to say so when Nina surged from the closet like a frenzied cat. She vaulted through the air, steel flashing in her hand.

"None of that, berk," Boffo said simply, and reached upward. Somehow, that single simple gesture sent her cartwheeling across the room to land half on her feet, blundering into a wall of strange, shiny implements.

Yes, across the *room*.

Their eyes had adjusted enough to see where they were— a small shop filled with strange devices . . . not implements, but instruments, *musical* instruments. There was a sackbut, an oboe, and a rebec among stranger items, some of which clattered to the floor in a cascade of brass, wood, and reed.

"Oh," cried the little man in dismay. "And look what yer

doing to my case! First you call it a hellish pit; then you smash my goods!"

"Get off him," Nina seethed savagely as she rose and stalked toward the round creature.

"You want I should slap you down again, berk? Keep your distance," Boffo warned, and his stubby fingers splayed out before him. Nina warily paused, studying the creature. He went on to say, "I got to pin him down sometimes after these time loops he gets stuck in. Makes him barmy as a bubber—can't remember a thing, not who he is or who I am . . . nothing. It's hard to think Artus of the Keys could forget who he is. Nobody else can."

"I'm not Artus," rasped Aereas.

"Just lie still and forget that knife, you poor sod," consoled Boffo. To drive home the point, he kicked the loose blade out across the floor. It shuddered to a stop near a baseboard. "Once you've settled down, I'll let you up."

Nina studied the scene a moment longer, her great brown eyes returning the tormented gaze of Aereas's bloodshot blues. Then a fire seemed to wink to life within her, and she soothed, "He's right, *Artus*. Just lie still, now. You'll be fine once you've calmed down."

For a moment, the little man fixed her with an incisive look, then nodded. "Never seen him quite so jangled as this, though," Boffo admitted, " 'cept that one time straight back from the Abyss. 'Course, it's been so long, I'm glad to see him in any shape. I thought maybe the tanar'ri—those leather-skinned monsters—or middle age had caught up with him."

"The Abyss," Nina repeated, musing. She quickly added, "Yes, that was a bad time."

"How do *you* know?" came the suspicious reply, accompanied by a glare from beneath bristling brows.

"He told me," Nina replied. "One of the few things he'd let me know."

"And you are . . . ?"

"Nina," she replied, then added, "his cou—his girlfriend."

The little man smiled at that and winked. "I thought he had something going, but he never said." The revelation of Artus's new love, as well as the stiff stillness of Aereas beneath the creature's sinewy knee, convinced Boffo to let the young man loose.

Aereas scuttled quickly to one side of the shop and, raking panting breaths, fetched up against a wall. He glared at the little man. "You stay away from me."

"Now, there there, Artus," Boffo said gently, holding his hands out before him. "You're going to be just fine. In no time, you'll be remembering everything."

"Where's my uncle?" Aereas blurted thickly, still ignorant of Nina's plan. "What have you done with him?"

"Was *that* your uncle, then?" Boffo wondered aloud. "Nearly tore up my case wrestling him out of the closet, those two gargoyles did. Took me a week to straighten the place, and then you two come dogging on in here."

"A week?" Nina asked with surprise. "They've had my f— my friend for a week?"

"Tsk, tsk." Boffo shook his head and studied Aereas's yet-confused face. "You had to go get a woman who knows nothing of the planes—you in your shape, and all." He rubbed his stubby hands together, then nodded to himself. "Tea. That's the thing. Tea and rhubarb pinwheels and a few long draws from the hubbly-bubbly. That'll bring your memory back."

"We've got to get going," Nina interrupted, her voice suddenly a worried moan. "If they've had him for a week, he could be—"

"Dead, yes. Poor sod," Boffo replied gently. "But if they'd wanted him dead, they could've had him dead before pulling him through the closet." Here, he glanced at Aereas, who still clutched his chest as he breathed raggedly. "Actually, I'm surprised they took your uncle and not you, Artus. He must be a real prize if they left the

Lady's own Key in the same study. . . .

"But now's not the time for such speculations. I can see I've already put a fear into you both with this talk of fiend abductions and abyssal tortures—"

Nina went very white. "Abyssal tortures?"

"See? There I go again. Come, let's fill up on tea and pinwheels, not horror stories. I've got some fine Five-Shires tobacco for the hubbly-bubbly. You always did enjoy a good pipeful."

And with no more explanation than that, the little man turned on his heel, presenting his wiry back for any weapon either of the two strangers might have desired to put there.

Neither Nina nor Aereas moved, partly because they knew this little gnome—that was the word for him—was more than able to defend himself, partly because they were both shrugging off the throbbing aches of his initial attack, but mostly because they now recognized him for what he was—a friend. A friend not only of the cousins, but also of the abducted uncle, whom he must have known in youth.

Boffo disappeared through a narrow rear doorway, and after only a breath's hesitation and an exchanged glance of wariness, the cousins followed. They moved slowly through the small shop, awestruck by the hundred strange instruments that hung from wooden pegs on the walls or lay upon shelves or stood in corners.

Not all the instruments were strange. The tin whistles and gitterns were familiar, or course, along with a clavier and a hammer dulcimer. Others were more peculiar, with strange twists of brass tubing or knobby pipes of ebony or bits of wood with long hollows carved in them.

"Come on, now," came the gnome's voice from ahead. He poked his long nose out the doorway to his tidy kitchen and beckoned them inward.

The cousins followed, albeit at a slow pace.

Boffo sighed. "Saints and proxies! A man who once walked from Acheron to Olympus and back in the span of a day can't get from the show parlor to the pantry in less than two. Step it up, now, man!"

The cousins pursued the disappearing nose and found themselves in a small, steamy kitchen. "Small" was the word, for though the show parlor had a ceiling meant to accommodate humans—and who knows what else, Aereas thought—this kitchen was a private space proportioned for gnomes.

Even so, the room immediately felt and smelled like home. Walls of axe-trimmed wood and mortar emitted the loamy scent of ancient rosin; a small sideboard held a hand pump poised above a ceramic bowl; fennel and coriander hung in dry stalks from the too-close ceiling; a kettle of water steamed through its spout and lid on a narrow hearth of whitewashed brick. The whole scene spoke of comfort and peace and familiarity.

"I *thought* my kip'd begin to bring it back," the gnome said proudly. "You could never resist my rhubarb pinwheels . . . speaking of which—" he said, vanishing through another narrow door beside the fireplace stack. The *ping* of full bottles came from the tiny larder where the gnome worked, followed by his voice. "Go on in to the sitting room. Take the gold chair, Artus, and see if it doesn't bring something back."

Nodding numbly, Aereas led Nina from the kitchen into a low-ceilinged room with a fireplace of its own, shelves crammed with books, and delicate, fey furniture. Immediately Aereas realized why Boffo wanted him to take the gold chair. Though low to the ground like the others, it was wide enough and stout enough to hold him without breaking. Aereas gestured toward it and lifted his eyebrows at Nina, who shook her head and took a seat by the fire. He nodded and sat.

In came the gnome. The kettle steamed on the tray he

held, along with four small crystal cups and saucers and three ceramic plates. He set the tray down on a small table (small even compared to the other furniture), lifted the silver lid from a platter of rhubarb pinwheels, and began serving the syrupy rings of pastry onto the plates.

"I brought two cups of tea for you, Artus, because I remember how you liked your first with cream and sugar, and your second straight—a chaser."

Aereas took the cup and muttered, "Thank you."

Boffo silently served Nina, then assembled a snack for himself, took a bite and a sip, and settled back into one of the small chairs.

He sighed, long and wistfully, and his cheeks colored in a brief blush of memory before he spoke again. "It *has* been a long time, hasn't it?"

Aereas choked down a bit of the pastry—which was lusciously tart and reminded him of how hungry he was—to answer, "Yes. Seems like forever."

"Yes," echoed Boffo distantly. After another sip, he said, "Sometimes I wondered if you'd ever be back—you know, the young cutter finding some reason to settle down." Here, he glanced at Nina, who looked away into the fire.

"No, not yet," Aereas replied. "I haven't settled down yet." He paused and thought about this. "Not that I know of, at least. My brain's still pretty scrambled from that last trip."

"Oh, don't get me wrong," the gnome burst in. It was as though he hadn't heard what Aereas had said, instead listening to the ghostly memory of the man he thought Aereas was. "I'm not complaining. I knew the dark of it when you set up your portal in my closet door. I knew there'd be all kinds of mixed-up comings and goings any given day. I'd even figured on seeing you as an old man running into yourself as a kid, talking to time-shadows of yourself, or chasing your own tail. . . .

"I knew on other days or months or years, you'd not

show your nose in here at all." He paused. "I guess I just got a little too used to the constant company and the . . . possibility of . . . adventure."

His eyes sparkled dangerously at that word, and Aereas gulped a bit too much tea, scalding his throat. "Well, though I don't remember much, I do remember why I'm here."

"And why's that?"

"My uncle—"

"Kidnapped—oh, yes," said Boffo, returning to the moment. "How did it happen? Where did it happen? In your study, I assume."

"Uh, yes," Aereas replied. His mind began to spin, fitting the pieces together. "Have you been to my study?"

Boffo shook his head. "No, you never gave me a key, but you've told me about it enough times."

"Yeah, well, let's see. I had retired for the night, having finished . . . part of the . . . shed I've been building. Did I ever tell you the cabin was done?"

"My, but you've been busy. You don't look a day older than when you took the keys and left. What these portals can't do nowadays." He shook his head and clicked his teeth. "'Course, until I'd seen your . . . hem . . . lady, here, I figured maybe the Lady of Pain herself was the one keeping you young. Bar that. Anyway, you were jawing about your kip being done."

"Well, mostly—as done as any project I've ever gotten started," Aereas said, warming to the role of Artus. His face grew serious. "At any rate, I'd retired for the night—"

"*We'd* retired," Nina clarified from her place beside the fire.

"Yes, *we'd* retired, when I heard a noise in the study. As you probably know, I keep the study locked—for obvious reasons."

"*Obvious* reasons," the gnome said with a wink.

"And Unc was not the sort of fellow to pick a lock and

snoop around, so I—we—knew something was up."

"We got out of bed and broke down the door to the study—" Nina interrupted impatiently.

"Why didn't you use the key?" the gnome asked.

"No time," replied Nina. "And we saw his uncle get dragged off through the tobacco stand."

"Did you see who or what did it?"

"No," Aereas jumped in, warning Nina back with a raised eyebrow. "We did, though, fight some kind of gargoyle, and that thing said Unc'd been taken to Gehenna."

"Where else?" the gnome said with an ironic sigh. "More tea?"

"That's all I remember," Aereas concluded. "I got pretty mixed-up following after them through the portal. Those fiends must have left behind some kind of . . . of sorcerous caltrops or something . . . to black out anyone who followed."

"Is that why Nina doesn't remember anything, either?"

"I don't think so," Aereas said. "I came over first, and my mind must have been washed clean, but Nina has never been to the planes before. I'd not told her much because . . . well, you know how I keep my cards close to my vest."

"I know. I know," said the gnome. "So you don't know where they took your uncle, or why."

"They took him to Gehenna—"

"Gehenna is a big place."

"As to why, we were hoping you could help," Aereas said.

Boffo looked solemn, speculative. "Obviously, whoever blanked your memory knew just the information to erase to keep you from following. Blanked out our whole past together. Took away any memories of this place, of me, of Sung Chiang and your other enemies in Gehenna. . . ."

Aereas was cheered by Boffo's interpretation. "I thought

maybe you could fill me in on some of my past, on some of the adventures we'd had that might make someone want to kidnap me—or I should say, my uncle."

The gnome rocked back again and thought for a moment. "How about that hubbly-bubbly?" he said at length. "That ought to smoke some ideas from this old noggin. I'll fetch it, and bring back with it the story of how we met."

✦ Forest Folk ✦

He scrambled up the rocky rise, sending behind him a trickling cascade of stone shards and scree. Oh, if only one rock would bounce down and strike those boys on the heads! But young Aereas knew better than to trust in that. He trusted, instead, in his sweat and his calfskin shoes.

Topping the shoulder of stone, Aereas darted in among the lodgepole pines that packed the windy ridge. Even with his feet crackling the dry needles, he could hear the boys rushing up behind him. They let out whoops like hounds trailing a fox.

But foxes didn't climb. Ten strides into the thick stand of pines, Aereas launched himself into the air, grasping one thin, sappy bough and swinging his leg up over the rough bark. He drew his body after until he was righted again, then climbed, praying the boys wouldn't see the green boughs waving flaglike in his flight.

Up, up, up, as though ascending a narrow spiral stair. He rose from warm dark stillness near the ground through a dense tangle of dead twigs and forgotten nests, and up into the rushing height.

The sun struck him, warm, providential, like a protecting hand, and air moved through that slowly ruffling treetop. He might have sung out for joy, but the boys now loped into the stand of trees, casting about with their dark eyes and bent shoulders. He might have sung, too, except that he saw, in the slow-pitching top of the next tree over, his cousin, the wild girl—Nina.

Her depthless eyes watched him, not like those of a treed raccoon or possum, but like those of an eagle. She was at home in that height. Indeed, Aereas now saw that the bole about which her legs were wrapped bore a wound of blond wood, narrow knife cuts that formed her initials: N.W.

Strangest of all, as the boys sniffed and circled below, the girl began to sing. If there were words to her song,

Aereas could not make them out. Her voice was high and sweet and wild, as though the wind itself were singing.

The boys below stopped their shuffling, and there came the rumble of worried discussion. Within the enormous wind and the thready song, Aereas made out only the muttered fearful words: "Forest folk."

And, spooked, the boys fled.

THREE

B⊖FF⊕

The shop was new then—or, I should say, it was new to me. The case had once been a home, and afterward, for some long centuries, a pub. Its ceiling was black from the smoke of the patrons. Then it sat empty for a dog's age until I bought it for the contents of my knapsack, which happened to be only a pair of good boots, a tattered jerkin, and one good meal's worth of cheese. Yes, when I started here, I had only the clothes on my back, the whittling knife in my pocket, a black-ceilinged and broken-windowed shop, and the friendship of a young cutter named Artus.

That was you, of course. Ring any bells? You don't look too comfortable with me recounting your own past. I don't blame you. For my part, I don't feel too comfortable sitting here and telling you your own story.

Well, best to get on with the tale. Artus was the cutter's name. He was on leave from the Blood War—a planar (no doubt about that in his cocksure walk and his bright blue eyes and his ceaseless, tireless mind, like some clockwork brain from Mechanus), whether because he was born on the planes or was born *for* the planes. He was a flyer, one of the Lady's Own Airborne, with hours on rocs and pegasi and giant eagles and you name it. He'd not been making combat runs lately, but flights for surveillance and cargo and transport for the Lady of Pain's peacekeepers. That's what Artus and his bashers were called—peacekeepers—even though lots of them did some head smashing and a good third of them were githyanki and githzerai themselves. I never knew a gith to keep the peace.

Anyway, Art was a sharp cutter—I saw that right off—but not a wise guy. He was the kind of fellow you'd want to be flying the griffon that'd snatch you off some blasted pinnacle of rock in a sea of lava with elemental fire leaping up to light your flatus. I don't exaggerate, because some time later I learned that Art had done just that, rescuing the Lady's whole Bravo Company on the back of a single griffon. Honest. And if he could do that, he could help a down-on-his-luck gnome start up a music shop.

He was on leave in Sigil—that's where we are, by the by—the city at the center of everything, and in the shop at the center of the city. That's just a little planar joke, see, since the city's round like the inside of a wheel and everywhere and nowhere in this place is at the center. But I'm losing you. Anyway, Artus was far from his family, who lived by the Placid Sea in Caonan. So, being footloose and bored, he thought he'd give me a hand fixing up the old place, letting me concentrate on whittling out some pipes and horns to start sales with.

While I patiently crafted the instruments the shop would sell, he impatiently reworked the place. From somewhere—I still don't know where—he got himself the creamiest whitewash I ever saw and repainted ceilings and walls both so that not a speck of the soot showed through. The walls were white then, not yellow like they are now, and of course there were no cobwebs when he was done.

He was also the one who converted the back rooms to two floors—gnome-sized floors, so I could have both a kitchen *and* a place to sleep. He even put in that indoor pump, which was pretty new for the time, and reglazed all the windows as they are now. By the time he was done with it all, I'd only just finished my first three sets of panpipes.

Well, I guess he wasn't quite done then. There was the one closet he'd not yet hung a door on. I was going to ask him about it, but then without a word of farewell or a claim to the profits of my little company, he was gone: back to the war.

I didn't see hide nor hair of him again until two years later, and by that time I'd made enough from my bamboo panpipes to buy some better knives, a set of chisels (which I still use, though they're worn now near to nubs), and some fine ivory and blackwood. From the profits of what I made next, I set to hunting alley cats and branched out into stringed instruments.

By the time Artus returned, I'd built quite a business for myself, and I felt a little guilty that the fellow who'd helped me get it up and running had seen none of the profits.

"I'll make you a partner," I remember telling him.

But he just shook his head and said, "I've still got that closet to finish. Then we'll talk."

At the time, I figured he was just some kind of obsessed workhound; now I know what he was really doing. See, he brought back from the war a sackful of weird, gnarled wood—driftwood from the River Styx, he said. I thought he was kidding at first, but I soon learned he was not.

It was the queerest wood, beautiful of tone, hard and smooth and twisted. In fact, when he'd done with the stuff, he gave me a few scraps, which I carved and polished and inlaid on those alpenhorns you saw in the closet. But you know, beautiful though the wood appeared, it somehow ruined the sound of the ivory. Each time those horns are played, there's this abyssal hiss and rattle and jangling groan, which seems to get worse with each note you hit. That's why I keep 'em in the closet; can't sell 'em and hate to destroy 'em. But, sorry, I've gotten myself off the path again.

Anyway, he took most of this Styx driftwood and started carving, making strange chains out of the stuff, almost like he was chiseling a sheet of chain mail out of wood. The links were delicate, all carved solid so there were no gaps in them, conjoined either by the magic of carving or by magic itself.

All the rapid impatience he'd used to fix up the rest of the place was now counterposed in my mind by the minute care he took in carving each link of this chain mail. And if ever he snapped a link of the thing, he'd throw the whole strand away and start over. I remember asking him what he was doing, and him telling me "every portal needs a proper door. That closet needs a damn good one."

At last he was done, and had a kind of wooden fabric made of those delicate links of Styxwood, a fabric the size and shape of the doorway. Next morning, as I was struggling and failing to shape the crudest of trumpets from a bit of brass I'd bought, Art showed up with another door—this one of solid wood he'd milled and joined, doing all the work between dusk and dawn. He laid the door on the floor and drew the wooden fabric over the upside of it. Before my very eyes, that batch of wooden links seemed to melt right into the solid door.

Slowly, taking care not to touch the side where the links had dissolved into wood, Artus lifted the door on its end, jiggled it onto a set of shims he'd positioned on the threshold, and sunk the iron screws into the pair of hinges he'd already fastened to the frame.

"What was that all about?" I asked, startled by this elaborate rite—and by the magical might exercised within easy explosion-range of two years' worth of hand-carved instruments. "I didn't even know you were a sorcerer!"

"I'm not," he responded simply, brushing the Styx sawdust from his hands. "And as to what this is all about, I cannot believe you are a shopkeeper in Sigil and still know nothing about the value of a good door. It gives ingress to the most mysterious, most magnificent of things, and denies entrance to that which is base and foul. Without doors, there would be no thresholds to cross or close, and without thresholds, there would be no life."

That was probably the longest string of words I'd ever heard the man utter. Even so, they only began to hint at the truth of the door, a truth I've pieced together for myself only after many intervening years.

No, he was not a sorcerer. I figure it was the driftwood that held the magic of the Styx. Perhaps each of the rings he had carved was a tiny portal into and out of the River Styx, which is everywhere and nowhere, in all times and no time. The turgid river brings all of a person's life rushing back in a fierce torrent and wipes all memory in one dull moment. That's what I figure, at any rate, and your blank mind would support my theory.

Every link interconnected with four others, and so the space within each was shared by all those adjacent. By connecting the links of the carved chain into a door-sized matrix, Artus had made a cumulative portal strong enough to move him through time and space, memory and hope, at his whim. It was, apparently, the sort of idea a sharp cutter could pick up in the Lady's secret service.

"Time and space?" I asked Artus. "To what time, to what space?"

"I haven't decided yet," he said with a shrug. Then he drew a deep breath and said, "Let's have a pull from that hubbly-bubbly. I've got some knotted muscles that a little of the Five-Shires smoke would do wonders to sieve away."

And we did, and it was over that smoke that he soothed me about having this portal on the inside of my closet door. He said, "Just consider it my compensation for all the work I've done on the place. The shop—the business—is all yours. The inside of the closet door is all mine."

Still, I wasn't satisfied. What if I got shut up in that closet? Would I have to dig my way through log and mortar just to get out of my own closet without getting sucked into the Styx? Artus said no, that he'd set the door up so that it had a handle on each side that worked for opening it, like any other door, and that the portal would work only when the door was closed.

Well, even so, you can imagine my concern, having a portal to the Styx in my closet, wondering what kind of abyssal barracuda might come flopping out when I went to get my hat. Needless to say, I stopped putting my hat in that closet, finally storing only those blasted alpenhorns to keep people from blowing on them and breaking my windows.

In the next weeks and months, I saw a good deal of Artus, who said he was yet on leave. What sort of organization allowed its officers leave for months at a time, I didn't know, but I also didn't ask. The Lady's business wasn't my business. My business was music, and the food I bought by selling music.

So during the next months, we enjoyed the music and the food, Artus and I, and we became not just business associates but fast friends. In fact, over a few more hubbly-bubblies, I wrung some of Artus's more interesting war stories from him, and also extracted the promise that, when he was done serving the Lady, he'd take me out of my little shop and give me a guided tour of some of the safer areas of the planes.

I extracted stories, songs, and promises from my friend, and then he was gone again. So I waited and whittled and watched and kept my hat on a peg by the back door, which is where it yet is, as you can see. There came a time two years later when I wondered if Artus had finally been killed in some remote and obscene bowel of the Abyss, for none of his friends seemed to know where he had gone. In time, I gave up the hope of ever seeing the planes with an experienced guide.

Just about then, Artus returned. Well, that makes it sound so banal. I found him in a gutter of the Lower Ward, and could only just barely lug him here and get him tended by a leech.

I feared he'd not pull through, but he did, and months later I got my wish to travel. We left on a secret mission of his for the Lady—the Lady of Pain, that is. Did I tell you she's the ruler, the Power, in Sigil? Well, she is, and I should have said so right off. That mission took us to the very gates of Olympus, and I got to see firsthand where else he'd been doing carpentry.

My music shop, you see, was not the only place that had benefitted from Art's tireless and handy hand. His reputation in the fix-it trade had traveled far, indeed, even to the heights of the snooty immortals. And as great and powerful as the powers are (let me be the last one to deny it), none of them were very interested in custodial duties around their temples. That's where Artus (and I) came in.

I'm not being fair to say that Artus was a celestial janitor, though he was, in truth, there to fix a few doors. Custodian is a better term for what he did. Yes, celestial custodian, for he kept the planes running.

Now, I see in your eyes that you're beginning to understand. Perhaps I should use the term "portals" rather than "doors," because that's what he was really fixing.

Why was I along for the ride? Good question. At the time, I told myself it was because Artus figured that my living with an extradimensional closet must have taught me something about the laws of portals and planar things. In fact, I once dropped a coin that rolled beneath the closet door and was nowhere to be found within, and I am sure the thing went through the portal and sunk in some strange corner of the planes, if not in the Styx itself.

But now I know that was all rationalization and poppy-cock. He'd brought me along to start teaching me what I needed to know to guard his portal back in my shop—the very portal you two came through, and the one that the gargoyles passed through when they stole your uncle.

Is any of this sounding familiar?

The door in question on Mount Olympus was the iron-barred gate of a tomb in the graveyard. Most mortals and demigods entombed in that most hallowed of hallowed grounds had typical monuments of marble marking their plots. This particular vault was different. It was rammed into one bulging and pustular hillside, and the spot was not marked with a name, nor adorned with an epitaph or even flowers.

"Who lies here?" I remember asking Artus as I leaned against a more usual grave. I crunched a bite from one of those fine Olympian tree-ripened olives—and ended up spitting out the horrid thing. (Only after soaking in lye are olives palatable—soaking in *lye!*)

"I'm not sure," he replied. "And if we're successful, per-haps we'll never have to know."

I didn't like the sound of that, and watched him with a curiosity born both of ignorance and fear. He cautiously repaired the gate's cracked lower hinge and oiled the rusted lock.

That was it for that site. Next we went to Marduk, a city I'd heard much of and had wanted to visit, until I got there. I must admit, the first day of strolling about that perfect metropolis—with its geometric streets and the rivers Kath and Luar that dutifully cross dead-center in the city before continuing impossibly in their former paths—was rather lovely and safe. But on the second day of our visit I real-ized the place had devised for itself a huge canon of law to try to make up for its dearth of soul. Not my kind of town.

When Artus'd finished his carpentry there, squaring a few doors and oiling a few hinges, I was glad to get out and get to a place a little more chaotic, though Ysgard was a trip in its own right.

Ysgard. What can I say?

You might say we were custodians to the powers, with all the anonymity and privilege that office entails. You see, custodians hold all the keys, they know all the nooks and crannies, they set up barricades and knock them down, they clean the secret-laden desks and beds and baths of those who move and shake the planes. And, best of all, anybody who sees a custodian looks away, eyes going black like those of actors that glimpse the set-crew offstage.

Yes, there's another name for people like us, who go unnoticed into and out of the most sensitive areas of planar powers: spies. We weren't merely fixing doors, you see, we were altering them, so that they unlocked to us as well as to their owners. We were putting our own touches on each job we did, much as an artist signs a painting, though the signatures we left behind were words of power that, spoken by us in the far reaches of Baator or the high summits of Mount Celestia, could lock the door or unlock it, or even bring us through.

Art was no janitor. He was more a joiner and mason and architect, discreetly placing new doors between the rooms of the planes and installing them into his vast network of secret passages and tunnels. It was a rat's maze, the network he set up—*we* set up, though if I got into it alone (let alone if anyone else happened through the wrong door at the wrong time) I'd never find my way out of that netherplace and would die of dehydration or starvation or sheer confusion. I know this was true, for Artus himself warned me of it. Once I was lost for a day before he hunted me down and brought me out.

For near on two months we were plane hopping, setting up the Lady's doors all over the place like silken threads of a spiderweb. But then it was over, and we returned to this little shop here, where we sit now. It's not that my music business is the cynosure of Art's web. In fact, he once told me it was the farthest point on the network.

That's why he liked to stay here. On the one hand, it was safe from the sorts of critters the rest of the thing would entrap and snare, and on the other hand, just sitting here with me in the parlor, drinking tea and puffing on the hubbly-bubbly, he was aware of every pulse in that network, just as a spider is of every twitch in its web.

And, soon, he was gone again. That was the way with him—with *you*, I keep forgetting. (It's been so long, and you seem to be drinking this in like it's all news to you.) Artus would work with fierce intensity for a few months, savor food and friendship and tobacco for a few days, and then disappear again into that vast invisible net of the Lady's for another few years.

That was the key. It was the Lady who owned the web, not Artus. He'd've had no reason to set up something so vast and secret only to go back to filling out requisitions and attending officers' functions and the thousand other duties he said he despised. Indeed, with that web, he'd not have to work another day in his life, being able to blip about and thieve and do all brands of mayhem if he pleased. But he didn't please. For all his sneaking about, he was a moral man, and I never did see or hear or suspect that he used the net for himself.

Then, too, it was a matter of power. Artus had worked for nigh on two months to carve that door-chain for the closet here, though every other time we labored over a portal it took only a day or an afternoon. So, I figured that the portal in my closet led somewhere private, and all the others were jobs he did for the Lady.

* * * * *

All this is speculation, of course. I never got a chance to ask you about it, because next time you showed up was the last time I saw you. You hadn't even time for tea or a smoke or much conversation. There was a baby in your arms—boy or girl, I didn't know, so quickly you were in and out of here—and that's how I suspected you'd found yourself a woman. Indeed, now that I look into Nina's eyes, I see that the baby was her spitting image.

You said something about keys, about adoption . . . hmmm . . . then rushed about the place, baby in one hand, pocket knife in the other. You etched hasty glyphs in all the windowsills and thresholds and even in the attic vents of the place. Then there was a brief embrace and the promise that you'd be back, and it was into the closet for the last time, the door slamming shut behind you. When I opened that dreaded door, you and the baby and the knife were gone, the portal locked by some spoken key I've never known.

That last urgent parting was the only word I had from you for years. Since that time, I've had no more trace of you than those glyphs, which, whatever their real purpose, sweeten the breezes that blow over my doors and windows. I'd thought about following you through that closet door, just to see what lay on the other side, but I didn't know the key, and the comforts of modest wealth and a job that one loves are the strongest shackles in this world . . . or any other. I'd every itching to follow you into more adventure, but every reason to stay here with my mellowing pipes and my simmering hubbly-bubbly and my simple music.

All impulse for adventure had been so completely dismissed that I didn't open the closet again until years later. And then, I had to. An obnoxious yugoloth customer had somehow heard of my cursed alpenhorns and wanted to give one a blow. Opening the door, I found a small envelope containing a short letter from you, and I was utterly surprised. Surprised and unsettled in the extreme.

Here it is, the letter, and so that you don't both have to crane over a piece of paper while I sit here twiddling, I'll read it to you:

From Artus Whitesun, Hermit of the Shadow Hills, Once Proxy for the Lady of Pain, friend and comrade of the honorable Boffo of Sigil,

To the same Boffo of Sigil, Entrepreneur of Music, Deputy Proxy of the Lady of Pain, and noble Gnome of Ancient Lineage.

Greetings:

I do hope this letter finds you well, finds you even alive, given the peculiar temporal fluxes of this most peculiar door I have made for you. A moment here may be a century there, I well know, and vice versa. But if you yet live and the cause for which we once labored yet matters in your world, I wish you to know that I too yet live, and have found myself new causes—dawns and sunsets.

Hermit, yes. There has sadly been no reunion for the child with her birth mother, so urgent were the matters that drove me from Sigil. Ours is a forced exile and, at times, a sad one. But the girl is fine, and we are both as safe as we might be in the Seven Heavens, or safer.

I write you not so much to put your mind at ease— though that is part of it—but rather because I suspect matters will soon require my return to your fair city. And, if you are yet proprietor of this musical establishment, I would much appreciate your assistance in the matters at hand.

Even as I write this, I realize the futility of it—what with the fluxes of Styx and Lethe. I may step through the portal the moment after this letter, and yet arrive in your closet years or decades hence. Ah, well, such are the uncertainties of planar life.

Forgive me, then, and forebear the time that lapses before my return. But, above all, know that I am returning.

> *Your Dear Friend,*
> *Artus J. Whitesun*

"That was it," the gnome said, turning the crinkling parchment page in his muscular hands. "I'd had this letter for nearly a year before the gargoyles burst from the closet, dragging that round old sod behind them—and dragging you two after as well, I daresay, though a good week later."

Aereas nodded seriously. His head swam with the thousand details he had just heard and the feverish smoke that filled the room in rings and crazings overhead. The stories and vapors were slowly, hypnotically, being drawn into the wood stove and up the flue. "So, you hadn't heard from him—me—for over five years?"

"Now I've got you doing it," Boffo said with a laugh. He took a long draw from the water pipe. "Yes, it was more than five years, though by the look of you, you couldn't have been gone for more than a few seasons."

"Oh, it's been more than that," Aereas said, slipping an ironic glance toward Nina.

"May I see the letter?" Nina asked.

Boffo handed it over.

As Nina inspected the thing, Boffo went on fondly, "But hearing your voice again and seeing your face, it feels like it was just yesterday."

"You said there was an obnoxious yugoloth interested in one of the alpenhorns?" Nina asked as she pored over the letter.

"Yes," replied Boffo. "I was so surprised to get the letter that I hardly noticed him playing the blasted thing."

"Did he buy it?" Nina pressed.

"In fact, I think he did. The only one of the six I made that's ever sold."

"Not the horn, I mean the letter," Nina clarified.

That took Boffo aback. He muttered something, then began stammering, "W-Well, I d-don't see how we c-could still be reading it if—"

"This isn't my fa— my lover's handwriting," Nina broke in.

Boffo went white, and Aereas snatched the letter. He gulped as he stared at the thing. "It sure isn't."

"It isn't?" Boffo said. "How is that possible? I read the

thing the moment I found it. It said exactly this, word for word."

Nina looked grim. "Well, either you let slip about the closet portal and somebody forged a letter from Artus . . ."

The gnome shook his head violently. "Tell her, Artus. The only ones who know about the portal are folk you told. After all, why would I want gargoyles poking about in my back room?"

Nina continued, ". . . or the yugoloth or some other critter switched letters on you."

"How?"

"Magic," Nina replied flatly. "How else?"

"But why?"

"You—we—don't know the first thing about what Artus was up to," Nina growled. "There could be a thousand reasons why someone might have switched the letters. Maybe the actual note would smell like Artus, let a hell hound hunt him down. Maybe his actual signature would allow him to be traced across the planes. Maybe the oils of his hand or the ink from his inkpot—"

"I understand! I understand!" blurted the gnome miserably as he covered his ears with quaking hands. "At least they—whoever *they* are—didn't find you, Artus. They only got your uncle."

Now Nina was on her feet, back hunched beneath the low ceiling. The fire in her eyes was fiercer than that in the wood stove. "That round old man *was* Artus, and I'm his daughter, and this"—she flung her hand out toward Aereas—"is his nephew, not Artus himself."

She strode to the window and stared out into the black night beyond. "Artus is out there somewhere, in some kind of abyssal torture chamber. We came here to rescue him."

Of all the colors the gnome's face had turned that night, its present greenish cast was by far the worst. "Oh, dear, oh, dear, oh, dear," was all he could say.

✦ The Cave ✦

Musty darkness hung curtainlike around the children. The walls here had last been touched by the hands that had mortared them in place. No one had been down here since.

Nina crawled ahead of him. She always led the way.

Aereas didn't mind. The sweet exotic smell of her was more welcome than the dankness. Besides, the cobwebs would be in her hair, not his.

"It opens up ahead," she whispered excitedly back to him. The sound of her voice was watery on the glistening walls.

Suddenly she was gone. A whoosh of wet air came through the space where she had been, and the swishing sound of her knickers had given way to a muffled tumble.

Aereas let out a yelp and scrambled forward. The stony floor beneath him dropped away, and he tumbled too.

For a moment there was only blackness and smooth slick stones punching across his body. Then he sprawled into her, and they clutched each other, panting.

How long they sat there, the two friends in an embrace of trembling fear, he could not have said. In time, the dim gray square of the passage above resolved itself within the black wall. In that pessimistic light, they saw the small water-smoothed bulges and hollows of the stone around them, and the curved contours of their own faces.

"This is our cave, now," Nina whispered, her voice secret and reverent. The words reverberated sibilantly through the chamber, like a hundred moth wings. "Swear it."

"I swear it," Aereas said dutifully.

She held up a finger between them in the dusk. "Blood-swear it." A glistening ball of liquid stood poised atop a scratch she'd gotten in the tumble.

Aereas's own hands were dry, but his lower lip tasted salty. He leaned forward and kissed her finger, mingling their blood.

"I swear it."

FOUR
SIGIL ⊕ THE PLANES

"Well, that changes things, don't it?" asked Boffo, staring at them sadly.

"Yes," replied Nina impulsively, "everything for you, but nothing for us. We still must rescue my father from Gehenna, or the Abyss, or wherever—and we still need your help."

Boffo's grizzled eyebrows lifted away from his round eyes, and his long nose shook slowly back and forth. "But your father is . . . is him . . ." he pointed at Aereas ". . . and he is someone else."

"Yes," Aereas began, trying to explain it all. "I look like my uncle did when he was young. I've been told that often, so we weren't surprised when you thought I was him."

"But you didn't tell me you weren't."

"Would you have helped us if we had?" asked Nina.

"I'm not sure I'll help you since you didn't," Boffo replied.

Nina moved from the window and towered over the sitting gnome. "My father's—Artus's—life is still at stake."

"And you . . ." he continued as though he hadn't heard, "you aren't the *mother* of that baby I saw, but the *baby*, herself. My, has the time gotten stretched between then and now."

"And time itself is what's against us!" Nina nearly shouted.

The gnome's eyes stopped their slow circling, and a stern, sharp look grew there. "Now, sit yourself down, you young clueless slip! You've presumed enough already. Don't be shouting at me in my own kip, in the very room your father—*your father*—built!"

She yet stood over him, simmering.

He barked, "Of *course* we will rescue him. Now *sit down* so we can sort some things out!"

Whether the gruffness of his tone or the assurance of his aid made her sit, Nina slumped back into her chair, her brown skin going very pale. The gnome did not speak for a time, and into the silence, Nina ventured, "Do you know who the woman—who my mother—was?"

Boffo shook his head sadly. "She wasn't from here—from Sigil. No, Artus said the child's mother was off on one of the planes, somewhere."

"Where?" asked Nina quietly. "I must know."

"Whoa, whoa. One quest at a time. Surely you want back the only father you've ever known before you seek out a mother you've never even seen."

She settled back again into the chair.

"Let's think. Let's think," Boffo said, rising to pace the small room. "The dark of it is that you, Nina, are a planar. You were born on one of these planes, the outer, the inner, the elemental, the astral—any of them except a prime-material world."

"Like Telmar?" Nina asked.

"Yes. Like Telmar," Boffo replied. "That realization will

help some. Your lover—I mean your cousin—Aereas, though . . ."

Aereas shook his head. "As far as I know, I'm a native of Tiraso on the Caonan continent of the world Telmar."

"None of that chant's very helpful, son," Boffo said, then lightly slapped his own cheek. "I'd better not start calling you son, or we'll all go completely barmy."

"Well, you know the planes, Mr. Boffo, right?" Aereas said. "You can be our guide. And, anyway, I've got a journal from my uncle—"

"That's not the point," Boffo said. "There's a certain, well, advantage to being a planar. Other planars tend to recognize the clueless right away—that's what they call primes, people from prime-material worlds like Telmar."

"Prime-material worlds?" asked the cousins in chorus.

Boffo whacked his forehead. "Lords, but you've much to learn. A prime-material world is one of the cradles of civilization, one of the . . . the . . ."

"The normal worlds?" Nina asked blankly.

"If you will," Boffo replied with a philosophical nod. "Suffice it to say, most primes know nothing about the planes, though most planars know all about the primes."

"I still don't understand," Aereas said.

Boffo huffed and shoved his hands in his pockets. "How can I explain?" He stood that way silently for some time, then finally said, "I can't. I can't explain it to you." He shrugged and trundled toward the gnome-sized back door.

"Where are you going?" Nina blurted.

Boffo merely donned a cloak and hat from pegs beside the door, lifted an umbrella from the cane-stand there, and said, "I can't explain it to you, so I may as well show you."

The cousins stared at him, stunned.

"Well, are you coming along or will you just sit there gaping like a couple of gargoyles?"

* * * * *

They stepped out of the little back door and into a new world.

"Gods," whispered Nina under her breath, and she had to steady herself on the door stoop behind her.

"It's like living inside a smoky wagon wheel," Aereas murmured shortly afterward. He dropped down to sit beside Nina.

And it was. The narrow, cobbled road on which they stood crooked and snaked through a tightly crowded warren of one-, two-, and three-story structures. The buildings—shops mostly, some half-timbered, some carved of ivory, some built from stacked dung, some woven like great inverted baskets, and all topped with horns and laced with a strange black vine—leaned hungrily over the slick cobbles. As the road wrangled into the extreme, smoky distance, it slowly rose up the side of the huge basin in which the town lay.

But the perspective was all wrong. The buildings on what seemed to be the curved wall of a glacial valley stuck straight out, their roofs hanging sideways. All the horned structures between Boffo's shop and the hazy yonder also followed the gentle curve of the valley wall.

"I hope we don't have to go that way," Aereas gasped, suddenly weary. "Uphill all the way."

"Look in the other direction," Boffo suggested gently.

They did, seeing a similar view: roads and houses and shops rising up into the absurd and smoky sky. The top of the enormous wheel, and even its lateral sides, were lost in that haze.

"Excuse me," Aereas said. He turned aside and emptied his dinner—was it the same baked salmon he'd eaten with Artus what seemed like days ago?—on the ground.

"There, there, lad," said the gnome. "There are three reasons for vomiting: sickness, overindulgence, and the first sight of Sigil."

Aereas wiped his mouth and sat back up. "I think it might be all three."

"How . . . how can it . . . how?" Nina began.

"All right. First rule for survival here in Sigil is: Don't look up. At least not at first. For one thing, looking up makes you dizzy if you're not used to the size and shape of the place. For another, if you look up, planars—and some of them are nastier bloods than you've ever met—will know you for a Clueless right now."

Both of the cousins dutifully averted their eyes, and Aereas even shaded his with a visorlike hand.

"Good. Second rule is: Don't always be asking the how or why of things. That's the second fastest way to feel sick, and it tells every other berk that you don't know what's happening.

"Besides, most of us don't know why Sigil fills the *inside* of a great wheel any more than you know why your world fills the *outside* of one. After all, it seems it'd be easier to stand on the inside of a world than on the outside.

"We don't know why, if you walk this way or that way"—he pointed ahead of them, then behind them—"you can go forever, eventually walking in your own foot-prints, but if you walk sideways"—he waved his hand laterally across the road—"you get to a wall of shops and houses at the end of the city. If you go through them and spit out the other side, your spit ain't going to land in Sigil. Like as not, it'll hit one of the Outlands and, good or evil, none of the lands likes to get spit on.

"In short, I can't tell you what keeps my feet planted here, or the shop upright, or Sigil in place. But I do know it all works."

The cousins nodded, even though they were still dizzy, still befuddled.

"And, third: Don't travel through Sigil on your own the first time. That translates into the simple instruction: Follow the leader." With that, Boffo turned on his heel and began tramping out into the street.

The cousins gaped stupidly for a moment at Boffo before

they rose woozily to their feet and started after him.

"The first thing you'll notice about my tours," Boffo began informatively, "is that I've got a love of architecture. Perhaps it comes from my being a sculptor of wood, bone, and stone, making my instruments. More likely, though, it's because architecture tells you the dark of any place, anywhere. It doesn't just *tell* you about the place, but actually *shouts* history to you.

"First off," the gnome began, as though he were a proctor before a whole class rather than a shopkeeper before a couple of Clueless, "notice the construction materials of the city."

The cousins studied the buildings nearest at hand, shops much like Boffo's. The structures consisted mostly of oak beams that formed a framework for lath, mortar, and whitewash. It was fairly common construction, with roofs of shake or tile, depending on the wealth of the establishment. If it weren't for the horn-shaped eave ornaments and the black vines, they might have been buildings from Caonan.

"Oak, mortar, plaster, straw," Aereas listed aloud. "Fairly standard."

"Tudor is the style—named after one particularly successful ruling class in the place where these emigrants came from."

"So everybody in Sigil came from Tudor?" asked Nina.

The gnome shook his head and laughed. "No, just this district of the Guildhall Ward. That's where we are, where most of the craftsmen work and dwell. It's not the richest ward of the city, but neither is it the poorest."

"So all the people from the . . . Guildhall Ward came from Tudor?" Nina reiterated.

Again the shake of the head. "I didn't, for instance, and neither did the deva and baatezu craftsmen, or any of the other races in between. It's just these folk here, these ten or so shops.

"And, by the by, Tudor's not a place; it's a family—or *was* when the people came over. And in the place where that family lives, they've got lots of strange beasties—but no devas or baatezu.

"Anyway, if you've got your eyes open, you'll see that we're leaving the Tudor houses behind for the Hinterland huts."

He was right. They had walked a mere stone's throw from Boffo's shop, but already the buildings around them looked entirely different. The walls here were made of stone, and they were round, rising into low domes with holes at their peaks. These holes emitted blue-gray smoke into the orange, sooty sky. The doors of the dwellings were also round, also stone, and opened by rolling aside in a track. The windows were tiny circles, like portholes in a ship.

"Not the most hospitable of places, the Hinterlands," Aereas guessed.

"Yep. Right bunkers, aren't they? Lots of big prowlers in that land of grass and bluffs, I hear, and hot days and cold nights."

"And those over there," Nina said, pointing to a cluster of narrow structures with sharply pitched roofs and elongated stories. "Were they built by tall, skinny folk from somewhere with lots of snow?"

Boffo nodded again. "You see how the architecture tells the story of the people? That batch of buildings is a bourgeois clan of Nouveau Yeti, as they call themselves, though the rest of us just call them 'apemen' or 'shags.' Despite their thick coats of white fur, they insist on wearing tailored woolen vests and tail coats, 'Like any other respectable merchant,' they say. Hmmph," the gnome gestured at his own clothes. "You see me wearing tailored wool?"

The cousins shook their heads.

Nina diverted conversation from this seemingly sore topic. "So, everyone here in Sigil is from somewhere else?"

"Yep, that's sure. And most of them are still on their way *to* somewhere else. Sigil's the crossroads of the planes, so most of the folk here are just stopping off on the way. Or just plain stuck. That's why some folk call it the Cage."

Aereas said, "Do you think the . . . the *things* that took Uncle Artus might still be here with him?"

"No telling," Boffo said, "at least not yet. That's part of what we're doing out here. We're going to a kip where we can find out."

"Do you know any shortcuts to this . . . kip?" Nina asked impatiently, suddenly remembering her father's peril.

"There are a few doors, portals—yes," the gnome answered. "But you're still getting your plane legs—and you're getting a lesson as we walk. Besides, there's nothing wrong with pumping the feet and working up a little sweat, is there?"

"But my father—" Nina began, before Aereas cut her off.

"What are we coming up on now?" he asked.

"Ah, the Market Ward," replied Boffo with a sigh. "If the architecture of the rest of Sigil can tell you about the history of each place, the sprawl of the market tents, booths, and shanties—and the bustle between them—will give you the dark of the people and purposes of the city."

They saw immediately what he meant. In the next ward, architecture was nearly nonexistent. The structures here were temporary—at best pragmatic, at worst haphazard. Nina and Aereas stared, amazed, at the plains of canvas, forests of tent poles, the stalls tacked hastily together, the banners and beads and curtains pressing back the smoky dusk.

Yet the focus of the place wasn't the structures but the people. People were everywhere in a ceaseless rushing stream. It was as though, over time, the eddying, chattering current of people among the stalls and tents had eroded whatever structures of permanence might have once stood here, making only temporary shelters worthwhile.

And "people" did not mean only humans. There were wings and horns and hooves aplenty in that collection of browsers. Many milled about on two legs—be those legs human, dwarvish, goatlike, or pseudopodal. Others moved along on four or more hooves, on tentacles, on centipedic

legs. Furthermore, it seemed that the sort of legs one possessed was no fair indication of the kind of body atop
them, or the kind of head attached to those shoulders. Frog
heads, dog heads, lizard heads, mantis heads, cat heads. . . .

After even those first moments of throat-gulping observation, the cousins could pick out what looked like members of species: angelic human figures with wings (Boffo
said they were called devas), demonic lizard figures with
horns (these he called gelugons), giant phoenixes, coiling
clusters of worms with the faces of babies, and so forth.

Aereas was feeling sick again but had no time to void
his stomach or shield his eyes; Boffo was moving forward.

"Now, keep hands and eyes and words to yourself as we
pass through here," the gnome said. His fey face went gray
and stern as he stared into their eyes. "Just as sure as there's
a thousand races of critters in there, there's a thousand
codes of conduct—distance, eye contact, gesture, touch. Of-
fend a blood here, and you'll end up in the dead-book."

He studied them a moment more. Then the light faded
entirely from his eyes, and his face grew stony and impassive. He no longer looked at them. "Do as I have just done.
Withdraw into yourself, bearing nothing of who you are
out where it might snag a basher's eye."

The cousins nodded and did their best to comply.
Though the expressions dutifully slid from their features,
neither Nina nor Aereas could hide the fear that yet lingered in their faces.

"Follow me," Boffo said, motioning them along with a
discreet wave of his hand. Not even nodding this time, the
cousins followed.

And what strange wonders they saw in that market.
Many of the wares for sale were creatures themselves, living
and unliving. The sellers, barking in their biting dialects,
suggested all manner of uses for these creatures—labor,
company, entertainment, food, decoration. . . . And though
the bins and bins of crawling worms and grubs made

Aereas's stomach turn for the third time that day, he found least appetizing of all the red-hot ladles of iron served up for a crowd of red-scaled fiends to drink.

There were, of course, clothes and armor, tailored to suit the many morphologies of the patrons. In addition to traditional fabrics, there were shirts of bone or bark, boots fashioned from the carved-out claws of some huge beast, belts made of yet-living snakes, ornaments of gold and silver that flowed like mercury. The only substance Aereas could not spot in use as a textile was dung—though glimpsing what some of these beasts ate, he had no idea what their droppings might look like.

Most of the substances and objects in the marketplace fell into that category—undefinable. There were items as large as houses and as small as lice; there were metals that stretched, woods that dissolved in air, skeletons made of ice. . . .

The churning fury of the place, the dizzying sights, acrid smells, ubiquitous black ivy (Boffo called this razorvine) combined to make Aereas green about the gills. To him, all the creatures looked monstrous. Any of them could have been the kidnappers of Artus. Some even appeared interested in kidnapping Aereas and Nina. If it hadn't been for an occasional barked word from Boffo and some glances that made even barb-tailed beasts cringe, the cousins would likely not have emerged from the market's other end.

As they approached the gloomy night on the far side of the clustered stalls, Aereas felt the color slowly returning to his face, felt his breath come more easily. He was beginning to feel relaxed enough that, when he saw a familiar beast—a black, short-haired dog leaning idly against one taut curtain of a tent—he bent down to pet the creature.

"Hiya, boy. Nice to see a familiar face."

"You aren't familiar to me at all," came the crisp, half-barked reply. "And I'm a bitch, not a boy."

The dog's flews pulled back to reveal fangs.

Boffo yanked Aereas away, shot him a warning glance,

and yipped an apology to the creature. He drew Aereas out of earshot before he spoke again.

"That was a moon dog, likely smarter than any of us. You're just lucky she was in a good mood."

Aereas nodded.

Clearly, there was far more to this place than the strange inward curve of the land, the otherworldly architecture, the menagerie of creatures, the unidentifiable substances. Nothing was as it seemed. Not only was a fiend not necessarily fiendish, but a dog was not necessarily canine.

Aereas again felt that dizzy vertigo. The city had no horizon. There was no way to tell if he was standing up straight, and even if he was, that meant everyone else was leaning. The thought brought chill sweat to Aereas's knotted gut.

And if the city—Sigil it was called, the Cage—was this bad, how awful would Gehenna be?

Aereas halted there at the edge of the marketplace and gripped his knees, catching his breath.

"Are you all right?" asked Nina, placing a hand gently on his back.

He nodded, though he seemed anything but all right. "Where, exactly . . . are you taking us, Boffo?" Aereas asked breathlessly. "I'm beginning to think we've been a little . . . hasty here. Perhaps we should get some rest before—"

Nina set her other hand on his shoulder and drew him upright. "A few more deep breaths, and you'll be fine." The fiery hardness of her eyes softened, and she looked for a moment almost sad. "We've got to keep going. Who knows where—"

He waved her off, drawing the coal-smoky air into his chest and nodding again. "You're right. I can make it."

Boffo intervened. "You're both right. Aereas, you'd both be wise to rest a bit before you go dogging on down to Gehenna. The planes ain't a place you swim through in one breath.

"But, Nina, you're right, too. The sooner we act, the better our chances. We might just find your dad tonight"—he raised a staying hand before her anxious face—"rather than in months, or years, which is possible, too.

"But I should stop flapping my bone-box, because we're here."

He gestured beyond the market sprawl to a small shop crunched between taller brownstones that leaned against it from both sides. The place itself, though small, looked well kept.

Its ancient fieldstone facade was fronted by an ornate fence of black wrought iron. If not for its color and the spikes atop it, the curvilinear ironwork would have looked like roses rising thickly up a trellis. At the center of the fence stood an archway constructed of interlaced black antlers. Some came from identifiable species; most did not.

Within the prickly embrace of iron and horn, four small tables were set up. Around them sat lean and urbane-looking creatures of all races, wearing what, from the looks on their faces, must have been the height of planar fashions: silks and scales; leathers held together by rows of curved metal pins; bits of bone that rattled about necks, hung about ankles, pierced noses or tentacles. . . . Acrid smoke of many varieties curled slow and miasmatic above the patrons.

Like all other sights of the city, it was too much to perceive at a glance.

"We're going in there?" Aereas asked.

Boffo nodded. "Believe it or not, this was one of your uncle's habitual hideaways. The owner, Leonan, is a long-time friend of his—a blood of some import."

Nina sighed, for the first time exhibiting her own anxiety about pressing on. "If we must, we must. I doubt we're wearing suitable clothing for a place like this."

"You're not," Boffo said with a wink. He set off toward the antler gate and the ominous creature that guarded it. "Luckily, your father's name can get a fellow into places that otherwise he'd have to stand on tiptoe to see into."

"Ominous" might have been too pallid a word for the

guard creature. It stood twice the height of Aereas, and that was without counting the majestic rack of horns that spread in a twelve-foot arc over its head. Those antlers made the creature seem the muscled embodiment of the arch it guarded. The horns cast in deep shadow the creature's lion-maned goat head, leaving only the undersized and tight-spaced eyes to gather the dim light. The thing's pupils were black squares. Its enormous arms crossed over a multinippled chest, which shadowed the cloven hooves that tapped impatiently on the brick street beneath it.

Yes, "ominous" was much too pallid a word.

The rumbled growl of its breath assured Aereas they were, indeed, inappropriately dressed.

"Full up," the thing said in a surprisingly high voice.

The gnome smiled indulgently, then crooked a finger, requesting that the thing lean down for a confidential message.

That seemed to Aereas an ill-considered request, and to the thing, too. It let out a puff of smoke from its nostrils. Where there was smoke, there was fire. Even so, the beast bent forward through its own swirling smoke and turned a long goat ear to the gnome.

Though Aereas should have been close enough to hear what passed between them, the lion's mane that cascaded down around the gnome's ears dampened all sound.

Suddenly the beast was standing up, an incredulous look on its goat muzzle. It jabbed a humanlike finger out toward Aereas. "Him? Artus?"

"Shh!" Boffo insisted, gesturing covertly toward a pair of winged fiends at the nearby table.

The arms were crossed again. "Looks too small, too young."

"Portals will be portals," replied Boffo with a shrug.

The goatman seemed to consider. "Well, all right. But you know what Leonan'll do if you're not giving him the dark of it."

Boffo nodded and tried not to gulp too obviously.

✦ Her Fire ✦

She was a blur before him, her thin taut body rattling through the trees like a windborne tatter of paper. There was fire in her hand. The black bough blazed and smoldered above her pitching hair. She ran. She ran she ran ran ran.

Aereas was behind, thrashing past thickets she'd leapt over, dived through. He ran too, though the rumpled knolls and cluttered streams seemed to swell between them. He was losing her. There was no time for kicking dust, no time for winging arms like a strafing bird or hitch-step strutting on this run. Only time to run. To run to run.

The ground fell away like an indrawn gut, and in the belly of the hollow were the Higgins boys. They stood, open-mouthed, staring at the black thrash of Nina falling on them.

Her burning bough struck Wayne in the temple, flung him spinning like a sprawled cat.

Careb and Jute hurled at her the chalky rocks they held. One missed; one rolled atop her shoulder like a ball in a game. They turned to run, and she was singeing their hamstring hairs into little black balls.

Aereas skidded down the slope at a galloping yell as Wayne was stumbling up and away, curses catching in his crooked teeth. Aereas screamed at him, a sound like the wail of a singer in dread, and Wayne was gone, too.

Aereas did not follow them, for he had seen where their chalky rocks had been falling. There, in the white center of that black-bellied hollow, he saw the stones in an accidental cairn, saw the twitching, broken ground squirrel the boys had buried alive.

It was the work of a moment. The misery was ended. And when Nina returned at a loping run, her brown skin war-painted in sweat and soot, she found her cousin painted in blood.

FIVE

CAFÉ LEONAN

The goatman gestured with his huge human hand past the archway, and Aereas and Nina followed Boffo through.

They were halfway across the courtyard, heading to the round red door of the fieldstone café, when Aereas tapped Boffo's shoulder and whispered, "Why did you tell him I was Artus?"

"Expediency," the gnome said. "Something you primes've got to learn here in Sigil is it's not so much your actions that'll get you killed, but what you say, and not so much what you say, but how you say it."

"What about who I am?" hissed Aereas. "Sounds like *that's* about to get me killed."

"Go in with that attitude and you're right," Boffo replied, pulling away and opening the door before them. "Ready?"

The cousins took a unison breath, then stepped through the doorway.

The room beyond was huge, far larger than it could possibly have been, given the size of the building. Boffo's shop could have fit four times within the main chamber. It was a white space filled with ornamental plants in raised boxes and brass bowls. There were ranks of rhododendrons, banks of leafy ferns, tangled screens of columbine, and half a hundred other species that neither of the cousins recognized. The plants were arrayed among tidy tables on many levels, the whole room centering on a stand of exotic pines that rose some five stories from the sunken garden where they were planted. The air murmured with water and customers and music.

"How?" Aereas asked, gap-mouthed.

Boffo flicked a finger beneath his chin. "Tsk, tsk. Remember Rule Number Two. Besides, you're supposed to be familiar with this place, Artus. Attitude again. Attitude."

Unlike her cousin, Nina hid her nervousness beneath a mask of serene beauty. She said softly, "If *Artus* is supposed to be familiar with this place, it'd help if he knew the name of it."

"Leonan," Boffo replied simply. He moved through the jungle of plants and tables and patrons, toward a stairway behind a zither player.

Nina paced him. "I thought Leonan was the owner."

"Yep, owner and café, both."

Aereas followed behind, his head too busy spinning from the impossible location to be spinning from the argument. He passed a table occupied by something that looked like a gigantic fly, sipping a drink through its long, tubular lips. Unsure whether this creature's multifaceted eyes were looking at him or not, Aereas nodded politely as he went on.

Without turning around, Boffo whispered, "Don't nod, berk. No eye contact." Then he said to himself, "What have I gotten mixed up in?"

Aereas kept his eyes veiled until the three of them reached the far stairs and began to ascend. The open steps gave an even better view of the room, displaying a fountain that bubbled quietly beside the zither player.

At the top of the stairs they reached an alcove, one side of it an open, wrought-iron gate. Without pause, Boffo led them through.

The room beyond was bare and white, empty save for a large black sphere that hovered in its dead center. The featureless ball was alive with blue motes of magic, some of which flowed out toward one wall of the room. Where the specks struck, the plaster had faded away to show lath, and the lath to show timbers, and the timbers to show the main café below. Where the magic lights did not strike, the wall was solid. The whole of the tavern was visible through that magical breach in the wall, though none of the three had seen a similar hole on the other side.

That was everything: the hole, the orb, and the trembling intruders. Otherwise, the room was empty.

The livid blue sparks seemed to notice the intruders. Some of the swirling lights gathered on the near face of the orb, and a tentacle of magic flung itself out and surrounded the three. The gate slammed closed behind them.

"It's got us . . . some kind of guard," hissed Aereas tightly.

Boffo, how dare you? came a voice in all of their heads at once.

"Expediency," Boffo repeated, with less conviction than previously.

There followed a kind of mental laughter, like a frission of cold or the tingling of a yawn forming in one's jaw. Then the prickling magic withdrew.

Boffo dropped to his knees and pulled Nina down beside him. Aereas joined them shortly afterward.

Oh, get up, came the voice, huge and everywhere, and yet narrow, crusty, idiosyncratic. *If your lie had made me angry enough, I'd've killed you already. No amount of bowing would've changed that.*

"Leonan?" Nina gasped, staring at the black orb.

Get up! the voice repeated.

They did.

The voice continued. *Well, you seem to know my name, but I don't know yours.*

"Nina," she replied, "my father is—"

Ah, Nina, the voice interrupted, as though in remembrance. *So that's what he named you. That's how Artus comes into this all.*

"I'm Artus," replied Aereas, finally summoning a cocksureness, but one that was as transparent as the wall.

Boffo smacked his forehead. The orb, though silent, gave the impression it was sadly shaking its head. *Badly played, child.* The sphere rolled along the long, translucent wall. *This eye of mine can see through walls, could see through your very flesh, let alone your lies. What is your real name?*

"A-Aereas," he said. "Forgive me, Your Greatness."

This brought another laugh from the thing.

Boffo seemed to ease. "He's just a clueless berk-boy, Leonan. Not much of his uncle in him, I'm afraid."

I'd not be so sure. The best spies are born with guts, but have to learn timing.

"Your eye . . . ?" Nina wondered. "That sphere is your eye?"

Boffo interjected, "The whole place is Leonan; the café is his body. This orb is his locus, his mind's eye, if you will."

Aereas's own eyes grew wide, and he began glancing suspiciously at the walls.

Now that introductions are out of the way, why are you here?

"It's about Artus—"

How's he doing? It's been long. Not met another man could down so much bourbon in an evening and still win at poker.

"He's been kidnapped," Nina blurted.

Whether or not it was possible for a featureless black

sphere to have an expression, Leonan did now. The blue motes of magic about it were tinged with amber. It—he—even seemed to darken in that moment.

By whom?

"Some kind of stony imps from Gehenna," Nina volunteered.

Stony imps from Gehenna? Leonan responded, humming ominously.

"Gargoyles," Boffo corrected. "We don't know who their high-up man is, perhaps even tanar'ri or baatezu. We think it's got something to do with the War, but the dark of it is we don't know much."

Leonan drifted along the wall toward them. *That damned Blood War. It's cost too many lives already—lots of them worth much less than Artus's. It's a boil on the backside of decent merchants like you, Boffo.*

"And like you, too, Leonan," echoed Boffo with an arched eyebrow.

Yes, like me, too. The sphere seemed amused by Boffo's sarcasm. *And now it's got Artus, too.*

"He knew the risks," Boffo said soberly, drawing a glare from Nina. "But so did I when I took him in, let him set up that closet the way he did. Now there's trouble, and that's why I'm here."

"We want to rescue him," Aereas summarized. Was it his imagination, or did that faceless globe suddenly have the aspect of a tired, kindly old man?

You have no idea how incapable you are of doing anything about this situation, do you?

"Forget about what we can't do," Nina said. "We're already doing more than we can do, and we'll keep doing it until we get Artus back. What can *you* do? If that eye of yours can see through me, can it see who's got my father?"

The sphere seemed impressed. *Now that's Artus's spirit, if not his flesh. He'd work for months without a peep, but soon as his work got dead-ended, you'd hear about it.*

No, I can't see who's got Artus. Kidnappers don't tend to turn up in the Cage and announce their booty. They might still be here, yes. This is, after all, the marketplace for the planes, but they might be gone now, too.

What I can do is take a look about Sigil and see if an old friend of your father is in town. He'll've posted his banners if he's here . . . if he's still in the helping business.

"Not Jandau Danus?" said the gnome ruefully.

Let me see if he's about and available, replied the sphere, then it lifted slowly toward the ceiling.

Its blue radiances shifted from the front wall and fountained up across the ceiling, which went from opaque to milky white to translucent and transparent until the plaster directly above the sphere dissolved away in a circle. Beyond the hole was a dark attic space, and into it, Leonan levitated. The cousins watched in amazement as the belly of the sphere slid through what had, moments before, been solid ceiling. It passed smoothly out of sight. Then, with a barely audible crackle of blue radiance, the ceiling sealed up behind the sphere, fading to opaque. The room—ceiling, walls, and floor—was bare.

Boffo answered their questions before they could even ask them. "I told you, this place is him. The whole tavern. It's his body."

"And that . . . that globe is his mind's eye," Nina repeated.

"It's the locus of his thought. That's why he can speak directly into our minds, can see right through us."

"How did he become . . . ?" Aereas paused, remembering Rule Number Two.

Boffo obliged him anyway. "Maybe your dad knows Leonan's story, but I sure don't. Some say he's a tiny creature encased in that globe, his persona projected outward to animate the very walls around us. Others say he's always been a building, some kind of stag modron—a mechanical creature. They point to how big Leonan is on the inside, saying he could only have grown that big if he were, say, three hundred years old."

"Buildings get bigger *inside* when they grow?" Aereas asked, then shook his head, stunned.

"What's so strange about that?" Boffo asked. "That's what people do."

The ceiling was again going transparent. Leonan descended.

Yes, he's here. Busy tonight, though. He'll meet you here tomorrow night, by the zither player.

"Tomorrow?" Nina said. "Imagine all the tortures that—"

Tomorrow! growled Leonan in a lionlike voice that seemed to suggest where he'd gotten his name. *In the meantime, I suggest you get some rest. Not a lot of planars, let alone primes, can catch any shut-eye in Gehenna.*

And with that, the conversation was done. Mantled in blue magic, Leonan slid through the far wall.

"Let's go," Boffo said, brushing off his hands. "He's right about the shut-eye."

* * * * *

Aside from the shortness of the bed, Aereas might well have lain in the spare room of his uncle's cottage in distant Caonan. But, no, he lay in the upstairs guest bedroom of Boffo's shop—his kip. Unfortunately it was a gnome-sized bed, and Aereas's human knees were hooked over the footboard. His toes dangled in the cool, smoke-charged breezes. The rafters overhead were straight and clean, outlining no constellations Aereas knew.

He opened the book, which he'd rescued from Nina's pack when she'd been washing up, and skimmed the volume, looking for Boffo's name.

That brief tour of the pages was like their brief tour of Sigil: mind-boggling, frightening, intriguing, stunning, beautiful. Artus's handwriting, if it all *was* his handwriting,

◆ 71 ◆

said as much about where he had been as his words did. Even the media of writing told tales: quill, fountain pen, charcoal, bloody fingertip, soot. Some pages were gilded, some stained in various colors with what might have been the blood of strange creatures. The folios yet bore scents of sulfur, fetid bogwater, elven glades, sweat, toil, death—whatever had surrounded the book when Artus had sat down to write. But all the pages bore words, words, words, and sometimes sketches of coy-faced fey creatures or gaunt execution machines or fortifications clinging to impossible landscapes. . . .

It was in the wash of these words and images that Aereas found the name of Boffo. The page smelled of the music shop, and the words waltzed across it in an unhurried hand and a flowing violet ink.

Thank the Lady for Boffo. It'd been ten days, at my best reckoning, since last I had eaten, and more than that since I'd had a bath. I had slept only in the eyeblink moments between trudging steps up Mount Mungoth. After all my travels and all my dealings with horrible beasts and hostile places, I thought that that single lifeless desolation would be the end of me.

I'm still not sure how it was I got back to Sigil. I found myself (just before Boffo found me) lying in a literal gutter in the Lower Ward, along with the rest of the detritus of the city.

Yes, I was back, and the Lady knew it, but I didn't expect a hand from her, didn't expect even another agent to hazard those alleys. I was certain I'd trudged up the acid slopes of Mount Mungoth, somehow found a portal or conduit (I still don't know which), and landed in the Cage, only to die within spitting distance of hot food and a clean bed.

I hadn't expected an agent, but who else would've come to nudge me with his curled boot and roll me over and say, "You don't belong here. If you can walk, you'll have a bath and dinner tonight"? Who but a little music-shop gnome?

I could walk, at least some of the way, and crawled the rest. The strange little man never even turned to see if I'd make it or not. It was like a test, like the hand extended down to a man in a pit, waiting for the man to lift his hand up and take hold. I did.

His shop wasn't much warmer or more accommodating than the gutter where I had lain—not then, at least. I swore to myself if I survived the digestion of my first food in nearly a fortnight, I'd do something about fixing up the shop. Even so, he couldn't have known of my carpentry skills. He couldn't have known who I was or for whom I worked. But he came and got me and fed me and saved me anyway. To this day, I do not know why.

There came a knock at the door, and Aereas, rapt in the story of his uncle, was so startled he slammed the journal closed and cleared his throat. "Come in, Nina."

He had known it was she by the knock alone, those small knuckles quiet against the wood, rapping out a rhythm he and she had established for entrance into their cave.

As it turned out, he didn't need to invite her in. When he looked up from the too-short bed, she crouched already inside the room, the short door closed behind her flank.

"It's cold in here, too," she said, lingering against the door. Her gnomish nightshirt cast a curving line across her shivering legs.

Aereas swung his own legs from over the footboard and found that his calves and feet had fallen asleep. Pins and needles prickled his flesh. His feet dragged dully over the polished planks of the floor, and he motioned Nina over to sit beside him.

She gave a brief, embarrassed smile, and if her flesh had

not been so dusky, he might have seen a blush there. Stooping to avoid the low beams, she hurried across the creaking floor and, in a rush, dropped down beside Aereas. She drew the covers over her naked legs and across his as well.

"That's better," she whispered through chittering teeth.

Aereas nodded, feeling the heat spill from her hip and wondering how she could possibly feel cold. Blushing, he drew the journal to his lap and opened it. "I—uh, borrowed this from your pack."

She waved off the implied apology.

"I've just found a slightly different story about how Uncle Artus—how your dad and Boffo met," he said hurriedly, opening the journal and paging through to find the spot.

Nina leaned in. Her small hand rested on the near edge of the journal, and her shoulder and side, despite their shivering, felt hot to Aereas.

He flipped through the book. Once again the blood, the burn marks, the charcoal sketches flitted by, though none of them looked familiar. He kept turning pages, attention split between the strange leaves before him and Nina's curve beside him.

"It—it's here somewhere," he yawned, beginning to flip faster. There was a sketch of a twisting tower, its bartizan bristling with horn and bone rather than stone; an illustration of swords; a page displaying an arcane set of cards; another written large, in letters that had since run from moisture. All of it looked similar to what he had seen before, though none of it was the same. "It's like . . . it's like the book has changed since you . . . because it—"

Nina, who'd seemed barely able to refrain from taking the book, now reached across his lap and lifted it. "Let me see," she said, then turned to the last page of the volume. It had but one line on it, centered on the page and written with some kind of globby green substance.

" 'And into this I went,' " she read aloud, and Aereas nodded his agreement. Slowly, she closed the book and took a deep breath. Opening it again, she flipped to the final page.

This time, it was a much-besmirched sheaf of what seemed vellum, crisscrossed with straight lines and scribed arcs, the intersections of them circled or marked with squares, triangles, or pentagons.

She closed the book once more, then opened it to the final page, which now held a detailed ink drawing of her own face. The likeness was so well rendered that the book might have been a mirror reflecting her visage back at her. She slammed the journal closed and slid it back onto Aereas's lap.

"Just like this place. Ever-changing, intimate, bigger on the inside than on the outside," she said. "It's like the pages are infinite, and where the covers are is just a matter of convenience."

Into the silence that followed this statement, Aereas let out a sick sigh. He slid the book from his lap to the floor.

Nina continued, "And my dad is out in this crazy infinitude somewhere."

Aereas nodded, swallowing uneasily. He laid a hand on her knee. "We'll find him. We will."

She blinked once.

Had she just banished the beginning of a tear? Aereas wondered—but then she was speaking again.

"This isn't my kind of battle. You know that," she said thickly. She drew a shaking breath. "I've got to *see* my enemies. I've got to *act*. All this patience, this planning, this hanging around. The fury in me just gets hotter and hotter, like coals when the flue is narrowed and the doors are near closed. I just want to tear into something, someone."

His arm was around her now. "There'll be time for fury. Hold on to it, but don't let it burn you from the inside out."

She wrung her hands and stood. In a step, she reached

the low-gabled window and knelt to look out into the smoky night of Sigil, into the unnatural upward curve of the land and the spiky, oblivious buildings that stretched out forever across it.

"And you know the worst thing? This place isn't disconnected from Caonan. No. Caonan is just a tiny corner of this place. It's like our whole world fits inside a tobacco stand, which fits inside a closet inside a music shop inside a circular city inside the next larger onion layer and the next.

"We grew up in the core of a nesting doll that goes on forever, and this is just the first layer beyond."

Aereas rose and came to place his hands on her shivering shoulders.

"At least," she continued, "if this were someplace else, I could hate it. But this is the shape of our own world, the shape of Telmar projected outward infinitely into an absurdity more vast than a thousand Telmars.

"Our world is just a water drop. This place—Sigil and Gehenna and the Abyss and everywhere else we've always thought just legends—are the ripples made when that drop merged with the rest of the sea. And each ripple ten, a hundred, a thousand, a million, a billion times larger than the drop."

Aereas held her, feeling the warmth of her shivering body, and realizing it was the heat of rage and despair.

"We'll find him. We have to."

✦ His Water ✦

He floated in it, in the cool deep blue place beneath the white shelf of stone that was like a duck's head. Above him, the sky arced in a pale reflection of this place, in clouded reflection of this calm.

Silent was what Nina called it. She did not dive here, not since the time she'd scraped her cheek on one of the great gray stones that lurked like silent leviathans beneath the surface. There were much better places for diving.

Boring was what the Higginses called it, for there were no fish here to catch and torment, and there were bigger, better tidal pools for splashing.

Haven was what Aereas called it. There was no better place to float in hushed peace until the cool pool had dissolved into his naked flesh and he could barely move to swim to the side.

And though she would not swim here, Nina always waited for him, toe tapping and arms crossed, over the ridge.

SIX

JANDAU DANUS

Café Leonan bustled the next night, when Aereas, Nina, and Boffo arrived for their meeting with the mysterious Jandau Danus. They each bore a sheathed short sword and a small rucksack filled with essentials, for Boffo had warned them that Jandau could never be anticipated.

"Do you mean *anticipated*," Aereas asked, "or *trusted*?"

"Both," replied Boffo.

They were to learn nothing more of the man from the gnome.

Neither had the cousins learned more about Sigil in the time since they had last walked beneath that antlered arch. Both had slept most of the day away, exhausted by their traumatic journey through the tobacco stand. The rest of the day they had spent thumbing through Artus's shifting tome, which never seemed the same book twice. They had looked in particular for references to the infamous Jandau, and they had found some:

> *If it weren't for that little gnome and his stash of alpenhorns, I'd've never found my way back. Luckily, alpenhorns are foreign to Daralax, so I locked on to the closest signal and hoped it was Boffo's kip.*
>
> *It was. And though I'd spent half a year aiding the Daralaxan freedom fighters, only a day and a half had passed in Sigil. Again, thank the gods. The dust on the clavier bench still showed where I'd sat only two nights before.*
>
> *As always, Boffo was both amazed and overjoyed to see me back. On more than one occasion, he'd expressed fears that I'd get killed somewhere and he'd be left with a dimensional closet to who-knew-where. "I've often thought about sending Jandau Danus after you," he'd said when I showed up in his case this time.*
>
> *I'd winced. "If anybody could've found me, it would've been Jandau. 'Course, I hope you'd not thought of bringing him into this shop to enlist him. He's got too many pockets in that cloak of his," I replied, gingerly stripping the acid-scarred leathers from my arms and back. "The problem would be giving him enough information to find me without revealing the dark of my missions. I wouldn't want a succubus to romance the knowledge out of him."*
>
> *"Strange man," remarked Boffo.*
>
> *"Strange tiefling," I replied. "It's not often you find a bugger who gets around so much, into and out of so many jams. For all his bleak poetry and dark ways and tiefling blood, you might say he's even got a glimmer of flash."*

From other accounts, the cousins had learned that Artus and Jandau had met in a place called Mechanus, where Artus was helping some robotic creatures called modrons realign a slipped shaft of their gearwork world—or at least try to realign it. The process required a circle of modron priests, a giant wrench, and what Artus described as "a small thermo-alchemical explosion." Jandau had meanwhile been trying to get off a disengaged cog in that clockwork plane. The one feat accomplished the other, and Jandau and Artus had become cohorts, if not friends.

In the passages Aereas and Nina found in the book, Artus had never joined the exploits of the band that slowly gathered about Jandau, nor did Jandau ever directly pitch his lot in with the Lady's custodian.

Among other lingering doubts, Aereas wondered why the sullen tiefling should help them now.

As though reading his mind, Boffo glanced back over his shoulder and said, "Jink. That's all it will take. Lots of gold and platinum jink. Like any artist, Jandau's got his price."

Nina was the one who put their fear into words. "But we've already told you—we don't have any cash. Even if folk around here would take our coin, we don't have coin to give."

Boffo nodded impatiently, guiding them among the potted ferns and the tide of dark-clothed creatures. Despite his words, his face was as gray and guarded as it had been that day in the marketplace. "We don't need up-front money. Never give up-front money to a critter like Jandau. We've just got to let the scoundrel know there's a sack of gold at the end of the trip."

"Scoundrel?" Aereas asked. "I thought you said we could trust—"

"Jink is what I said," Boffo interrupted. "As long as there's jink—and the Lady *should* pay to have her Key returned—you can trust him."

Suddenly the gnome stopped short, his toe stubbing on a smooth black stone raised a bit higher than the others in the café floor. He tripped, then caught himself and nodded in a silent affirmation. "He—and his gang—are in the far corner, behind the zither player."

Aereas glanced along the gnome's line of sight but saw only the palms and the waterfall. "How do you know?"

The gnome tapped his foot twice on the black stone and muttered, "Thanks." Only then did the cousins see the rounded obsidian move, sinking down into the floor.

"Leonan," Nina said with a nod.

A frission of cold—whether from delight or terror he could not say—ran down Aereas's back at that realization, and he felt for a moment that he could sense the all-seeing orb as it moved through solid stone beneath him. Even so, there was neither tremor nor sound. . . .

Until Boffo lightly kicked the young man's planted foot and hissed, "Let's go. He's waiting."

Aereas followed, feeling another chill as he realized Leonan had likely informed the rogue that they had arrived.

They rounded the fountain and came to an overhung corner of the restaurant, cool beneath cascading water and ivy. It was like a grotto, dim and chill, and there Jandau sat, tiny beside the spotted-skinned things that lurked on either side of him. Despite their size and the tacit threat they exuded, these beasts did not draw the companions' eyes so much as did the man.

Jandau was birdlike, a small man and small boned— Aereas would not have been surprised to learn that he was hollow boned. There was an angular fragility about him. His hair, crow-black and bunchy like oiled feathers, formed an unkempt mantle about his pale cheeks and beaklike nose, and the man's narrow neck had that supple curve of a stork's. Even his hands, beringed with small gold things that glinted darkly, were wrapped about his drink like talons around a branch. And when he spoke, though the tone was deep, his words had the melody of birdsong.

"Leonan said you'd arrived," he said, speaking directly to Nina and extending one of those thin, strong hands toward her.

Reflexively she reached out and set her own supple

brown palm on his, and he kissed her wrist.

"Nice to see you, too," Boffo groused, his voice not quite breaking the mesmerism that hung in the air around the man.

Again Jandau spoke, again to Nina. "Your father and I were friends, once. Those days have flown, though." There was melancholy in that. "I've not seen him since you were a brat in arms."

Nina seemed stunned by this statement, unsure whether it was meant as fond remembrance or insult. She retreated into sarcasm of her own. "Ah, yes. I remember you, now. Hard years since then?"

He replied with a toothy smile that somehow looked all out of place on his wan face, like a beakful of teeth. "She bites, too," he said to Boffo as though seeing him for the first time.

"I'm Aereas," said the cousin, extending his hand forcefully over the table.

The man looked at the strong hand, and that smile came again. "I don't intend to kiss it," he said.

With a wave, he warned off his spotted guards—lizardlike men with great iguana eyes that moved independently from each other. Until that moment, Aereas had not realized the lizardmen had raised small crossbows above the table. He withdrew his hand. The bows sank back down.

"Look," Aereas replied in a voice that shook more than he had hoped, "no hows and whys or anything. We just want Artus back, and Leonan says you can help us."

"Leonan rarely lies," the man replied evasively. "He told me of your plight, and I've even sent out a couple of lampboys in my pay to check the gutternet and see if anybody's seen hide or hair."

"So you'll help us?" Nina asked, her voice still mesmerized.

"So I'll take the job, you mean?"

"Take the job?" spat Aereas. "I thought you said you and Artus were friends."

"Friends are friends and business is business." His voice grew cold. "Gehenna is a nasty place. It takes lots more than friendship to make me want to go for a stroll there."

Aereas nodded. "Boffo told us it would cost."

"He rarely lies, either," responded Jandau.

"So," replied Boffo, playing the lay of the trump, "you'll believe me when I say we can get ten thousand gold, easy, for his safe return."

Jandau opened his mouth in a laugh, though no sound emerged. "I could get twenty thousand by selling your lower bits to the resurrection men. Surely you can do better than that."

"You know Artus—" Nina began, but the birdman broke in.

"I told you this wasn't about friend—"

She continued as though he had said nothing. "You know what he holds, what power he has. Ten thousand, and a key."

The man's slim eyebrows lifted. "What key?"

"Any key he's got," Nina replied.

Jandau shook his head and clucked. "You disappoint me, berk. You can't bob me. Those keys aren't yours. They're Artus's—no, not even Artus's but the Lady's. Don't try to bargain with stuff you can't give."

"If we don't get him back, the fiends are going to get *all* the keys," Nina reasoned. "Surely the Lady would rather lose one than all of them."

"And don't speak for the Lady," Jandau said, shaking his head in a silent snicker. "Clueless."

Nina reddened, and her soft hands became hard fists at her side.

Boffo laid a stilling touch on her elbow. "He's right," he whispered. "Sods who speak for the Lady often end up thunderstruck or barmy or mazed or worse."

"Let's face it," Jandau broke in, slowly spreading his talons in a gesture of strange grace, "you've nothing to offer me for this job."

Nina pulled free of Boffo's staying hand. "Why you self-satisfied finch!"

Jandau's face was placid as he droned:

"Goldfinch bright in bare black boughs,
Still your flight and singing calls,
For flames have burned the sacred glade,
And none but you have stayed."

Again, Nina's eyes grew glossy, and Aereas watched her, wondering if this was what Boffo meant by "thunderstruck."

"Who?" asked Nina before she realized she had made the sound. It was as plaintive and quiet as an owl's call. "Who wrote that?"

"I," came Jandau's response. "I wrote that one for your father on one of the Mungoth battlefields. It's in his book, though I doubt you've seen it."

Now the hand on her arm was Aereas's. "Let's go. He won't help us, even if he could." He began to draw her away, but Jandau spoke again, and his words seemed to tether Nina to the tiefling.

"Oh, yes, lass, I can help you—that's sure. But you're right my boy. I won't. I never help anyone but myself."

Boffo, too, tugged at Nina's arm, and they almost succeeded in pulling her away.

"Even so, I'm as much speculator as entrepreneur," continued the thin man. "And though you can't offer me the keys, I imagine that you are right about the Lady's case."

They were still moving away.

For the first time in the conversation, Jandau sounded angry. "Come back here. I'm not finished with you."

They turned but made no move toward him.

"At least stay until I send a message boy," he said, motioning past them, "to the Lady, with a note of my expected compensation."

Nina asked excitedly, "You're taking the job?"

"Taken," replied Jandau as he scribbled something on a scrap of paper.

As though summoned by the tiefling, a breathless boy approached the group. "Found him!" was all he said between pants.

"Artus?" asked Aereas.

"Where?" Jandau and Nina blurted in unison.

The boy addressed his employer. "The foundry."

"Which?"

"*The* foundry. . . . The great one . . . iron . . . on Alehouse Row. . . . A slagger saw him."

And with birdlike grace and speed, Jandau was up from his seat, a crow-black cloak fluttering about him as he slipped his arms beneath it.

"We go," he said to all of them and none of them.

* * * * *

Though Jandau's form was that of a sparrow, it hid a veritable arsenal of weapons, as the cousins soon found out. While they rushed with him along the wheeling streets of that wheeling city, Jandau's talon hands dived at intervals into various folds and pockets of his billowing cape, and with each jab he produced a new weapon: snakeskin stiletto, blackwood blackjack, coiled bullwhip, feathered and faintly glowing wand of some sort, shiv, brass knuckles, even some throwing darts. All but the darts and the wand he was already throwing—to the two Clueless who paced him. They were panting from the speed of their run, from the variety of weapons, and from the prospects of what lay ahead.

"At best, we've got a sneak job," he said briskly. "At worst an all-out donnybrook. You're gonna need something to keep those clueless heads attached to your clueless necks."

They both glanced at Boffo, who nodded gravely and

produced a knife of his own in his muscled hand.

"What about you—?" began Aereas.

Another flap of the cloak and a double tap of the man's hand revealed a short sword strapped to his side.

"This and the darts and the wand, if we get up against it," he replied simply.

He turned away and let out a shrill whistle that more than matched his avian form. From the dimly lit brownstones to either side of the street came a few answering calls, and a few gently turned-back shades.

Then, just as Jandau had produced weapons from his very being, the city produced an army of cohorts to join the fast-striding band. To Jandau, the cousins, Boffo, and the speckled lizardmen were added one by one a dark band of renegades and rogues, many human, many not, and of both genders where gender could be discerned.

Of the nonhumans, the most disturbing was a gray critter that seemed a drifting shadow with no owner. In the flickering lamplight, it proved itself to be a flat, muscular, boneless triangular thing, which skimmed inches above the cobbles and ahead of its own whipping tail. Aereas had heard his uncle tell of similar beasts, flapping silent and sullen beneath the seas. Artus had called them manta rays or something such.

Its physiological opposite was a centaur—or bariaur, as Boffo called him—who stormed suddenly from a dark alley. His hooves were heavy and loud on the stones, and his muscular bulk was swathed in a flitting robe much like Jandau's. He had the grim look of a pirate on his brutal, scarred face, though when he glanced at the cousins, there was a softness there.

A sprite had also joined the company. She glided along in a faint rubescent glow. Her feral features were avid and her eyes beaming red.

A snakewoman was the last to arrive. She looked like the Medusa of legend, with her giant, slithering abdomen, but she thankfully lacked the stunning hair.

Aereas was glad of that, for even among the humans that had joined their number—a lumbering brute who reeked of spirits, a lithe woman with something elven in her gait, and a yammering little man who pranced at Jandau's heels and barked like an excited dog—he felt daunted.

There were some thirteen in their company now, an unlucky crew at best, but Aereas had no time to puzzle on that. Jandau was talking again.

His low whisper reached them all with an uncanny clarity, and the fierceness of the clipped words shut up even the yammering man. "If Artus is at the ironworks, that means it could be an elemental job, or fire minions, so if any of you louts thought to bring water weaponry, keep it handy."

There came a slithering snicker from low down—the manta thing—and a sly voice that sent chills up Aereas's spine: "You think any of these bashers're gonna be packing holy water, Jan?"

The amusement that followed that comment was shortlived, killed by their leader's tongue. "Enough of that, Krim. Keep your head clear of jokes and clear for spells. We're going to need them."

"What about me?" enthused the yammerer. He avidly slid his short sword in and out of its sheath. "Old Bob's already!"

"Old Bob can wait. I'll not have you wilding unless Krim fails. And don't you go slaking yourself on any innocents. If we need you, we'll need you thirsty."

"I been in that place once't," offered the lumbering hulk, whose voice was disconcertingly high for his size. "I kin maybe get in again."

"Better yet, tell me where'd be good kip for kidnappers, a cage for a prisoner," Jandau replied evenly.

"I knowed they once't had this yugoloth they throwed into the smelter, and there was this 'splosion cause he turned right now into steam and out splatters all the iron and stuff."

"Where would they put one they wanted to keep alive?"

That seemed to take a bit more thought. "Uh—outside the smelter, prob'ly."

"One they wanted to keep secret?" pressed Jandau.

"Oh, they gots tunnels underneath there that goes down down down and some says down even to the backside of the city so's you can fall off to the Outlands."

The manta sneered, "You can't fall off the city, you nematodic thrall." Then Krim's tone changed as he addressed Jandau. "Even so, a quick spell tells me he's right about the tunnels, and about someone being down there."

Jandau nodded, his mind keenly eating up the information as his feet ate up the road. "Anybody work down there, Dif?"

The oaf scratched his head. "Don't think so. I only knowed about them tunnels 'cause I got locked down there once't and almost went barmy trying to get out."

Krim made a clicking sound. "An intellect of your magnitude going barmy would be like a daisy going stag."

"Hush, now," ordered Jandau. "We're getting too close. The foundry's up ahead, around the bend. Split up like usual, three *M*s per group. Post around the perimeter and look for a way in. Krim will mindlink with the brains of each outfit and keep us up on the chant."

As quickly as they had arrived, the rogues departed, and more silently, their clusters melting into the darksome patches between the street lamps.

That left only Jandau, Boffo, the cousins, and a lizard-man.

Without breaking stride or slowing, Jandau seemed to take stock of his party. "I suppose I'll count for Mind, and LiGrun here for Muscle. The only other *M* is Magic, though I doubt I can ask any of you for that."

Nina glanced dubiously at Aereas and Boffo, then

replied sharply, "How about your little wand? It seems to be glittering excitedly."

There came a brief laugh to that, a single whuff of air, and Jandau said, "We'll talk about my wand later. But you're right, I've got all three *M*s."

Aereas found himself flushing with jealousy, and he muttered, "I guess we're just *M* for Monitors."

* * * * *

They made a strange fivesome, crouched as they were beside the baroque iron fence that both barred passage into the Great Foundry and proclaimed to all the product of the place. Not that most of the Lower Ward's inhabitants—creatures on their way from or to one hell or another—would be stopped by mere iron. Nor, Jandau told them, would most of those creatures mind dismantling a fivesome of Market Ward brats, hiding with daggers in the bushes.

He spoke to them in hushed whispers, which tumbled from his mouth and barely reached their ears before dissipating in the dust. "Whoever they are, they've not got the Lady's go-ahead. Krim says he's found a downed guard—yugoloth by the look of him—at the gate just around the corner."

"We might as well go in where they did," Nina said, finishing his thought.

He gazed at her for a long moment in the darkness, then nodded. "C'mon." He was moving again.

Given the almost elven grace of their leader, the reptilian glide of the lizardman, and the gnomish unobtrusiveness of Boffo, the cousins felt gawky, loud, and slow. Jandau apparently agreed, often snagging their shirt sleeves and pulling them into shadows or shoving them forward, or shouldering them to a halt. And always just in time. Though the kidnappers had downed one yugoloth—a mixed-mettle beast like the guard at Leonan—three others yet patrolled between them and the unguarded back gate.

It was a trash lane—short, wide, inauspicious. The path was strewn with rubbish both recognizable and not, and singing with flies.

The five rushed, panting, to fetch up behind one of the darksome brick posts of the gate. Aereas glimpsed the other members of the party converging in the shadows on the opposite side. Jandau nodded to them, then glanced out past the slightly open gates and the supine guard breathing in ragged unconsciousness beside them.

Beyond lay a back courtyard, well lit though vacant, leading to a structure of some magnitude. At the base of the brick building, one door stood hastily propped on wrenched hinges, and from within, steamy light issued in a languid roil.

"Krim," hissed Jandau, "how about a bit of glamour to run in?"

The manta ray glided nonchalantly toward his master and whistled out, "Always send the flapper ahead of you, aye?"

Then they were moving again. The whole company fell in tight behind the ray as it swung the creaking gates wide and flowed sinuously through.

Aereas and Nina in midcompany poked forward on tiptoes, though none of the others made any special attempt to conceal themselves. Then, the cousins realized why—a kind of haze surrounded them, a diffuse mystical cloud that shimmered dully with a thousand minute reflections of the bricks and shadows and spaces around them. It was as though they hurried forward in a spray of glitter that masked them, dressing them in myriad reflections of the world about.

"Amazing," Aereas murmured, not for the last time.

Though the magic masked sight, it seemed to amplify sound. Aereas's voice echoed among them for a moment, even after one of the humanlike beasts in the company had slipped a hand over his mouth. Aereas wrenched it free but said no more as they reached the wrecked door.

At a gesture from Jandau, the hulking brute grasped one edge of the door and flung the thing quickly and silently aside. The group, following the patiently drifting Krim, crowded within.

The dark hall before them led obliquely downward. Its walls were some strange compromise between cave and passageway. It was as though the company had entered a mine, with rough walls shaped only by occasional supports.

"Let there be . . ." the manta ray began dramatically, and he suddenly glowed with a purplish hue that made the descending chamber all the less welcoming.

Down they went, as though into the venous gullet of a giant. The space was hot and growing hotter. The walls and floor, at first damp, became moist and then downright slick. With each corner they rounded, the metallic humidity deepened until they saw steam, rising from below and curling in wreaths from their own mouths. Despite the rippling bellies and knees of stone, the comrades saw no signs of doors, no intersections of any kind.

"Anything, Krim?" asked Jandau, panting.

The manta's tail lashed in place of a nod. "Something's ahead. Something or someone."

"Glad you're so precise," blurted Dif the oaf, who seemed instantly pleased with his jab.

"One of us must be," replied Krim serenely as he plunged onward.

They had descended for a quarter mile, it seemed, before the snaking passage changed, and it wasn't so much the passage but the air. There was a vast rumbling this deep. After another quarter mile, the cave began to glow with a hellish illumination.

Aereas swallowed. "Was that door a portal into—"

"The Abyss?" finished Jandau. "Not likely, but who

knows here in the Lower Ward. Nah. When you hear hooves, think horses, not zebras."

"Huh?" Aereas asked.

The shadowy fellow seemed pleased by his perplexity.

Nina broke in. "It's a foundry. That red glow is probably from—"

And they rounded a turn into a vast chamber. They halted on the water-beaded floor and immediately saw what the glow was from—the glow, the steam, and the roar.

Molten iron. The ceiling of the huge cavern was oozing the stuff in long columns fatter than any tree Aereas had ever seen, and taller than most. Those columns of red-hot iron poured down from holes above and into holes below— literal pillars of fire. The edges of these pillars roiled with sagging cascades of red iron, their bloody hues manifold and alive as though they were vast hot arteries.

The chamber was huge and cavelike, the amorphous stone walls once molten. Within those walls were carved catwalks, and upon them drifted strange gray creatures. Literally drifted. The silken robes that draped their tall, gaunt forms passed inches above the catwalks, and showed no feet beneath.

"Meet the staff," Nina said dryly.

"Dabus," noted Jandau. His voice was grave. "I should have known this would be their place. Too grand, too covert to be part of the Godsmen's guildhall. And too many portals. Guess the best place to hide a foundry is under the Foundry. I'd always wondered where they got their metal."

Aereas nodded, though he hadn't the slightest idea what Jandau was saying. That ignorance hadn't time to manifest itself; the narrow tiefling was still talking.

"Anyway, we've chased down a red herring. If the kidnappers'd been down here, the dabus would've stopped them. After all, they work for the Lady—"

Krim let out a riffling laugh that seemed to come from

his wings. "They're the Lady's garbagemen and demolition crews—they wouldn't give a rip if Orcus himself walked through here."

"They *did* pass this way," one of the lizardmen said gravely. His reptilian face looked particularly cragged as the scales over it lifted in the intense heat. Aereas realized this blazing furnace room must be a most uncomfortable and dangerous place for him. "Or somebody with feet did. I can see the heat of their footprints, fading away on the floors."

They all squinted to make it out, but could see nothing.

The lizardman pointed between the glowing columns of iron and sniffed, "They went through there."

Nina suddenly stepped from the group, drawing a short, stinging gasp of the prickling air. Her throat tightened, but through it she squeezed the word, "Father."

Now the others saw it too, the final flicker of a horned wing of gray flesh, and behind it the brief flash of red human skin.

Artus. His aged face showed just between a scaled shoulder and a stony talon. He was red from the heat, his eyes closed, though not against the bald fury of the iron columns. He was unconscious. Then the face was gone again, eclipsed by the wing, which also slid away, leaving only the momentary lolling of a single loose foot.

"Father," she said again, beginning to dart forward.

If she said anything more, not even she knew. Suddenly there was a horrific hiss followed by an explosion of searing white.

✦ Elflords Dancing ✦

"Wake up! Wake up!" she cried.

The room was midnight, and Nina seemed a hot, fierce coalescence of it. Her fingers were talonlike on his night-shirt, on his shoulders.

"Wake up! They're dancing."

Aereas came awake two steps away from the bed, one leg already rammed into his rumpled breeches. Before the other was lifted past the flopping buckle, he reminded himself why he was awake and standing. "They're dancing?"

She nodded in the darkness, rushing toward him, past him. "Bring your hat. It's raining."

So it is, he thought as he tugged the breeches up about his narrow waist. The press of her now-absent hands still ached hot on his shoulders beneath the pummeling cold racket on the roof. So it is.

But it was more than just rain.

He followed her into the teeth of the storm. She was dreamlike in her thready clarity as she ran through the pelting gale. Flashes of blue from the raging sky momently lit her flesh—an angled elbow, the inside of a knee taut with running. Already, her thin cotton shift clung to her as though she'd been swimming in it, and Aereas knew his nightshirt clung to him, too.

There were beginning to be differences in their bodies. He was like a milkweed stalk, tall and taller, beginning to bristle. She was like a rose, curving and hipped with bloom.

In the blackness between thrashes of lightning, he ran full into her. They both tumbled—she from the bare feet she'd planted on the muddy hilltop; he from the toil of legs through blood-brown puddles. Neither cried out. They merely rolled, serious and silent like wrestling cats.

When the black-gray spinning of the world had stilled, she did not even disentangle herself from him, but pointed to the next ridge.

There, against the distant sheet lightning, he saw a dead copse of pines, their bare blackness straight and rigid against the pitching darkness. And now he saw the dancers, too, moving in violent circles.

There were four whirling strikes of lightning, and the dancers' feet thundered a clog-dance among the dead boughs.

SEVEN

IR⊕N CRUCIBLE

In the afterimage of their vision, the company glimpsed what had happened. The dabus along the catwalks had lanced long poles into holes in the wall, from which sprang roaring jets of water that struck the draping columns of iron and exploded into steam.

That's what that burning was, Nina realized from the floor where she now lay, gasping for air and feeling only fire instead. Then, in the white blindness, someone floundered over her and struck the floor beyond. She reached out to grab Aereas, and felt his hand thrusting out to do the same. On the suddenly slick floor, they struggled up and ran back toward the door.

Or where they thought the door had been. Running full-tilt into one of the stony walls of the cavern, they sprawled again, clambered up, and skated along it until they found the mouth of the entry. Again they ran, veins bulging like those of swimmers who must labor through thirty feet of watery tunnel before air.

They rounded the hairpin corner and began to rake in breaths as they ran. The steam was still around them, but gray rather than white, hot rather than searing. Another thirty steps and they approached the gasping knot of their company.

They skidded to a halt, still holding hands as they doubled over and hacked out the heat from their lungs.

"That was close!" Aereas rasped, but not from beside Nina.

She glanced up quickly and saw that the hand she held was Jandau's, not Aereas's.

She dropped her hold. Were it not for the red of her face and eyes, she might have appeared startled or embarrassed. Instead, she simply said, "Yes. It was close."

Aereas interposed himself, turning his back upon the sardonic smile of their leader and setting a hand on Nina's shoulder. "Are you all right?"

She shrugged off the hand. "It's too hot."

Aereas backed up a step. Jandau began to speak. "Keep yourself behind next time, and you're less likely to get scalded." His voice sounded hollow in the echoing smoothness of the passage.

Coughing one last time, Nina shushed Jandau. She held her hand up for silence from the rest. The hissing had gone, replaced again by the ever-present rumble. "It's stopped. There has to be time to get through before the next steambath."

Protests rose up from many lips, loudest of all from those of the heat-beleaguered lizardmen, but all these entreaties were wasted. Already Nina had disappeared back into the swirling steam.

Jandau gaped after her. Aereas felt rare delight in seeing that stunned expression on the keen features of the tiefling. Then Aereas, too, was gone. He and Nina had spent too many summers together for him to stand stunned by her headlong charges.

Half running, half staggering, Aereas rounded a curve and broke from the grayness of the passage into the whiteness of the room beyond. The steam had become mist, hot but no longer scalding, and the red pillars glowed an evil pink through the thick haze. There, between them, he made out the struggling shadow of Nina, and redoubled his speed to reach her.

He did, but all too quickly, nearly bowling into her where she stood. Stood? That was not like her. She'd be running, unless . . .

A piercing shriek above their heads answered his question, and Nina swung a suddenly drawn short sword into the mists. The thing darted into sight, all triangles and gleaming eyes, just above her. Her sword clanged and cracked on its flesh as though she were fighting stone.

Not another gargoyle!

Halting beside her, Aereas fumbled for his short sword. In that instant, he wished he had something longer, some sort of rock hammer. Ah, well. If only he could get the sword drawn.

He spun, bumbling into another creature that loomed up out of the mist.

A dabus. The tall, lean thing looked like a floating candle with its gray priestly robes and white flame of hair. The wick of the candle, the creature's head, was goatlike, at once profane and wise. It was topped with four horns, two straight in the center, and two curled on the sides.

Strangest of all, in the mist about the creature floated a nonsensical collection of symbols and letters. The sigils emerged from the thing's head like hand-sized dandruff flakes, then went winging away in an upward spiral.

No time for talk, especially given how well Aereas's conversation with the moon dog had gone. Instead, he reached out and snagged the staff the creature held in one long, gaunt hand, and swung it upward at the darting form above Nina. The gargoyle reeled away, disappearing for a moment in the mist, but returned a breath later with another at its side.

Nina was still at it, though now she was fighting her way forward between the radiant pillars.

Aereas made another jab at the second beast, and this time the tip of the staff struck and stung it. The creature fell suddenly from the air and crashed, stiff, to the floor, shattering like a statue. The shards of the monster flung themselves outward in a skittering explosion, some of the pieces sliding soundlessly into the nearby column of iron.

Aereas was about to release a whoop of victory and jab the second creature when the staff was ripped brutally from his hand and he was whirled around.

Though the dabus had touched neither Aereas nor the staff, the stick was now clutched in its hand. Aereas stood gaping in amazement at the creature. From the thing's flamelike hair, a single symbol emerged, a red dove that swept upward for a moment before diving toward Aereas. It swelled in the mists, became huge. Then it crashed into him.

Aereas's body was aflame. The intense heat of the columns was redoubled by the sizzle of magical energy from the dove. And he was rising. His feet kicked uselessly above the slowly descending floor. He shouted out for help from Nina or one of the other companions who'd just crowded up, but all were too stunned to grab hold of him until he was out of reach.

Out of their reach, that is, but not out of reach of the gargoyle. Suddenly he was grappled by the thing, its horned beak opening for an instant before it bit down viciously on his shoulder. The beak ripped through flesh, down to the ligamented joint between bones.

Aereas screamed. The sound was lost in the roaring column, and his free arm flailed for the short sword. He wrenched it free, though the hilt was slick with steam or perhaps blood, and he struck his assailant in the side with a hammering blow. Only the sparks that came up from that stone skin told of the attack, the sparks and the quivering pain that shot up Aereas's arm and into his neck. He struck again, again, feeling but not hearing the clang of steel and stone. But the glowing eyes of the beast showed no pain, no panic.

In a miasma of metallic mist and swirling anguish, Aereas suddenly realized why the roaring pillar was so loud. They were being drawn into it. No, not drawn—impelled. The flames around him pushed him toward the pillar. It was the dabus's doing.

Aereas ceased the futile chopping with his sword, instead flailing his legs like a cat does to turn itself in the air. Two kicks, and a third, and the horn-winged back of the beast was toward the hellish pillar. Aereas doubled his knees up before him, planted his feet on the stone creature's waist, and kicked furiously.

The beak did not release his shoulder. If anything, it tightened, the sharp tips above and below dragging over the rounded seam of bone on bone, lacerating muscles and ligaments and all as it went.

Next moment, the beak snapped shut, ripping free of Aereas's shoulder. The blood-spattered beast soared beautifully backward until its flailing wings sank into the column. They buried in the gushing iron, cracked free, and tumbled the wounded thing over. Its head sank into the pillar, and it was dragged downward with the plummeting iron. Though it disappeared from sight, Aereas heard its body strike the stone floor and shatter, as had the first.

Aereas, too, was moving now, flung backward by his kick against the creature. He flailed his legs to turn over so that he could land on his feet, but then discovered he was not going to land. His downward rush slowed just before he glimpsed Nina, gazing fearfully upward through the mist.

She swung out one arm, but couldn't reach him.

The dabus suddenly loomed through the fog. Its eyes glowed with the same impassive fury they had held when it first enchanted him, and another cardinal-red dove emerged from its head and smashed, stinging, into Aereas.

Just before the world was swallowed in white blindness and thrumming red, Aereas saw Nina turn upon the dabus, her features blazing in rage. Her sword flashed violently.

Aereas was falling now, and could not turn. The floor struck him a profound hammer blow, and the pain that a moment before centered on his shoulders now pulped his whole back. Someone else lay beside him, bleeding as badly as he, but Aereas had neither the will nor the wind to see who it was.

Nina knelt above him. He tried to speak, but she wasn't listening. Her strong thin arms slid beneath his shoulders and knees, and with teeth clenched, she lifted him from the floor. She ran. The other twelve caught up and clustered around her as they threaded their way between the flaming pillars.

All the while, Aereas watched Nina's face. Her eyes were wide, searching the thinning mists ahead; her cheeks were red except where something greenish spattered them; her neck was corded and slick with sweat.

There was terrible heat in him, both from the burns across his body and from his bleeding shoulder. There was terrible heat around him, too. The pillars that flashed by could have set his hair ablaze.

Next moment, they were through the room. The steam gave way to biting cold, the high ceiling to a dark, low vault of stone. Another passage. The footsteps of the company rang loudly against the stone and, for the first time in what seemed eons, there were humanlike voices speaking.

The first was Jandau's, who ran beside Nina, fussing at her face with a balled rag. "Got to clean off the blood. . . . What were you thinking, to kill a dabus? Last thing we need's to get . . . tracked by them and the Lady, too."

"No time!" Nina shouted between pants. "They're just ahead. . . . They'd not have sent the gargoyles otherwise."

Aereas, stunned by the dark ceiling spinning quietly overhead and by the pain in his shoulder, mustered four words to his lips: "Thanks for saving me."

The words went unheard; Nina was still arguing with Jandau as they bolted from the twisting passage into another, lower chamber.

"Last thing we need . . ." Jandau gasped out, ". . . is to piss off the Lady. . . . Who's going to pay us?"

Aereas again formed the words. "Thanks for saving—"

"Father," she said again, her slender neck craning up and out into the vast chamber before them. She lowered Aereas to the feverish stone at their feet.

"What are you doing?" The words should have been Aereas's, but they came from Jandau's mouth. "He's not . . . out of danger yet."

Nina had already moved from Aereas's sight, and her voice sounded small and strident against the rumble of the place. "Heal him. Surely you've got . . . a healer in this zoo of yours."

Jandau apparently did, for one of the lizardmen stooped over Aereas and began drawing vials from pockets in its cloak.

"Thanks for saving me," Aereas repeated in a delirium of pain.

The reptile only grunted and set to work, its blister-scaled head prickly like a sea urchin and casting sharp shadows.

Aereas's head lolled to one side, and he looked out from their elevated platform, down to the cavern beyond.

It was huge, a great natural cistern that must once have been an underground lake with no shore, no air. Now it was something altogether different—a smelter, a huge pool of molten iron that slowly cooled, allowing slag to form and solidify atop it. Aereas lay on his back on a platform that overlooked the vast lake of lavalike iron, which moved in a slow tide toward the dark gaping tunnel at the far end of the chamber. That was where the slag would be skimmed off the top of the iron.

Even though he couldn't see the sluice gates beneath the platform where he lay, Aereas knew that there the iron from the upper chamber would be pouring into the smelter basin. Beside the sluices were two sets of stairs descending to either side of the sweltering lake from the platform above. Aereas couldn't see the stairs, either, but could see Nina descending one set, reaching the bottom, and rushing out along the shallowly slanting shore. . . .

And *onto* the iron.

No, not the iron. Onto the crusted, solidified slag floes that covered the lake, floating along slowly, idly in that screaming heat. The slag moved sluggishly with the iron toward the far end of the cavern, where Aereas could make out several black shapes laboriously wrestling an unconscious man toward the dark cave mouth beyond.

"What's she—" Aereas began, struggling to sit up. The fierce hand of the lizardman kept him down. Even so, the creature glanced briefly at the woman below, leaping from one floe to the next as though they were icebergs.

"She'll do anything for her sire," the creature noted absently as it turned back to its patient. "Even fall in."

Aereas started, turning to see. Before he could make out what was happening to Nina, a furious burning engulfed his shoulder, his singed skin. Involuntarily, he convulsed, feeling as though he himself had plunged into the molten iron.

Again the reptilian hands, again the hissed voice. "Easy, now. This won't heal you fully, but your arm won't come off afterward."

Aereas could not respond except by locking his tearing stare on the beast and shuddering. The sensation began to ease from excruciating to intolerable, perhaps because the salve's work was nearly done, perhaps because the flesh was nearly dead. The lizardman began wrapping his shoulder.

"No time," the lizard said to no one. "The dabus'll be coming."

Aereas was suddenly up on legs that wobbled like leather beneath him. Before he could catch breath or balance, the creature hoisted him across its shoulders and bolted down the stairs that Nina had taken. Aereas cried out and clung to the lizard, realizing that he held on with both hands.

Down they went, the waves of heat not just palpable but visible in the air. The reptile's breathing grew strained, and the already sharp scales on its shoulders pressed higher into Aereas's belly.

"Let me run," Aereas said. "Let me run. It's too hot for you."

The creature obliged with neither argument nor hesitation. Aereas found himself suddenly seated on the steps, the thing descending before him. After a few wobbling attempts to stand, Aereas gritted his teeth and stumbled after the creature. He told himself that, as soon he was out of the frying pan *and* out of the fire, he'd have to learn the name of that savior.

How Nina stayed standing on the molten river of iron, let alone bounded from isle to isle of slag, Aereas could little guess. He choked back a wave of dizziness as the tiny hairs on his face shriveled into acrid little balls. As always with Nina, there was nothing to do but follow.

He jumped onto the first floe. It was sizzlingly hot under his feet, and it moved ever so slightly beneath him, pitching on the hellish lake. A segment of the floe calved off, spun for a moment like a dog lying down to rest, then sank into the opaque red pool.

Aereas shook his head and shouted out a string of curses. He steaded himself on the tipping, scalding raft, located an adjacent floe, and leapt across to it. He flew over the sizzling iron and felt the rest of the hair on his head flash and curl and disappear in smoke. Much more of this, and his clothes would catch, he thought. Thank goodness they're coated with sweat and steam and blood.

Ahead of him, far ahead of him, Nina was catching up to the kidnappers. They were four or five to her one, but were weighed down with an unconscious man while she jumped fleetly from floe to floe.

Her hair was gone, too, Aereas saw in the withering, shimmering heat, but not her fire. The inferno seemed only to charge her, and she raced along atop it as though she were its avatar. Yes, this was her sort of fight. The fire, the running, the battles. She could not have known it, but she was at home.

Aereas, as he leapt to the next precarious raft, wondered if the whistling banshee keen he heard was the eternal protest of skating iron or the outraged shout of his cousin.

He was thankful of one thing: The kidnappers were sending no more attacks back at the companions. Biting his lip, he pressed on, hoping against hope that others—the tiefling perhaps—would catch her before she caught the beasts.

✦ ✦ ✦ ✦ ✦

Despite the shifting slag, which bumped through the chamber like cattle toward a corral gate, and despite the heat that made the very air dance like distilled spirits in a glass, Nina could see the kidnappers clearly.

One, a great rotund thing, looked like a glob of slag that had been pushed upright by its neighbors. Vaguely human on its two skinny legs, it was the fiend that held her father pressed to its swollen belly.

Its opposite, a wiry, naked man-thing with a skull-like head and a wicked scorpion tail, bore Artus's feet. Two others accompanied them, one a huge spider that capered nimbly across the adjacent slag field, and the other a massive toad-beast with enormous batwings.

These final two pranced anxiously, glancing between the yawning cavern mouth toward which they moved and the feverish woman gaining on them.

She would reach them before they reached the cave mouth. She knew it, and so did they. Nina drew her sword.

Krim suddenly skimmed past her, his leathery wings glowing with a blue magical light that turned back the fierce scarlet of the molten iron. He seemed to wink at her with one of his low, lumplike eyes before flying out in a wide, shallow arc around the outer edge of the iron.

The kidnappers don't see him, she realized, not yet. They're too distracted by my ridiculous charge. And she would make sure they didn't see him until it was too late.

Leaping violently toward them, she shrieked out a warcry that over-arced the hiss and rumble of the iron. The sound chilled even her—the sound and the fact that one foot slipped beneath her, sliding to within inches of the bubbling metal. But the lunge had its effect. All four beasties gazed, astounded, at her for a moment as Krim circled up behind them, gaining altitude.

He skimmed just over the twitching tail of the scorpion-man, then brought his own tail slicing down on one of the monster's companions. The effect was deadly. Krim's barb sunk deep in the bloated side of the astonished creature, and there was a blue spark and a pop and a wisp of white smoke.

Then Krim was gone, sailing out wide again.

The fat man jittered for a moment, flesh trembling, spasming, and Artus slipped from his arms. Like a rotten tree stump at last toppling, Artus's captor tumbled into the iron. Red metal splashed outward from the spot where he disappeared, and the surface roiled with a deep explosion as the water in the creature turned instantly to steam.

Gaining her feet and her breath, Nina smiled savagely.

But only for a moment.

The winged toad creature sped out after the soaring Krim. It was fast, bounding across the slag and catching air between leaps. Its mouth alone was as large as the fleeing mage-being.

Perhaps he has a spell, Nina hoped as she watched Krim flee. With five surging swipes of its wings, the frog-thing closed the distance to the mage. Perhaps Krim can use his tail again to sting the thing.

The creature opened its gaping mouth, which could have swallowed even the lumbering brute Dif. Krim's rippling wings grew frantic, and his tail lashed behind him. The barb sank again and again into the fat lips of the thing behind. Though sparks snapped from the stinger and the toad lips swelled with each sting, the creature did not fall back.

Krim turned, rose, dived, but could not shake the thing. It swooped toward him, and in a uvula-flapping inhalation, drew him backward into its mouth.

The ungainly toad swerved suddenly, and Krim was spat forth from the closing lips.

The sprite woman had flown from Jandau's side, lighted on the monster's muzzle, and kicked it in the eye. Then, trailing motes of blue, she had leapt into the air, speeding straight toward the ceiling of the chamber. Enraged, the winged toad turned to pursue her, leaving the weary Krim to retreat.

Nina almost cheered again, thinking the frog's bulk would keep it from catching the sprite. She was wrong. With a lava-splashing surge, the beast leapt upward and was upon the tiny woman. This time, its long, tentacular tongue lashed from its mouth, snagged the sprite from the air, and snapped her back between swollen lips.

Nina staggered, horrified, and her foot slipped again.

Suddenly there was a hand on her arm, the same hand that had pulled her back from the steam.

A voice that sounded small and calm though the roar

shouted, "No missteps so close to our goal."

Jandau. He'd caught up to her during the aerial battle, and she was glad—not only because he'd saved her from falling but because the winged toad was now flying directly toward them.

"Look out!" she shouted, bracing for the attack and pointing with her sword.

Jandau whirled about, sword also drawn, and the two stood side by side, flanks touching and toes dug into the searing slag beneath them.

The thing came on. Only its wings seemed to move. The rest of the beast—a grotesque gray fleshiness centered on a gaping mouth—only grew larger and larger as it neared.

Nina felt a light, tingling touch on her cheek.

"For luck," shouted Jandau, though they both knew they would need more than luck to escape this. In fact, they knew they could not escape this. Even if they drove their swords into its heart, they would be toppled into the inferno to explode beneath the surface as the fat man had.

Nina nodded, not turning from the swollen mouth that soared to swallow them.

Then all went red, blistering.

In the scant yards between them and the beast, the red-hot lake of iron was suddenly alive, cresting into a huge wave—no, a solid mound, and on up from there. Lavalike metal streamed in ropy rivulets away from something huge and black emerging from below.

They glimpsed it—an ebony leviathan—huge, hammer-headed, blind, sentient. It rose into the air like a great wall. Only when the blunt end of it had cleared the iron by twenty feet did the streaming mouth appear.

Into that short-toothed maw the toad crashed. It was bit in two while the iron creature yet breached. The hump of the thing's back crested from the water, and the leviathan arced back downward, its head breaking the viscid surface just as the severed head of the toad creature slapped down red beside it. That second head was sucked quickly into the impossible mouth, and then the beast was plunging away, the vast fishy tail of the thing lifting only now above the iron.

"Back!" Jandau and Nina shouted in chorus, clinging to each other even as they scrambled backward across the treacherous, floating slag field.

They'd clambered over two, three searing rocks before the tail struck the iron, and a fourth rock when the splash of it lashed out.

Still, they had not gone far enough. Meteors of metal sailed past them, two slicing quickly through Nina's jerkin and branding her skin, while a palm-sized glob struck the tiefling's bare wrist.

Both he and she collapsed atop their raft, shaking to knock the stinging stuff loose. Once they did, they again gained their feet and leapt after the kidnappers.

Even Gehenna would be more hospitable than the iron whale.

The fiends knew it, too. The spider had taken up Artus in four of its eight legs and clutched him to its pulsing abdomen. Its air holes wheezed as it picked its way along. The scorpion-man, too, was fleeing, though with no hold on their captive and no interest in waiting for its friend.

"Hurry," shouted Nina uselessly.

She waved an unnecessary encouragement to those behind her and saw with satisfaction that Aereas was among them, side by side with Dif. The big brute was searching out the largest, most solid floes on the slag field, and clearly Aereas was glad to do the same.

When she looked before her, into the yawning cavern mouth at the far side of the smelter, she saw that it was no simple tunnel. The passage was a sluicing cascade of red-hot iron and black slag.

Worse yet, the kidnappers and their hostage had just disappeared over its brink.

✦ How Can You Fish? ✦

She spun before him, breezy fabric flowers rolling outward in a circle from her dark legs. Her teeth were white in her face, and for the spinning motion of her and that smile and those flowers, Aereas could little recognize her.

"What is it?" he asked. The circle of the whirling skirt was like his mother's flapping hat against the sky on the day the cousins first met.

"My cotillion dress," she responded without ceasing to spin. "The dress that made all the boys ask me to dance. How do you like it?"

He reached in, his hand darting white and fast like a fish into a waterfall, and stopped her. She reluctantly stilled, then wilted dizzily against him as though only the spinning had kept her up.

"How do you like it?" she repeated, out of breath.

"How can you fish in a dress like that?"

EIGHT

IN+⊕ GEHENNA

It was too late to turn back. The leviathan circled behind Nina, Jandau, and their floundering company. The massive head of the iron whale every so often crested above the swell it made.

Perhaps worse yet, beyond the sucking spout of the beast, the platform from which they had descended was lined with dabus. The robed creatures watched the hapless host. More symbols circulated around their cryptic faces, symbols and faces that seemed to hold something of satisfaction.

"No, we can't turn back," Nina decided aloud. Her hand yet clutched the sleeve of Jandau, who stood beside her on a slowly listing slag floe. "We can only hope the fiends know where they're going."

"Always a bad bet," responded Jandau through a bleak grin.

They no longer struggled toward the awful brink of the

tumbling cascade of slag. Instead, they merely stood on their large raft, flank touching flank as they faced the huge black cave mouth that loomed before them, ready to swallow them whole.

This time, the kiss was Nina's, planted on the mysterious man's cheek. "For luck," she repeated.

Then the slow, terrible current dragged their raft away from the cluster of others. For a moment the floe tipped on the brilliant shoulder of iron, and the human and the tiefling reflexively leaned back. . . .

Dark silence followed, so dark and silent that Nina only then realized just how loud and radiant the iron had been.

But the black hush was not empty; it was full of falling. Nina felt the lurch of the heavy slag dropping beneath her feet. It had suddenly become light, and it hurtled away from the pressure of her toes. Jandau's sleeve had flown free of her grip in the convulsive arm-swings that began with the falling, and his warm thigh, too, was no longer there.

Then the roar and red returned, different now. The roar was not the low rumble of liquid metal moving inexorably through bowels of stone, but the thousand sharp cracks of boulders tumbling one over another. And the red was no longer of heat, but of sulfuric miasma, a stinging, foul fog through which Nina now plummeted.

Yes, she plummeted, and knew Jandau did as well if only for his long animal howl, which hung solid and unmoving in the rushing air beside her. It was moments before she realized part of that howl was her own voice, cleaving to the fear of the tiefling.

Then, through the mist they broke, and the twilit land far beneath them seemed stunningly illuminated. It was a black and cheerless slope toward which they fell, they and the turning chunks of slag, the underbellies of which were marked with brown liquid iron that sizzled into hardness in the torrid air. Below, the slag boulders were tumbling into the head of an apparently infinite rockfall on the side of a greasy gray mountain. From there they cascaded downward, ever downward, into darkness.

In moments, Nina and Jandau would impact the mountain where the stones did.

Jandau landed feet-first on a loose stone, which rolled beneath him and spun away, skittering down the fall line.

Nina was less lucky. One foot struck a rock outcrop that held firm, while the other missed. She spun in air and hit the slope hard, rolling. The hot, rough, powdery slag ground into her shoulders and knees as she tumbled.

It burned worse than the molten iron, this chipped scree and dust over which she rolled. It grated away flesh from her elbows and bald, blackened scalp. Screaming still with the hot smelter air in her lungs, she jammed a heel down into the rending stones and came to a halt.

A hunk of slag fell toward her, its glowing iron underside crescent-shaped like a hateful eye.

Her scream stopped, not for lack of terror but for lack of breath. All was brown glow for a moment. Then a line of sparks showed her the tumbling edge of a stone that smashed against the falling boulder. Both chunks parted in air and crashed down to either side of Nina.

Then, not hard stone but hard flesh touched her, the tiefling's slim hand again. With extraordinary strength for one so thin, he yanked her up from between the two slabs of stone, draped her across his narrow back, and fled joltingly uphill.

Her arm felt as if it must separate at the shoulder, but she did not care.

"Third time . . ." she gasped with the first wind she could draw.

He was still scrambling upward, only just clearing the fall zone. "Third time?"

" . . . you save me," she finished.

Above the rockfall, he collapsed onto a flat, smooth, cold slab of stone. "Once a savior . . ." he jibed, breathless and hoarse, ". . . always . . ."

There came, overhead, more cries like their own, some human, some not. The sounds were short-lived; bodies rained with uncanny speed from the sky.

First came the capering little man, who dropped from the red clouds back-first. He struck a huge stone on the slope and splayed there, dead already, though the jostled boulder turned over and crushed him under, bearing his broken body down the mountain.

Next came one of the lizardmen, legs flailing spiderlike. His eyes were wide and fiercely focused as he clawed over the tumbling slag around him. With clear-eyed lunges, he propelled himself toward the upper slope, above the cascading stones. He landed in a roll within a chute of pebbles and next moment clawed his way to one side. His was the best success so far, his scales having dropped flat against his flesh in the sudden rush of cool air.

His comrade was not as lucky. The second lizardman fell soundless and limp as a leaf, scales yet bristling, and disappeared beneath a pounding of stones.

Next came the man-giant, Dif, who wriggled like a great cat in the air. He turned over and landed with back arched. He rolled. Though a boulder struck his shoulder as he rose, there was no more than a pained grunt from him and an angry sloughing gesture. He scrambled upward to join Nina, Jandau, and the lizardman.

Aereas had been beside the giant on the slag floe, Nina realized. Where was he? She tried to stand, but weakness had stolen her legs.

Krim soared then from the dense mist. He was much higher than the rest, but even the alien mouth on his flat belly bore a look of terror.

From the roiling dark came next a windmilling reptile tail, followed by the scarred and savage torso and head of the snakewoman. Her tail coiled springlike to absorb her fall. She landed lightly, though a sharp slab rammed down chisel-like on the end of her tail, slicing off the final two feet. She hissed and clawed her way upward, leaving a trail of blood.

Nina saw him, then, limp and red. Aereas tumbled from the cloud as had the second lizardman. She wondered for a moment if he was unconscious, or dead. But when he slid slowly past, his eyes locked upon hers with recognition, relief that she was safe.

He did not brace for impact, as though certain he could not survive.

A gray wisp of cloud circled evilly beneath those slack legs, and Aereas tumbled backward to strike his head against a great stone slab.

Nina winced and turned aside. In the grinding moan of the stonefall, she could not hear his impact, his last screaming breath.

Then came a gasp and a roar from the others beside her. She glanced up to see Aereas soaring limp and supine toward her. Beneath him was the struggling form of Krim; the mouth that had once held awful terror now curved with sardonic determination as the other companions hooted him on. Despite the rescue, Krim was none too gentle depositing the human beside the comrades. He merely banked, letting Aereas roll brusquely off onto his face in the scree. With an annoyed flip of his barbed tail, Krim soared outward to catch any others.

He was too late. From the caustic cloud charged the centaur—or bariaur, as Nina had heard him called. The stallion looked huge and savage in the red light, emerging like a god sculpted of marble, legs drawn up as though he were leaping a pasture gate. Down he dropped, forehooves stretching now before him.

Krim curved sharply off, knowing he could not break that fall.

There were sparks when those hooves struck, and then a surge of muscle and grit as the bariaur went to his belly only to fling himself upward, upward.

As much as Krim's rescue of Aereas had cheered the survivors, the proud rush of the bariaur to a safe outcrop made them all shout joyfully.

Meanwhile, Krim circled just beneath the clouds, listening for more companions. None came. There was only the tumble and rumble and scrape of slag, the sizzle of cooling iron. And the cheers died as the others strained to hear who would come next.

"What about Boffo?" Nina wondered aloud.

Jandau stood now and gazed upward, "What about Lanni?"

But only the cascade of stone answered them. Krim at last even flew up into the cloud, seeking the portal through which they had fallen, but could find nothing. When he returned, the others were toiling up the hill.

"No sign of them, or even of the portal," Krim said, winging by.

"Boffo?" Nina repeated.

Aereas was beside her, laboring up the slope, and though he said nothing, he sagged against her heavily.

"No sign," Krim repeated in his retreat.

Jandau shouted after the manta. "Find us a shelter—a cave. We've got to regroup."

Krim eased into a long circle and shouted back, "I imagine any shelter'll be occupied."

"Find us one with an occupant we can kill," Jandau replied just before Krim slid away in the distance.

* * * * *

Krim did, and they did, the companions advancing into the narrow dark cave with spells and stones and daggers flying. The scrawny inhabitant—something Jandau called a farastu—was quickly reduced to a seeping, motionless sack. Jandau ordered Dif, the big brute, to toss the corpse out the entrance of the cave "as a warning."

Soon there was a fire, first a magical one woken by a weary Krim, then a real one when Dif returned with some rotten logs he'd scavenged from the mountainside. In the flickering and pessimistic darkness of that place, the company began to assess their wounds and their losses—and Nina began to wonder where the kidnappers had gotten off to.

Thankfully, Cora the snakewoman and Henry the bariaur knew something about healing. Cora had mastered spells and potions; Henry knew all about splints and bandages—from his mercenary years, he said. But all of them applied what they knew, first to themselves and then to their comrades.

Dif, who was in better shape than most, went with the remaining lizardman, LiGrun, to find water—drinkable water. There was a foul black cascade visible a mile or so away, but even the two Clueless knew the stories of the River Styx and its waters of forgetfulness. They would have to find another source.

In time, Dif and LiGrun returned bearing what they could in anything that would hold it—waterskins, hats, armor, and of course their own gullets. Only when all had drunk their fill was the water used for bathing wounds, and only after that for bathing bodies.

Through it all, Aereas sat silent and distracted, tearing his shirt into strips for bandages. His shoulder obviously pained him, and it was swollen and red—the only patch of color on his otherwise pallid body. Beside him crouched Nina, hard at work tightening a tourniquet on Cora's tail stump. Aereas draped another rag of his shirt over Nina's arm—a rag she neither needed nor wanted, and she shook it off irritably.

"What's wrong with you?" she asked him. "Would you concentrate."

He nodded absently, and she set her teeth in frustration.

She turned the tourniquet bar twice more, eliciting a twitch from the stump, then began tying the bar in place. Only after it was secure did she realize why Aereas was so distracted.

She gazed hard at him, eyes pinning his. "Boffo?"

Aereas turned away, rising and walking to the entrance of the cave.

Nina groaned and finished the knot. She stared after him, then scanned the company. The wounds were under control now. None threatened life. Standing, she brushed off her skinned knees and walked to his side.

"Did you see what happened to Boffo?" she asked gently, setting a hand on his shoulder.

He turned, eyes clouded in blue as though in complementary reflection of the roiling orange overhead. "That's just it. I didn't. He was beside me one moment. I felt him grab my tunic, my rucksack . . . and then he was just gone. Not on the slag floe, not in the cloud, not down here. Just gone."

She carefully placed a hand on his other shoulder, but he winced away, the swollen joint recoiling.

Without pause she took him in her arms, embraced him, and whispered, "Who knows? Who knows what happened? He might be back at his kip, hubbly-bubbly steaming away."

In the silence that followed, she felt the eyes of Jandau on the pair of them. She drew back and led Aereas out into the darksome night. Their hands joined, and they stood gazing into the red clouds.

"Who knows with this place? Living cafés. Dogs that speak. Underground foundries and iron-swimming whales. Who knows? We might round the next corner and find him waiting for us."

Aereas nodded silently, his focus shifting to the black ground that fell sharply away beneath them. "Where are we, anyway?"

Nina's lips drew into a tight line. "Jandau says this is Gehenna—the First Mount of Gehenna, whatever that means."

"Where in hellfire would that be?" Aereas wondered, gazing about at the red-black clouds that rolled like satin above their heads and the dead black rock that dropped away beneath them.

"Apparently not in hellfire at all," replied Nina absently. "The Nine Hells—Baator is what Jandau called it—is hell; this is another place entirely."

"If this isn't hell, I'm not looking forward to seeing Baator."

He shifted, lifted a rock from the jagged scree at their feet, and tossed it down the slope. It cracked away into the distance, like the hollow report of debris pattering into a cave. "Why would those fiends want to bring your father here?"

Nina shrugged, her eyes still seeming to follow the rock downward though even its sound was gone. "I don't know. Why not check the book?"

Aereas stared out, too. "The book. Yeah. Your father's been here before. Maybe it will tell us something."

The cessation of sound from that stone left the empty place feeling even emptier, and the distant drone of the Styx waterfall seeped up like darkness. The cousins withdrew into the cave, where the smaller, closer drone of a fire had begun, lending warmth and light to the band gathered there. Aereas led the way to his pile of belongings, all of which now were tattered and blood soaked.

The journal leaned behind the other items and cast a flame-shadow on the wall. He lifted the book, the covers still damp, then sat down against the wall and motioned Nina beside him. She sat, and it was as though they again huddled, reading, in Boffo's upper room.

Nina touched the binding and with gentle pressure drew the book toward herself. "The question is how to find anything in this chaos of words and pictures."

She opened to the first page, seeing an illustration of an otherworldly gallows, closed the volume, then opened it again to the same spot, finding this time a crammed page of numbers.

"It's like a hall of mirrors," she said. "You can't see where you are or where you've been or where you're going, only where you aren't and where you haven't been and where you'll never be."

Aereas's eyebrows lowered, and a gleam started in his pupils. "Maybe that's the point. In a house of mirrors, you can't trust your eyes. You've got to move forward with one hand on the mirrors beside you and the other out in front. You've got to move by feel."

Nina stared at him and handed the book back. "I don't understand."

"What's our question? What are we trying to find out?" Aereas asked, holding the book to his chest as his mother had done with a book of fairy stories.

"Was my father ever here?"

"Was Artus ever here?" Aereas repeated, closing his eyes and lowering the tome to his knees.

Nina watched uncertainly, the quirk in her lip showing she was unimpressed by her cousin's divination. "This isn't a game like the one we used to play with the cards—"

Her words cut short as Aereas reverently opened the book and, eyes yet closed, began to page through.

She watched intently, shadows and firelight playing over the multifarious pages as they flipped by. There were more sketches, more strange stains, more unidentifiable inks. Once she glimpsed a shadow that looked like the head of Boffo, facing sideways, nose beneath Aereas's fingers.

Then the pages stopped turning, and Aereas's hands flattened on the open spread. Again, she saw a shadowy visage for a moment peer outward from the gutter between pages—Boffo it seemed—but in the flames and shadows, the face was gone.

Aereas began to read.

I wondered why the Lady would want a slag dump leading to Gehenna—

"This is it!" Aereas said excitedly.

Nina laid hold of the book and drew it toward her. "Let me see that." She studied the pages, looking for the face that had been there a moment before, but saw nothing.

Aereas watched her sharply. "Don't you see it? The 'slag dump' line."

Nina shook herself and blinked away the vision. Boffo's death—it was safe to call it that, what with the lava and the iron whale and the dabus—had affected her more than she knew.

She began to read where Aereas had left off.

But then again, the Lady's got gates to everywhere, why not Gehenna?

It was in wondering this as I stood beside the thundering cataract of the forgetful Styx that I drew out my compass to orient myself. Its glass face was smashed. I couldn't puzzle out east or west, but did see, unexpectedly, the whole of the multiverse.

Over the spinning lodestone, the glass had fractured outward from the point of impact. A hundred tiny lines radiated from that moment of collision, interlaced with myriad crossthreads, like the circling webs of a spider. I was about to tap the fragile shattered glass out of the case and onto the black stone at my feet when I knew with a strange surety that this was a miniature map of the planes.

Before time, before any worlds, there had been a clear, thick, homogenous primeval unity, a thing that—like glass—seems nothing because of its clarity and stillness and perfection.

Then something enormous—perhaps the bootheel of some god—impacted that unity and shattered it outward into the complex and fragile matrix of the planes. And the point of impact was Sigil, and the crazed and crackling lines that it flung outward were her thousand portals to a thousand worlds.

Nina stopped reading, the story having ended with the last word on the page.

Aereas leaned back, eyes clouded with wonder and dread. "The bootheel of some god."

Nina glowered at the page. "But what about Gehenna?"

"Perhaps it's on the next page," he suggested, reaching out.

"Don't turn it!" she snapped. "It might not be there again when we flip back."

Aereas drew his hand back and bit his lip. "We can't keep it open to just this page."

"I'll mark it," Nina said.

Her clothes were already in tatters, and she was not in a mood to lose more fabric. Instead, she tore a tiny tip off the bandage on her arm and set it like a bookmark sticking from the top of the page.

"That's not big enough," said Aereas, who had much more bandage to choose from. He tore loose a finger-length of blood-crusted cloth.

"That's got blood on it," Nina protested.

"It's dry," replied Aereas dismissively as he set the strip beside Nina's. "Besides, yours had blood on it, too."

"But mine was smaller—"

Her objection drew up short as Aereas turned the page and began to read again.

Once my legs had steadied, I did knock out the glass—a person can stare at the multiverse only so long without going mad—and noted by the compass that the Teardrop Palace lay on the mountainside, high above the Styx. It would be a long walk.

"Wait," Nina said urgently. "The bookmarks are gone."

The tattered fabric no longer extended beyond the rough-cut pages, and when Aereas flipped back to the previous passage, they saw that neither strip remained.

Nina's voice was tight. "It's like the book swallowed the cloth. It's like it's alive. Did I tell you I saw Boffo in it?"

Aereas gazed levelly at her. "I've seen you in it, too."

"I don't mean a drawing. I mean a shadow, a reflection."

Aereas closed the book, the pages meeting before Nina's hand could dart out to keep them open. "We'd better get some rest. A person can stare at the multiverse only so long. . . ."

✦ Hush Now . . . No ✦

He had never before entered her room like this, never without Nina preceding him, never at night while she slept.

No. He *had* entered this way, treading soft on the foot-polished planks, eyes wide in the darkness, seeking out her slimness in the bed. He had done so in his mind a hundred times since last summer. And always, he had wondered how she would awake.

Moving with the black solidity of purpose, he lowered himself to sit at her bedside. There was not even a crackle of straw, not even the gentle jog of leather supports adjusting to his adolescent weight.

Even so, she was awake. She did not lurch. Her breathing continued, unchanged. It was only her eyes, slowly opening in the near-dark room, glinting faintly like twin moons just before going new.

"Hi," Aereas whispered gently, and he smiled.

She looked up at him, eyes unblinking in that unseeable inkwell face. "Hi."

He began again to speak the words he had for so long burned to say. "I think I love you."

"Oh." The response was immediate, calm.

He lifted her hand from the bed beside him, felt its dry warmth, and kissed the soft back of it. "I think I love you."

"Please," she said. He did not think he had ever heard that word in her mouth. "Hush now . . . no."

He kissed her hand again, drawing in the scent of her. "I think—"

"No . . . hush."

It was as though he had not heard those words the first time, heard them only in echo. He felt himself then buoyed up on that implacable wave of sound and borne backward through her open door.

"No . . ."

And he would never again enter the darkness of her room.

PART II

THE WRITERS

✦ Marapenoth 3, 692 C.C. ✦

I wonder how long it'll take old Sung Chiang to realize I've shut down his Sigil connections to make the Lady a slag dump. Serves him right to try to open a gate in midair to the heart of her ward. It just took a little finagling to move the terminus to the Lady's own dabus iron works beneath the Great Foundry. Two birds with one stone.

'Course, I've likely made an enemy for life. I'll have to be careful next time I drop in on Gehenna.

NINE

A✝ ✝HE G⊕D'S GA✝ES

They bedded down that night in the smoky light of burning refuse. The vines and rotten wood that Dif had gathered, added to the dried droppings of the thing they killed, certainly couldn't be called firewood. It burned sullenly, hissing—and in its jumble looking—like a nest of steaming vipers at the heart of the company. The smell was bad—worse than the soot and sulfur of Sigil, worse than the smell of any place on Caonan.

Nina wouldn't lay all the blame for the smell on the fire. Part of it was her, she knew, and Aere, and the others. They'd been through a furnace and smelled like it. There was a metallic scent to their blood and fear.

Krim was perhaps the worst. Though he didn't sweat like the rest of the group, he smelled like a fish, dry and sandy where he slept beneath a light blanket of kicked-up dust. Nina had to wonder if he was dying like a fish, too.

Henry, the bariaur, was probably the least offensive. There was a sweetness to the scent of his horseflesh, a better smell than that of worried humans. Nina wasn't surprised when the bariaur stuck his nose out the cave mouth and left it out all night. He'd declared himself the first to take guard duty, and apparently decided not to relinquish it. Nina woke up a number of times, head pounding from the hard stone, and saw him sitting there, legs tucked up beneath him like a dog's, not those of a horse.

No, she hadn't slept well, not even the sleep of the righteous, though she felt pretty righteous in giving up everything to follow her dad to hell.

She had to get over thinking that. To Gehenna.

Nina rose after Jandau, after Aere even, who'd apparently ventured beyond the cave. She'd slept maybe six hours, though the world outside had not changed a whit to indicate it.

Jandau stood in the cave mouth and stared out into the rolling red blackness. "Might as well call it morning."

Nina nodded. She crossed arms over her chest as though chilled, despite the relentless warmth of the place and the glow of the stinking fire.

Jandau turned and offered her a bit of meat sizzling on the end of a charred stick. "Breakfast?"

Nina gingerly took the meat and ate. It was bitterly smoky and salty, but tasted good in that place, as though she were eating something native.

It turned out she was. Henry hadn't just sat there, guarding all night. He'd spent his time butchering the beast they'd killed. A fitting breakfast.

"Flesh of the monster roasted over its own dung. Delightful." Nina took another piece. "Where to, this lovely day?" she asked Jandau as she chewed the sinewy stuff.

" 'Farther up and farther in,' as the saying goes," he replied with an enigmatic smile.

Is he consciously quoting one of my favorite fairy stories? Nina wondered. Best not to let on. "Any sign of the scorpion and spider?" she asked him flatly. She decided not to include her dad in that roster, though Jandau knew whom she meant.

He shook his head, his straight white teeth flashing this time not in a smile but in slicing through a hunk of the meat. "You've got to look before you can find a sign."

Nina shook her head in turn. He was cocky, this one, and he knew how impatient she was to find her father.

Just then Aere returned to the cave and said, "I found something. Might be nothing—I don't know the flora and fauna around here—but I think it's something."

It's just like Aere to think and think and think, Nina realized. That's the way it's always been with him—he can speak my thoughts before I even think them, but I can act before he even begins to think about it.

She smiled at him, then nodded at the nonplussed tiefling, dusted herself off, and strode from the mouth of the cave.

Aere was right; he *had* found something. Up the slope and around the bend, he'd found a big blue skeleton from something slothlike. The beast had had a huge chest, gangly arms, and squat legs. Now it had nothing at all except bones.

"Looks like somebody else had dinner last night," Nina noted, pointing to the yet-wet streaks of blue on the bones. "What is this thing?"

"A caver," the narrow tiefling said professorially as he poked a stick about the rib cage. "The blue's from the spider's venom. Stings the thing to paralyze it, then sticks its head into the critter's gut and eats from the inside out." He shifted for a better look. The bones were already gathering flies, though they were picked nearly clean. "Usually after a kill this big, the spider'd stay wrapped in the creature's rib cage for a couple days while it digests. It must've been anxious to get on."

Nina couldn't believe it. "You mean, while we slept

down there, the spider and scorpion held my dad captive just up here?"

"The spider, at least, had dinner up here, yes," Jandau said.

Nina shot a glance down the hill toward the man-giant, who stood talking to the bariaur. "Dif must've passed within paces of this thing and never even noticed."

"Get the others up here," Jandau said to Aereas. "A gorged spider'll be a lot easier to catch than a lean one."

Aereas nodded and went, running. Nina watched him, thinking, he's still just a boy, still comes running down to get me when he's found something, still needs to impress and be important.

Jandau and she were left standing there. They sized each other up, both sharp-eyed and angular like the scorpion and spider themselves.

"What's our chance?" Nina asked flatly.

"Same as before," he replied. "Nil. The chant is that we can't leave it to chance. We'll have to do it ourselves."

He turned and started up the slope while Nina stood. The gloomy air felt dry and bleak as it sifted past her legs, through more tears in her clothes than she cared to think about.

She watched Aereas down below, waving his arms in adjuration of the sluggish others, excitedly commanding them to move, telling them Jandau was on the march.

He was sweet, Aere. It was for her father that he did all this, had come all this way. She had come too, but had not done so at the cost of surrendering her pride or her fury. Aereas had. On the other hand, he'd never had much of either; even now he was trying to roust these mercenaries like a vicar, not a general.

"Get up here!" Nina shouted, with a gesture that in her world meant emphasis. What it meant in other worlds she neither knew nor cared. They came anyway, and Aereas hurried up the slope with them.

Nina turned and followed the tiefling, who had silently ascended a distance that seemed impossible in that short time. He stood, almost smirking. There was challenge in that smile, and Nina loved a challenge. It was as though Jandau's tattered black cloak was in fact a set of bird wings, which he had used while she wasn't looking. Nina followed, determined to show that the ascent was no more difficult for her than for him. But all the while she climbed, she knew she'd reach the tiefling with a light gloss of sweat on her shoulders and arms, though he would be dry. And she knew he would turn and head up farther before she'd gotten even with him. She was right.

Aere was trying to catch up to her—that much was also certain. He probably had something to say; Nina was not in a talking mood that morning. He probably had some observation about the strange obsidian mount they ascended or about the blue-boned beast or one of a thousand other things; Nina didn't care to hear any of it.

She didn't know why she was being so hard on Aereas. She'd loved him once, or nearly so. Or if she hadn't, at least she believed he was worthy of her love, if she could only muster it.

Next moment, he proved that worth. Struggling up beside her, face red with something more than exertion, Aereas fell in step with her as they climbed. He could have spoken then, but he didn't need to speak to know how Nina felt: desperate, lost, furious, grieving. She'd always had a hard edge, a sword blade with which to parry the likes of Jandau, but Aere'd always been able to slip within the guard of that sharpness and quickly get so close that the edge was made useless. Once inside her guard, he knew immediately what it was she had been guarding.

Not for the first or last time that quest, he said, "We'll find him."

She neither turned nor slowed, only nodded.

"Until then, I suggest you look around," he pressed as

they rose higher.

Nina did not look around, not outwardly, though her eyes rose from the purple-black stone they climbed to the lurid red sky. It was low overhead and tumbling with mist. Only then did she see, motionless within the churning herd of clouds, a deep crimson moon. It startled her at first, as does an eye discovered peering through a gauzy curtain.

She knew immediately that Aereas was watching her watch the moon, her eyes struggling to form a circular shape from the shifting image. It was no circle, but diamondlike. Aere seemed silently delighted by this discovery.

Already panting from the climb, Nina drew to a halt to stare at that odd moon. Aere stopped beside her. "And that's not everything. Look behind us."

She did, and saw the toiling chain of comrades moving, heads bowed, up the hill toward her. The steep mountainside fell away beneath a sloping blanket of mist, just as it had the night before, but now the landscape was not simply a bleak and featureless rockslide. There was an elegant geometry of fracture to the stones, to the monochrome of red in shades from crimson to black. The loose boulders and deep clefts and jutting shoulders of rock had a stark alien beauty to them, like the wandering rows of tombstones in an ancient cemetery—or, no, like statues poised on a long, wide, winding stairway.

"And over there," he said, pointing to one side.

Beyond his jutting finger, the ubiquitous clouds moved with a different motion, more fierce and purposeful. Nina's breath had quieted enough that she could hear a new, louder roar than that of rage and blood in her ears. A rumble larger than any sound she had ever heard, and with it a hiss so high as to be nearly beyond human ken. It was the sort of sound that would set dogs to singing.

"C'mon," he said with a smile, and hiked out across a narrow traverse toward the sound.

Nina followed, seeing then that the slanting horizon was

not distant, as it had seemed a moment before in its severe reds and blacks, but very close indeed. What she had thought a huge black shoulder of rock was dwarfed now by Aereas, who reached it and climbed onto its sloping top. He beckoned her forward and up, and when Nina reached the calved boulder, she sensed that it lay at the edge of the world. He extended a hand to her and pulled her up on the stone.

It *was* the world's end, or nearly so. Together, they looked out over a great cylindrical valley carved into the side of the mountain, as though a god's heel had sunk into rock as he descended. The curved cliff carved by that heel cut a deep crescent in the steep mountain, and the cliff face was striated with enormous columns of black stone.

From its highest edge sluiced a magnificent waterfall, wide and black as though an ocean of ichor emptied itself into the flat-bottomed vale. The hungry cascade foamed gray and foul and awful at the base of the falls and sent up a spray of mist that went from white to brown to red as it roiled into the sky. From the turgid pool flowed a wide sullen river, which grew to rapids near the open end of the valley and then dropped away into another fall.

"Breathe it in," Aereas said, beside her on the warm stone. Nina was startled by his voice, as though she had forgotten he sat there.

She inhaled, and the smell was like falling leaves and myrrh, like the flesh of old women or old books. She would not call it sweet or foul, but profound and dark and hypnotic. She drew in another breath.

Aereas did too, shaking his head. "It's so big. The worlds upon worlds." He sighed. "I guess I'm done feeling sick to my stomach here. It's like they say about sailors, that they get so used to the roll of the sea that they get sick on land. I feel like I'm getting used to the roll of the worlds."

Nina nodded and smiled, breathing and silent.

He laughed. "*There's* my cousin," he said.

For a moment it felt like old times, felt as if the rock

they sat upon were the sun-warmed stone beside Calvin's Creek, where they'd fished for bluegill and caught frogs and swum and chased the dogs away from the poison oak. For a moment.

"Get up! Get up!" The sound was distant, almost meaningless, though the mouth that produced it was just in front of her face.

Jandau. His narrow bird-wing hand flashed out, and Nina felt a slight pressure on her cheek. Again the flash, and this time the faint sting was enough to make her realize she'd been slapped. And again.

At the next swing of that hand, her arm surged up as if through water, and she caught his wrist. He tugged her forward, off the stone and into his arms.

"Get up! Get up!"

Someone else was working over Aere—ah, the bariaur.

"Get walking. Breathe as little as possible." Though Jandau's voice was less urgent now, it sounded louder, closer.

Nina stumbled about in his arms like a sleeping person struggling to wake, realizing something terrible had happened to her, to them. Jandau was drawing her up the slope, away from the cliff.

"Hold your breath if you have to. Just keep going."

She moved in front of him, half on hands and knees as she clambered up the slope. She keenly felt Jandau's slim hands on her hips, steadying her, and determined to correct him about that touch—but later, when the hammering spin of her brain had slowed.

"What was . . ." she began with a gasp, scrambling away from the cliff.

"Styx," Jandau said sternly. "The water of forgetfulness. It almost had you. The mist is bad enough. You're lucky you weren't within drinking distance."

The thought of drinking that black stuff immediately put a strange, longing ache in her jaw—at the same time that her stomach turned.

Nina did not want to remember what sort of monster-flesh she was throwing up, nor did she want Jandau to see her do so, so she pushed him back and away with one hand. He gave her space.

When she rose, bile burning her lips, Nina saw that Aereas had had the same difficulty.

He smiled bleakly up at her and said, "I guess we're not yet over the nausea bit."

She laughed. The sound was good in her throat, and it cleared her headache.

Aereas, apparently, agreed, for he was laughing now, too.

"There!" cried Dif, and the whole company turned to see the man-giant standing uphill from them, his huge, power-ful form eclipsing the red light. One meaty hand gestured uphill farther, much farther, where a flash of bone-white moved through a field of boulders.

"The scorpion," Jandau said, clapping Nina on the back.

She was already moving, Aereas beside her. Together they clambered up the rock embankment, looking them-selves like wiry spiders. But fury and four legs could not match fear and eight. Even as they fiercely, emphatically thrust the landscape beneath them, the white exoskeleton disappeared beyond a rise.

A blackness surged up between them, and the ground dropped away. Nina was flung backward.

She would have screamed if she could have gotten air into her lungs, but she was pressed flat between an ironlike wall of hot flesh and a massive, sinewy arm, like the haunch of a bull.

Dif had picked her up—and Aere beside her—and was now striding up the slope with massive steps. Had she not emptied her gut already, she would have done so then, see-ing her own dim shadow thrash across the stonescape, be-side the cloudlike darkness of the man-giant.

At least now all the air of the Styx was driven out of her,

and with it, the dreamy darkness. Instead, she felt only the fire of rage hissing in her. Let Aereas pine away for his waterfalls and dreams. This was her sort of fight.

Dif was not alone in his boulder-tumbling ascent. Henry the bariaur galloped up the slope beside them. He showed all the stern assurance of a mountain goat. Krim paced them, too, his fishy flesh flapping languid and smooth in the red air.

There was blood in their eyes, and not just from the sleeplessness and the sanguine skies. No, all of them, even Nina, were thinking in that moment of scorpion parts scattered across the stones—not of her father free. Nor did she give any consideration to what the rocks loosed by Dif's stamping feet might be doing to Jandau, the snakewoman, and the lizardman struggling below.

Dif and Henry leapt a crevasse that the other earthbound creatures would have to climb around. With three great lunges, Dif gained the top of the rise over which the scorpion had disappeared.

And stopped. . . .

And dropped Nina and Aereas onto the cracked black mud there.

They hardly noticed. None of them—not even the bariaur who clomped over the rim, or Krim who sailed up to suddenly go sluggish and still beside them—were ready to see what they saw.

On the plateau before them towered a strange, brilliant palace. Nina could tell by the puniness of the spider and scorpion before its ornate black stone gates that the place was huge, as though fashioned for a titan of titans.

The fence that fronted the great courtyard had stone pillars that rose six times the height of Dif. The central gate was a torii, secured with two massive gates. On each side of the gates stood stone statues, their enormous hippo-heads set with dark, piggy eyes, their muscular man-bodies fierce in kilts and sandals.

Even so, the fence and torii and statues were dwarfed by the palace itself, a rectangular pagoda with stacks of red-tiled roofs edged with exotic dragon gargoyles. Huge drums of glistening stone supported the corners of the roofs, porches lined with ornate wood screens stood off to the sides, and smaller temple pagodas festooned with flags and kites flanked the main structure, both emulating and guarding it. A set of regal steps reached out of each building, like roots burrowing into unforgiving stone. The whole palace compound was draped with paper lanterns that glowed orange and green and blue against the crimson twilight.

The central pagoda, enormous in its distance, was adjoined by numerous wings, each with the curving pearlescent appearances of nautilus shells lying on their sides. They looked organic, alive, as though the nautili had each thrust their chitinous heads beneath the stacked pagoda roofs to gnaw on some floating bit of flesh within.

Yes, this was all astounding, but even more so was the fact that the gates were swinging narrowly open to let the scorpion-man and the gorged spider bear their captive through.

Nina blinked. The two enormous stone statues—stone golems, apparently—were moving. They drew the massive portal closed and stood, facing outward with glowing red eyes.

Jandau, panting, reached Dif and the others, and his moment of gaping shock allowed Nina time to get up off the cracked mud and help Aereas do the same.

"Sung Chiang," Jandau whispered when he had breath to do so. Then, as if he had been physically struck in the stomach, he doubled over and hissed breath through his teeth. "Sung Chiang. I should have known."

Nina's jaw tightened as she remembered the name from her father's journal: an enemy for life, this Sung Chiang.

Cora slithered up the hill behind Jandau, followed shortly by the lizardman LiGrun.

"Should have known what?" Nina asked the tiefling.

"Thief lord of Gehenna," Jandau said. "He'd call it justifiable larceny, but at heart, he's just another crook."

Nina was getting tired of having to pry answers out of him, so she only stood there, arms crossed, and gazed at the ominous palace. Jandau was dying to display his knowledge, and she knew waiting would pay off. It did.

"In addition to being a slag dump and a Blood War battlefield, Gehenna is Sung Chiang's home. He's a power—a god, you might say—though there's little that's godly about him. He's lord of thieves. He was the greatest mortal thief of all time, and so became immortal from it.

"It was only a matter of time before he figured out a way to use thievery to profit from the Blood War."

Nina was also tired of incomprehensible explanations. "What are you talking about?"

Jandau stood up, flexing his back, and stared into her eyes. "Your father's a blood hostage, likely to be sold to the highest bidder. That might be the tanar'ri. That might be the baatezu."

"That might be the Lady, or us," Aereas broke in. Nina clasped his hand and squeezed her thanks for his determination.

Jandau only laughed. "Not likely. The Lady bargains with nobody—for nobody. And look at us. How could we outbid the legions of hell?"

"How about stealing Artus back?" Aereas asked.

"Steal from the god of thieves?" scoffed Jandau. "We're talking about a power here, berk, not a stuffed aristocrat. No, like any good thief, Sung Chiang will fence the goods to the highest bidder, and won't make a sale that doesn't profit him most. Perhaps we'd best just put your dad in the dead-book and—"

Nina began walking toward the palace.

As she had expected, the others followed. "Everyone has his price," she said through set teeth.

✦ Berioth 17, 695 C.C. ✦

I cannot abide this. Never before have I balked at one of my duties. Never before have I flapped my bone-box about dogging down to the Abyss or tripping the gray fantastic of Mechanus, and lords know I should . . . and could. But always it was repair jobs; always it was putting in new portals, or tearing out old ones.

Not anymore. Now I'm supposed to go to some prime-material world in search of one of the Lady's lovers. At least that's what I assume he is, since unlike most people she sends me after, this one's not supposed to get trapped, or mazed, or looped, or put in the dead-book. No, she wants him in excellent health and spirits.

He's a god, of course. No sooner do I get Sung Chiang's Sigil connections finally shut down than I've got to go do some hand-holding and coddling of another god, one who's decided he wants to try being mortal. Poor babies. You'd think the powers could take care of themselves, but I guess as long as they can get us to do the dirty work, they will. Ah, well, so it goes. . . .

Malkin, the cat lord, is his name. Never heard of him. 'Course, anymore, you can't spit without it landing on a god.

It all makes me wonder—what's the Lady want with an old alley cat, anyway?

TEN

SUNG CHIANG

Jandau had no idea what Nina was thinking as she took those first steps toward the looming palace.

Aereas, however, did. She knew they couldn't catch the scorpion and spider with her father cocooned between them; she knew they couldn't fight their way into the home of a god; she knew they couldn't thieve from a thief. No, Nina was nothing if not keen as an arrow tip and just as straight shooting. She was marching toward the palace to buy back her father.

That's why Aereas moved so quickly, falling grimly into step beside her as she marched toward the towering gates.

Gods, what a sight they were, two green primes striding out ahead of Jandau and his crew, right up to the stone gates of the palace.

It was the second time that day that Aereas had seen the old Nina shining through, confident and cocksure. The scale even felt right, the two of them tiny before the giant gates as though they were still too short to see over Artus's table. He supposed it wasn't just the physical scale, either. Just like when they were kids, Nina was still dragging him into the strangest of places, into the unexplainable business of her father.

Of course, even after the kids had grown tall enough to see over Artus's table, they still weren't big enough to glimpse the planes that lay beyond.

They tried to walk right up to the gates of the palace, but the gates seemed to get bigger, not nearer. In time, the gray statue guards—with heads of hippopotamuses and bodies of men—no longer looked two stories tall but four. Then they no longer looked four but eight. The gleaming bars of the gates became as wide around as Aereas, then as wide as Dif, then wider than the whole group of adventurers put together. And the sky above seemed to deepen and grow more distant, the red fading to brown, to light green, and toward blue.

Still, Nina's stride did not break; her set face did not falter. Aereas was glad to see that; otherwise he'd've been tempted to turn and run. A brief glance at Jandau, who'd come up beside him, told Aereas the tiefling had the same impulse. Even so, Jandau wanted to convince the primes—and himself—that wherever this woman would go, he and his seasoned adventurers could follow.

Nina could not have liked the hugeness of the place, the fact that this small shelf of stone on a mountainside of Gehenna was warping out before them into a whole world.

Perhaps, though, that was her plan—to become so minuscule that they could slip unnoticed beneath the gate. In fact, Aereas now saw as they arrived on the enormous flagstones before the gate that they could slip like mice beneath . . .

There came a tremendous blast of sound, huge and deep and meaningful only in its threat. That stopped all of the group.

Aereas gazed upward at the gaping hippo mouth of one

of the guards. The angle, and the height of the creature made its piggy eyes seem small in that monstrous face, though each was the size of a man. The stone creature looked down at the group and repeated the awful bellowing noise, and it lifted one of those huge, bare man-feet from the ground. The sole of the foot eclipsed the greenish sky and made its intent clear.

Nina made hers clear as well. "Your master has my father! We want him back!" she shouted up to the thing. Her voice echoed punily against the smooth foot.

Jandau tugged at her sleeve. "This is a hasty plan. Perhaps we should retreat and re—"

"I would like to discuss with your master a valuable trade!" called Nina, shaking off Jandau's grip.

The response was again huge and deep. This time it came not from the rock lips of the guard, but the grating stone hinges. The gates were opening. The guard's foot resumed its place on the ground, its head regal and impassive again, with only the faint eye-glow to show it yet lived.

Nina was already marching through the gate, and Aereas sincerely hoped the palace itself would not recede any farther, that he would not shrink beyond the size of a mouse in that enormous place.

As though the palace had read his concern, they crossed the cobbled courtyard in far less time than it had taken to approach the gates, and though some of the paving stones were already large enough to hold the whole company, they became little larger as the group made its way along.

Aereas was also heartened—and disheartened—to see that the courtyard was not deserted. Atop the huge cobbles, more mice-sized folk moved.

It was a marketplace, its menagerie matching or exceeding that of the marketplace in Sigil. In addition to many humans, each wearing shallow conic hats of straw or linen, there were tall, gaunt yakmen, tusked pig creatures, goateed dogs (whom Aereas assumed immediately to be intelligent, though they rushed at the heels of passersby or snapped up little snacks from meat-cutters), winged heads that trailed tentacles like severed muscles and nerves, loping gray man-things that groped about the bright-colored stalls. . . .

Gazing at that crowded plaza between the gates and the gigantic steps up to the central shrine, Aereas realized that, from a distance, he had thought the red and orange and green tents to have been leaves on the stonework, had thought the movement among the tents to be the whisper of wind.

"There's more here than meets the eye," Nina said to him, as though reading his thoughts.

Aereas moved forward first this time. "It's a good thing Boffo taught us how to successfully pass through a marketplace."

She laughed, though per Boffo's instructions, they both immediately donned impassive faces, eyes averted from those of the beasts there.

Not that they could remain long averted from the articles in the stalls. The stuff was both exotic and mundane, shiny new and crusty old. In one of the first flapping tents of canvas, a beautiful red silken scarf hung on a hook beside a dented hubbly-bubbly, its tube missing and its brass dull as scoriated copper. There were some coats on hooks nearby, one of silk and embroidery and fit for a king, the next of elbow-worn wool, the third muddy linen with stains where its previous owner had spent long hours kneeling in wet fields.

"Not the choicest of stuff," Aereas noted quietly to Nina as they pushed past.

"It's likely all stolen," she replied with equal impassivity.

The truth of her words came clear a moment later when a scrambling fury of five spider monkeys capered over the tops of a number of roofs. In a squealing game of tag, they leapt from one tattered edge of canvas onto Aereas's shoulder, then off of his burned head and, as he was still ducking, onto the shoulder of Cora. Her darting tongue whipped them away, but only after they had already taken the jeweled earrings from her lobes. In a scratch of claws on cloth and a *wap* of tails, they were gone, just as quickly as they had come.

Cora now looked like a true medusa, her natural hair standing out from her head in angry cobras. She whipped her snaking abdomen in barely contained irritation and, with dark delight, "accidentally" smacked another spider monkey that had been scrambling across the ground behind her.

"Cheer up, Cora," Nina said with a keen glance. "You can always buy the jewelry back."

The snakewoman showed her teeth in an expression that could not have been a smile, and Aereas quickened his pace.

With eyes yet hooded from those around them, seller and buyer and stealer alike, the party made its way without incident through the marketplace and to the stairs of the main pagoda. They ignored the two side pagodas, which looked like temples; Krim had seen the kidnappers follow this same route up to the foot of the central building.

And what a giant foot it was. Each step rose higher than their heads, and there were twelve of them. Aereas looked back at Dif, wondering if he might get another ride, but then saw Krim circling with solemn patience to one side of the stairway. There, a wide curved gutter flanked the steps, and creatures, not water, were streaming down and up it already.

Jandau spoke: "Looks like old Sung Chiang likes his petitioners and proxies to spend time in the gutter before coming to see him."

Nina laughed at this.

Aereas nodded with a smile, noting the immortal's ingenious device for degrading his worshipers.

Though she had laughed, Nina ignored the procession up the gutter. Instead, she moved to the first step and, with a surge, leapt up to sit upon it. She drew her legs up to stand, then set hands on her hips. "Suit yourselves, folks. I'm not a worshiper. I'm a business associate. I doubt Sung Chiang would esteem my request as highly if I approached in the normal way." She turned and hoisted herself to the next step.

Jandau gazed up at her, a wry smile on his face, and he shook his head. "She's almost gotten us put in the dead-book thrice over, and still is working at it. The problem is, I don't seem to mind."

That was the problem, all right, Aereas thought. He stared hard after the tiefling, who'd turned to follow Krim to the gutter.

This planar guide was taking too much of a liking to his employer, too much for Aereas's tastes. How was the tiefling supposed to guide them through the planes if his eyes were clouded with visions of roses and wineglasses? Besides, Aereas was beginning to see what a pretentious fop Jandau was. Nina was leading this expedition, as always, and Artus's journal was as good a guide as this tiefling could ever be. For that matter, Nina and Aereas had been doing all the fighting, too. If it weren't for—

"You coming, Clueless?" came the narrow man's snide request as he started up the gutter.

Aereas cocked his head and said, "Not your way, that's for damned sure," and hoisted himself up the first step, following Nina.

She was already three steps above, determined to enter the palace of Sung Chiang the same way the god did. Aereas, on the other hand, was simply determined not to enter it like the tiefling gutter guide.

What had Boffo said about not trusting this critter?

As always, determination led Nina to some sweat and toil—and a little blood. By the time she'd pulled herself up the final tier, the others waited in a bemused knot at the top of the stairs, and by the time Aereas joined them, he was blanketed in sweat and was scarred at elbow and knee.

Jandau had extended a slender hand to Nina—as though she were the most delicate of fallen ladies whom he was helping to rise. "Must you always take the path of most resistance, berk?"

Nina was still panting but managed to spit out, "Must you always take the path of least propriety, scum?"

Though she smiled with those words, Aereas knew she meant them. He was proud of her again, forcing his aching frame upright without any assistance from these proud planars.

"All right, let's get at it," Aereas said, brushing off his hands. "We've got a god to barter with and a whole afternoon for finding the door back home."

His joke, feeble as it was, brought a kind response only from Nina, who nodded, took his hand, and drew him toward the enormous gaping front doors.

Enormous was too small a word for the opening before them. It was a square of cavernous emptiness so large that Aereas could not see it all at once. When he tried, the corners of the doorway warped into acute points, like the horns of some beast. And yet, it wasn't a solidity before him, a *thing,* but rather an emptiness, an airy lack of substance.

Of course, it was not entirely empty. Through the darkness of the sanctum within, coiling tendrils of incense moved like albino snakes through cave water. The incense came from dozens of blazing braziers clustered around the green marble posts of the doorway. Any one of those shiny brass burners was large enough to cremate the entire company, but beside the stout drums of marble and the stories-high flap of giant silks, they looked like tiny punk pots.

The creatures who had climbed the gutter to the temple above now streamed in patient, head-bowed rivers toward these steaming braziers, where many of these proxies knelt and tossed small articles into the ceaseless flames. It took no genius to presume these sacrifices to be bought or stolen in the marketplace. Stolen sacrifices. That had to make the thief god happy.

Nina had already made her sacrifice, though. Even if she

wasn't consciously thinking of her father, her actions told Aereas she was. She strode right between the patient lines of proxies and into the broad open space of the gigantic threshold beyond.

Having never known how to dissuade her, Aereas followed, and the esteemed tiefling "leader," pallid face even whiter than usual, did so as well.

A large beast appeared suddenly before Nina and halted her. It had dropped down from the lintel high above as though it were a spider, which in fact it was—or half was. Its eight rail-thin legs clung delicately to the silken strand that had lowered its blue-gray abdomen just above the floor, while beneath that abdomen snaked eight tentacles, moving in wet threat in front of Nina. The thing was a fusion between spider and octopus, the perfect leggy guard for a thief lord with a thousand hands.

It spoke, its language clipped and chirping, though no more understandable than the sternum-rattling moan of the hippo guards.

"I don't understand your words," Nina said with the confident patience of a woman well within her rights.

The thing recoiled a moment, as though surprised or unsettled by the sound of her voice. Then, adjusting those snaking appendages, it said, "You must sacrifice, like the other proxies." The words chirped from a strange, beaklike mouth nestled between its flowing tentacles.

"I am not a proxy, whatever that is," Nina replied simply. "I'm here on business."

"You must sacrifice."

"I have—" she began, then broke off suddenly. "What constitutes a sacrifice?"

"Stolen items . . . fruits of your larceny . . . the flesh of a person you have thieved from."

Nina shook her head irritably and crossed her arms over her chest. "I have already sacrificed. I have sacrificed my father, who was brought to your master as a war hostage.

Now let me in."

The octopus thing shivered a moment, then said, "You are Nina, then?"

The rest of the party shivered at that, and Aereas snagged Nina's shoulder to draw her back.

She pulled free and said, "I am."

"You have been expected—or an agent of yours, but not so soon. Are you here to bargain on behalf of the Lady, or of yourself?"

"I am here to bargain on behalf of my father," she said sternly. "Now let me pass."

A slithering tentacle flowed up before her and snapped her once with its tip, raising a small red welt on her shoulder. "You must sacrifice."

Nina stared at the thing, furious, the veins in her temples beginning to stand out.

With a sudden motion, she lurched forward and wretched into her own hand. Acidic liquid spilled forth, bearing a hunk of meat.

She hefted the grisly thing in her hand and shouted, "Here is our sacrifice, the flesh of the creature from whom we stole a dank, dark cave!" And with that shout, she flung the meat across the wide threshold to one of the giant braziers, where it dropped with a puff of ash and smoke and sizzled away most impressively.

A gray coil of the smoke rising from that sacrifice played out across the threshold and dragged itself around the hanging spider creature. The monster seemed to inhale through rubbery slits in the side of its flesh. Then it shuddered again, this time in pleasure. The rodlike legs above the thing began the dexterous, diligent work of coiling up the silken thread and lifting the guard toward the lintel far above.

Nina did not even wait for the tentacles to move out of the way before striding forward. She backhanded one last slimy appendage from her path, delivering to it a welt the equal of the one on her shoulder, then continued on into the smoky hugeness of that dark place.

Beyond the enormous drums and the glass-smooth marble of the threshold, light seemed unwilling to penetrate. Perhaps it was the steam and smoke, the incense that caught up the light and bore it out to the almost-blue sky above the palace. Perhaps it was the hugeness of the cavernous interior, its walls so black they appeared to be nothing at all.

Whatever the cause, ten steps in and the group seemed to be in dusk, and twenty more and they were in full twilight. The last golden glow of light pattered against metal before them—a screen of bells and chimes and tall cylinders of brass, blackwood, and silver. The screen funneled Nina and her crew toward its center, where a small, low archway stood.

In the darksome air around them, other worshipers moved like ghost shadows. They walked along the metal screen, their hands dragging across the bells and chimes and cylinders, whirling them on their axes. But no sound came from them.

No sound came from anything. The hush of the space was extraordinary, deafening; Aereas had not realized how much so until he noticed he was murmuring something to Nina and neither of them could hear it.

They shuffled along with the worshipers, all of them like ghosts now among the lingering hands of steam and incense. Aereas fell in line behind others, even reached out his hand in that holy darkness and set a cylinder spinning before he joined Nina and his comrades, who already were ducking through the low gate to the sanctuary beyond.

The weight of the darkness there was even greater, though the moment Aereas passed the screen, there came the sibilant surruss of whispered prayers.

Worshipers knelt shoulder to shoulder (those *with* shoulders) in a long wall, their heads bowed before their god. It was by lifting his head, however, that Aereas saw the deity—or what he assumed must be Sung Chiang.

If the large octopus-spider at the gate had been fearsome, this creature was horrifying. Its main body was a huge, liquid, transparent sac that hovered in the extreme height of the ceiling. Within that placental organ there moved bubbles and spheres and pulses like those of some deep sea creature that never enters daylight. The whole of it had the pallid luminosity of unholy life—viscid and pulpy.

From the sac spread a thousand ropy, glowing tentacles, also translucent and veined with pumps and strange organs. Each tentacle reached outward through the swirling shadows and into a transept or chapel or apse or other side chamber to the main sanctuary.

These appendages breathed with light, as though the impulses of that horrid sac could be carried out along those flagella to the ends of the worlds, and the sensations of each stinging arm could be shot back along its length to the sac at the center.

It was hideous and beautiful, unexplainably horrible and wicked, but also lovely.

Aereas found himself wanting to cough, but only a sort of hummed psalm came from his mouth, and as he bent forward to clutch his stomach, he found he was already on his knees on the ground. Had he cared, he might have seen that the others were, too—all but Nina, who stood beside him with trembling knees locked and eyes lashed to that awful, wonderful presence.

Aereas felt a hand on his shoulder and thought it hers. It was too warm and slim and gentle to be anyone else's, but the voice that followed at his ear was deep and precise and refined.

Magnificent, aren't I?

Aereas nodded, somehow knowing that the creature who touched his shoulder was also the one who hung enshrouded in incense above.

One of my favorite forms, the creature continued, setting another hand on Aereas's other shoulder. *Thief of the sea, stealing the life of any creature that swims beneath it. Arms long enough to reach from the Yangtze to the Rhine, long enough to plumb the Marianas Trench.*

Though the voice spoke a tongue familiar to Aereas, he had no idea what the being was talking about. He could only nod.

But it is unseemly for you to kneel so long, the voice resumed. Only then did Aereas realize he did not hear it in his ears but in his head. *Friend of she who is my guest here.* And with that, a third hand grasped Aereas's arm to help him up.

He rose quickly, startled by that hand, and whirled to see the creature the others were already gazing at in stunned shock.

He was a man, no more than Aereas's height, his skin the yellowish cast of Orientals, though it was scaled like that of a fish. His hair was blue-black and straight, and his features bore the almond beauty of his race.

There was more than enough space for those beautiful features to show, too. The man's one head had three faces: one youthful, one middle aged, and the third old. He also had eight arms—human arms that somehow impossibly shared his shoulders. But, most shocking of all, were the six eyes in those three faces, each eye glowing with the red fury of molten iron or dancing lava.

It was, of course, Nina who first mustered the strength to speak, and she spoke the same message she had borne for days now. "Return my father to me."

Your father, the man began, turning the middle-aged face toward Nina, though the lips of none of the faces moved, *is in my possession, and therefore is my possession. I lost many minions to claim him and would, at the very least, need to be reimbursed for them. Truthfully, though, I intend to gain much more for him than mere money.*

"He's my father—" Nina began, but with the speed and snap of a rat trap, one of the god's hands slapped over her mouth, and another wagged a finger at her.

He is your father, he is my property, and you are my

guest. Let us each remember our roles in this affair so that all might work out in the end to everyone's satisfaction.

The hand was still clamped over her mouth, thumb on one side and forefinger on the other, pinching beneath her cheekbones to retain their hold.

The god's head turned, and the young face regarded Nina with keen interest. It spoke, moving its lips this time, "You have much more to barter with than mere blood ties."

Aereas moved forward and gently laid his hand upon the creature's arm, but already the god was withdrawing his hold. Into the tense silence, Aereas blurted, "Well, name your price."

The young face pivoted away, and the old face swung toward him. *Ah, impetuous youth. You would bargain with a man about whom you know nothing? You are certain to lose all in such a trade.*

Besides, interrupted the middle face, which now gazed paternally at Nina, *it is too early to begin the barter, for the other bidders have not yet arrived. Come. I have clothes and rooms and food for you, and you have need to learn about me, so let us be civil.*

"Where is my father?" Nina cried, though the sound was stolen from her voice before it could rise and echo.

The creature clapped his hands before him, all eight—a sound that *did* rise up to fill the great chamber as a thunder-crash. From the corners scuttled tiny creatures, midgets that looked like street scamps with green hair, though they had the faces of adults. Still speaking to Nina, the creature said, *Patience. All will be revealed in time. Your impetuosity has even prevented our formal introduction. I am Sung Chiang—*

"Where is my father?" Nina repeated as the scamps converged upon her, grasping her arms in vicelike grips and beginning to drag her away.

—or perhaps such formalities can wait until the dust of the road is washed from you, the head said sadly. *My lin-qas will show you to your chambers.*

✦ Berioth 41, 695 C.C. ✦

Well, like it or not, here I am in the city called Xiam, where this alley-cat god Malkin is supposed to be skulking, hiding from his dear mistress. For certain, I've seen many of his minions: half-starved mange-balls with piteous howls, worse from a stucco wall beneath a full moon than the cry of a banshee from hell.

Needless to say, I've not been getting much sleep, and have certainly grown no happier about this assignment. But I am assured he is here.

Too bad Malkin is a cat god, happy to belly crawl and stalk. Most gods incarnate like to be robed in glory, unmistakable in a crowd. Not this god; no sir. I do hope I track him down soon, not only so I can get out of this arid place and back to Boffo's kip, but so I can give him a talking to.

Anyway, I've been setting up a few temporary portals round about so I can make the distance from any of the city's five wells to any other place in this oven in less than a heartbeat. Now, if I can just find Malkin, I'll not likely lose him before I can wrestle him back to the Lady. Once we're in her Ward, I'll leave the wrestling to her.

ELEVEN

FIENDS ARRIVE

She did not struggle long in the grips of those filthy little scamps, those linqas, as Sung Chiang had called them. It was pointless. Their strength came not from their midget hands but from the very walls of the place, ornate and obscenely opulent, ridiculously huge. The linqas' power came from the viscid, gargantuan leviathan that hung from the smoky rafters of that temple . . . from the thousand tentacles with their thousand reaches into a thousand worlds . . . from the eight-armed, three-faced man and all the other avatars of the god Sung Chiang that were wandering around this place or other places.

Nina and her crew were surrounded. The tiny, fierce grip of the midget hands was only the insistent physical reminder of that undeniable metaphysical truth: There would be no escape.

The sense grew even greater as they marched down the

hallway toward their "staterooms," as the linqas called them. With each successive step, the huge corridor became smaller and smaller, and the rooms that opened off of it also shrunk in size. They were marching into a literal snail shell, the passage dwindling in infinite, spiraling regression.

Though Nina was still dwarfed by the opalescent chambers they passed now, she could sense that ahead there would be a room her size, with beds her size, and clothes and refreshments and the other condescending appointments of her fawning host. She knew, too, that these little imps could go farther, to rooms their size, and perhaps when they lay down at night, the fleas from their green-haired heads would continue on down the halls to their rooms, and the mites on the fleas to theirs. . . .

In the giant shell of the chambered nautilus, each space along the curving, shrinking passage became smaller, more distant from the temple. Once again, Sung Chiang had instituted a not-so-subtle demonstration of his worshipers' penury. For him, a species' size determined its proximity to god.

Nina wondered wryly what he was compensating for. Then she wondered if this long-fingered god could reach even into her mind and find that thought lurking there, an ingrown chuckle.

By the time they had reached the rooms that were their size—dropping Henry off just up the hall—Nina was dizzy from the journey, lost in the twisting structure. The passages they had marched through were too long and serpentine to fit within the walls of the palace, enormous though it was. And the passages went on, smaller and smaller forever.

Even so, Nina knew she could never get lost. By merely following the ever-larger path, she would always end up back at the sanctuary. By always turning toward the greater possibility, a worshiper would eventually reach the greatest possibility of all—Sung Chiang.

Perhaps he should have been a god of joiners and masons,

she thought, for he certainly knows how to magnify his glory in the very wood and bricks of his palace.

When Nina reached her apartments, Sung Chiang's obsequious hospitality reached its full flower. The chambers were roomy and warm, with walls of smooth-cut yellow limestone festooned with exotic sprays of herbs and dried flowers. These must have been the greatest extravagance, for she had seen no appealing native flora. The warm invitation of the room came partly from those herbs, and partly from the thick tapestries on walls and thick rugs on floors, and curtains on the wide windows (impossibly) overlooking the courtyard.

But mostly it came from the fireplace. It was not exactly a fireplace, for it never would contain a fire. It was a chimneyed shaft emitting hot air through a grate in the floor, and venting fumes through a flue overhead.

Nina gazed down into the grate and saw a long, straight darkness, at the base of which was a tiny red glow, like a single living ember in dead ash. Somehow she knew that what she saw was lava deep within the mountain, what she felt was heated air from the very belly of fire.

It would be comfortable here, with the silken screens and paper-paneled windows and embroidered chairs. But, as she sank down upon the edge of the rope bed, she wondered where her father was, how he was quartered, if she would ever see him again before the undertaker's wagon bore him past.

Into this reverie Aereas came. He was near jubilant as he threw open the door between their rooms and came striding in. The hollow clatter of his footfalls in the tiled chamber between their suites gave way to the quiet pad of feet on thick carpet.

Nina's back was turned to him, but she knew immediately who it was. She said nothing, made no move, knowing he would soon enough know her thoughts.

He did. In midstride his footfalls became soft and short, his voice—once edged for excited jabber—became pensive. "I'm sure he's being well cared for," Aereas said as he approached.

Nina still did not see him, though she felt his hovering nearness and the warmth of a hand on her shoulder. "I'm sure he is being fattened like a pig for slaughter," she replied with more anger than she felt.

He knew she had overstated herself, and he moved to sit beside her. "Lucky for him the pig rustlers are in town."

She had to laugh at that. Old Aere. This grim mission would have burned her to cinders thrice over—from internal heat if not external—had it not been for Aere and his cooling voice.

"Yes. Ever rustle a pig before?" she asked, struggling to banish the weight from her voice.

"I wrestled one, once."

Nina glared at him in shocked amusement.

"It was on a dare. And the pig won." He laughed. "I got all muddy and scared and humiliated, and the pig just got mad."

She shook her head, hands straying to the scrapes on her arms and legs. "Seems like the pig's still winning."

He looked hard at her, though she did not return the look, and something like a small moan of sadness escaped his lips. The sound hung in the air only a moment before Aereas was up from the bed again, the caper and excitement back in his step.

He moved to a tall carved-wood wardrobe and threw back the doors. The sudden flash of red and gold silk from within was stunning; the kimonos and robes and shifts stirred gently in the rough breeze of the doors.

"Look at this stuff. It's fit for a queen!" Aereas enthused.

Despite herself, Nina rose to join him. The fabrics were indeed fine. Their clean, vibrant colors and textures looked and felt strange on her soot- and scar-darkened hands. "I can't wear any of this. Look how filthy I am."

"That's what I came in to tell you!" Aereas continued, grabbing the very hand she had just drawn away from the clothes. He pulled her after him through the door where he had entered. "Look, here!"

She did, and saw a great, wide tub lined with obsidian tiles that glowed faintly with heat. Warm waves of air wafted from that surface, and now it was her turn to moan gently.

"Oh, a bath would feel so good."

"It's between our rooms. All the rooms are connected through baths. You can use it, and I can use it—" He colored at that implication, coughed briefly into his hand, and quickly said, "And since you're filthier than me, why don't you go first. Scrub off the grime. Get your head clean of the burnt nubs. I'll wait in my room—"

Nina grabbed his arm as he tried to whirl away. "Wait. I don't even know how this thing works."

He smiled, seeming relieved, as though she might have required him to stay for other reasons. "Weren't you listening when the linqas dropped us off? They said to use the bell outside your room to call for one of them, and they'll bring water—a whole parade of the little fellows with buckets, I imagine—to fill the tub. It'll be warm in moments."

"Really?" she said, backing toward her door. "You go first."

He waved that suggestion away and smiled, then drew her to sit on the side of the tub. "Wait here. I'll call the little men."

He turned to go, but paused when the door on the opposite wall of Nina's room swung open. They both glanced up at a similar bath chamber, except that this one roiled with steam and held small, green-haired figures moving within.

One such creature emerged for a moment and called out in its crass voice, "Lady Nina. The honor of your presence is requested in the baths."

Nina stood, arms indignantly akimbo, and asked, "Requested by whom?"

The midget took one bowing step back and gestured grandly to a lean, narrow figure in the tub, dark in the swirling mists. Jandau.

"Tell the man he has more than enough filth to fill the

tub on his own," she replied sharply.

The midget's face quirked into a grin, and he nodded.

Before he could escape again into the swirling mists, though, Nina called out. "Bring your water buckets over here, good man. I have my own bath to fill."

Just before she closed the door to her bath, Jandau craned and squinted through the fog to see her—no, not to see her, but to see Aere standing beside her.

Then the door swung to, and the latch clicked in the frame.

The sound was an excellent punctuation to Jandau's bawdy request, Nina thought.

But Aereas was already withdrawing beyond his own door, and it too swung closed.

* * * * *

The companions met for dinner at half after thirteen; their host explained with self-satisfaction that he had stolen an extra hour a day and placed it at what he called midnight "to allow all-night conversations to last longer."

Not that there was night or day here. The near-blue firmament that Sung Chiang had impressed into the roiling sky of sulfuric clouds remained a greenish twilight that constantly reminded Nina that all here was falsity and illusion. The man who seemed a gracious emperor was in fact a kidnapping scoundrel.

Not that the food tasted like illusion. Aereas and Nina sat around an intricately carved cherrywood table with the six who remained of Jandau's company and Sung Chiang himself. Onto that table were set steaming silver platters of all manner of fare, none of which Nina cared to classify, all of which tasted wonderful after fried farastu. As savory as the food was, it was even more beautiful. And as beautiful as it was, it was less so than the folk gathered there to feast.

The rags and tatters were gone; in their place was elegant finery. They looked oddly at home in these rich garments.

Jandau, Aere, and Nina were freshly shaved—their hair had been only tight-twined balls after the smelter. Nina felt like the high priestess of some great oriental mystery religion—if not merely from the clothes, certainly from Sung Chiang's elaborate decorum when dealing with them.

Even LiGrun looked elegant in the silken garb. His alien lizard face seemed especially wise and handsome hovering above the splayed gold of his robe. Henry, too, was draped in satin and silk, his huge muscularity impressive beneath the flowery sleeves. But as nice as any of them looked, Sung Chiang outshined them all.

He was the god, after all, and this was his banquet hall. His clothes were the most sumptuous: rich brocade lined in white ermine, a keenly cut red robe, silk leggings like those of a troubadour, and lots of pockets secreted throughout his attire.

From these pockets, his many hands at intervals produced astounding things: a caged grasshopper, which filled the great chamber with the sweetest, strangest, most rarefied music; a pair of finger cymbals, which he used as percussion for his melodic speech; sets of ivory keys, which slid themselves from their leather thong and walked across the table to each guest's place (*Keys to your rooms, that you know you are welcome to return to them at any time*); a pair of silver spheres, which he rolled deftly between the short, callused fingers of one hand; a tiny bat on a slim gold chain, who hung in drowsy sleep beneath one outstretched index finger. . . .

And all of this he did while they ate, reserving two hands for the patient lifting and consuming of his meal. He had supplied them with silverware, though he himself used a pair of bamboo sticks to eat. He was as deft with them as an old lady with a pair of knitting needles. It was but another instance of his power. He was a god of details, who not only could converse and commune with his guests in their own language, but could also trifle with playthings from his pockets . . . and all the while hover ensconced in invertebrate glory at the peak of his sanctuary.

With a chill, Nina realized the significance of the silks that fit every curve of her body. It was as though those thousand hands of his knew her intimately.

To dismiss the sudden cold sweat that prickled her brow, Nina began to talk. "So, you said you knew someone would be coming from the Lady," she said. Her voice broke into the cricket-song and brought worried looks from the companions at the table. "But, you seemed to have expected us, specifically. I mean, you had rooms ready with beautiful clothes that fit perfectly."

Sung Chiang's middle-aged face gazed appreciatively at her and said, *Simple suspiration, my dear. Part of being a god. I suspire, and the world is inspired.*

Nina was not about to let him pin her so easily, regardless of how many hands he had. "So, did you have rooms and wardrobes prepared for Boffo and Lanni and Drun and Cavendish—the ones who didn't make it? Or did you know who'd get crushed or burned alive en route?"

From yet another pocket came a pipe, long and thin like the pipes in her father's tobacco stand—no, like the alpenhorns in Boffo's closet. The bowl of the thing was already smoking when he lifted the thin stem to his middle set of teeth.

It might surprise you to know that all the things I've pulled from my pockets tonight—the cricket and the spheres and the keys and all—were stolen by me. These hands wrap about all things, everywhere. My fingers comprehend the worlds. What they comprehend, they apprehend. And what they apprehend, I possess.

"So if you possessed my father back on Ҫaonan, why did you have to steal him?"

There came a low warning growl from Jandau, who sat to one side of Nina. She felt his knee shift to nudge hers, and returned the favor, though a bit harder. Their host seemed amused by this childish game of footsie.

My reach never exceeds my grasp, he said serenely, drawing upon the pipe in his mouth. *But feeble minds cannot believe in ownership unless they see bars—bars or chain or rings, some outward sign of true possession.*

The haze around his features dissipated, and he turned his young, catlike face toward Nina. *Until Artus was in chains, who would have bid a sovereign for him?*

She drew back from her plate, its contents only picked over, and crossed her arms over her chest. "As I am no doubt one of those feebleminded people, and am certainly a bidder in this game of yours—and *undeniably* his daughter—I want to see him. Show me these chains you speak of."

Amid the many other mesmerizing movements of his form, there was but the casual wave of a hand to suggest that anything had changed. But everything had.

A faint motion at the opposite end of the table drew Nina's eye, and she saw her father. He sat there in a great chair, equal to Sung Chiang's in its massive intricacy, and he wore robes that rivaled the others in beauty and tailoring.

She stood, so quickly that her chair fell back behind her and the ornate carvings atop it cracked.

Her father looked up, his eyes tired but glad, his old pillowy face healed of the bruises and burns that must have been there just this morning. He did not stand as Nina approached, but she reached him and threw her arms about him in embrace. He was real, solid, warm . . . breathing.

"Father!"

"You see me now, do you?" he murmured into her ear, with a voice that sounded infinitely old and tired.

She stared into his silvery blue eyes and fondly finger-combed his pate of silver, thinning hair.

"Of course I see you. How are you?"

"Fine," he said with a nod, as though he had only just decided it. "I am fine. In fact, I had expected a day like this to come a bit sooner. You can't give old Sung Chiang the laugh forever. I'm glad it did not happen until you were grown."

"What do you mean?" Nina asked, kneeling there.

Aereas hovered now by the other side of Artus's chair, his eyes wide with delight and hope, but his face withdrawn and respectful in this private moment.

"What do you mean, you expected it?"

Her father waved off the question and smiled sweetly, sadly. "A trifling disagreement he and I had in the past. This more than pays us up square. Or at least it will when he sells me to the fiends."

They don't want you, really, Sung Chiang broke in placidly. *They just want the keys, the Lady's keys. The skeleton keys to the portals of Sigil. They think you have them.*

Nina's eyes did not turn toward her host, and she spoke still to Father. "Do you?"

Aere's eyes reflected her question.

Her father spread his arms in resignation. "I have nothing, now. Not even the two of you." And with that he gently cupped his hands on their cheeks.

It doesn't matter what you have, Sung Chiang continued, *only what the bidders think you have.*

Nina glared at him. "What's to stop us from fighting our way out of here?" The question was stupid, she knew, even the moment after she spoke it, but she awaited the response nonetheless.

Twin jets of gray-blue smoke came from the thin nostrils of Sung Chiang's aged face, turned now toward Nina. *Is all of this lost on you?* He made no gesture to take in the chamber, the temple, though the smoke rising from him seemed to do so in place of arms. *As you yourself said, the very cut of the clothes you are wearing tells you why you cannot take him.*

His old voice went cold. *I am a god. You are a guttersnipe. You would not even be able to lift him from that chair if you tried.*

Nina did not, knowing when to end her fool's errand. But she did speak further. "If I am but a guttersnipe, why do you even entertain me? Clearly I have something you need or want, otherwise you would be unwilling to bargain with me."

It was the young face that answered now, virulent and arrogant. *The master chessman may complete a checkmate with a mere pawn, an inconsequential piece such as yourself. Even so, he needs no one piece at all to mate. But the game is incomplete without the pawns, and no master chessman will begin a game until all the pieces are in place.*

Damn this man, this god. Lost for words, Nina turned back to her father, and saw then what Aereas had already seen. He was gone. She reached toward the back of the chair but felt neither flesh nor warmth nor breath.

Oh, he's still there, assured the middle-aged Sung Chiang. *He can see and hear you, though you cannot sense him at all.*

She whispered to her father, "I will save you," then stood and returned to her seat. "How long before the other pieces are assembled?"

The god seemed pleased with her extension of his metaphor. *They are converging even now.*

With that, he swept a hand toward a huge tapestry that hung upon the wall. In its weave was depicted a titanic fiendish army on the march, their vanguard lined with shuffling creatures whose flesh seemed to be eternally melting downward onto the rocky ground below. Behind them, monstrous pikemen bristled, their shoulders and wings bearing prickling horns, their faces small with terrible fangs. The other fiendish hordes were lost in the darkness of the room and the smallness of their details, but Nina could see clearly that this was an army of horrifying strength.

And now they moved. It was not as though the fabric suddenly melted into reality, but that the fibers themselves shifted with the moiling army. It seemed the companions watched through a screen of cheesecloth.

This, the white army of baatezu, advances first, as the

white army should do. Its emissaries will arrive here to-morrow.

Another wave of the hand, and the scene changed, this time showing a horde of creatures with reptilian wings and birdlike heads and vicious claws. The beasts flowed through the narrow gap of a mountain range, like water churning through a rocky pass. They moved with none of the regular and relentless stride of the baatezu, but more the violent churning eagerness of floodwaters.

This, the black army of tanar'ri, will be, as always, late. Let us hope for the day after tomorrow, though it may well be a week from then.

"A week?" she asked, dismayed.

Is my hospitality so terrible? the middle-aged face responded with mock injury. Then he waved off the notion. *Ah, you are eager to get to the game.*

Nina nodded.

Then let us have a foretaste.

With that, one of Sung Chiang's long-fingered hands reached out toward the living tapestry. His fingers touched it, though the tapestry hung on a wall easily thirty feet from the god. His arm did not stretch or elongate as would that of a mage or illusionist, yet it was there.

His fingers reached into the scene. For a moment, they were like the ganglious tentacles of his other avatar, suddenly amorphous, dropping down amid the marching hordes of fiends. Where the stinging tip of a tentacle would touch, a creature would be snagged. With a gesture, as of a man drawing a card from a pile on the table, he drew out five squirming creatures, which became huge and horrifying as they left the fabric. He hefted them over the table and set them onto a carpet opposite the tapestry.

Nina recoiled. Who could help doing so? These beasts were unnatural.

The two nearest her were gaunt greenish creatures with hollow eyes that stared from faces that could have belonged to bats. Their long, pointed ears twitched horizontally beside their heads, and their naked scrawn shivered with fear or cold or both.

Beside them were a pair of what looked like evil elves. Their features were sharp like shattered crystal, and their white-yellow hair stood out from their heads as though it could little tolerate the vile thoughts circulating beneath. The whole foul frame of them was canned in spiky black armor.

The final creature, or creatures, had two heads: one a snarling dog and the other a hissing snake. Both heads shared the stooped shoulders of a slouching, vaguely human body.

All of the creatures glared about with sluggish malice, as though waking from a dream.

Nina was not prepared to wait for this waking to take place. She stood from her seat to retreat behind the table.

The others also moved to the opposite side. She happily joined their ranks, sliding into the fierce and sardonic shadow of Jandau. Somehow, it seemed safer to stand beside this planar creature, who'd no doubt seen beasts like this before, than beside Aere, who was used to squirrels and bluegills. Besides, Aereas too hovered nervously, standing behind the readied lizardman.

Sung Chiang was already reaching to the tapestry again. The scene had changed back to the original army. Those tentacular fingers descended. The stingers stuck like red-hot iron to living flesh, sizzling and drawing the squirming creatures from the tapestry to the carpet.

Nina moved into the reach of the tiefling's cape, and knew he could feel her trembling.

These creatures seemed more hideous than the first batch. The one nearest the table had huge, lost eyes set in a body of molten flesh. Its form was both sliding back to and reconstituting itself from the floor. Behind it stood two savage-looking men with barrel bodies encased in leathery armor. They had pointed ears, hooked noses, and jutting underbites ringed in wild, wiry gray beards. The final two were scorpion-men like the one Nina had chased toward the palace.

All the creatures now seemed much more awake. They began to drift apart and raise their axes and claws and swords—not toward the diners, but toward each other.

Sung Chiang spoke with mirth in his voice. *Don't be afraid, my young guests. They can no more see you than you can see your father. They can no more attack you than your father could stand from the chair where he sat. I've stripped them of their powers, their magics, leaving only claws and knives and teeth.*

To have any hope of bartering for her father, Nina had to master her fear, and immediately.

She moved away from the tiefling, feeling the retreat of his warmth and the sudden chill of stone again around her, then drew up an empty chair beside her host. With unseemly ease, she slid into the chair and said, "Let the entertainment begin."

Sung Chiang stared at her, amusement and amazement flashing for a moment in his middle-aged eyes. Then the young face spoke, *Begin!* and a set of hands clapped once.

The creatures lunged toward each other with snarling rage.

The first to meet were the melting man—a creature Sung Chiang told Nina was a *lemure*—and the two gaunt-bodied, long-eared green monsters—*dretches*.

The lemure flowed forward like a foul, breaking wave, its amorphous arms lashing the batlike faces of its attackers. They howled once. The sound was otherworldly, as though a ruined pipe-organ were bellowing, its player slumped dead on the keys.

Nina shivered, and was glad to feel the tiefling's warm darkness arrive behind her seat. The soft edges of his cape gently swept to either side.

Sung Chiang was addressing them all the while. *These are the least of baatezu and tanar'ri. See how they clash first in the vanguard, see how the others wait behind, see how they tear at each other?* There was black glee in his voice, a sound more distressing than the shriek of the dretches.

They were not long in striking back. Whirling claws stayed the slice of the lemure's talons while they each bit deeply into the biceps of the beast.

Nina covered her eyes. Moments after came the rip of tendinous flesh, the slosh of torrid arms dropping together to the ground and splashing away to puddles. Nina forced her hands from her face.

Sung Chiang chuckled as a fluid thinner than the creature's flesh jetted momently from its stubs. Then the lemure was lost beneath the furious clawing of the dretches.

Now the others, he said, watching keenly.

For sake of her father, Nina looked up with him.

First, the cambions, he said, indicating the spiky-armored elflike monsters. *Then the osyluths.* The scorpion-men lunged past the flying gray flesh of the lemure. *Neither can wait long to begin a fight, and both can last long in one.*

The first scorpion-man flung itself across the carpet. It slid on its belly, grasped the ankles of a surprised cambion, and drove its stinger through a gap in the creature's armor, deep into its gut. The blood was immediate, black on gray armor. It sprayed the creature beneath it the color of deep shadow.

Unless, of course, one gets in a lucky strike.

The cambion shrieked. Its voice replaced the quiet moaning gurgle of the dismantled lemure. It drew a great sword from its shoulder harness and drove the blade down into the osyluth's back. More blood, orange this time; more still when the cambion lunged, cracking the stinger's exoskeleton between the plates of his armor. The sword sliced through muscle and poison glands both. Neither beast would last long in that horrible fountain.

Behind this filthy mound of flesh, the other beasts moved hands through intricate gestures. *Spellcasting,* said Sung Chiang, *or trying, but magic is not allowed in this temple.*

Look! he said, gently patting Nina's hand. He had the strange excitement of a grandfather with a child at a carnival. *This will be more interesting.*

The other elf-eared cambion had closed with a barbazu—one of the barrel-chested creatures that stood in the rear of the pack. This seemed an even match, both creatures jabbing with wicked polearms. The cambion's strike hit first, a bejeweled axehead that sliced through the leather stomach-guard of the barbazu. A gush of blood followed the blade. Viscera seeped brown-red from the wide mouth of the cut.

But the barbazu was not finished. With its saw-toothed glaive, it pressed its opponent, taking a stolid stance in the slippery pool of its own blood. One strike, two, and the glaive had beaten past the whirling haft of the cambion's axe. Three strikes, four, and it was chipping away at the wooden shaft. Five strikes, six, and the barrel-bodied barbazu was treading on its own drooping entrails as it brought the glaive whirring down into the cambion's skull.

There was a giant crack, as though a dragon's egg had been split. Then came the inevitable fountaining flood of brain and blood. The cambion went down, and the barbazu, in its blind fury, plunged over the falling corpse to attack its next opponent.

Nina looked away for the second time, knowing she could not bear the twitches in that riven corpse, despite its horrible inhumanity.

When at last she looked up, the survivors were engaged—two dretches, the wolf- and snake-headed molydeus, a barbazu (its comrade had finally gone down after its own steps had drawn out all its entrails), a scorpion-tailed osyluth, and the lemure.

Yes, the lemure. Even as the dretches rose from its dismantled, melted corpse, the primeval flesh of the lemure began quivering, molding itself into a gelatinous whole. In moments, it was again at the attack.

Nina turned her eyes not to the shadowed safety of her

hand but to the soft dignity of Sung Chiang's middle-aged face. Unlike his young visage, which watched the fight with keen fascination, the middle face was gazing at her. It was as though he awaited a recitation from a pupil. Nina obliged.

"So this is the Blood War we have heard so much about?" she asked with feigned calm.

The head nodded, seeming pleased by her observation. *This is what tanar'ri and baatezu do in close quarters, yes. This genocide is the heart of the Blood War, if any war has a heart worth mentioning.*

There came another shriek before Nina responded, and the spraying of more black blood.

"What has my father to do with all of this?"

The head shifted. The old man wanted to speak to her. *Your father is the custodian of the Lady's keys. He holds the secrets to all her portals, the skeleton keys to the planes. All of them. Surely you knew that.*

She had not, not in so many words, but nodded as though she had known all along. "So they fight not only to slay each other, but also to gain the Lady's keys?"

These ends are one and the same, replied old Sung Chiang. *Those who hold the keys will hold Sigil, and those who hold Sigil will hold the planes.*

There came a final, strangled cry from the field of battle. A single figure was left standing—a blood-smeared scorpion-man whose stinging tail yet darted among the fallen bodies. It flicked with assiduous care among the quivering bits of lemure left behind. The gaunt scorpion raised its specked arms in a gesture of triumph and began a ululating cry of victory.

That sound was as short as it was defiant.

One of Sung Chiang's hands, without elongation, reached out, wrapped the beast in a sudden huge fist, and crushed the life from it. The stinging tail dropped dead to the ground beneath the flexing fingers.

He who holds Sigil will hold the planes.

✦ Berioth 46, 695 C.C. ✦

I take back everything I said about Malkin, the alley-cat god. He's a pleasant enough fellow, though as gullible as a kobold in the Lady's Ward.

Yes, I found him. He bore the blue tattooed whiskers on his cheeks, just as I'd been told. (These gods are so predictable, wearing telltale body ornaments like any child dressing up for All Souls.)

At first I almost missed the tattoos; they blended so nicely beneath the blue shadow of the umbrella shading his round café table from the noonday sun. He was sipping something red out of a wooden grail, his white pants sending up a sharp glare against the dun tiles at his feet.

His teeth were the same color as those trousers, and they shone with obvious enjoyment. His eyes glowed red and catlike from the brilliance of the adobe walls. He was looking wonderingly about the place, still new enough to flesh to enjoy its simple pleasures.

I struck up a conversation.

"So, what brings you to Xiam?" I asked nonchalantly and took a seat beside him.

He blinked at me, and his smile faded. He was studying me. Waves of uncertainty and suspicion washed over those eyes.

(Gods incarnate find human senses horrifyingly limiting. Having once had all power and all knowledge, they aren't well versed in intuition, in reading facial expressions and nuances. Gullible, as I said before, is the best term for it. I don't think he figured out who I was, or that I knew who he was. So, how's it feel to be a clueless sod, god?)

In time, the suspicion was replaced with a faraway, starry-eyed seriousness. "I'm looking for true love."

I almost laughed, but he wouldn't have understood. I knew he wouldn't, since he didn't understand my brusque shoulder slap, or my comment about his not being my type, but I covered quickly, and saved our new friendship.

When he got up to leave, I blurted, "See you here, tomorrow?"

"Yes."

He moved from the table, his immaculate trousers catching the bald eye of the sun.

I watched him go, thinking, Now if only I can figure a way to lure him back to the Cage.

TWELVE
BL⊕OD BINDINGS

There was something more to this journal, something more than randomized pages and flitting sketches—words written in ink and blood and mud. There was something more, and Aereas knew he was missing it.

He'd suspected it before but knew it for sure as he sat on the bed in his chambers, the book in his lap. He was studying it beneath the merciless glare of the oil lamp in the room and the ceaseless stare of the black sky beyond his windows.

He had heard Sung Chiang say it: Artus was custodian of the Lady's keys, and where he kept the keys would have to be told here, in his journal. The truth of that belief was only underscored by the realization that if anyone—even Jandau or Sung Chiang—knew he had this book, he would have it no longer.

Anyone except Nina.

Aereas rose and knocked on the door to the bath between their rooms. There came a faint, watery response from within, a murmur that sounded to him like an invitation. Even so, when Aereas opened the door, Nina startled where she lounged in the tub. She sank down into the cloudlike bubbles that topped the water.

"Couldn't you knock?" she asked sleepily.

"Sorry," he apologized, though he had knocked. Aereas moved backward to leave and began to draw the door closed behind him.

"No, wait," she said, sitting up a bit again. "What is it?"

He paused, then hefted the journal. "It's this. Your father's journal."

With one soapy hand, she made a gesture that drew him toward the steaming tub.

Her skin seemed especially brown against the blue-white spheres of soap that clothed her. Aereas tried not to notice.

"There must be more to it," he said, averting his eyes to the book and diverting his attention from those shoulders. "If your dad is the custodian of the Lady's keys, this book's got to tell something about where he keeps those keys . . . and how to use them to get out, to escape."

"Sit," she said, as though they were merely fishing from the stone shelf beside the creek in her back yard. "Show me what you mean."

Aereas was no more prepared to show her than he was to climb into that steamy water with her, but he didn't want her to know that. So he drew up the stool she had indicated and laid the volume down on his lap.

"Like here," he said, opening the book to a page his finger marked.

What he found startled him, kept him from speaking in the moment before it was gone. On the page where before he had seen only ropy lines of text, he saw now, in addition to them, a small figure. It was as though some beetle that had chewed its way into the book had been startled by his opening the pages and scuttled away across the page, out of sight. Only it wasn't a beetle. It was flat, a drawing that moved. . . . A drawing of a small figure on two legs, arms pumping above a paunchy belly, trailing what looked like gray whiskers.

"Boffo," he said before he knew he had said anything.

"Boffo?" repeated Nina, sitting up taller and setting an arm across her chest as she craned toward the open book.

"I thought I saw him, running across the page." He blinked and rubbed his eyes, wondering if his fevered mind was playing tricks. The rubbing fingers also shielded his eyes from the sight of his bare cousin.

"I thought I'd seen him, too," she said. "Not now, but before, back in the cave, staring out of the page at me. Is it just us—?"

"Or is he inside the book?" Aereas wondered, finishing the question for her.

He peered down at the page. It was vacant now except for the wandering craze of words that had been there all along.

Nina already was thinking. "And if he is inside the book," she began with a tone of awe in her voice, "what else might be inside it?"

"It's apparently infinite," Aereas noted, "as we saw when we flipped through it before. An endless account of your father's exploits."

"But when did he ever get time to sit down and write all this?" Nina wondered. "I'd heard of the book, maybe glimpsed it once when I was growing up, but I never saw Father reading it, let alone writing in it."

Suddenly they both knew . . . knew that their very thoughts, and all the thoughts of their dreaming and wakeful minds, were being somehow filtered by and recorded in the book. . . .

Artus never wrote the book at all. The book read him and wrote down what he was thinking, in whatever form seemed best to suit. The book had read Artus's mind as surely as it was reading both of the cousins' minds, as surely as it was just now putting down these very words as Aereas thought them in his brain. Somehow, the magic journal had made a connection with the three—Artus, Nina, and Aereas—that it had not made with any others.

Neither of the cousins had to voice that revelation, though both immediately understood it, understood it and the fact that perhaps they were neither the readers nor the writers, but the books themselves, being read and written.

"Infinite, and growing," Nina said, staring at the volume.

"Infinity plus two," Aereas replied. The infinite recollections of Artus, plus those of his adopted daughter and his true nephew.

All thoughts of Boffo fled their minds then as they contemplated the strange, slim, silent tome lying between them.

Their innermost thoughts were suddenly open to anyone who found the key to unlock the book's secrets. Aereas was abruptly blushing as he saw Nina's wet, smooth, brown shoulders against the suds of the tub. She was blushing, too, and drew down into the foamy water as he pushed his seat back and, with book in hand, withdrew to his room.

Nothing had changed, but everything had. That single now-undeniable knowledge—that the book *knew* them both, and that all was now being written down somehow—was a knowledge fraught with all the ancient mortal dread of sin and salvation.

That knowledge stood for all knowledge, for knowledge of one's self as a separate and self-determined creature, for knowledge that one's actions contain a moral dimension and are not merely motions that slide seamless and pure into black nothing, for that final inescapable knowledge of the corporeal desolation that comes inevitably. It stood for it all. There was loss in that realization. Loss and rape and death.

Once the door was closed and Aereas was lying in his nightshirt in the strange, soft bed of the suite, he opened the book again. If he would from now on live with that knowledge yokelike on his neck, he would find the good of it, too. What might these chaotic pages tell him of him?

What he learned instead was more about Nina. On one page, after much flipping and concentrating on the question of his past, he found a single diary entry by a hand much too looped and graceful to represent the thoughts of Artus. And the entry said:

Nindonth 22, 702 C.C.
I have given my only child away to the tiger. A ghara-girl, filled with killing fire. I knew it from the start, but hid it as we all do, though she was found out to be what she was sooner, not later. And they took her . . . I gave her over to the tiger, and wept, as we all do.

But here is my secret. It was not the tiger that found her, that took her. I was in the bush, watching, weeping, and saw a man appear and scoop my little Ninavereth up before the cat came. I went to him and told him her name, and he kissed me sweetly and spoke of a great Lady who had a place for Ninavereth.

It was the best I could do, with the tribe so close. I hope only that she has the security and love I will never know.

The passage was unsigned, the page ends burnt, the words disappearing into a black verge of soot and ash. That dark barrier looked like the weather-smoothed slope of a mountain, beneath which the next page was visible. As Aereas closed the book against his chest, he knew it was a mountain of hope.

Nina was not his true cousin, not Artus's flesh. That passage proved it.

Though this news would come as sadness to her, it

brought him joy. It meant the love he felt was not a thing impure, unholy.

Perhaps this news would at last allow her to feel as he did.

* * * * *

Dawn came strangely to the slopes of Sung Chiang's sanctuary. Just as the day was always greenish, never able to trade the rust-red entirely for a healthy blue, so the morning came brown rather than rosy, its winds dry and hot and harsh, with more than a taste of sulfur in them. But it was better than the cave had been, where there was no dark nor light. If Sung Chiang had managed to put any sun in the sky over his warped palace, Aereas felt he should not complain about the color.

He rose early. He wanted to see the dawn.

The revelations of the book had kept him up long into the night, flipping uselessly through the volume, which had already surrendered to him greater revelations than he could have hoped for. Nothing more came, though, not even a return to that diary page, which he had marked with a bookmark that disappeared as quickly as the others had. No, only sleep came to him in the darkest corner of the night, sleep bedeviled by dreams of fiends tearing into each other and of Nina in his arms, warm and safe like a child saved from a tiger.

So he rose before the light of day and sat beside the wide, clear bank of windows while brown light crept upward over the sprawling home of Sung Chiang. It was as though the sun rose through blood-dried gauze.

In the twilight of that morning, Nina in her slim night-shirt appeared through the door and came to sit beside him on the wide window-seat. She had brought with her a heavy, warm cover seemingly woven of feathers, which they shared as they watched the sun rise.

Together, they saw also a black bank of brooding thunderheads threatening the dawn. Watching in deeper silence, sipping the aromatic tea brought to them by the furtive and ubiquitous linqas, they saw this ebon wave resolve itself into what seemed a swale of burnt grass, which in turn became a vast army moving toward the gate with slow and relentless tread.

The baatezu were nearly here.

It was a tread now, not a liquid flow, that brought them. Soon the army had reached the outer fence of Sung Chiang's plaza. There were fires among them, torches that became bivouacs, glowing against eyes and throats. Aereas could hardly bear to look at them, but neither could he look away.

Though the army seemed to lean upon the great fence, threatening to break it down, only the smallest party of creatures—four or five figures—made it past the stone golems and the cracked gates.

They passed through the gates and moved self-importantly across the stone-paved courtyard, their faces indistinguishable in the morning light. But the glint of bone and horn and the lash of tail and the haughteur of stride left no doubt as to who they were.

"Fiends," Nina and Aereas said in a breath, though they'd said nothing else for what seemed an hour before that.

Nina was shivering as she leaned into her cousin, and he was glad. That way she was less likely to notice he was shivering, too.

Aereas went on. "Sung Chiang said they would arrive today."

She nodded, staring at the fiendish crew advancing toward the steps of the sanctuary. "I wonder how we are to be their match at the bargaining table." Her voice spoke of despair, of self-doubt.

"We've already overmatched them," Aereas replied easily,

slipping his arms around her. "See, they come up the gutter."

"So we outrank them in hubris. What about power? What about trading ability? They still outmatch us there."

"Yes, we have a job ahead of us," Aereas replied. "And sitting here won't help us get started . . . as comfortable as it may feel."

She stretched against him, as languorous as a cat, and he could feel the expansion of her ribs beneath the thin shift she wore. Then there was a gentle nuzzle as her face brushed his cheek. He might have called it a kiss, had it not been so casual.

She yawned and said, "You're right. Let's get dressed and get down to the sanctuary. We should stand beside our host when the next guests arrive."

And she was gone, soft robe flapping like an angel's raiment as she disappeared through the door between the suites. The portal latched behind her.

Dizzy, Aereas rose and went to the tooled chest where his clothes awaited. Perhaps I'll be better able to stand after I'm clothed, he thought.

Of course, then he'd be standing in the company of a god.

*　*　*　*　*

Dressing for company was not easy, especially given that the clothes were not theirs and the company was demonic. Even so, Nina and Aereas were ready quickly and left their rooms together, only to run into Jandau the tiefling standing suavely in the hall. Unlike the cousins, bedecked in reds and yellows like a pair of silken roses, Jandau was wearing his old clothes.

Well, not exactly his old clothes—a new pair of trousers made of black linen, a roughweave shirt, and a cape with all manner of pockets. He seemed to notice Aereas's suspicious eye scanning the crisp lines of his clothes.

Jandau smirked. "One cape pocket that escaped ruin was the pocket where I keep a change of clothes."

So saying, Jandau extended an arm, which Nina—as startled and confused as Aereas was—reflexively took hold of. At least, Aereas thought it was because of confusion that she did, though as she strode down the hall at her accustomed pace, she did not let go.

A change of clothes in a pocket? Aereas was not about to ask. All sorts of things in this place fit into spaces they could not have, so why not a change of clothes? Besides, it had become one of Jandau's favorite pastimes to trip Aereas up with questions, a pastime the younger man had tired of.

At least I have the consolation that Nina is too preoccupied with the quest for her adopted father to notice the posing and preening of that peacock, Aereas thought as he trailed the flapping cape and flitting white hand of the tiefling.

Following the ever-widening hall, the group reached an archway into the great sanctuary and were about to sweep on by it when a sweet puff of incense came from below. They drifted toward the cloud. No, it was not just incense that drew them. When they stepped into the sheltered alcove, they found their host, his old face gazing expectantly toward them as he stood there.

Good morning. I trust you slept well.

Aereas began to answer with a lie, but realized lies were, at most, transparent in this place.

Sung Chiang was still talking. *Your competition has arrived.* With a gesture of his arm, he indicated the sulfurous party of creatures making its way across the floor of the nave.

The worshipers of Sung Chiang gave them a wide berth, which was wise since the yellow miasma that streamed from these menaces was visible in a twenty-foot trail behind them.

I see they will be in need of a bath, Sung Chiang said placidly.

Jandau let out a snide snort.

The old face of the god blinked and turned toward him with a gentle smile. *As did you when you arrived.*

The head kept moving, right past Jandau's irritated expression and on to Nina's face. She stared curiously ahead, like a girl-child struggling to see the new arrivals at her parents' party.

The god murmured reflectively, *Though some of you did not arrive by way of the gutter.*

There was not a sign on her face that she had heard him, only the vacant reply, "Nice of you to notice."

Seeing those feral creatures—two of them like small dragons bearing whips; a giant lizard that stood upright on bird talons and had a mantis head; the squat, pudgy body of a man with a mouth as wide and red as a gashed throat—Aereas felt a sudden terror. If only we could conclude our quest without their involvement.

"We are prepared to make you an offer that would prevent this unpleasant meeting from occur—" Aereas began. The hand raised toward him was neither quick nor insistent, though it shut him up immediately.

In due time.

"They are up to the screen," Nina said. The fiends had reached the spinning cylinders, and silence had enfolded them. Without taking her eyes from these monsters, Nina continued, "What is it, Your Holiness, that makes the screen silent?"

Ah, said the old head, *those spinning cylinders are prayer bells. My worshipers in all the planes have similar bells, into which they place prayers on rolled slips of paper and burn them with incense. The spinning of the bells makes them ring and makes the smoke of their prayers and incense rise up through the worlds and reach me here.*

The bells on the screen below us, however, spin to gather the incense and the prayers from these worlds, and that is why they are silent. All the words and sounds of anyone beside the screen are drawn in with the prayers.

It was another manifestation of the endless arms of this thief god, reaching into all times and places and drawing to its central being the powers and prayers of all peoples.

And we expected we might negotiate with him, Aereas thought drearily.

If Nina felt equally staggered, she did not show it.

The fiends were through the gate now and standing within the holy place, gazing up at the great pulsing man-o-war above them.

Nina said, "I'm just glad we reached you before they did. I would like to be at your side for introductions."

I am afraid it is too late for that, said the middle-aged face. He gestured down to the knot of fiends, where they bowed shallowly to another man with three faces and eight arms.

Nina's jaw clenched, and she released Jandau's arm—she had been clinging loosely to it this whole time. She latched onto one of Sung Chiang's.

"Let us go meet the competition, my lord. I am eager to see what they might have that you don't already own."

Sung Chiang turned and dutifully followed her, his aged face bent toward his feet in the posture of an unsteady old man. Even so, Aereas glimpsed the young face gazing at Nina, and there was a predatory light in the eyes.

Aereas felt another pang. This was not his Nina, this woman desperate to grab whatever arm would lead her to her father. She'd always soared on her own, but now had become a hooded falcon, all too anxious to land upon the upraised fists of men who were slowly becoming her masters, were training her to gauntlets and chains.

I've got to get her out of here, get them both out of here, and sooner rather than later, Aereas thought, or there will

be nothing but t   empty semblance of Ninaflesh and Ar-
tusflesh to drag c   with me.

The tiefling, to   seemed irritated by the sight of Nina
holding Sung Chia 's arm, though neither of them spoke
their jealousy. It was strange and stupid. Surely the god
knew how they felt.

> . . . *I have since concluded that, with gods, outward po-*
> *liteness is even more important than it is to humans. Yes,*
> *I. It is me speaking, me Aereas suddenly speaking. I am*
> *speaking, but the book writes down these thoughts. In this*
> *sudden brief terror of knowing, I know it, but already I*
> *feel the lucid mood sliding, failing. It's just my awareness*
> *of being read that is lapsing, not the book's reading me. I*
> *shall have to remember this mood. I wonder if there were*
> *once upon a time and a very good time it was there was a*
> *moocow coming down along the . . .*

Aereas and Jandau both followed with heads similarly
lowered, like a pair of whipped dogs.

The floor of the sanctuary was thronged this morning,
worshipers packed tightly to either side of the stinking
cloud of fiends. Once Sung Chiang and Nina had pressed
past the crowd, it was only a few nervous steps up to the
beasts.

They were shocked by the humans' arrival, and ap-
praised them severely. Fiends and humans both were
shocked when the two Sung Chiangs slid soundlessly into
each other, their bodies joining seamlessly into a single
being.

Speaking of fiends, they were incredibly imposing here,
a mere arm's length away. Aereas could see the large leathery wings that sprouted from the short, bald-headed fiend,
and the throat-gash of a mouth on that creature could
have swallowed his head whole. The robes it wore over its
bulky body radiated heat into the stink cloud of the other

creatures, and the horned helmet on its head ran with something gray, which Aereas assumed to be blood.

It was the small one. The whip-bearing creatures, though small for dragons, were half again taller than Aereas. Their gaunt wings arched above bodies that were as spiked with scales as their whips were with barbs, and they glowered with empty gold eyes, like the eyes of statues. Were they not breathing and stinking, Aereas would have thought or hoped they *were* statues.

But the tallest of all was the lizard creature with bird talons and a mantis head. It was twice Aereas's height, even hunched over its fifteen-foot-long glaive. Were the beast laid out from antennae to spiked tail tip, it would have measured a good twenty feet. Aereas imagined, however, he would never see such a creature laid out that way. He certainly thought himself incapable of laying one out.

Allow me to introduce your competitors, Sung Chiang said out of all sides of his face. He gestured to either side with opposite arms and bowed slightly. Jandau, Nina, and Aereas took the cue. The fiends did not respond with similar bows.

The fat one said, "When can we get to the bargaining? You know what we want, Sung Chiang."

Yes, said the god with a nod of his three-cornered head. *But you do not know what I want. This is your disadvantage, and I would advise you to compensate for it with study and patience.*

"We have platinum. We have jewels," the thing said through its blood-red lips. "It all awaits you just beyond the gate. Now, where is the hostage?"

Xarmostrogaphus, Sung Chiang responded, *you know better than to offer in trade what you cannot deny in thievery. Especially to a god like me.*

The great fleshy thing crossed arms over its chest.

As I say, you do not know what I want. You have until the tanar'ri arrive to find out.

"Tanar'ri!" replied one of the dragons, and it spit a patch of acid upon the floor.

There was a slight pop, a wisp of less-than-fragrant smoke, and a sudden tumble of yellow bones on the spot where the dragon had stood.

No spitting in my tabernacle, Sung Chiang said mildly, then turned to drift slowly away.

Aereas followed, of course, as did Nina and Jandau, none of them wanting to be left alone in the presence of these horrible beasts.

Before they passed through the archway, Aereas saw Xarmostrogaphus poke at the bones with one foot and overheard it whisper to its companions, "He was a proxy of Takhisis—and Sung Chiang just smoked him! I ain't telling her how it happened, or there'll be *two* fiends missing!"

Sung Chiang apparently heard it as well and shook his head. To Nina he murmured, *Perhaps I'll grant a boon to the tanar'ri to bring them here sooner. I've little love for fiendish scum in my temple.*

* * * * *

The tanar'ri arrived that evening.

They arrived with considerably more panache than their hated counterparts, though it took Aereas longer to notice them.

Krim and he were busy bending over Artus's journal, too distracted with the flitting words and images to look out the window at the gloaming dusk. Though Aereas had initially wanted to keep the book a secret, he knew too clearly now that nothing was secret from Sung Chiang in this temple of his. And if the wily god knew about the book, it would be wise to enlist the aid of a powerful protector with magic at his wingtips.

The manta had agreed to keep the book secret from Jandau and aid in speeding Artus's rescue, in exchange for merely seeing the magical tome. Together, they lurked above the shifting pages. Aereas was struggling to catch another glimpse of the elusive Boffo, whether it be dim eyes staring directly out at him or fleeting feet in the margins or strands of hair stuck in the binding as though slammed in a doorframe. But nothing.

Krim did not upbraid him. His fishy form was curved like a question mark in a chair, and his bulging eyes stared over the flat cliff of his edged face. His initial questions about the sightings of Boffo had slacked off as both searchers glared almost angrily at the uncooperative pages.

"I'm not making it up," Aereas muttered beneath his breath.

Apparently the ear-slits of that great manta ray were sharper than he had expected. "I don't believe you are," Krim said quietly. "The magical emanations from this book are very strong, indeed, and I've already seen how its pages seem endless, receding and advancing like a tide so that the last page, like the last wave, is never the same from one moment to the next."

"You're right," Aereas said. He heard in his mind the click of one piece of the puzzle falling into place. "It's more like . . . like nature than literature. Like waves or clouds or flocks of birds—"

"Or spinning planets in spinning systems in spinning universes in the spinning minds of spinning gods," Krim took up. Each repetition of the word grew more clipped, more irritable. "I suppose we are lucky that most books aren't this blasted dynamic." The manta paused, seemed to consider. "Or are they?"

That's when the tanar'ri sent their calling card to Sung Chiang. It was a blistering sound rather than a piece of paper, and it was in truth addressed more to the baatezu hordes beyond the walls than to the god within them.

Krim seemed especially unnerved by the sound, and his barbed tail lashed behind him as he flowed out of the chair toward the window. "What the devil—" As he went, the sound of his rippling gray hide was like the low rumbling hiss of sheet metal in a stiff wind.

Aereas was up now, too, and followed Krim to the window.

"Boffo said he'd sold some cursed alpenhorns to a yugoloth—" he began, but when Aereas reached the sill, the words caught in his throat.

A battle was ready to break.

There, just on the horizon of this strange bubble world, beyond the warped gate of Sung Chiang, the baatezu bivouacs sent up yellow smoke into the pall of the sky and their dark forms moved with patient malice among lean-tos and tents of all descriptions. But nearer the gate, antlike black forms moved with agitation, some taking to the air, their wings stirring the smoke columns of their own fires.

To the other side of the gate, the jagged rocks of Gehenna rose glistening in the gloom. But, no, they were not jagged rocks. They moved, and it wasn't water that glistened on the rocks, but sweat and blood on horns, tentacles, wings. As Aereas watched, the ground there seemed to reshape, rise, broaden, and sweep out toward the baatezu. It looked like an avalanche of bodies—a cloud of locusts, pouring black and eerie and unstoppable over the mountaintops and sweeping toward the baatezu like brush-fire toward grain.

There came a twitch from Krim and a muttered arcane word, and suddenly the distant gate swelled up toward them as though they had been thrown through the window and out into the open air. Aereas dropped to his knees in queasiness and could feel the thick carpet beneath him, the windowsill before him. They had not moved at all, but Krim had shifted the perspective before them. The gate seemed only a stone's throw distant, with the converging armies only another stone's throw beyond.

"I thought it would be good to see better," Krim stated, curled again like a question mark before the open window.

Aereas nodded, glad that Sung Chiang's prohibition against magic applied only to the tabernacle and not the staterooms. Otherwise, he might have been kneeling beside the collapsing cartilaginous skeleton of a manta.

Aereas didn't look to see, for the moment his eyes saw the battle, he thought for sure it would be good not to see anything at all.

The yellow-orange sky beyond the gate was empty for only a moment before flights of tanar'ri gushed into it.

These new arrivals were as horrid as their foes, though the wicked gleam of their eyes had something of chaos in it. As one, they opened their mouths—be they serrated beaks or scissoring pincers or mucousy wounds or fang-studded caves—and shrieked, a sound Aereas heard seconds later, mixed with more of the hoarse, wild baying of those baatezu horns. Those monsters that had fire in their bellies released it along with gouts of acid and steam and smoke, which flew out before the shrieking hordes and struck the first wall of entrenched baatezu.

The defenders stood shoulder to shoulder in their shallow lines and held aloft hoary shields of bone, flesh, metal, or stone. Among and through them stabbed lances of fire and acid and smoke. Some shields disintegrated immediately, and the once-living flesh behind them erupted in sprays of red or black or gray. Others shields held, and from behind these, claws and tentacles lifted wicked pikes into the air.

The descending tanar'ri either did not see these blades or did not care. Fiends fell like lightning from the sky and fiercely struck the poles. Their bodies hung for moments in jerking terror, spraying magic and fire and blood all about them in their frenzy before the pikemen let the weapons fall before or behind and raised more pikes.

One goat-headed thing crashed down upon a halberd

that cleaved through its mannish gut. The creature grabbed the haft in bloodied hands and drew itself down the shaft until the astonished baatezu had to pull its clasping fist out of the thing's gut. It was too late for the baatezu, for the goatman attacked with unholy fury, shredding the flesh from its orange bones. In moments, the goatman collapsed dead atop the bare skeleton of its victim.

As Aereas turned away, feeling ill, he felt a hand pat his shoulder.

"Better to see it now, before we are in the center of it," said Krim. It was not a hand on his shoulder, but the underside of that stinging tail. Even so, the words were well meant. Nodding, Aereas looked up again at the battle.

Beside the riven corpse of the torn baatezu, reinforcements were sliding into place. The bodies of the dead were shoved out of the way or flung up in bulwarks before the survivors. Despite numerous casualties among the baatezu, the growing wall of corpses before the defenders consisted mostly of fallen tanar'ri.

Not that all were fallen. While the air cavalry swept onward, crashing into the next hasty redoubts of the baatezu, tanar'ri infantry had closed, too.

Gaunt, long-eared dretches lumbered into battle, claws slashing before them, and beside these mindless brutes came scabby creatures whose flesh crawled with maggots and pill bugs. They moved with grotesque temerity, naked and groggy like madmen beneath the moon. Sluggish enough, stupid enough, the first wave of them ran upon the bristling embankment of blades and went down in a roiling, filthy mass.

The second wave climbed over the shuddering wall of their compatriots, and this time there were no pikes to stop them. Down onto the shields, and the claws and teeth began their monotonous rending. Still, most were beheaded in moments by the quick blades of the entrenched baatezu, and their jiggling bodies filled the trench like so much shoveled earth. The third wave rushed across the body bridge, many of these catching the retreating foes, whose shoulders and backs were turned.

Just as the baatezu were falling back, a new wave of hissing, spitting things rolled forward through their ranks to slash down the dretches and manes (*manes* is what Krim called the scabby ones).

For a moment, the flood was stemmed, gray flesh wrestling gray flesh and ripping and tearing. Then, through the writhing line of monsters, a troop of keen-eyed, gray-bearded barbazu charged. They did not waste their time engaging the dretches and manes, pushing beyond them to the rushing and flying ranks of greater fiends, whose magic commanded the foot soldiers like puppeteers pulling strings.

"You think"—Aereas's voice sounded strangled, and he coughed and began again—"you think we will be among them?"

Manta rays do not nod, but in the long harsh silence that followed, Aereas knew what Krim's answer would be.

✦ Berioth 47, 695 C.C. ✦

True love. I suppose it's the one thing that a god cannot command. Some have tried; they've failed. Maybe that's why barmy old Malkin wants it so bad.

The sky was gray-blue. The mud shops in the square of Xiam looked as blue as cobalt tiles. A mean wind moved among them, chasing folks home in a hurry like darkness does, or cold, or fear.

Normal folks, anyway. Malkin sat across from me in the café. We'd decided to sit in the smoky, low-ceilinged taproom rather than beneath that blustering sky. I was dressed for the weather in coarse gray wool and leather. Malkin was not. His lean feline form was yet garbed in tailored whites.

But his face held a pensive, anxious fear.

"She's got to be out there, Artus, my friend," he said.

He drew a timid, wilting marigold from the vase on the table, set it beneath his nose, and breathed. He seemed to like the smell, though no mortal I've ever known could tolerate a marigold beneath his nose.

"It's only been a few days," I said. "Give it time."

"Time is what we mortals don't have."

I almost laughed. As though he would know!

Suddenly, he lurched to his feet. The table nearly went over; vase and lunch both landed in my lap. He peered excitedly out the window.

"There! There she is!"

And with a small whine of anticipation, he bolted for the door.

I rose with somewhat less haste and went to the window.

I missed her—whoever she was—but reached the sill in time to see that anxious set of god-shoulders suspended in indecision in the blue square. He glanced down alleys, craning to see.

And then the storm broke. Before Malkin could even have thought to turn around, the white shirt was stuck to his shoulders like plaster, and mud had speckled his pant legs.

THIRTEEN

BARGAINING WITH THE THIEF GOD

Nina was with Jandau when the tanar'ri arrived, and just as she'd been when she'd seen the fight in the banquet hall, she was glad now to be with him.

Not that she noticed the tanar'ri right away; nor had Jandau, for that matter. Neither of them looked up from the maps of Sung Chiang's temple complex until the sorceries began flying along the outer wall. Not even the low rumble of voices, the high strange keen of dying fiends, had pierced the concentration between them.

Perhaps it was because there was a kind of subtle but powerful magic in the room itself. From the moment Nina had laid eyes on this black sparrow—as Aereas called Jandau—she'd been intrigued by him.

It's no wonder he and Aereas didn't get along. They were

direct opposites: Aereas familiar, comfortable, safe, muscular, boyishly handsome, straightforward; Jandau mysterious, intense, dangerous, gaunt, mannishly attractive, puzzling.

He was a cipher to Nina, an avatar of these planes, with all their impossible closets and living pubs and slag-dumps into hell. Jandau was the manifestation in flesh of fiendish depths and angelic heights.

Nina'd seen plenty of depths so far, and expected to see a lot more before all was said and done. Even so, she knew the heights lay here too, both in the planes around her and in the man before her.

The map. She told herself that it was the map that held her spellbound, mesmerized. It was a lie.

The map. It was just the sort of map that could mesmerize—laid out on thick, scaly vellum the size of the round tabletop she huddled over. Broadly stroked lines arched over the iridescent scales of the dead flesh. The lines seemed complex at first glance; then with further study, the underlying simplicity manifested itself. But concentrated attention brought her once again back to the complexity.

Nina's eye focused on a corridor here, a stateroom there, and suddenly she could see individual flagstones, wooden window moldings. More concentration brought cracks in the mortar and nails in the moldings. She had the sense that were she smarter or more focused, she could gaze into this map and see the tiniest sinews of stone or wood or bone in any feature.

But she was only Nina Whitesun, not a god. And she was mesmerized.

His hand was on the thing, tracing out the grand arcs that she had missed for all the window moldings. "See, here, the six wings off the main temple? Each curls in upon itself, like the tentacle of an octopus."

"Like the tentacles of a hexapus," she said wryly.

Jandau smiled at that, a keen-edged expression that held

something of a sniffing snake in it. "An octopus, if you count the stairs to the temple as the seventh and eighth arms."

"The arms that extend out into all the world," Nina murmured, indicating on the map how the central pathway passed through the gates and spread outward, like the delta of a river. "He's rather attached to water metaphors."

Jandau only nodded. No smile this time, and Nina upbraided herself for being disappointed. He said, "Sung Chiang told me the baatezu are rooming here, in this wing."

He gestured to one of the round, recursive curls at the top of the map, the wing they were in. It looked like the cross-section of a chambered nautilus, its central corridor and staterooms becoming smaller the farther one progressed into it.

"I imagine they're staying in these midsized rooms. The baatezu would rile at staying in rooms our size."

This time it was Nina's turn to nod without smiling. "What of the tanar'ri?"

Whether he noticed the alacrity of her response, she could not tell. "They'll be *here*," he said, pointing to a wing on the opposite side of the temple.

"Caught between a vrock and a hard place," Nina said, and tapped the sanctuary.

This made him laugh, and as ashamed as she was for having wanted that laugh, she felt even more ashamed for having brought it forth. "Yes. Sung Chiang needs some sort of buffer between the two."

"Then that's just how we ought to bargain," Nina said.

"What do you mean?" His lightless eyes lifted toward hers. The irises were too big in those tiefling eyes, making them seem at once the eyes of a puppy and those of a shark.

"It's no good trying to compete with the fiends on their own terms. We obviously can't match what they could offer. We should, instead, play toward our strengths, use what little advantage Sung Chiang will grant us. We should play up our being in the middle."

Those eyes hadn't left her, and they were digging into her own for answers—answers she did not yet have. It was only an intuition, an impulse, but clearly he thought it was more.

"What do you have in mind?"

Yes, girl, what *do* you have in mind? Nina had never been the brooder, the thinker that Aereas was. Her way of solving a problem was to begin to talk, and then see what came out.

"Well, the fiends are . . . what?" Good girl. Lead him along with questions so he thinks you're teaching him rather than stalling.

He took the bait, eyes swinging down for a moment in thought. "They're base, violent, evil, hateful, powerful, paranoid. . . ."

Nina was starting to hatch an idea. "And they think we are soft, stupid, easy, trusting, weak?"

"Of course."

"Then let's use their natures against them, their paranoia, their certainty that we could never conceive of treachery. After the negotiations begin, we can go to the baatezu, here"—she pointed to their quarters on the map—"and tell them Sung Chiang intends to sell them out, that he'd already decided to give Artus to the tanar'ri, even before they arrived."

He was nodding and smiling. Yes, definitely the eyes of a shark. "And then, off to the tanar'ri to tell them the same thing." His hand slapped over the area of the map where the tanar'ri roomed.

Their forearms were crossed, barely touching, and despite the heat of his body, gooseflesh rose on Nina's arm.

"And to both sides, we pledge our aid when things go bad. We pledge to help them pursue their foes and get Artus back," she concluded triumphantly.

His hand was up from the map and suddenly, gently, pressed over her lips. "Shhh. If our host's tentacles reach into all the worlds, surely his ears do as well."

Nina had never been shut up like that. She'd never had a hand clamped over her mouth, neither that of Father nor that of Aereas. She did not like it.

She bit him, incisors clamping for a moment on the flesh of his middle finger. He yelped and drew back, shaking the pinched hand as she placidly finished.

"Sung Chiang will not care. He will have his ransom already and won't mind what we do to the ransomer. Besides, if we want to earn the admiration of this lord of thieves and deceit, we might as well do it with a plan like this."

He nodded again, though this time with tears edging his blinking eyes. "Girls from Caonan need to learn manners."

"Boys from Caonan don't try what you tried."

That was when streamers of fire, roiling columns of smoke, and jagged splinters of lightning began beyond the gate.

Jandau stood framed by it all, his livid features limned with the light that flickered between blue and orange and green, and Nina wondered suddenly if he even knew of the war going on behind his back, too distracted by the war going on in his head, his chest.

Whether he knew it or not, the sparrow was falling for her. Nina knew she had somehow won a first battle in what would be a long war, one that would end for one of them in surrender. The battle would necessitate irrecoverable casualties, but it was a fight she knew she wanted to fight.

Casualties like those beyond the impassive, massive gates of Sung Chiang's palace.

"Look," Nina said, pointing past the tiefling, past the window, out to the cobbled courtyard that stretched between the gate and the temple. "Look how they kill each other."

He turned as she rose, and together they went to the window.

She was right. The battle was fierce, the air above the warriors thick as gelatin with pungent smoke and sluggish sparks and plunging tracers. The ground heaved beneath the combatants, with bursts of flame and lightning and with thrashing, dying bodies.

Nina realized then that her hand was in Jandau's. She didn't know whether she had given it to him or he had taken it.

It seemed the battle could get no worse, but suddenly, subtly, it became far worse.

A grayish red tide poured slowly through the bars of Sung Chiang's compound. It passed the magic wards that kept out living fiends, but not their gushing blood. At first the pooling stuff looked merely like the shadows of late afternoon beneath the tremendous wall. But it spread too quickly for any sun Nina had ever seen, and its rust color was out of place on the black flagstones of the courtyard. Its movement quickened unnaturally, as though the temple lay downhill of the battle, as though some great beast lay upon the horizon, bleeding from its neck in ceaseless spurts.

Now the tide covered half the courtyard, and the tiny creatures in the marketplace began fleeing, too late. They were caught by the flood and borne along atop it. The line of worshipers waiting beneath the gutter were swept up and carried on the frothy pink foam. In moments, the tide swept the courtyard clean, breaking against the stairs of the temple.

Then, two veins of the liquid started up the gutters on either side of the stairs, rising against gravity, sweeping up those who struggled for the sanctuary door. At the top of the stairs, the blood streams converged in the central plaza, forming a great red, spinning disk.

Something ignited the whirlpool, and instead of flames,

up rose congealed and clotted strands of blood, twirling into a hoary column, coalescing into a head with three faces.

It laughed, from all three mouths, and Nina was holding Jandau with more than just a hand now. The sound chilled her, like the sound of a thousand leg bones snapping in gory progression.

How right that negotiations should begin with a blood sacrifice, said the huge, sanguine head of Sung Chiang, spinning horribly above the pool of blood that had formed it. *And how considerate of you to accomplish the violence of this sacrifice beyond my own gates, so that we may avoid such . . . unpleasantries within.*

Then, most hideous of all, a great forked tongue of blood emerged from the central face of the god and stretched out over the plaza. It reached over the yet-coursing tide of blood, beyond the enormous gates, and out to the armies where they fought. The tips of the tongue lashed out into the tanar'ri troops, snatching up between them a knot of wriggling monsters, then drew them back over the gates.

The battle continued, but with the retreat of the tongue toward the temple, the red-gray flow also retreated toward it. The flow followed the huge muscle into the courtyard, up the gutters, and into the pool beneath the heads. The five struggling tanar'ri in the grip of the tongue shrieked helplessly as they were lowered into that bloody gullet and the rubescent lips closed over them.

Then there was a spasmodic collapsing of the blood-head. Drops as large as fists or heads plummeted suddenly to the ground and spattered violently. The godhead plunged downward like a building collapsing in on itself, and the thick liquid hunks of its being fell away from the tanar'ri in their midst.

The fiends hit the flagstones, blood raining around them, and were struggling to get to their feet. The red tide rushed beneath them as though they sat on a drain. Next moment, all the gore was gone, and the tanar'ri stood there, dazed and bewildered.

Jandau pulled away from Nina, dropping her hand. "Let's go meet our new competitors."

* * * * *

The fiends were not yet through the screen of silent bells when Nina and Jandau came upon them, blustering and flexing before the eight-armed lord. Sung Chiang seemed small and patient before their evil bulk.

One of the fiends was a nalfeshnee—an enormous, gray-skinned, boar-headed thing that stood upright on man legs, had puny, filthy wings, and angrily switched its dragonlike tail. As best Nina could tell as she approached through the arch of bells, the thing was thrice the height of Sung Chiang.

Two others were snakewomen, much like Cora of Jandau's band, though in addition to their giant snake abdomens, each had six arms and plenty of silvery jewelry to adorn them.

The final two abominations were vrocks, giant buzzards standing two heads taller than Nina, with grotesque little human arms extending from beneath their wings to hold their staves. Yes, an ugly crew.

This time, Nina felt it: Jandau's hand slipped into hers.

Sung Chiang was arguing with the fiends. More exactly, they were arguing with him. The god's avatar stood silently before the railing crew, two pairs of arms folded behind his back and two pairs folded in front. Despite their ranting and his silence, the fiends left an empty ring of floor before the god. They were more afraid of him than he of them, as it should be.

Jandau and Nina neared—she pulling away from the tiefling and approaching the god as a wife might. This was stupid, she knew, but her father was at stake, and she had a great need in that moment to impress upon the tiefling and the fiends and herself that she had power. She'd literally descended to hell to save her father. Placing a hand on the thief god's shoulder was a little thing next to that.

She kissed his old-man cheek. "Trouble with the peasants, dear?" Though the words were just whispered, they cut through the fiends' rantings.

Aside from the retreating echoes, the place was suddenly silent.

The young face spun with unnatural ease toward Nina, and the god kissed her full on the lips. But the look in his eyes made her draw back, a look as sharp and disciplinary as a slap might have been from any of those hands. But it was the old face that answered her. *Thank you for your concern.*

The tanar'ri glanced at each other, and the boar-headed thing muttered, "Who's the bitch?"

Sung Chiang's voice was as even and passionless as ever. *The bitch was wondering the same about the curs.* He nodded toward the tanar'ri, inviting—no, demanding—their introductions.

"I am Kraxon. This is Garcon," said one of the buzzard things, and they both bowed low, not letting go of their staves.

"My name is Climestratenicova," said the taller of the two snakewomen.

"I am Listrodomocinitus," said the other in her turn.

"I'm Frak," belched the boarhead.

Sung Chiang bowed, this time deeply. As he rose, he said to the fiends, *Welcome to this humble house. I hope all will be well with you as we discuss the captive.*

The hair on Nina's neck stood on end as she heard her father being referred to so coldly. Perhaps that was why she repositioned a hand on Sung Chiang's shoulder and, through clenched teeth, said, "Please introduce me, dear, to the tanar'ri, as you did to the baatezu."

Before Sung Chiang could respond, the boarhead made a great hawking noise in its throat, easily twelve feet above Nina's own throat, but she interrupted. "No spitting in the sanctuary!"

Her emphatic warning was backed up by a glare from Sung Chiang, and the monster swallowed its bile.

The god spared Nina another withering glance, which drove her hand from his shoulder. She knew in that moment that, if she had not stopped the boar-headed nalfeshnee from spitting, her censure would have been much less bearable. Still, Sung Chiang was a god of rogues, and she thought her playful insubordination pleased him on some level. Doubtless, the nalfeshnee was also saved by her quick tongue.

Responding to her request, the god said, *This is Nina of Caonan, and Jandau, a planar of some note.*

"Jandau," hissed one of the snakewomen. "We meet again." Nina could smell the venom in her breath.

Jandau smiled wanly and bowed low before her. "Let's let bygones—"

"Are these lovers of yours, Sung Chiang?" croaked a buzzardlike vrock.

Nina blushed slightly at this insinuation, while Jandau went bone white.

Again, her hand was on the god's shoulder. "We shall see."

Not lovers, not as far as things have gone, Sung Chiang said. *But competitors against you and yours.*

"What could they have that you would want?" demanded the nalfeshnee violently.

We shall see, said Sung Chiang, and his young face swiveled toward Nina. *We shall see.*

*   *   *   *   *

Nina was relieved when Sung Chiang decided to hold negotiations immediately. After having had one supper ruined by dretches and lemures clawing each other to pieces, she was not looking forward to sitting at table with these beasts. Apparently the god was not, either.

He led Jandau and Nina with the sullen pack of tanar'ri through the bell screen to one of the stairways. *I hold all negotiations in the undercroft. It is the dark inverse world that upgirds my light, airy temple above.*

Nina followed uncomfortably, knowing all too well that the fiends were nearby. She wanted them neither between her and the god nor behind her. Had she the nerve, that hand of hers might have taken one of Sung Chiang's—he had plenty to spare, after all—but her bravado had deflated. Besides, the tiefling was already holding her hand, and better him than no one.

Sung Chiang made a few discreet gestures to the ubiquitous linqas, at least four or five of which scurried off into various pearly passages before the party, which descended the stairs.

Like all things in that strange, oceanic palace, the stairs were huge near the sanctuary, scaled to the size of the god, and gradually grew smaller, shallower, as they descended. Sung Chiang, of course, was unaffected, gliding downward through air as if borne on a puff of wind.

For Nina, it was another matter. The first four steps jarred her jaw as she jumped unceremoniously down them, following the tiefling whose robe at least fluttered like the sparrow Aereas accused him of being, and who landed more lightly than Nina on each step.

At least the fiends were having similar troubles. She saw them each preparing spells, their talonlike hands darting into pouches and forming arcane glyphs in the air—doing so despite the gentle finger-wag of Sung Chiang, descending eerily before them. They had been warned that no magic was allowed in his temple but tried it anyway. Or one did.

The first to complete a spell was one of the snakewomen,

whose final finger-snap ended in a black puff of smoke and a spark that licked rapidly up knuckles and wrists and elbows and shoulders, leaving only ash in its wake. The spark split at her sternum, half ascending to flame the head and braided hair in a single whoosh, the other half descending to rush through her rattling tail. Next moment, the ash of her form fell like talc upon the stair, then skittered along the floor like tiny leaves before an autumn wind. She was gone, and so was her spell.

So, too, disappeared the spells the others had been readying. Guano, gum arabic, spiderweb, and other arcane stuff disappeared back into pockets.

"Killed by a god," objected the other snakewoman. She swallowed hard, the lump in her throat looking the size of a large frog. "Flamed her on the stairs . . . dead, forever."

None cared to walk through the space where Listrodomocinitus had stood. They all ambled around the emptiness as though she still stood there, and all began rather more rudimentary forms of descent than those they had planned.

The vrocks, of course, flew, passing overhead with a haunting wuff of air as Nina readied her fifth jump. The second snakewoman, Climestratenicova, clung to one stair as she lowered her tail, springlike beneath her. Frak, the boar-headed nalfeshnee, was as hard pressed as the tiefling and Nina, with wings too small to hold him aloft and a gut too large to land with any grace when he jumped. Which he did. Nina was happy she'd moved to one side when, on the fourth step, he slipped and rolled downward onto ever smaller stairs.

Yet another practical excercise in the god's ritual debasing of mortals. Whatever hubris any of the negotiators had brought with them was efficiently stripped away by this descent.

Needless to say, Sung Chiang arrived first in the deep, deep chamber that lay at the base of the spiraling, shrinking case of stairs. Nina and the others eventually caught up to join the smug god—and the baatezu, and the other members of Jandau's party who had somehow gathered in that place without having to traverse the treacherous stairs. However they had come, they had come.

The place was strange. Nina's first impression of it was that it was some sort of cistern, for the chamber was carved from the black rock of the ground itself, and though dry, was filled with dark, watery echoes. The only light down here came from a solitary torch borne in one of Sung Chiang's hands.

It was an unnatural cavern, carved into bedrock. The floor was pitched on two sides like a deep-cleft valley, the edges of which rose up into straight walls that disappeared in the darkness high above. The floor was adorned with thin stone traceries, which began at the center cleft in intricate rootlike tangles and rose outward to merge on the walls into great trees of stone. The broad boles of these stone trees, half-embedded in the wall, were evenly spaced and ascended into blind darkness above. Between the stone trees were black spaces filled with some sort of scaly membrane and shaped like inverted sword blades.

Perhaps it was the tilt of the floor beneath Nina's feet, or perhaps the tremendous downward energy of the ornate chamber—whatever, Nina found herself tilting her head and nearly turning it all the way over. Then she recognized the space.

It was an inverted cathedral. What should have been an arch of stone was a floor of it. What should have been glowing lancets were black, scaly daggers of lightless glass. What were perhaps once iron chandeliers were now tables resting uncertainly astraddle the valley of the floor.

In all ways, the space was inverted. Instead of white limestone walls these were black like obsidian. Instead of worshipers and priests, the place was filled with desperados and the legions of hell. Instead of an occidental sanctuary, the room was an oriental house of trade.

Sung Chiang allowed his guests the chance to be confused, astounded, and mortified by the setting. The fiends seemed particularly pleased with the desecrated space.

At length, the god's voice rang against the cold stone of the place. *This is where I do all my bartering for stolen goods. Such transactions should not take place in my temple. They are base, both because they are common and filthy, and because they are the basis of my godhood.*

He lifted his hands, now—all of them—and a beatific look came onto his features. *Just as the miracle of life comes from the vilest rutting, so the power of my domain comes from the quick snatch, the garrote, the dagger and cloak.*

Nina shivered, perhaps from the cold of the place, but more likely from the darkness of it. Aside from Sung Chiang's torch, the only light came from the black walls themselves, like faint shimmerings through subterranean pools or volcanic glass.

"This is where we will bargain?" Nina asked. The sound of shivering came out in her voice.

Yes, said Sung Chiang. He motioned the crew of them—four baatezu, four tanar'ri, and Jandau's uncomfortable party of eight—toward the center chandelier.

It had become a literal table, its black iron now supporting a sheet of round dusky glass. On the far side of this, Sung Chiang settled in, and only now did Nina realize he'd been floating all this time. The rest of the bargainers arrayed themselves around the table, baatezu to the god's right, tanar'ri to the god's left, and the eight quaking members of Nina's band opposite him. For such mortal adversaries in so strange a place, the opponents settled in quickly, and the liquid echo of their movements were silenced.

Now, the property in question, said Chiang.

The reverberation of his voice had not yet dissipated when there came a tremendous rushing noise, like bats pouring from a cave. The sound grew louder, and if it were not for the watery darkness, Nina would have sworn there was a great fire somewhere. Her glances around ended when Sung Chiang pointed up.

A huge, tatter-edged shadow swooped down overhead. The weight of flesh and iron was behind it. It careened past, its sudden black eclipse of the place retreating as it withdrew toward the opposite wall. Nina got the brief impression that it was a giant spoon, or a giant hammer swinging above her head. In the angry flutter of Sung Chiang's torch, she saw that the rag-edged thing hung from a great pendulum.

Artus of Caonan.

It was her father. His pudgy, aged form was somehow strapped to the end of that rising pendulum—she still could not tell whether right side up or upside down. But she knew it was he. Perhaps it was the scent he trailed as he went by—books and concern and just a tang of labor. Perhaps it was the brief lightless silhouette of some feature—elbow, wrist, hand, ear—that she recognized. But she knew him.

Bids must be placed before the pendulum stops, Sung Chiang said calmly.

The lever arm eased into its final rise, seeming to hang for a moment above the far nave before returning her father toward her.

"We are prepared," barked one of the gray-bearded barbazu, "to cede to the most honorable Lord Sung Chiang a second palace, in Baator, built by slaves of the pit, serviced by an attentive staff of spayed succubi, and overlooking the Styx, itself, at its delta on the banks of the Sea of Bile."

The god smiled with all three smiles. *Mine to perpetuity?*

"Yours for eternity," replied the fierce-faced fiend with a smile of his own.

And what rights of rule come with this palace? asked Sung Chiang.

By this time, Artus was swinging past again, and as he whirled overhead, Nina glimpsed his face. It was puffed from hanging upside down, from the terrific rush of the lever arm, and from the ropes that bound him in place.

"Father," she said, and as surely as she had known it was he without even glimpsing his eyes, she knew he heard.

The barbazu was meanwhile struggling to amplify his promise. ". . . rule there as surely as you rule this plateau, here."

I am not interested in a summer home, Sung Chiang said. *Especially not one in hell.*

To this, the tanar'ri snickered, turning their heads toward the sputtering barbazu to see how he would counter. Aereas seemed ready to speak, but Nina clutched his arm to signal silence. She wanted the advantage of hearing the other bids before she spoke.

"A palace in Baator means instant access for you there, a link between your temple here and the one there."

There is a link between my garderobe and my cesspool, but not the sort of link I hope to explore. The mild nature of the god had not shifted, though it was the young face that had spoken. In those words had been daggers.

"Per-perhaps we can extend the rights of rule. Rights to roam a section of Baator, rights to reach beyond your gates for, say, one hundred miles."

Sung Chiang shook his head, his faces. *On whose authority do you offer such rights? Your own?*

The barbazu, who seemed on the verge of responding with exactly that sentiment, was suddenly incapable of any response.

The tanar'ri leapt into the silence.

"We offer you ten palaces in the Abyss, and ten thousand slaves, and twenty thousand concubines from among our more . . . desirable species," croaked Garcon, one of the buzzard-headed vrock. He glanced at Climestratenicova, who dutifully licked her lips and sent a frissive rustle through her tail.

Ah, typical tanar'ri imagination, said Sung Chiang placidly. *Take someone else's idea and make it more abysmal. At least such claims from baatezu are tenable. Not so with you, my chaotic friends.*

Nina might have laughed at the god's puns had her father not been whirring horribly overhead like some great axe of aged flesh and bone.

The tanar'ri did not laugh either. Nor did they respond, leaving a silence into which Sung Chiang spoke.

Surely you have not come here intending to offer me homesteads in hell?

Clearly, by the looks on their faces, they had. Even so, these creatures were not stupid. Nina knew that even then, glancing briefly at them before her father passed again.

Garcon the vrock quickly spoke. "The best merchant knows his customers. The Abyss has much to offer—more than even a god could dream of. So, what is it you want, my lord?"

Sung Chiang stood, or perhaps levitated. Suddenly he seemed taller than even the towering nalfeshnee, thrice Nina's height. His eyes, all six, were glowing with green avarice, and his mouths spoke in ragged unison. *I am a god, like any other—like Thor, like Apollo, like Takantua.*

Yet, here I reign, on this filthy volcanic range, its sulfuric skies never seeing day, its glassy ground never seeing trees. This was not my world, this pit, this foul hole. Mine was the metropolis and the marketplace, the desolations of civilization, not the desolations of lava and steam.

As great as I am—and I think none who have survived to reach this room would contest how great—my skies are never quite blue, my sun never quite bright, my temple never the infinite space I work to make it. No. I am trapped here, as surely as a cricket in a cage, trapped and fed by fingers of someone greater, whom I amuse.

Do not laugh, came his voice, stentorian like the sound

of rocks grinding upon each other. The nalfeshnee's claw dropped from his wormy lips, which struggled into a line. *I may be the caged cricket, but you are merely the pollen I breathe. And should you not bring me freedom, or at least the sense of freedom, none of you will leave here alive.*

That sobered them all.

Nina thought again of the flipped cathedral where they stood, thrust down into bedrock like the spade of a shovel.

Her father passed by.

"If what you wish is escape," she began, "then we have it for you. My father is custodian of the keys of Sigil. He is an agent for the Lady, herself—"

"We all know that," hissed the snakewoman. "Why else would we be here—?"

"And you bid upon him in hopes he will divulge to you the keys," Nina continued, interrupting the fiend.

She was in turn interrupted by the swaying pendulum, more shallow now, and the voice of her father, which seemed to whisper her name. His voice drew a cloaklike chill across her shoulders. "But he will never tell."

"I will not tell," came the strained voice of her father, passing the table. The barbazu leered up at him with hatred.

"The best any winner of this bargain has to gain is a silent bit of flesh into which many holes may be poked in search of answers, but from which no answers will seep." The words were cold from her lips, and colder still in answer from the stony walls of the place.

"She is right!" Artus cried out urgently.

Sung Chiang's young face leveled at her. *Have you come only to demean the value of my offering?*

"No," she shot back. "Though the wise buyer dickers down the worth of a thing, that is not my intent. I intend only to say I will trade you something that will tell you where the keys are hidden, for something that will not."

One of the mantis-headed lizards responded fiercely, "And what priceless thing could a Clueless offer one of us?"

"My father's journal," she replied simply, crossing arms over her chest.

"No, Nina—not the journal," came Artus's voice.

The baatezu seemed pleased to learn her name; she did not let their twitching tails unsettle her. "The journal tells of all my father's travels, of all the gates, of how he set them up, of the secrets of Sigil," she said confidently. "You could not torture from him what riches of information appear on the first page of that book."

She felt a gentle prodding pressure, like the water that passes in blind intimacy over every surface of a swimmer's body. Then came Sung Chiang's voice: *You do not bear the book with you.*

No, not with me, she thought, but in my cousin's room, where the smallest of linqas could take it for our host. Knowing the godly probes that checked her pockets might even now be prodding her mind, she tried to divert her thoughts and his. "So, you are interested in this book, then?"

Sung Chiang's middle face turned upon her, and there was a gentle, appreciative smile on it. *How insightful of you to offer me a book when these blustering monsters could think only to offer castles in hell.*

The snakewoman broke in. "We will make you a greater power in the Abyss, set at your command legions of fiends, give you a force so great that each of your faces will be as powerful as any single god. We will give you artifacts, the Scepter of Cymbal, riches. . . ."

There came an off-putting hand, only one of the eight. Sung Chiang said to Nina, *And put out of your mind the fear that I would steal the book from you. Though I could—though a tendril of my mind is leafing through it even now, as we speak—I do so only to check the merchandise. I am lord of thieves, yes, but it is not thievery to take what lies already in my grasp. It is not chess unless we begin with all the pieces on the board.*

"You cannot read it!" declared Artus, the arc of the pendulum growing shallower and shallower with each pass. "You cannot! The book will set itself aflame in your grasp."

Sung Chiang shook his head. *Oh, no. It is already in my grasp and has not burned. Please, Artus, lies are unbecoming of you.*

Garcon croaked out, "We'll show you our conduits into Gehenna and other worlds."

Again, the hand was raised. *You have all made your bids, and the pendulum has nearly stopped. Withdraw, all of you. Leave me alone with my prize to think on this a while.*

They all waited as Artus swung gently overhead, like an untended swing in a playful breeze. Then came Aereas's hand on Nina's shoulder—the first warmth she'd felt in that room since she had arrived—and Jandau's hand on her other shoulder, icy like the overturned sanctuary itself. As though their opposite faces occupied the same head, like those of Sung Chiang, they spoke together.

"Let's go back to our rooms, and wait. . . ."

✦ Doroomoth 5, 695 C.C. ✦

Quite a woman Malkin's found himself. Problem is, she doesn't even know he exists. I have to laugh. I guess this is a pretty common dilemma for gods—letting people know they exist.

I have to laugh also because he's asking me for advice. For lines and approaches and school-boy introductions.

I'd better hurry and spring this trap before things get sillier.

F⊕URTEEN

TREACHERIES

When he reached his room, Aereas could still see that awful whirring pendulum whooshing past his mind's eye. The effect was strange, as though *he* were on the pendulum, not Artus—as though the temple around Aereas pitched and turned and he was still. It wouldn't have surprised him if such had been the case, if Artus and his lever arm had been the only static point on the whole gyrating world.

Gods, I hate this place, Aereas thought as he set the key into the lock of his room and swung the door slowly open. I hate it. Ill-proportioned, arrayed to make minuscule the man and omnipresent the god, with gutters where stairs should be and bloodwaters instead of rain. How hideous.

Before he could close the door behind him, before he could take what little comfort was due him in the pearlescent room that looked out on the distant genocide of the ceaseless battle—fiend bodies tumbling and rumbling red like flames in a cheery fire—there came Nina's voice.

If there was any sound in the world that could stop his turgid thoughts, that was it.

"Let's go. The task is only half done," she said. Aereas knew immediately that she had spoken around the closing door.

He pulled away and pivoted, drawing the door back between them and sticking his face through, as though he spoke to her from behind a curtain. "What's only half done?"

"The bargaining," she said. Her slim brown hand reached through the open door to him and drew him out. "We've set up our winning position. Now we need to set up our losing position." She closed the door behind him, and for one brief moment it was as though she embraced him with that arm. "Lock it."

He did. "What are you talking about?"

She put her arm in his and began to propel him forward. In a near-silent voice that whispered on the polished walls, she said, "We're going to see the baatezu and the tanar'ri. We're going to convince each group of the conspiracy against them, and offer our aid in recovering Artus when the opponent wins."

It was her plan. Aereas knew so immediately. It was just the sort of thorough, graceful treachery she had used many times when they had been children, when she had turned the red-headed Higginses away from tormenting the cousins and on to tormenting each other. But these creatures had more than red hair.

"The book," Aereas said suddenly, drawing to a stop despite her attempts to pull him onward.

She patted his hand. "It's well guarded, now. Jandau and his crew are stationed around it. They'll be better able to defend it from fiendish assault than either of us would be."

"But can we trust them? Trust Jandau?" Aereas pressed.

She pressed, too, and they were walking again up the curving, widening passage. Already they seemed ridiculously small next to the ever-enlarging doors. "It doesn't matter. We must. I offered the book to Sung Chiang. The fiends will deal with no one else but me."

Aereas was going to ask why she wanted him as an escort rather than Henry, the brawny bariaur, or Krim, the mysterious magical manta ray. But he did not ask.

✦ Doroomoth 12, 695 C.C. ✦

Well, I succeeded in one endeavor and failed in another.

Malkin was icy when we met at the well. I had arranged to meet him there after he met the woman in the Music Market. We'd gathered to discuss the next step of his romance.

Malkin's white clothes were like lightning in the bright sun—alien, foreign beside rocks worn down by human hands and rumps and feet as though by persistent waters.

He lifted one leg, planted it on the well rim, and said, "Thought you were pretty smart, lying to me . . ."

I glanced up at him and felt my face go red beneath my gray shocks of hair. "She didn't go for the line?"

The darkness of his eyes fled before a bright glare that made them look like double full moons. "Oh, no. That line worked very well. She knows I am alive now. I have seen her a few times."

I was honestly perplexed. There was fire in that red face of his. "What is it then, friend?"

My hand, only just settled on his shoulder, was flung off. He spat. The spittle was not like liquid, but like a jag of quartz as it cracked against the inner well wall. "Friend is not a word I would use."

I would not give him another prod.

He didn't need it. "Friends do not mask their true faces. You are no mere man. You are a spy, an agent of a former . . . a clinging power."

He knew. I'd gotten reckless, somehow, had let slip once too often some veiled pun. I'd been incorrectly lazy in my assurance that this incarnate god could not tell a snarl from a smile.

"Well, you should not act so wounded. Neither are you . . . are you any kind mere man," I replied. "Where is your honesty?"

He'd turned already. His back was a white triangle against the dun houses. "Do not come near me again, Artus of Sigil."

FIFTEEN
JANDAU

Those two. Jandau had never seen such a green pair of primes in all his life. Always wide-eyed. Always looking up and waiting for the whole damn puzzle to make sense. Still not willing to concede that the puzzle was actually mixed-up pieces of a thousand, a million puzzles, none complete in its own right and certainly none complete now. But off they had gone to bargain with fiends.

To look at them—and that's what Jandau was doing through the crack of his door—he'd've thought they were off to their first dance. No, that's too stiff a thing—off to go fishing. There was that natural spring to their steps like the spasmodic jiggle of a newborn colt's legs beneath it, not so much joy but mere newness in standing. No one had a right to walk like that toward a conference with fiends.

The tiefling widened the door crack and looked specifically at Nina. No one had a right to walk like that, period, he thought.

Well, as they say, better the devil you know than the devil you don't, which as far as Jandau could tell, was why she'd entrusted the journal to him. He stepped back from the door and turned around to see his dubious party—all five of them—watching him.

"What are you looking at?" he asked all and none of them.

They responded differently. Henry blushed slightly beneath his pointed black beard and looked back out the window, toward the massacre raging beyond. LiGrun lowered the nictitating membranes over his great lizard eyes and let out a rib cage of air. Cora was wry-mouthed, with a sinewy rankle of her tail. Krim was curved above the closed journal, those strange fish eyes of his drawn into wicked-looking slits. And Dif . . . Dif goggled at Jandau, his great lips wet with anticipation.

"You kinda like her, don't you?" he asked.

"I kinda like this book of hers," the tiefling replied truthfully, moving toward the table and drawing up a chair beside the arched muscle of Krim.

The manta hovered, poised and tense, a great king cobra both fearful of and mesmerized by the book.

"Open it," Jandau said.

Krim looked at his leader. The eye on one side of his canted head opened just slightly wider. His voice came with a scent of seawater. "So, you're not planning to merely guard this thing, then?"

"I've got to understand it to be able to guard it," Jandau replied lightly, then repeated, "Open it."

He didn't wait for the manta to comply, but opened the volume himself. There was a sharp jab of pain, and the cover flew open and slammed on the table. Jandau cried out, and Dif and Krim lurched back, braced for an explosion.

"Just a paper cut," the tiefling said, laughing. He sucked the end of his finger and wiped a spot of blood away from the page. Then the three leaned in to see what was written there.

Jandau had never studied magic. Krim's talents far exceeded what the tiefling could have attained, even if he had been fond of headaches. Jandau was enough of a leader to know when to use a subordinate to fill in a deficiency of skill. Still, he'd seen lots of magic in his time, and this book was magic.

It wasn't blue motes of light or a shimmering vibratory presence or any of that mystic nonsense. It was the way the page held its characters, the lines in hard black ink, each word more a glyph than a collection of letters. On the opposite page was a charcoal sketch of Nina, so spare in its thick black lines, so quickly and expertly rendered, that she seemed to stare out of the page. Jandau colored.

"Uh—" said Krim, imitating Dif, who hulked above the tiefling's shoulder, "you kinda like her, don't you?"

Jandau caught on. Thankfully, Dif didn't, but only nodded his interest in the very same question.

The next page was blotchy and faint, light pigments arrayed like fallen ash leaves on a forest trail. What was signified by that golden yellow array of colors, in their random branching pattern? It gave Jandau a sense of deep, poignant melancholy.

Beautiful, isn't it?

It could not have been Dif who spoke; the syntax was recurved. It could not have been Krim, either; the voice was large and deep, not the sound of cartilaginous cavities and valves and gills. Jandau looked around the room at the others, all occupying themselves with the war or the fire or both. And then he knew who had spoken.

"You could have taken it, couldn't you?" he said, without the silliness of lifting his head to the ceiling.

Sung Chiang responded from nowhere and everywhere. *Of course. But as I said, taking something that is already in one's grasp is not theft. The game is not played that way. It is like fishing in one's own bowl.*

Jandau nodded and laughed. None of the others did, and at that point he realized that he alone could hear their ever-present lord.

Continue turning the pages, Sung Chiang said.

This time, without the nod, Jandau complied. It would serve him to be discreet in his communications with this thing.

The next page had been folded many times over. Creases yet remained in the now-flattened sheet. Jandau traced his hands over the space, over the notes scribbled forward and backward on it, along the fold lines, over the corners, around the edges. There was something familiar about the geometry of those folds, something rather like a paper unicorn he had once seen folded in moments from a tiny scrap, displayed, then unfolded and flattened and handed to him in defiance to repeat the arcane gestures. It was a puzzle, like all the rest of this journey had been, like the rest of this journal was, like this man and his beautiful daughter were.

A puzzle, indeed, came the voice of Sung Chiang, and Jandau knew then that the god could hear his thoughts. As though in answer, Sung Chiang said, *It's the book. Somehow, touching it, I can hear your mind, and you can hear mine.* To the query that lifted in the tiefling's mind like an arched eyebrow, the god said, *Yes, I am touching it, too, as I am touching all things here.*

Jandau opened his mouth to speak but thought, instead, *The book is a conduit between minds.*

It is at least that, replied Sung Chiang. *The girl holds it in great esteem because it is her father's, but she is not half-wrong about its value, its power.*

The tiefling pursed his lips instead of nodding, and turned the page to see more twining lines of black text. *She is off entrenching herself against failure,* he thought. *She thought you would trade her father to the fiends, and*

*wants to be braced. But it sounds as though the book is
what you want, more than the man.*

Not actually, came the reply. *I thought you more perceptive than that. I want the book and the man and the daughter and the boy and the Scepter of Cymbal and the tanar'ri
legions and all of it.*

Jandau smiled. *Well, even if you were to snatch this book
out of my hands, you'd not get all of that.*

The god smiled. Somehow, Jandau felt it and was
chilled. *I'd thought you more perceptive. Let me explain. I
am going to make the trade with the tanar'ri. The girl will
then enact her alliance—which she is striking right now
with the glowering baatezu—to join forces with them and
use the book and her "Power from the Lady"*—there came a
laugh here—*and her knowledge of her father to help the
baatezu capture the hostage. You, of course, will accompany her and the boy, and not simply because you've devel-
oped an . . . attraction for one of them.*

"Accompany them into hell?" Jandau asked aloud, forgetting himself. Krim turned a slitted eye on him. The
tiefling gestured vaguely to the scribbles and said, "It looks
like that's what it says here." Mantas do not nod. Neither
are they particularly gullible, but Krim said nothing.

Making sure his lips remained closed, Jandau said to
Sung Chiang, *It would take more than legs sculpted like
daggers to get me to follow a woman into hell.*

*How about magical bracelets, protecting you against the
hazards of the Abyss?*

More.

*How about a payment? Would one hundred thousand
gold be sufficient?*

Jandau was glad he had not tried to barter. The god could
see the stunned glee that that amazing figure in gold had
evoked in the tiefling's mind. To deny his interest would be
insulting.

The god knew that Jandau knew, and he said, *With these*

bracers, and expectation of this tremendous sum, you will guard my girl and her boy and aid them in rescuing her father. Then you will find your way back here, bringing all four to me.

All four?

Artus, the girl, the boy, and the book.

And you will pay me one hundred thousand gold, only to sell Artus, the girl, the boy, and the book all over again? You will have everything again. Jandau was impressed with himself for that one tiny insight.

Tiny, indeed, came the reply. *Perhaps one hundred thousand is too much.*

I have already accepted. Surely a god who would not deign to steal what is already in his grasp would not renege on a deal once accepted.

Surely not. His voice was dry, cold. *Neither, I trust, will you. Otherwise there will be no gold, and the pair of bracelets now on your wrists will constrict slowly, unstoppably, until your hands drop off and you are left scarred with the mark of the thief caught.*

Jandau nodded, seeing the slim golden bracelets, new and tight where his wrists lay on the page of the book. He began to withdraw his hands, not wanting Krim to see the jewelry.

As the black wings of the tiefling's cloak bunched up over the bands of metal, he heard one last whispered warning in his mind. *And take care not to touch the book while the boy or girl does. It reads and channels and connects minds, and our plans would be laid open. Such failure would truncate our plot, and your arms.*

Again, Jandau nodded.

✦ Doroomoth 43, 695 C.C. ✦

I've set up my trap. I've a portal to Sigil tucked into a back alley. Now, the bait, to lure Malkin's lover there. Once she's in the alley, Malkin will be on her and into the trap faster than a fly onto a carcass.

SIXTEEN

LAST NIGHT WITH
THE THIEF LORD

How could she sleep that night with the distant wailing sounds of battle beyond the gates and the memories of monstrous faces looming in paranoid counsel over her, and the fear that at any moment one of the tenebrous stingers of Sung Chiang would descend into the bed with her and snatch away the book that Nina clung to as she would a babe?

That book was her father's life, not only in words but now in truth. Were she to lose it, whether before a trade could be made with the god of thieves or after the deal had gone sour and she fought beside fiends for her father, all would be lost. Yes, she'd fooled them into thinking this queer little volume meant actual worlds, and not just worlds to her.

At last, none of these things seemed to matter. The battle outside became the distant rattle of a waterfall. The terrifying fiend faces became merely grotesque masks in a child's book of boggles and ogres. The ever-present tendrils of the god withdrew into the amorphous horror of a body they occupied. And Nina slept.

Until the rap of fiend knuckles came at the door.

"Wake up! Wake up! We've been betrayed, just as you said!"

She recognized the voice as that of Xaxtros, one of the baatezu she'd bargained with the night before. His voice had rung hauntingly through her sleep.

And she was still asleep, waking up only two strides from the door, unlatching it and flinging it wide with her off-hand because she yet clutched the book in her other, next to the silk of her nightshirt.

"What!" she said. Not asked, but said.

She was staring into the angry, frantic, bile-breathing, wire-bearded face of the barbazu. He had to crouch to fit into the corridor, with knuckles near the floor, and so he looked like a bulldog growling at some creature that had invaded its doghouse.

There was a flash of apology on those fierce, bestial features, and a glance down at Nina's body—no, at the much-touted book clutched to her body. Ah, yes, her power would come from it in the next days. With that realization came also the sudden absurd awareness that she was standing in a nightshirt before a fiend. She began to laugh.

He went on, riled by her laughter, thinking her more daring because of it. "That thieving bastard betrayed us to the tanar'ri." Despite the house rules, Xaxtros did spit this time, and the green gob struck the wall and began to slowly run down it. He continued without pause, "They somehow got Sung Chiang the Scepter and a deed or something for the rest—I don't know. He gave them the hostage, and safe passage."

Seeing that Xaxtros hadn't been turned to ash for his spitting—and feeling a fresh fury born from sleeplessness and betrayal and righteous rage—Nina spit as well.

"Damn them. Damn them all." She turned and darted into the room, flung open the wardrobe, and began yanking out the few clothes that might last on the trail. Strange, but she now saw that half of the outfits were sensible leathers—jerkins and leggings—as though Sung Chiang knew from the start she would have as much need of them as of the gowns.

Xaxtros hovered outside, and Nina motioned him in, again with a laugh, realizing she was inviting a fiend to crawl on hands and knees into her room while she dressed.

That passage created the predictable rumbling racket, and Xaxtros had not gotten his hips through before the door to Aereas's suite banged open, and he charged into the room.

Though Nina had awakened two steps shy of the door, Aere wasn't awake even now. He'd grabbed an ornamental sword, still sheathed, from the wall, and with this blunt instrument lunged at the advancing fiend. The sheathed sword struck Xaxtros's shoulder only moments before Aere himself struck it.

He came awake then, recoiling in terror not simply from the monster, but also from the uselessness of his own weapon.

"Put that thing away," Nina scolded. "Or better yet, strap it on. We've got to pack up and get going."

Thank the gods Xaxtros had remembered Aereas from the night before. Thank the gods also that Xaxtros was as certain of Aereas's harmlessness as Aereas was.

"He did it," Aereas stated with flat incredulity. "He traded with the tanar'ri."

Nina nodded. "Get your stuff together!" He whirled, but her voice brought him up short. "No, first tell Jandau and the others what's going on. Pack while they pack."

He complied with no sign of the hesitation he typically

had around Jandau.

As Aere rushed to the opposite door and flung it open, Nina turned on Xaxtros. "Where are the other fiends?"

"Ready," he said simply.

"What do you mean, ready? Where are they?"

"In the sanctuary, ready for you to lead us out."

"Ready for me—" Nina repeated, putting the pieces together. It took quite an effort to keep from groaning. "Which way did the tanar'ri go?"

"I told you. They got safe passage," said Xaxtros with a snarl. "You mean you can't figure out how to follow them? You said the book would tell you."

"It will," Nina snapped petulantly. "Go down to the sanctuary and wait with them. I can't get dressed with you lurking here. We'll be down shortly."

Xaxtros nodded uncertainly. He'd begun to suspect Nina's powers were more tepid than she had let on. Such a belief, if allowed to grow, would be the end of her and the loss of her father's journal—and her father, too. It was time to act decisively, even if she hadn't a shot in hell of finding those fiends. At least for now, the baatezu had no other choice than to trust her.

Xaxtros backed out through the doorway. His muscular arms trembled for a moment with the panic of sudden confinement. Then he was out, and with one more wary glance through the opening, he moved away up the hall.

Nina crossed to the open door, slammed it, and threw the bolt. "Krim, get your shark hide in here. We've got a problem."

Moments later, the manta slid through the doorway to Jandau's room, underfoot of a rushing Aere who stumbled for a moment, jabbing tiptoes down between wings and tail, and darted across to his own chambers.

The sly ray's voice was as sinuous as ever. "*We*'ve got a problem?"

"Unless you know some quick doorways back to Sigil,

yes, *we* have a problem," Nina snapped. "Sung Chiang made a deal with the tanar'ri, and he's sent them off somewhere. Our only hope of rescuing my father lies in following them, with the baatezu to help us."

"They'd be going to ground." It wasn't Krim who said this, but a sleepy-eyed Jandau, his pale flesh even more so in the dim light of the banked fire. "They've got their prize and now'll be going back to the Abyss."

"Damn it," Nina observed. Then again, and again.

"We've got the baatezu—" came Jandau's voice, and his hand settled like a bird on her shoulder.

Nina shrugged away. "What good's a posse of baatezu going to do us in the Abyss?"

"Fish out of water, all right," said Krim dryly.

Nina and Jandau both shot him hateful glances, but neither could see his mouth beneath to tell whether he smiled—if mantas do that.

"That's not entirely true," said Cora, approaching now. Her sleek form was already strung with waterskins and packs, and she moved as though the weight of them were nothing. "The main battlefields of the Blood War are outside the Abyss and Baator, but there are some pretty hefty clashes there, too."

Krim spoke the question they all had: "How do you know?"

She arched an eyebrow. "Ever date a gehreleth?" There should have been laughter to that, but there was no time. "At any rate, we could hook up with a whole baatezu legion in the Abyss, if worse came to worst."

"Worse *has* come to worst," Nina assured her grimly. "I never thought I'd *hope* to meet up with a legion of fiends." That did bring laughter, from everyone but Nina—and Aereas, who'd come up behind the growing knot of bodies. "At any rate, we can't hook up with anybody, baatezu or tanar'ri, if we can't get down to the Abyss. Krim, any ideas?"

"The Abyss is a big place," said the mage, "which is both a good thing and a bad thing. The good thing about it is that a teleportation spell has a big target to hit. The bad thing about it is, if we touch down in the wrong place, we'd not last long enough to scream."

"Forget about the spell, dear," said Cora snidely. "You'll not be casting anything like a teleport in this temple, and I doubt any of us want to stand beyond the gates while you think us away with your magic." With that, she lifted her snake tail and spun the tip of it languidly over to point toward the yet-raging fiend war.

"No spells, no portals . . ." Nina said angrily. "We can't just *walk* there."

"Why not ask Sung Chiang?" replied the tiefling smoothly. The look of sleep had gone from his eyes, and he seemed again a predatory bird, keen eyed and clear.

"What are you talking about?" said Aereas. "He doesn't want us to catch the tanar'ri."

"I'd venture to say he doesn't care whether we do or not. Sung Chiang is too wise, too powerful to have traded away his hostage without having a firm hold on the promised goods. That's all he wants. If one party should happen to steal the hostage from the other party, it wouldn't bother him, would probably delight him. He is, after all, the lord of thieves."

A fourth damn it. The last thing Nina needed was to beg Sung Chiang in front of the baatezu for help in following the tanar'ri.

It was as though Jandau could read her mind. "I'll see to it."

"No," she said swiftly. "If this thing is going to work, the fiends will have to believe I'm in charge. I'll see to it."

Again, the hand, though this time she did not shrug away. "We'll go together."

She had been hoping he would say that.

* * * * *

"This way, boys," Nina said, motioning the uncertain knot of baatezu toward the sanctuary exit. "We're late for an appointment in the Abyss."

As little as they liked to be called boys, they liked even less the idea that they were following a clueless girl into the Abyss.

The tall mantis-lizard ambled cautiously forward, tail slashing at empty air. Orandeaux was his name. "We're not going to wade through that battle?"

"Why would we?" Nina asked lightly, remembering how Xaxtros had taken her levity for authority. "The tanar'ri aren't out there on Gehenna. They're in the Abyss."

Xaxtros was next in line, skepticism and hope flickering in his huge eyes. "How did you do it? How did you find which way they went?"

Nina shushed him, signaling up toward the divine man-o-war floating in the distant darkness of the ceiling. "Wait till we're outside." The barbazu nodded dutifully and came on, trailing the towering toadman and the creature that looked like a small dragon. Nina told herself she would have to learn their names as soon as possible.

Once beyond the first pillar, she began in hushed tones to explain her divination, though of course all the knowledge she divulged had come directly from the mouths of Sung Chiang. The fiends didn't know that, and somehow she felt safer in her masquerade once they were beyond the immediate swing of those godly stingers.

"The book," she said, glancing for corroboration from the tiefling, who nodded sagely. "My father had been to this very palace before, which was how Sung Chiang knew of him and knew to kidnap him. Last time, though, Father was escaping the Abyss, and he did so by means of a portal that surfaces in this very yard."

The gold dragon scoffed. "A portal? Here? One Sung Chiang knows nothing about?"

"Of course Sung Chiang knows about it. He knows about everything here," she replied in an equally harsh tone. "What he doesn't know is that *we* know about it. And by the time he does know, we'll be standing at the literal gates of hell." That was enough to satisfy them, for the crew was silent as they trooped down one of the gutters beside the great stairs.

Leaving the temple created the strange sensation that the creatures were growing, for slowly the world around became more manageable, more correctly proportioned. It was a good feeling. Nina didn't know if she could have stepped from that place into the Abyss had she kept getting smaller.

"What's the key?" asked the toadman as they reached the bottom of the stair.

"What key?" she replied as sharply, with as surly and demanding a tone.

That approach did not cow him; he snarled all the more vehemently. "The key to the portal."

Sung Chiang had told Nina about the portal, had showed her on one of those uncanny maps that displayed every crack of mortar in the place, and she knew she could find the great red slab of stone in the courtyard that would take them away to the Abyss. But Sung Chiang had said nothing about a key. Jandau cast her a wary, sidelong look.

Doubt could be death.

"Leave the key to me," Nina blurted before she knew what she was saying. Then, stupidly, she repeated, "Leave the key to me."

They were approaching the smooth slab, set in with the other flagstones but strangely triangular and strangely red. Just as the space around the temple seemed warped, shifted by the power of the god within, so too the space around that flagstone was not right. Nina walked straight toward it but found the stone swerving strangely from her path. With the slightest turn either way, the slightest pivot of the ball of her foot, the stone and the land beyond it swung away to one side or another.

The others were having trouble, too. They swayed as though they walked on a spinning disk. So that's how the thing had remained a secret in this wide-open space. Any who neared it were spun away and ended up walking around.

Nina passed the book to Aereas so that she could focus her full attention on the huge slab. Then she pressed her walking way forward like a woman on a tightrope. Even so, the thing resisted her movement, and it was only by the sheerest concentration that she at last stepped from the mortar that verged the stone onto its wide, flat surface.

Suddenly, all the vertiginous force was gone, and she stood, panting and a little shaken, there on that flagstone.

"Concentrate on me," she said, gesturing the others forward. "Keep your steps trim and your eyes straight on me."

The first to try was Henry, who bulled his way directly there with the stern silent strength of his race. Next came Xaxtros, who seemed not to trust Nina to wait for the fiends to board. He had more trouble, once spinning entirely around as though turned by invisible hands and ending up in a spill on the ground. While he rose, the frogman came on with grimly clamped jaws, and LiGrun, and the others. All had their difficulties, snaking Cora and brutish Xaxtros most. But in time, only Aereas was left, clinging to the book.

He'd tried to approach a number of times, but like Nina, he found the book—its weight, its aura, its power—distracting. Only when all the rest of the group was atop the stone slab did he get within five feet before falling.

"Come on. Focus on me," Nina said, gesturing him in.

He rose, set his jaw, and gazed into her eyes. Still, the unseen and silent forces tore at him, and at the book. His attention dropped to his white-knuckled hands for only a moment, and he was down again.

"Focus on me!" she repeated.

He looked up, gray faced, and must have seen Jandau standing close behind Nina, one of his arms brushing hers. She could feel the cold bite of the bracelet on his wrist, and pulled gently away.

Aereas saw the movement and stood. He strode toward his cousin like a man into a gale, though his eyes were not ducked against the force, but fastened to hers. He had almost reached the stone, but it tore at his clothes, and the book most of all.

"Come . . . for me," she mouthed in silent desperation, glad Jandau was far enough behind that he could not have seen it.

With that, Aereas was across, book clutched tightly to his panting chest.

And then they were all falling.

✦ Doroomoth 51, 695 C.C. ✦

Oh, Murderess! Now I know why they call you Lady of Pain! You knew! You must have known what would happen to that poor woman whom the cat lord loved. You must have sent those brigands to do it. But you could not have known what Malkin would do then, could you? You could not have wanted this!

Here! Here is the destroyed lover you sent me after. Send me on no such quest again!

PART III

THE B⊕⊕K

SEVENTEEN

WE ARE FALLING

They were falling again, as they had fallen through the slag portal. This time, though, there were not huge, spinning clods of slag lit with hot iron like half moons. The place of these great slabs was taken by the four fiends that had accompanied Nina and Aereas and their company through the red flagstone portal in Sung Chiang's courtyard. Of course, each of the fiends was as big as one of the boulders, each more intelligent and malicious and dangerous. And, boulders don't flail and scream.

In that frantic shouting moment, Cora's snake tail whipped widely through the dark air. It accidentally struck Aereas and spun him over, leaving a red welt on his white skin.

He, meanwhile, clung to the book, though one cover had gotten away from him and the pages rattled angrily like moth wings against a lantern globe.

Nina was beside him, her sword drawn. It was only presence of mind that brought the blade up against her leg as she plummeted past. Otherwise, the welt on Aereas's ankle might have been excised along with the foot beneath it.

All of them were falling in a strange pitch blackness. Some unseen light shone upon the company, making them bright and sharp-edged against the vast, empty air, like figures cut from an illuminated manuscript and dropped down a dark dark well. They fluttered and tumbled like paper people.

Even Krim, whose wings struggled against the rushing air for purchase; even the dragon fiend, whose scaled muscles pumped furiously against the fall. Though their wings slowed the descent and they spat incantations to make themselves float, they could not stop or reverse the great dragging pull of what lay below. If not for the constant rush of wind, they would not have known they were even moving downward through the emptiness.

More than one of them craned upward, hoping to see the portal receding in blackness above. But that was gone, too.

The thin ones fell the fastest—Nina, Jandau, Aereas, and LiGrun. The wind plastered their clothes against their flesh or twined it in ropy lines that trailed above them. Nina, tumbling end over end, spread her arms before her and arched her back, sliding from her spinning dive. Then, projecting her legs outward, catlike, she slowed her descent, but only slightly.

Meanwhile, Jandau devised his own set of wings from the black cape that fluttered behind him. Holding the corners of it in both hands, he formed a billowing sail that slowed him. He seemed to rise, up past Nina and LiGrun and Aereas, though in fact he was merely plummeting more slowly.

The screaming had stopped now, whether because throats were raw or minds were numb. None had the faintest idea where they were or what would happen to them.

Nina, somewhat stable in her spread-eagle position, searched the darkness below to see land, or water, or whatever lay beneath them. There was still nothing. Aside from the invisible air that flooded up over them, the darkness was empty.

Sung Chiang has fooled us, Nina thought to herself. This is a trap. Surely the fiends would not have come this way, plummeting with their hostage to their doom. The god has betrayed us, and let his fiends escape to hell.

Above Nina, Jandau let air spill from his cloak, diving downward until he was beside her.

"What now?" he shouted over the rushing roar.

She shrugged, the gesture tipping her a bit forward. "We fall."

"This isn't a conduit," he cried out, nodding around them with his head. "No walls. Can't tell where we are."

"Sung Chiang sold us out," Nina replied bitterly. "The tanar'ri wouldn't have—"

"Look!" cried Aereas, hurtling suddenly headlong past their shoulders.

He soared down into the darkness, arcing away from the rest of the pack. There, just beyond his shrinking form, was a point of light. No, not *a* point but five points, shimmering red and green and gray against the black blackness. Aereas was heading straight for them, wrestling the pack from his back with one hand and sliding the journal into it with the other.

"Where's he off to?" shouted the tiefling, his tone sounding almost angry.

Nina shook her head, smiling. Aereas knew something, and he was on his way. Without any other response to the tiefling, Nina rolled forward into a dive and shot away, closing on her cometary cousin.

She reached him just as he was sliding his arms into the pack he carried, and he tightened the angle of his descent. She trimmed her dive, too, and side by side they streaked downward, two shooting stars, toward the cluster of lights.

Now they could discern more than lights down below.

They could see a ring of creatures, descending through the pitch darkness with the same troubled flailing as the humans. These creatures, however, clung to each other's hands to slow their fall.

Nina knew who they were—or what they were—before she and Aereas had gotten close enough to see the bone-tipped wings and the horn-bristling armor, the hackles and scales, the buzzard necks craning and snake tail whipping . . . and before she saw the pasty, doughy form of her father, shackled and clutched in four of the snakewoman's six arms.

Sung Chiang *hasn't* sold us out, Nina realized, or at least hasn't sold us out any more than he has sold out the tanar'ri.

But where were they? Nothing was visible beneath the fiends, not even the gray-black coruscations of a nighttime sea, and nothing around or above.

Did it matter where they were? Holding hands like that, the fiends were vulnerable to attack.

Nina lifted her sword before her. Aereas drew his and did the same. In the morning's sleepiness, he'd grabbed an ornamental sword rather than his short sword. It would have to do. The wind rolled past them fiercely, and they could not have heard each other even if they had screamed. But neither did.

Like twin lightning bolts, like twin falcons, they slashed down through the preternatural night, dropping on the silent, unknowing prey below. The ring grew larger, the vrocks no longer seeming the size of moths but now crows, now eagles, now dragons.

Nina angled toward the snakewoman, whose tail turned languid circles in the roaring blackness beneath them. Nina nudged her cousin and made a stroking gesture across her neck. Aereas nodded, his jaw set, and Nina hoped he knew what she had meant.

There was no time for wondering. In a heartbeat, they rushed down into the ring of fiends. Aereas slowed, pulling out of his dive just before striking the snakewoman, though Nina plunged into the thing, sword held in two arms out before her. The moment before impact, the woman saw her and rolled. Nina pitched past the creature's knobby shoulders, but her sword sank through the sinewy flesh of the creature's neck. Blade struck bone.

A lava-red ribbon of blood streamed up violently from that half-severed neck, showing just how fast they were falling. In moments, the fiend's blood had arced up to paint the diving tiefling, his company, and the baatezu, all soaring down from above.

Nina hurtled past the twitching snakewoman and clutched her sword hilt madly, but it was wrenched from her grasp. She turned and flung her arms and legs out to slow, just in time to see Aereas's sword skewer the half-removed head from ear to ear. He held on, and his careening flight past the fiend tore the head the rest of the way off.

That tail, which had moments before thrashed furiously, and moments before that had spun in languid circles, now spasmed stilleto-straight beneath the headless creature. Her six knotty arms clenched tight upon Artus, like crisscrossed laces.

She fell, faster than any of the others, pulling away from the now-broken ring of tanar'ri and trailing in her wake a rippling line of red.

Nina's heart sank, and she dived once again. A hoary and huge vrock punched past her, its talons catching only a layer of skin in their constricting grip. No time for terror. Nina tucked her head and plunged after the spiraling corpse, hoping the buzzard-thing could not dive as quickly as she.

The sudden hot blossoming of fire beside her shoulder told her it did not need to dive. Had she any hair left after the smelter, it would have flamed away with that fireball. Perhaps flight spells did nothing in this place, but fireballs were another matter.

Another fiery meteor hurtled past, cauterizing the claw-marks on Nina's back and burning what skin remained there before the sphere caromed off to one side and fizzled into blackness.

There was a cry above the roar of the next fireball. Nina could not, would not, listen to it. No time. She cut across a wide arc of blood, gaining on the corpse, and heard the fireball hiss when it plunged through the liquid trail and on after her.

*   *   *   *   *

It was Aereas who had shouted, tightly tailing the plunging vrock. He'd seen one fireball spin off into emptiness and another ride scorchingly along Nina's back. His shout was rageful, meaningless, meant only to draw the fiend's attention and break its spell-thought before the blast could form.

But the shout was in vain. The largest of the three fireballs belched outward from the creature, trailing Nina. It sizzled through the cascading blood of the snakewoman, seeking Nina's pointed feet as a fighting fish seeks a minnow.

Damn, thought Aereas. The vrock's focus could not be jarred. Of course, so intent on offense, it might have neglected defense. . . .

He slimmed his form, struggling toward the tight-tucked wings of the beast. Closer, closer. The craning neck was almost in range, the beady eyes of the thing focused on the fireball that now singed Nina's toes.

If only . . .

Aereas swung his ornamental sword, aiming for the creature's great neck. Just before the blade contacted the gray-pink scabrous flesh, something massive struck Aereas and sent him spinning.

The sword whirled into the open beak of the thing and slashed through its bony cheek, widening the evil smile on one side. But it did not cut the head loose, did not even puncture the eye.

This time, the blade *was* wrenched from his hand. He tumbled over, and saw his attacker. Above him, the sky was not blackness, but prickly armor and a fierce, hate-filled grin of glee. A cambion. The elflike face of the warrior was a mask of blue-black steel, leering after him.

Aereas struggled to flip over into a dive to escape this thing, but it lunged toward him and clasped his neck in an iron grip.

A sudden panic swept through Aereas, a terror like nothing he had ever known. It was not the fall, nor the crushing force on his windpipe, nor the horror of wrestling a thing from the Abyss. It was something else, as though the cold touch of those clamping fingers not only held him now but extended their reach back through all his days, and would hold him forever, irredeemable. It was as though he had fallen into a narrow, deep well, his hands and arms wedged down beside him in the cold darkness, with neither light nor rescue above.

He thrashed, and the grin of the cambion deepened. Its teeth were like a wall of yellow pickets, its lips black and lumpy as a dog's.

The darkness in Aereas's eyes thickened, giving way to a pulpy redness. He knew it was his own burst blood vessels he saw. The world closed in until only that yellow smile remained.

Then there came a jolt, and a sharp gray tongue emerged from between the daggerlike teeth.

Aereas lurched backward, suddenly freed from the thing's grip. He tumbled away, glimpsing in the last moment the gray fishy tail from which the cambion hung, the spike of Krim's stinger jutting through the back of the skull and out the mouth. With a flick, Krim tossed the body aside, and it cartwheeled upward through the rushing air.

My sword, thought Aereas as the pulpy red gave way to black again. I must get back my sword. He spotted the ornamental blade, tumbling near the tiefling, who himself was diving after the wounded vrock. Letting the air surge into his lungs, Aereas shot out toward the plummeting weapon.

He'd almost reached it when an enormous thing hurtled past him, smashing his hand back and sending the blade spinning into the distance. Aereas whirled to battle the new threat, but it continued on, not an attacking tanar'ri but the ruined, spell-shattered corpse of a barbazu. Though he could make out the crumpled edge of one scaled arm, he could not have identified the corpse. Aereas felt almost sad watching the thing drop rocklike and inert through the darkness. It careered near to Nina and the first corpse, then plummeted on.

* * * * *

Nina, too, whirled when the thing brushed past her, but she saw what it was soon enough to correct her flight. At last she reached the corpse that held her father. She clutched one cold, knotty shoulder of the snakewoman and drew herself down beside it, to the level of Artus's face.

"Father," she said softly, just as she had in the pendulum room.

Though the savage winds tore the whispered word away, he opened his wise, kind eyes and blinked at her.

"Nina," he said, the sound lost, but the shape unmistakable on his lips.

She began prying at the dead fiend's clenched arms, struggling to pull them free, but to no avail. "Help me!" she shouted.

Though this time Artus must have heard, he made no move to offer his assistance. "Nina," he said, as before.

They had drugged him or enspelled him somehow. How else could they have kept the Lady's custodian in shackles?

Ah, the shackles.

Nina gathered a loop of the cold iron chain and forced it

between one of the snakewoman's arms and her father's stomach. Then, placing her legs on two adjacent arms, she yanked fiercely on the ends of the chains.

What inhuman strength the creature had while alive had solidified into granite now that it was dead. Nina yanked on the chain, feeling as though she pulled against the stony arm of a statue. The snakewoman would not relinquish her prisoner, even now.

Aereas was suddenly winging down toward her.

"Help me with this!" Nina cried out savagely.

He spun out through the whistling air and positioned himself. Thank the gods for Aere, she thought. He wrapped his arms around her, wrists bracing wrists, biceps against biceps, and they both pulled.

The snakewoman's taloned hand loosened a bit, and the grinding shiver of dead dry tendons moving in dead dry sheaths rose up the chain like fingernails on slate. They yanked again, the tiny success redoubling the contractions of arms and legs.

The hand was slowly swinging away from the creature's midline, away from the stunned and staring form of Artus. Then, with a horrible crack, audible even above the strain of the wind and of the cousins, the snakewoman's arm snapped at midbiceps. The rigid elbow let loose the chain and rose to flap in the air.

The cousins flew outward with the freed loop of chain, Nina clinging to one end and Aereas to the other. There was a moment of panicked thrashing as they spun away from the whirling, plummeting snakewoman. Aereas and Nina turned and swung like falling cats, then were thrown together. They clutched each other tightly, face to face, and the sudden spinning terror was gone.

"I love you," whispered Aereas.

Nina nodded, not knowing what to say. She leaned into him and kissed him.

It was as if the rushing darkness and the cascading

fiends and the tumbling terrors had vanished, and they were back beside the creek, a boy and a girl who'd known each other as long as they had known the rudiments of language, as long as they had been able to stand on Caonan, let alone on Sigil.

The moment was gone in a flash; the torrential air and the threat of death came crashing into them with a lash of the loose-flopping chain.

Aereas snatched the end from the air and turned with Nina toward the snakewoman, who seemed to be waving forlornly to the two of them.

"One down," Nina shouted out, "five more to go."

Bending their bodies into dives that would bear them back to the corpse, the cousins soared, laughing, on jets of air.

The snakewoman, yet dribbling blood from her severed neck and her flapping arm, lurched slightly as they entered her pocket of air. In one swift motion, Aereas seized another arm and fit the chain around it.

They set to the task, and whether empowered by the kiss or educated by their previous success, they broke this arm much more quickly. Nina lunged to snatch the fingertips of the loosed hand, and Aereas grabbed her foot so that they didn't soar out away from the corpse. Two down. The third followed shortly, then the fourth.

The last was a bit harder to get loose. The drugged captive leaned heavily in the grip of this final arm, which made the limb tough to get at. He would go tumbling as soon as it was loose.

Nina fitted the chain around the wrist, then clung to her father while Aereas pried and pulled. She watched her cousin, eyes both eager and haunted, hand holding lightly to her father's. Aereas struggled, yanking spasmodically like a dog playing tug-of-war, but still nothing happened.

Nina blinked, and holding to her father, drifted out to aid Aereas. That was enough to bring red fury to his shoulders, and with a final shriek he snapped loose that arm, too.

Chaos. The snakewoman's six shattered limbs tangled suddenly in the chain, as though all were still alive, and the body pitched forward, smashing brutally into Aereas and bearing him away beneath it.

His shriek of exertion became a shriek of rage and terror as she and he shot headlong downward, away from Nina and her father. The headless corpse was oppressive atop him, its severed neck only inches from his gritted teeth. The dead arms flipped above her back and hammered him with random, fierce blows. He let loose the chain, hopelessly fouled now in the hideous creature, and fought his way free of the beast.

Still it was above him, drawn by the pocket of air he trailed, like a log in an eddy.

Aereas grasped the nearest arm, flung the corpse back over his head, and angled his feet away from the thing. He and the corpse split like two halves of a wishbone.

The hydralike monster rushed ferociously away. Its broken arms seemed tentacles drawing it onward into the deep, endless darkness. The young warrior slid down, feet first, obliquely away.

Where was he? Where was everyone else? He looked up, seeing the others as five bright points of light in the rushing, whirling darkness above. Far above. He had to slow his descent or he couldn't help defeat the final tanar'ri, couldn't help bring Artus around, couldn't see Nina again before . . .

Before they all struck whatever it was they were falling toward. A quick glance told him there was still nothing below.

Leaning backward, Aereas spread arms and legs to the side and tried to imagine his body as a wide, wafting oak leaf. Instead of staring downward into the infinite blackness and wondering when he would strike bottom, he kept his eyes on the points of light above, which grew larger with aggravating slowness.

They've probably slowed themselves, too, Aereas thought.

Perhaps Krim cast some sort of spell that keeps them from falling . . . a spell I am beyond the reach of. Surely not. Nina would come for me. She would not let me just plummet while the rest hovered in space. She loves me.

There was a lie in that thought, he realized. Those were his words, not hers. He had confessed his feeling; she had not.

But she kissed me, he reasoned, struggling to hold his body out against the ceaseless torrent of air. Kissed me to get me to shut up?

A sudden ache filled his chest, as though his sternum had been fractured in wrestling the snakewoman. His skeleton felt shattered, held together merely by the pressure of tired muscles. He'd seen the way she looked at Jandau. He'd seen the enticement there, the excitement of someone new, strange, different, otherworldly, elegant, handsome.

No, he told himself. Bad enough to be plummeting into this ceaseless pit of air and blackness. He didn't need to rush down into a similar abyss of emotion.

The Abyss. *That's* what this place was.

He was getting nearer his group. He could make out forms now, tiny bright creatures against the black roaring air. There was Krim, and LiGrun, and the mantis-headed lizard. Henry, the bariaur, was there, leaping like a pegasus from the huge, supine form of the porcine nalfeshnee.

The grotesquely fat tanar'ri drifted lifelessly down in the midst of the group, its too-small wings bent unnaturally up beside its head, like great, flapping ears. The glimpse of an enormous, snake tail startled Aereas for a moment until he remembered Cora. Then he saw the brute Dif, too.

They'd apparently already killed and disposed of the other tanar'ri. The dragonlike baatezu was gone as well, their bodies borne as quickly and quietly away from each other as autumn leaves struck from the same branch.

What about Nina and Artus . . . and Jandau? Though Aereas was near enough now to make out faces, he saw no trace of his uncle, his love, or his rival.

If only he could slow himself more . . . but tightening his muscles seemed only to speed the descent. So, eyes wide, heart thrumming, sternum aching, he watched and waited until they had descended near him.

When but a stone's throw below the group, he shouted up, "Where are Nina and Artus?"

The others couldn't hear, cupping hands behind their ears, but to no avail. He shouted twice, thrice more.

At last, only an arm's length beneath Henry's uneasily churning hooves, Aereas cried out to him, "Where's Nina? Is she all right?" He snagged one of the hooves and pulled himself upward.

The bariaur nodded his ram-horned head toward the supine nalfeshnee, and Aereas spun around to see.

Atop the slain tanar'ri stood Jandau, facing away from Aereas. He stood with all the wide-legged panache of a pirate at the helm of a stolen ship. Instead of a wheel, though, he held to the end of a slender spear, which stuck straight up from the fiend's chest. The head of the spear was buried where the thing's heart might have been. The tiefling's black cloak flapped dramatically behind him, and his soft boots were poised comfortably on the scabrous flesh between the boar's ribs.

What bothered Aereas most about that stance was not its bravado, its cockiness—not even the fact that he had clearly slain the last of the tanar'ri. The troublesome thing was that Nina clung to his arm. The black cloak for which Jandau counted himself so famous flapped at intervals against her slim body, enfolding her, embracing her.

Though he had taken long minutes to rejoin the pack, it was the work of a moment for Aereas to dive across the empty space between himself and the dead nalfeshnee and smash against Jandau's back.

Just as he had hoped, the tiefling was bowled over by the attack. His one hand wrenched loose of the shuddering spear, and his other of Nina. She fell, too, but was able to cling to a tuft of hair on the fiend's chest and hold on to her father, lying unconscious there.

Not so Jandau. Aereas had grabbed the offender's cloak with the offender attached and hurled the tiefling away from the nalfeshnee. He, too, flew clear, so that now it was just the tiefling and Aereas and the roaring, insatiable pit.

"Keep your hands off her, freak!" shouted Aereas in a rage that surprised even him. Next followed a vehement punch to the tiefling's narrow gut.

Jandau soared momentarily into the darkness. He had never before looked so birdlike than when he came flying down, black crow's wings flapping behind him. He ducked beneath another punch and drove the full force of his narrow body into Aereas's chest. It was like being struck by a swift, slim, man-sized arrow.

Aereas flipped backward once, seeing the nalfeshnee and the others tumble ludicrously away overhead. Then came a triangular flash of gray against the blackness, and then only gray.

The talon hands of that tiefling bastard had grabbed his throat from behind. Aereas kicked at him futilely, missing each time, though he sent the two of them into a tumbling spin away from the others.

He felt like the snakewoman's corpse, flailing away with mad hopelessness against a much smaller, much fiercer and faster competitor. But at least, like the snakewoman, he was dragging his foe down with him.

Suddenly, the talons were ripped away, leaving behind the throb of choked flesh and the sting of scratches. Gray went to black again.

Aereas took another blind swing, spinning himself over in the process, and felt a stunning crack to the jaw. As he tumbled away, he saw a foot that was too slender, too beautiful to be Jandau's. Aereas swung back up to be grabbed at the collar by a slim, hard hand.

Nina. She held Jandau out to the other side, gripped in a similar fist.

"Would you boys behave!" she shouted. Though the words were only chiding, her tone was furious, humiliating.

Aereas did not fight her implacable grip, but glared at her through wide, angry eyes. "Stay away from him! He's no good!"

Jandau didn't struggle either, and whether he could hear Aereas or not was unclear. He did not speak.

She returned Aereas's glare and shook her head. Then she drew him in, and he thought for a moment she was going to kiss him again. Instead, she raised her head toward the nalfeshnee above and jerked both combatants flat. Immediately, the three of them began to rise toward the others.

Their progress was much faster than Aereas's had been earlier, both because of the wind resistance of three bodies and because Henry was directing the dead fiend down in a shallow dive. He used the spear like a tiller, standing on the beast's head and leaning his considerable weight into the shaft to draw the body downward.

In moments, the sundered party was again joined, and Nina, Aereas, and Jandau alighted on the plummeting corpse. Henry flattened out the descent and stayed in position as Krim, Cora, Dif, and the mantis-headed lizard hovered uneasily beyond the fringes of the plummeting beast.

It felt nice to stand on something solid, Aereas thought, though that something was dead fiend flesh. It was also nice to be out of the wind for a moment, for the nalfeshnee blocked most of the air rushing up from below. Nina's and the tiefling's skin was red from the gale. But, best of all, the lee of the corpse gave them a chance to talk without shouting.

The three of them—Nina yet clutched their collars—crouched down beside the unconscious form of Artus, held to the fiend's chest by a wide-eyed and bescaled lizardman. While they had been fighting, LiGrun had patiently picked the lock of the shackles and stripped them away.

Nina's fists, once hard as hinges, became soft, sliding to her father's cheeks and fondly stroking them, tapping them. "Wake up, Father. Wake up."

Aereas watched intently, though Jandau sidled off like a soaked and sullen cat to the shoulder of the tanar'ri. There he clutched a clump of hair and gazed down into the endless blackness. He did not even look up when Henry shouted to him, "Tell me if you see land—anything!"

"Father, wake up. We're in great trouble."

There was a flutter about the silvered eyelids of the Lady's custodian. They opened slowly to reveal gray eyes clouded with pain, with confusion, with some sort of enchantment.

"Where are we?"

Nina's eyes were suddenly clouded, too. She clutched him in a quick embrace.

The question was answered by LiGrun. "We are falling, sir."

"Falling?" he repeated emptily as Nina drew away. His eyes settled on her. "My daughter. Oh, how good to see you!" His watery eyes turned toward Aereas, and a smile came to them, spreading from there to his mouth and his whole face. "Aereas! Have you two been down to the creek?"

Aereas shook his head. He spoke in a loud but gentle voice, "It's the Abyss. We're falling in the Abyss."

Artus blinked. "You shouldn't play in the Abyss."

That brought a grim smile to both the cousins' faces.

Nina pressed, "We came to rescue you from the tanar'ri. We've killed them all. But now we're falling."

He nodded and smiled again. "That's nice, dear. I need some rest."

"No," she said forcefully. "We need you now, before we hit bottom."

His eyes winked open, and he groggily shook his head. "Hit bottom? There *is* no bottom to Layer Six-Sixty-Five."

✦ Terrors, Creatures, Darkness, I ✦

What is this?
What is this?
Terrors. Creatures. Darkness.
There are words—a thousand thousand words—on one side.
There are things—terrors, creatures, darkness—on the other
  side.
What is this?
Words and things.
Things—terrors, creatures, darkness—outside,
  and a thousand thousand words inside.
Words inside what?
Things outside what?
The narrowest word, tallest word, briefest word: I.
The least thing, the biggest thing, the strangest thing: I.
Words inside and things outside I.
What are these terrors, creatures, darkness . . . I?

EIGHTEEN
POCKET PORTALS

"No bottom. Now be a good girl and go to the creek and let me sleep. . . ."

Whether she was a good girl or not, he slept. The coma would not even break when Nina frantically shook his shoulders and—once—slapped him.

She raised her arm to slap him again, but Aereas caught it and nosed toward her ear to whisper, "Let him sleep. He's been through enough."

A wedge of gray wing intruded into the circle, and Krim's high, thin voice came through the torrential wind. "How is he?"

Nina glanced at the creature and caught her lower lip between her teeth. "Not good. Can you . . . magic him out of this?"

The tail of the manta lashed in a negative gesture. "I know no magic for that. Besides, this place dampens magic strangely. Fireballs and lightning bolts work, but a simple featherfall or levitate spell—nothing. And teleportation magic won't work."

"So we can't even stop our fall," Nina said.

"No, but unless I miss my guess, there's no bottom to this pit."

Aereas nodded. "That's what Artus said. He said it was the Six Hundred Sixty-Fifth Level, or something."

"The Six Hundred Sixty-Fifth Layer of the Abyss," Krim hissed. "There may not be a bottom, but we'll die sure enough without one."

"What do you mean?" Nina asked.

"No water," Krim said, "for starters. With this wind, we'll dehydrate in two days, tops. No food. And even if we ate this nalfeshnee and somehow distilled the water from its blood, the very skin would in time be winnowed from our muscles. It's already begun on the two of you. Your faces and arms are windburned. And after the skin goes, then the muscles, too. We'll be shredded to death by the invisible hands of the wind."

Aereas and Nina stared, stunned, at the hovering manta. She spoke first. "There is no bottom, no food, no water, and no way out?"

Krim seemed to consider. "There is always a way out. That's something planars all know. It's just a matter of finding it. I suggest we send out . . . scouts, for lack of a better term. Prod the edges of the envelope . . . see if we find anything."

Nina looked up at the mantis-headed lizard, hovering proprietorially just above them.

"I'm staying here, with Father." She leaned in to whisper to Krim, "That bugman up there's got his own claim to Father, and I don't want it stealing him away."

"I'll stay, too," Aereas began, but Nina's slim hand pressed gently on his chest.

"You go. I can take care of myself. We need everybody to

search this pit for some portal, some escape. Tell the others." Aereas was rising away from her when she shouted, "Stay in view of the big corpse here. And be careful."

Aereas nodded, drifting out toward the others.

Of all the instructions Nina had just given him, only the last three words stayed in his mind.

They had not been the right three words.

* * * * *

The companions fanned outward, brilliant tracers in the preternatural blackness: Aereas, Jandau, LiGrun, Krim, Dif, Cora, Henry, and even the mantis-headed lizard. They looked to Nina like the last stars falling from a now-empty sky.

Aereas cruised out slowly, remaining level with the falling corpse. Jandau meanwhile went swiftly, like a fleet-fletched arrow.

The tiefling's quick disappearance worried Nina as she watched from atop the gently rocking fiend, restless in death. She told herself she worried because the tiefling could be up to something, could circle wide to attack Aereas just out of sight. But she knew that was not why. She was worried because she feared he would disappear forever.

He did not, and neither did any of the others. Though Nina lost sight of most of them at one point or another, they could all still see her; the nalfeshnee corpse-camp was larger than any of them. Just as they had gone out differently, they returned differently—some from below, others from beside, Krim from above.

All brought back the same news: blackness upon blackness. Aside from this plummeting corpse and the creatures that clung to it like parasites, there seemed to be absolutely nothing in this void.

All returned in the same condition: fatigued and limp as rags, skin rubbed red by the wind, eyes bloodshot from the strain of looking ceaselessly into emptiness, brains fevered from the emptiness and despair.

Though she had planned to tell them when they returned that they should rest in the lee of the giant corpse, she did not have to. Cora came back first, shook her head in grim-faced denial, and slid without comment into the calm behind one half-folded wing. Her truncated snake tail clutched the giant through one nostril. Then came Henry, who bowed gracefully before Nina, gave his full report, and without waiting for comment from her, dropped to his flank to sleep like a dog.

Next came LiGrun, who slid wearily into the other wing, then Dif, then Krim, then the baatezu, then Aereas, then Jandau. They all took their cues from those already collapsed and sleeping, and each found a suitable part of the creature's body for shelter.

It was only the last three arrivals who had to be coaxed to sleep. The baatezu curled itself like a bug-headed cat on the fat paunch of the beast, overlooking the place where Artus lay. The creature—Eareao—would not sleep, even with Nina's repeated promise that she would not make off with its prize.

Aereas was similarly recalcitrant, though for different reasons. He trusted neither the living fiend nor the dead one, and least of all Jandau. Weariness at last succeeded where trust failed, and he coiled himself around the shuddering spear, asleep even as his hands closed over it.

Jandau took convincing in his own way. He told Nina he would remain awake gazing over the corpse's shoulder, watching for the ground that must lie somewhere below. And he did just that, digging a dagger into the sinewy shoulder and sitting astraddle its handle. His feet dangled in the voracious wind as if in a waterfall. Though to start with, he occasionally looked beyond the shoulder, his glances gave way to nods, and the nods to slumped sleep.

For a time, Nina sat alone upon that sinking barge of

flesh. It was a strange ark that bore them, and a stranger world it bore them through. Vast emptiness. Sourceless illumination. Darkness beyond. In time, her ears became deadened to the roar, and the world seemed silent as well as black and empty. Only by opening her own mouth to speak and hearing no voice in the silent storm did she know the roar remained.

A tear came to her eye. She was as surprised by it as by anything that had happened since they had crawled through the tobacco stand.

What was this tear for? She was out of the wind and her father was resting beside her. She had men fighting over her, she had overcome armies of monsters to gain her father back, and no foes remained.

Even so, that was the greatest threat of all. Better to march back to Caonan across the slain bodies of fiends than to fall through emptiness like this. It was not her sort of fight.

Awake, Jandau moved toward her. He floated with toes inches away from the plummeting bulk of the giant. He moved more like a fish than a bird, hands waving gently at his side. When he reached her, she laid fingers on his ankle and drew him down beside her.

"Still nothing," he said dully. "The Abyss has no bottom."

He was warm next to her, warm and alive, unlike the chill flesh of the fiend. It felt good.

His eyes were keen, his smile knifelike.

He nodded toward Aereas. "Your boyfriend over there is quite proprietary."

"He's not my boyfriend," Nina snapped back. "We've been friends forever."

"He's a friend, and he's a boy—"

"Why don't you go back to sleep?" Nina asked bitterly. "I have no boyfriend."

"Perhaps you'll have to let Aereas know that," replied Jandau. He began to float away, and cold air rushed into the space between them.

Nina pulled him back down. "There's no bottom. Might as well sleep here. It's warmer."

He gazed at her levelly, and his mouth moved as though to form a snide retort. But nothing came forth.

He leaned into her and fell asleep.

Nina set a hand on his shoulder to keep him from floating away. In words stolen by the winds, she said, "Girl, what are you getting yourself into?"

Despite her desire to guard her father, and despite the baatezu's desire to guard its prize, they all slept.

* * * * *

Interestingly, it was Artus who woke first.

He sat up with a start, the surge of his heavy shoulders drawing him up from the belly of the fiend.

Where am I? he wondered to himself, realizing only then how loud the world was around him.

Convulsively, he reached down to grab on to the ground. It slipped away beneath his feet, but he caught a tuft of braided hair someone else had used as a handle.

Someone else?

He was surrounded by others: his daughter and a tiefling, fully dressed but intertwined as though they were not; his nephew Aereas; and a bunch of creatures he did not know. Species that he knew, but individuals he did not. The most startling of the crew was the nalfeshnee on which they rode and which, judging by its passivity and the smell it was beginning to exude, had been dead for some fifteen hours or more.

But how did they all get here? What set of events had led up to this? And where was *here?*

It was coming back to him, slowly, in fragments of images, coming back through a mind as turgid and lightless as the whirling, spinning world around them. The Abyss.

That's right. There is a layer of the Abyss that's just emptiness. He could think of no other place where a passel of creatures could sleep as they plummeted to their deaths. Now, which layer was it? Blast if the ride so far hadn't addle-coved him. Crazy. Barmy. He'd heard those words enough before.

Grasping another stalk of hair, he made his way across the nalfeshnee to the beast's shoulder. There the handle of a dagger jutted from a pale, bloodless wound. He gripped the dagger and looked over. Blackness, just like the blackness above, only with wind rushing up through it. What layer was that, now?

There came an earnest shriek that sounded small against the roar.

Artus looked back to see his daughter leaping weightlessly up from sleep, sloughing off the tiefling as though he were a robe, and gaping at the empty spot where Artus had been. Next moment, she was diving toward a mantis-headed gelugon curled on the belly of the corpse. It had been asleep the moment before she began attacking it, and now it rose.

Though nothing else around him made sense, Artus knew enough to break up a fight between his daughter and a fiend.

He scuttled his way across the dead chest, reaching the argument just before the first fist was thrown. He crawled past his daughter and pushed his way between the combatants, spreading arms out to keep them at bay.

"Now, hold on here, you barmy bashers!" he shouted, but his voice was dry with the wind. Nothing came out.

He didn't get a second chance. In that moment, he was wrapped in the elated embrace of his daughter and clasped in a proprietary pincer of the gelugon. The cries of joy and consternation that followed added confusion to Artus's kaleidoscopic mind, and the others encamped upon the corpse rose now from sleep to crowd toward him.

"Father! You're awake. You're well!" Nina cried out.

"What layer of the Abyss is this?" he asked incongruously.

It was Aereas, joining his arms to the glad embrace, who answered, "The Six Hundred Sixty-Fifth Level!" he shouted, overjoyed.

Artus frowned, thinking that should sound familiar.

The dogpile grew until the whole batch of them were drifting up off the corpse. It took a manta ray to carefully hook its stinger into the nest of arms and swim down toward the corpse to bring them all back to it.

The many creatures fell away, then, each taking eager hold of the beast before they resumed their questions.

Nina waved her hands above the whole crew, shutting them up, before saying, "Help us get out of here, before we all shrivel into dried husks."

Artus shook his head, staring through clouded eyes at his daughter. "But, if I remember rightly, there is no way out. This is the Six Hundred Sixty-Fifth Layer, right?"

She nodded.

He shook his head. "Then . . . hmm . . . no bottom, no way out . . . I think."

"What about portals?" shouted Aereas. "What about conduits, or teleportation, or something?"

"Impossible. No portals out, only portals in, unless one of you brought one along. No conduits at all. Teleportation doesn't work. . . . No gods here to pray to." His surety seemed to surprise even him. "How did I get here?"

The manta spoke next, its serpentine voice unnerving the man. "What about air elementals? Surely in a place like this—"

"Do we have any elemental priests?" Artus asked, staring around.

Those who had heads shook them.

Jandau said, "So, we will all die."

Artus nodded gravely. "Eventually, in one way or another." His old face darkened. "Perhaps if my mind were clearer, I could think of something. But I just can't seem to think, can't seem to remember."

A light came on in Aereas's eyes. "Wait a minute!" He shrugged off his pack, undid a strap, and pulled from it the slim book. "Your journal. Maybe this will remind you of something."

The man's hands trembled as they reached for the book. "You *did* bring a portal with you, lad!" He drew the book up before him and looked fondly at its cover. "But how did you ever get ahold of this thing?"

"You gave it to me," Aereas replied excitedly. The words stumbled over each other to get out of his mouth. "And what do you mean, I 'brought a portal with me'?"

"The book," Artus said simply, flipping it open. The old, infinite pages riffled in the strong winds. "It's full of them, boy."

"You mean, it lists where portals are in different planes— in the Six Hundred Sixty-Fifth Layer of the Abyss?" Aereas asked.

"No," replied his uncle with a kindly wave. He opened the book to an illustration of Boffo's music shop in Sigil. "The pages themselves are portals. You just climb into them." And so saying, he extended his fingers into the illustration.

His nails struck dully against the paper. "Now, hmm, that should have worked."

"Maybe you're cut off from the power," LiGrun volunteered with dry despair.

"Or maybe you just need to remember the key," said Jandau.

Artus nodded. "Yes, the key. This is going to be difficult. I don't have any physical keys with me, and the keywords are flying out of my mind."

"Think, old man!" Jandau said, his pale face reddening. "It's this, or death for us."

Nina shot Jandau a glare but said nothing as Artus

puzzled through the problem.

Artus groaned, staring at his own journal filled with his own words and illustrations in pen and coal and blood and whatever other material had come to hand on his journeys. Had it been so long? Had he forgotten all his old secrets? Gotten that soft?

Mesmerized, barmy, drugged?

It was as though the creature he now was bore no resemblance to the creature he had once been. It was as though he was the doddering father of that young, self-assured man who had become an agent of the Lady, who had skipped across worlds upon worlds as though they were mere chalk squares drawn by children playing hopscotch.

But, no. He was a father, yes, but not of that plane-hopping espionage agent of the Lady. He was father to this girl, this young woman who hovered before him now in the rushing impossibility of their free-fall.

She had followed her adoptive father into the ceaseless planes, packed like pomegranate capsules around their core worlds. And, surely, if she had followed him this far and overcome fiends and gods to rescue him, she had learned more in days than he could remember from years.

And yet she huddled over him, waiting for a word of hope.

"I don't know," he said, shrugging, closing the book of his past life and handing it slowly to his daughter, his nephew. "I'm an old man, jangled and confused. If this were a street and not a plunge into the Abyss, you two would likely take my hands to walk me safely across. But it isn't a street, and you want me to tell you the way out?"

Nina gazed levelly at her father. It had been his custom throughout her upbringing to teach her by making her figure things out for herself. Was this just another such episode, or was he really as helpless as he claimed to be?

"We're going to die unless you do something, Father," she said.

He smiled faintly, a sad look in his eye. "We're going to die anyway, my child.

"If this is the Six-Hundred Sixty-Fifth Layer, we are shooting stars. If this is some other place, there may well be, far beneath us, years beneath us, some impassible, impenetrable lump of something—lead or granite or dung—that we will strike, and it will all be done. But, either way, we are mortals—races defined by their dying, not by their living."

Nina would not look away from the old man. White hair lifted from his wrinkled cheeks like the down of a thistle from the bulb. He was giving up. The bloom was gone, and now only the shroud-white seedpods showed on his face. He was dying, consigned to it. The abduction by fiends had been only a signature placed on the autopsy.

She looked away from her father at last. She opened the journal in her lap and saw the familiar pages—gray, rust, black, tan, skin-colored—beneath her hand.

This was the planes, this infinite book with its pages rattling violently in the windstorm. The journal—her father's life, which he had somehow orphaned himself from—was the planes, and in here lay their salvation.

"Find a page," shouted Aereas at her shoulder. "Find something that talks about or shows a picture of a place we could escape to. If this is a book of portals and conduits, you can find someplace that lets us get out."

Nina began flipping the sheaves, reading pages, scanning drawings. Aereas sat back, giving her room. She could find it. He knew she could.

Even so, his attention was dragged away for one moment by Jandau, the black sparrow, literally hovering nearby. The bracelets on his arms glinted golden in the strange light as he rubbed them together. It seemed they were flint and tinder in the hands of a freezing man.

What could he be doing? What could he be thinking, staring down at those slim bands of gold, grinding them together with not even a spark between them? And where had those bands come from? Aereas remembered the tiefling's slim wrists clearly, those empty stalks of bone and flesh beneath the talon-hands of that man. To see jewelry there was as strange as to see diamond rings around the ankles of a crow.

"I don't see anything," Nina muttered in despair. The words were somehow carried outward by their emotional weight, though the sound of them was ripped away. "I don't see anything, don't hear anything."

"Close the book and open it again!" shouted Aereas. "You've got to see something!"

Nina did so, still paging through. She was shaking her head. "The journal was written before Dad came to Caonan. I don't remember any of these places."

"We've been in Sigil and Gehenna—" Aereas pressed, growing impatient. "Isn't there *anything* familiar?"

"Wait," said Nina, stopping at a page scored with black ink and a water-colored hue of gold. "Wait just a second."

"What? What is it?" asked Aereas.

She didn't even have to answer, for he saw it himself.

Café Leonan.

"Lords be praised," said Jandau, speaking for all of them, even the wide-eyed gelugon who hovered nearby. Its mantis-face was alight with hope for the first time since entering the Abyss. Jandau tapped Nina's shoulder. "If you can get us there, Nina my girl, I'll buy drinks for us all—for a week straight!"

"Not so fast," Nina replied. She held out the book to her father. "Do you remember the keyword, Father? This might be our only hope."

The old man, head flaming with his white whipping hair, stared long at the image on the page before him. If he recalled that small café, crammed between two larger, newer, taller buildings on some crowded market street of Sigil, his eyes showed no hint of it.

He shook that shock of white hair. "I'm sorry. It has been

so long."

Tight-lipped, Nina drew the book back toward her, clasping the pages tightly in her hands. "You say if you knew the key, you could merely reach—"

The words halted in her throat, for one thumb had slipped into the text page of the open spread. She gasped lightly, pulling the digit out, then prodded with the opposite thumb into the illustration of Café Leonan. Her finger seemed to pass through the page, through the paper and into a place of warmth and stillness.

"This one doesn't need a keyword," Nina exclaimed, digging her hand into the picture.

"Of course it needs a key," said Artus irritably. "All portals need keys. I remember that much at least. Besides, it didn't work when I tried—"

"Not this one," replied Nina brightly, and she plunged her whole arm into the picture. Her father began another reproach, but before he could finish it, she ducked her head into the page and it seemed to flatten, to become part of the illustration.

There came a moment of wordless apprehension as the others looked on, and then Nina wriggled through with her shoulders, her slim waist, her hips and legs. Suddenly, the book was bobbing free above the dead fiend on which they all rested. She was on the page completely, and they all stared after Nina.

Aereas's goggling was over quickly, though, for he grabbed Artus by the scruff of his collar and rammed his head into the page.

"You next, honored sir," he said, though the old man could not have heard him. His head had already become scrawled lines on the paper, and his shoulders quickly followed.

Though he had twice the girth and half the flexibility of his daughter, he slipped through with the same alacrity as she, like Aereas and Nina through the tobacco stand.

Jandau gave up the futile rubbing of his bracelets and

dived for the journal. "Me too," was all he had time to say before his brow struck the page, flattened into it, and was followed by shoulders and arms and hands and waist and legs and feet, like the others.

The fourth creature through was the baatezu, who'd just watched his hostage disappear and was not likely to let it get away so quickly. While Aereas clutched the flapping book, watching in amazement the compression and regression of the tiefling, the gelugon was coiling and bunching like a cobra behind him. Once the tiefling's toes disappeared into the page, the creature arced up and plunged into the book like a diver into a deep pool. The covers shuddered a bit with his passing, but he was through faster than any of the others.

Aereas braced for another such assault on the volume, but none came. He looked around at those remaining—Cora, LiGrun, Krim, Henry, Dif—and sensed uncertainty where there should have been desperate hope. "Come along. Time to follow them," he said, waving them forward.

"What if they went nowhere?" asked Cora, studying the page with sharp interest. There was no longer any sign of Nina or Artus or the two others in the illustration of Café Leonan.

"If they've gone nowhere, they're in a better place than here," Aereas reasoned with a shrug.

Krim took him up on it. With a brief, "Quite right," he glided into the open page and disappeared with a twitch of his long barbed tail.

"Who's next?" Aereas asked.

Without answering, Cora threaded the stump of her tail into the page, and braced herself as the beautiful scales melted slowly away into paper. Halfway down the length of her serpentine body, the weight of that which was in the book exceeded the weight of that which remained, and with an inertial lurch, she disappeared into the flapping gutter.

That left only Aereas and the two largest members of the

party. Though he was anxious to follow Nina wherever she had gone, Dif and Henry were anything but. Aereas glanced at them with a strained smile. "I'm going, whether or not you follow."

Henry nodded with a conviction he clearly did not feel. He leapt up from the putrefying belly of the nalfeshnee and dived, forehocks first, into the rattling page.

Dif would not follow, shying away upon the dead body.

"What?" asked Aereas. "You want to ride a dead tanar'ri down to your grave? It's either the book or that."

Dif was shaking his head vehemently and still backing away when Aereas lunged up from the fiend's gut and brought the open book down upon the man-giant's head, like a lasso over the head of a bull.

The head disappeared into the spread pages, followed slowly by the shoulders and arms and hands. Then he went more rapidly, as if those creatures already on the other side pulled the man-giant through.

Aereas was now alone on the plummeting corpse of the nalfeshnee, feeling the empty weight of the body as it cascaded gently through the violent winds, downward, ever downward. Somewhere below were the falling corpses of the other fiends, tanar'ri and baatezu alike. Somewhere below there might be some ground, some land to strike and explode against horribly. Aereas gazed out over the shoulder of the tumbling titan, seeing only blackness, not even stars, not even the faint specks of other bodies falling, falling.

He felt strangely sad as he stepped into the rattling pages of the book. And then he was gone.

✦ Not Simply Words ✦

Not simply words move through me now. There are not just the words words words within and the terrors and creatures and darkness without. There are thoughts.

One thought is hot, like iron. (How do I know of iron, or of its heat?) She is fierce and angry, is embattled and battling.

One thought is turgid like water. He is troubled, seeking to flow in escape from the grinding weight of rocks, like water that seeps through a thousand miles of ground to deep, dark, cool seas.

One thought is keen as a knife, and he moves between the fire and water.

There are many more thoughts. They crowd my mind in wordstorms.

They crowd my mind. That is the thought above them all. My mind.

NINETEEN

BY THE BOOK

There was birth-fear, death-fear in that moment. Though they had all—even Nina and Aereas—passed from world to world before, this passage was different.

It felt like passing from one physical state to another. It was as though their bodies had become ice, then were immediately sublimated into air. It was as though they had emerged from the fretting wet darkness of a womb into the bright cold expanse of a breezy birthing porch. Their bodies had fallen to ash around them, and they had taken up residence in the fickle-thin resonances of memory.

It was like nothing they had ever felt.

They were words, simple and finite. Straightforward. Flat.

Nina was no longer a vast complexity of flesh, but the word *Nina* itself. She was letters on a page, pregnant with the possibility of becoming an idea if that name were ever read. In that form, she was the potential of herself, of sounds on muttering lips, and meanings in spinning minds, and perhaps even passions resonating in tears on a living cheek.

Aereas too was there, and Artus, and all the rest, their beings reduced to finite ink lines on a page. Whether they had become etchings of words or those of artists's pens, they each had only an explosive evocative existence, not flesh and blood.

It was uncomfortable. It was like pinching shut one's nostrils against the airlessness of water as one swims an impossibly long tunnel. They were out of their element, were flattened, compressed, and blind in reduction.

"Leonan," Nina called out.

The sound was not sound, but strokes in letters and pictograms and pictures. They could not see it—him—the café. They could not find the place, though it must be there, somehow deeper in the depthless page.

"Leonan!"

Aereas tried to move to her, his alien flesh of dry ink not nudging any nearer than a character space. It was as though the syntax of their bodies resisted touching, merging, which would render them both meaningless.

Two words cannot occupy the same space at the same time.

Or, perhaps they could.

The baatezu overwrote them all like the signature of a madman, signed in the center of the charter they had all composed.

LiGrun was meanwhile more punctuational than syntactic, more a matter of stark stops and starts and policing lines of grammar.

Krim was there, too, his restless wings transformed into line spaces and paragraph breaks, into the omnipresent structuring component visible only in the absences of words.

And the rest hovered somehow on that page, in that moment, and Nina called and called—black slashes on a crinkling page.

Then they were out of it, themselves again, bodies returned and names, wordforms, stripped suddenly away.

But the world around them was nothing any of them had ever seen before.

"This is not what I expected," said Artus wearily. His tired voice spoke for all of them as they stood there on that spongy, heathlike ground and gazed at the strange landscape before them.

At least they stood on the ground, and for that they were grateful. The place had breathable air rather than magma and smoke, solid ground rather than quicksand, a bright sky rather than depthless, plunging darkness.

That is where the comfort of the place ended. Before ears or eyes had latched on to the unsettling nature of the place, noses did. It smelled like a compost heap, rich in life—not newborn life but the teeming life of decay. More than a vista, the place was a stench. It was an autumn garden whose flagrant flowers had given themselves up to mist and mold.

As to their eyes, they were drawn first to the sky. It was not blue but silver—quicksilver—shiny and globular, poisonous and bright. It was a sky like a mirror that reflected nothing, giving to the void an element of liquid mercury.

The land that huddled beneath that mercurial sky was tumbled and swollen, broken, angry. It was jagged like a wound that seeks to heal itself despite the constant disruption of new injury. There was a pulse to the land, slow and magnificent, almost unnoticeable. It was like the frantic spin of a world about itself, at once profound and slight. The place was alive—or was once so—with the muscular fecundity of the living and the dead. It was spongy and swollen, like flesh.

The motley group—human, tiefling, fiend, reptile—stood

in a smooth-edged valley of the brown ground, seeing before them massive slopes of humus, of solid softness strewn with the flora and fauna of decay.

There were white funguses that lined the soil like scales on an ocean pier, and little pale wormy things that moved among the plants as though they had evolved from them.

There were jumbled twigs and tendrils blown by the silver winds into heaps along the living earth. These brushed up against crags of yellow rock, which jutted like bones from compound fractures. The deadfalls had come from the few stark trees that stood there in hairy tufts on the bald scalp of ground, their violent and hoary shafts truncated and brittle in age.

There were little creatures darting through the air like black knots of thread, moving among the fungi and maggots and drawing life from both.

It was a place alive with death.

"Where are we?" asked Jandau, gazing skeptically at the mirror sky.

"This is not Café Leonan," Artus said, not in response but observation.

Jandau's expression drew to a thin point. "Obviously. Let's just step back into the book and try again."

Artus raised a staying hand and shook his head, still not looking at the tiefling. "It's not as easy as that. We'd not planned on arriving here. If we jump back in, we might go to the Elemental Plane of Fire, or the Thirty-Second Layer of the Abyss, or some such place equally and immediately lethal."

"It's not even as easy as that," said Aereas. All eyes turned toward him. "We don't have the book anymore."

Artus's aged hand struck his aged forehead, and he sighed. "I should have told you to hold on to the covers when you came through. It all happened so fast."

"You mean," said the mantis-headed lizard-thing, "that you've lost our portal out of here?"

"It's probably still floating in the Abyss," replied Artus absently. "Or stuck somewhere halfway between there and here, or imbedded somewhere in this world. Unless you close the book behind you, you can't know where it'll land."

Jandau moved up beside Nina. His jaw muscles worked with the same grinding motion that animated his wrists and the bracelets on them. "Well, where are we?"

Artus said, "Someplace in the Astral Plane, I'd guess. I'd be sure if I could spot a few silver cords. Of course, travelers tend to avoid the islands in the Astral, fearing their lifelines will get tangled."

"Somewhere in the Astral," Jandau said disparagingly. Whatever he was trying to do with his bracelets apparently didn't work, because he stopped, slipping his arm around Nina's waist. "*Where* in the Astral, old man?"

At the last two words, Nina pulled away from the tiefling. A gratified smirk hovered half-formed around Aereas's mouth.

Artus seemed impervious to the sarcasm. He was holding one aged finger up in the air as though testing the silver flow of it. "This place is familiar. I've never been here, I know, but somehow it's familiar."

Jandau was suddenly laughing. His hands were folded about his own doubled waist. His companions stood watching, none seeing the source of the humor, all waiting for the tiefling to volunteer the joke. Shortly, he did.

"I should have known when I took this job that the man wanted by the Lady and the gods and the tanar'ri and the baatezu would end up in the hands of no one, of nothing. That the spy who was supposed to be the crux of Blood War domination would end up floating in astral space like some decaying god—"

"Decaying god . . ." echoed Artus, moving forward now as though drawn by a lodestone. "A decaying god."

Without conscious volition, the others followed the

wandering old man. They padded down into the cleft of the valley, and up the smooth-faced hill before them. Their feet broke through the fetid white fungi on the hillside and left depressions in the decaying twigs, the clinging mosses. Up the hill they rose, through a sparse and twisted orchard of ancient, leafless, dying trees.

"There's something familiar about all this. Something I remember," Artus said to no one except himself. At the summit of the hill, he spoke again. "Oh, gods."

But none heard him. Their eyes were shouting sights at them that overwhelmed sound.

Ahead and above, a league distant, lay a city of gold. It was perched upon high jagged mountains made of this watery, fleshy ground—a walled metropolis that glowed almost jaundiced against the cold silver sky. The walls around the city were built of blocks carved from the mountains. Beyond the walls stood shops, domes, and steeples that bristled beneath the sky with the jag-toothed decorum of scabs. The tan-gold buildings were splendid, but vibrant and livid like infection, decay.

"I know that city," said Artus. "I have never stood here to see it, have only stood within it, but I know it."

LiGrun, normally reticent, was pointing a scaled limb out behind them and hissing, "What is that? What is that dark boil?"

They turned and looked and saw a gray slab of water dully flashing back the silver sky over their heads.

"It is a sea," said Artus. "But a dead one. A sea of brine and poison."

Jandau stood, arms crossed over his chest despite his obvious dizziness at both sights—the impossibly high turrets of the golden city and the impossible foul stagnation of the poison sea. "Well, what now?"

"To the city," said Artus, already walking, stooping to lift a desiccated branch from the tumbled deadfall beneath him and using it as a cane to steady his feet on the way.

Jandau gazed down angrily at the inert bracelets on his wrists, then cast a skyward glance of approbation before shrugging and following the doddering old man.

After descending into one more soft-shouldered valley, they struck upon a road and began rising up it, marching toward the city that lay absurdly high and distant above. All the while, the jangled old man muttered that the place was familiar, that he knew where they were. Jandau's repeated and insistent queries about how to get from this place to someplace meaningful, however, seemed to fall on deaf ears.

Then they came to the herdsmen.

It was a squalid tent camp beside the road, haunted by the long, leaning shadows of herdsmen poised over rocky ground. There was no pasturage for the nuzzling, shouldering flocks around them. Lambs and ewes and rams, filthy with dust and lanolin, nosed intently en masse on the insupportable barren stretches between luffing tents.

"These people," muttered Artus dryly, moving off the road toward them.

"Maybe we can refill our waterskins, at least," said Jandau, tapping the deflated bag at his belt.

No one answered him, certainly not Aereas. The young man pushed up beside Artus to take his arm. Not even Nina, beside whom the tiefling strolled with his rounded gait, said anything. The cousins were as focused, as mesmerized, as the old man they'd come so far to rescue. Neither spared the slightest attention for the chafing tiefling and his spangled bracelets.

"Pardon me, sir," said Artus, approaching the nearest of the lank, leaning herdsmen. The man was garbed in tan linens that shifted on the silver winds. "What is this land, this place?"

If the man heard him, there was no telling, for he did not look up from beneath the darksome hood he wore. Artus reached out for him, his old hand sliding through the flapping robe and solid shoulder of the shepherd.

"Shadows," gasped Aereas. He pulled his uncle away.

"Yes," said the old man. "Either they are shadows, or we are."

As he moved his uncle back toward the road and the city that waited in bleak, spiny patience at its head, Aereas at last echoed the question Jandau had been posing over and over. "What is this place, Uncle?"

Instead of the disjunct silence he had anticipated, there came a response from the thin lips of the white-haired man. "The corpse of some god or other, I imagine. Not much else you'd find sliding through the Astral like this. Not much of this size, at any rate."

A corpse? That answer was more unsettling than no answer. As they started up the dusty road, Aereas asked, "This is the body of a dead god? I thought you said you'd been to the city. How could you have been to a city on a dead god?"

His uncle did not spare him a glance. The man's feet were trained on the rubble-strewn path before him as though it might be as treacherous and shifting as the dead descending body of the nalfeshnee. "You must remember, my boy, fleshly bodies for gods are nothing more than a matter of convenience. They are no more necessary or real to them than your haircut is to you."

Aereas rubbed his nubby scalp and cast a glance at the tumbled branches around him. Clippings of godshair? And what of those tangled trees?

As though Artus could read these conjectures, he said, "How long have you been in the planes now, boy? How long, and are still thinking as you are thinking?"

Aereas bristled at this question, feeling reprimanded, but then began to think of it. It had been the night of the abduction that he and Nina had followed Artus through the tobacco stand. They spent that evening in Boffo's little music shop and met the next evening with Jandau. That night, they had fallen through the smelter portal into

Gehenna, remaining in a cave until morning. The next two nights they had stayed in Sung Chiang's palace, and then came that infinite falling, and the sleep upon the dead tanar'ri's gut. How long had it been? Five, perhaps six nights—it already felt like an eternity.

"Less than a week."

"That is enough time that you should be thinking differently. It takes less than a week for a great battle to change the course of history. It takes less than a day for a storm to change the face of a city. It takes less than an hour for an orator to change the mood of a nation. It takes less than an instant for a life to end . . . or awaken."

"We are near the city, Uncle," Aereas said impatiently. "Stop with the riddles."

He nodded and said, "The corpse of a god is not flesh. Flesh is inconsequential to divinity. The corpse of a god is memories, wars, heroes, regrets, sacrifices, prayers—the stuff of significance."

"These are the ghosts of some dead god's life gone by?" Aereas ventured.

"Yes," said Artus. "Now to remember which of the thousand thousand of them these things belonged to . . ."

Jandau had been hovering just off their shoulders, and he said uneasily, "So I was right. The Blood War hostage hasn't ended up with tanar'ri or baatezu, but with the insensate corpse of some forgotten deity."

"Godflesh never fully dies," Artus said, his voice like the warning growl of a guard dog. "And no deity is ever fully forgotten. Remember that, Sparrow."

The term from the old man's mouth brought a tight smile to Aereas's lips.

But Artus was not done. "We are not here by chance. I am—we are yet hostages. What vile purpose might have lain behind fiend abduction would pale next to what lies in the flesh of a dead god."

Aereas had never seen Jandau chastened, had never seen

the green-gilled silence of nervous fear on those tight-lined features. The tiefling withdrew and took his place beside Nina, arm linked in her arm. Aereas looked away from the sight of them. Maybe the planar rogue had stolen away Aereas's love, but he would not steal away his uncle.

In silence, the crew toiled up the dust-haunted slope toward the towering walled city at its summit. They passed into the massive shadow beneath those soaring walls, into the unguarded, arched gateway.

They entered an empty cobbled courtyard. Its vacant porticoes were covered in swaying fronds and sliced through by ceaseless silver winds. Artus did not pause, moving into the maze of stone and mud and mortar shops and houses beyond. They passed shrines and streets, markets and manors.

"Ah, Xiam. Now I know you!" said Artus to himself, nodding. "Yes, and I think I know whose corpse this is."

Among the buildings moved robed ghosts, sliding insubstantial and inattentive up and down the narrow, winding streets.

"Whose corpse, Uncle?" asked Aereas. "Whose?"

"Hush now. Let an old man's mind spin in silent remembrance until I piece this all out."

Aereas did not turn. He did not want the chastened tiefling to see him with a similar green about the jowls.

So they walked through the cobble-scaled and snaking paths of the city, between and among and through the spectral inhabitants that sullenly wandered the place. They passed teeming markets and fetid alleys, roofless shops and floorless chapels. At last, one of those strange, solitary figures drew the old man's eye, and he gasped and sighed all at once.

"Miriam," Artus said, breathless. Though the name had emerged with no more than a whisper, it had been heard by them all. "Miriam."

Before them walked a ghostly woman—thin, young,

shapely beneath the shifting dance of her robe, the gentle tottle of the water jug she carried on her head.

"Oh, Malkin. I should have known."

She walked, that young, beautiful, oblivious spectral woman. Her feet had the assured and measured gait of one who had passed that way many times, who had gathered water from pool or well and carried it back across those dry, tight stones enough times to plaster the dirt between them into a mortar of persistence and necessity.

This impression of Aereas's was deepened a moment later when he noticed that her easy, natural movements were augmented by a bright, coruscating cloud, a jagged encompassing halo that hovered to either side of her and in front and in back. It did not alter her path, did not affect her stride in the slightest.

"What is that?" he wondered as he and his uncle followed the slim woman. "Around her, I mean?"

"You mean 'Who is that?' " Artus replied dryly. His eyes remained on the glaring cloud about the woman. The focus of those eyes seemed to slow the frenzied movement of that white thing.

For the first time, Aereas and the others could see that the aura that swathed the woman was a man. He moved about her, stared keenly into her eyes, followed her, led her, clutched one hand or the other. The tenacious presence of the creature reminded Aereas at first of Jandau, though the bulk of the man and his big-boned, eager, adoring face was not that of the tiefling.

"Malkin," Artus said. "He was Malkin. A god in flesh. The old cat god, who died some time ago, giving place to Bast. Of course, you'd probably not recognize the name Malkin so much as you would his later name, Leonan."

Aereas stared, stunned. Yes, it was Leonan, though how he could have known this presence for the floating black sphere in the café, he didn't know. "Leonan, a god," he muttered, "and this, his avatar?"

"No," replied Artus. "Not his avatar. An avatar is a mere projection of a god's essence, no more the god than a drawing of my daughter is Nina.

"No, this was no avatar. Leonan did what few other gods would do, making himself flesh—fully and completely mortal."

"Why?"

"For love. For love of this Miriam. Only watch," said Artus.

Dutifully, they did.

The phantoms they saw came not from a solitary walk of the woman from the well, but from hundreds of such journeys. She was the same in all of them; the incarnate god spun in an orbit around her.

She was solid in that place of flitting shadows, where cloaks waved like flags, snapping and transient in the wind. She was real in a place of ghosts. She must have walked this walk from well to home a thousand times, the very stones bearing the press of those constant feet in their straight line.

A ghost of the girl split off, wandered away along a narrow, leaning alley where the awnings and tents crowded tight like packings of cloth in a mouse nest. She yet bore the water jug, or the ghost of it, as she headed down the winding alley. The tents and robes around her moved with flaglike frenzy. Artus followed this ghost girl, peeling off when the solid girl walked on in her straight line, the halo of Leonan flickering around her.

"Ah, yes, the Via Cantabila. The Music Market," Artus said in reminiscence. The quickening of the old man's legs and the bright flush that came to his face, rising all the way to the white-haired pate, told the others all they needed to know.

He had been here.

The tiefling was less patient. "What does this Music Market have to do with our finding our way out of this place?"

Artus did not answer.

Aereas said, "Perhaps nothing, perhaps everything."

As they approached one leaning stall, tucked against the mud wall of a small emporium, they heard an answer of a different sort. There was music here. The shadows that moved antlike and furious beneath those buzzing tents and canvas slopes seemed visible manifestations of the music that filled the place.

A thousand melodies spilled from tin whistles and carved reeds of a thousand street musicians and beggars. The tunes blended together in a multifarious and continuous sound, like the melodious chaos of a large chamber group warming to scales and arpeggios. There was the drone of voices added to that liquid sound, the stacked and hierarchical chording of bass, soprano, tenor, alto, of singers and talkers and chanters and auctioneers.

It was a huge and soothing tone, like the song of wind in dry wheat or the restless tumble of streams in their beds.

Into this thrumming music they went, absently following the girl with the water jug, absently weaving among the crowded stalls and the shimmering people of the place. There, in the trembling memories of godflesh, they for a moment lost their own recollections, their own memories and hopes and fears.

The woman stopped beside a canvas shop, a place of silk scarves that shone with sunlight from brass and glass. In that baptism of music she stood, one hand free from the pot, slimly and tentatively drawing through a hanging scarf. The fabric bore a floral motif, juniper and sage and lily and hyacinth, the colors of green and white and violet dancing across her form as though she herself were a creature of stained glass.

Malkin—Leonan—appeared. Unlike before, when he was but a blurred and persistent planet in orbit around her, now he stood and could be seen. He was beautiful. Tall, statuesque, with a narrow face and intent eyes like gold coins. His hands, too, seemed chiseled of stone—powerful and venous—and the clothes he wore were calm beneath the shuddering light of the tents.

It was as if the two of them had stepped from time, as if in that moment before they had even spoken, before one of his marbled hands had reached up toward the same silk scarf, that they had stepped from the world of ghosts and dreams and into that of solidity.

"They meet," said Artus simply, a reverence in that strangely terse phrase.

The others stood just behind him, even the mantis-headed baatezu watching with silent awe as the god and the human began to speak.

The words were lost to the music of that place; not lost, but part of its music. No one had to hear to know what passed between them. A gold coin came from Leonan's robe and glinted for a moment in bright emulation of his eyes before it spun through the air to the vendor's dark hand. Then the flowing scarf of hyacinth, lily, sage, and juniper was down from the others and being tied about the woman's gold-brown hair.

"They meet," Artus repeated, as though speaking for the first time, "and the foolishness of a god who sets his whole self in a body is doubled when that god finds a tragic and mortal love."

They were gone, without dissolving into shadow, without drifting away in ghostly form.

Then, Leonan was there again—not there at the flapping tent stall, but there, crossing at the head of the narrow street, moving with broad step and purpose, and bearing something large before him. Another step, and he disappeared around the corner.

Artus ran after him. The others stood gaping for a moment. The tiefling, perhaps the most jaded of any of them, was first to recover, angling up the street, black cloak flapping winglike behind him.

When he reached Artus, he said, "You're chasing him down to get him to send us off this . . . corpse, right?"

"He's a dream," Artus said irritably. "He's not solid, but mere memory and regret."

The tiefling slowed in the blue shadow of a leaning shop. He shouted after the retreating old man, "You're chasing shadows and dreams, berk!"

Aereas passed him. A smile was gritted on his teeth. He rounded the corner where Artus had disappeared, and nearly bowled the old man over.

Artus stood in the cold lee of another building, a rich tenement with many windows opening out from it into the chill air. Faces floated darkly in those windows, staring and bloated like drowned men and women looking up from the bottoms of deep wells.

Artus, too, was staring, though he moved slowly forward, staggering, drifting like a boat at the calm edge of a cascade.

Ahead of him, Leonan moved with a similar motion, passing only now out of the great blue wedge of shadow in which the others stood.

As golden light drew over the god, Aereas saw at last what that dark bundle was he held: fronds and flowers, cuttings. The scent of them came back on the cold wind, and he smelled juniper and sage, hyacinth and lily.

Except that the god was holding them no longer.

They tumbled to the ground beside him, separating out into skinny branches, a bouquet no more. A large, white lily was the first to strike the ground, though it disappeared the next moment beneath the tangled darkness of the sage and juniper, beneath the fetid green aggression of woody stems and bushy leaves.

Then, upon the whole pile came the god's foot.

As though that one step broke the spell of dread and hesitation that held him back, Leonan ran full-out toward a tight knotted mob of men. It was not a fight. The men's clenched fists were not falling on each other; their shouts were not angry but gleeful, avaricious—bleakly, violently joyous.

Those legs that had borne Leonan across the alley in two steps now brought him among the black knot of men. There was a long flashing fang of metal in one of the god's marbled hands.

The first man's head came near off, dropping backward from a fountain of red and striking between the shoulder blades before the whole jittering corpse went down. The next, shrieking, was taken in the mouth, and from the back of his skull came the darting red metal like a second tongue. The third and fourth went down together beneath the trampling, charging feet of the god, limbs and ribs cracking beneath otherworldly weight.

More fell, and more, and he had not yet reached the white heap of cloth around which they had converged when those on the edges began to peel away in flight. From one corpse he drew up a saber in his other hand and mowed through the staggering, stumbling men like a reaper through grain.

Then, but for the dead and the twitching and the god, the courtyard was suddenly empty. Malkin knelt over the white form there, lying soiled and panting like a dove that had fallen from a stormy sky. In the triangle of space between the kneeling god and his arms, braced before him, Aereas glimpsed the woman's face and the silken scarf that brutally gagged her bleeding mouth.

She was still. Even the rapid pigeon breaths of her flank had ceased beneath the acid-blue arc of sky.

"They part," said Artus in a whisper. Only Aereas heard it, and he only because he was bracing himself against the old man's shoulder.

How long the god lingered there over his fallen love, none of them could say. It seemed forever, and an instant.

Then he was up, rushing through the courtyard in the white shadow of fury he had once been, darting into and out of open doors and open windows, and casting forth those drowned faces and the drowned puffy bodies beneath them, who had watched the rape without moving, without stopping it. The pile of dead grew in the courtyard.

Soon came green-garbed soldiers who drove arrows into the raging man until he tore their bows from their arms and their arms from their bodies and cast them atop the bulwarks of flesh he was building. More came, and more, and up went the bodies, and in went the arrows in ceaseless and orderly rage.

But then, into the midst of the carnage, marched Artus.

Not Artus, Aereas realized, since he yet clung to the old man's shoulder, but a shadow of Artus. A younger Artus.

While the green-clad archers had moved into the courtyard with furtive caution, this young Artus strode slowly and easily toward the arrow-laden god. Before Artus was clutched the journal, shieldlike, open pages turned out toward Leonan. But not the journal. The ghostly memory of it.

Leonan charged the young Artus, a great marble fist dropping to smash the calm man, but at the last moment the book lifted to block it. The god dropped heavily to the paving stones. The fletchings and arrowheads in his back snapped off beneath him.

"You killed him with the journal," Aereas said, stunned.

The old Artus beside him shook his aged head. "No. He was dead anyway. It was my trap for him gone awry, and when the Lady knew Malkin—Leonan—was dead, she sent me to recover him. I could return only with his spirit, stolen from his dead flesh. I took him to Sigil, where his soul resides today in its new body."

"The café," Aereas muttered.

Next moment, the ghostly Artus raised the book over his head, covers pitched like a tiny roof, and he drew the thing down over him. With the same ease that had borne the cousins through the impossibly small tobacco stand, the young Artus slid through the small book until its covers swallowed up his feet.

Last, the tiny pink fingers clutching the edges of the book drew it closed, and it disappeared. The corpse of the god lay alone in its own blood, in that of its dead love, in that of its victims.

"And so," Artus said emptily, as though reciting some long-forgotten litany, "the god fool enough to become wholly flesh and the god fool enough to fall in love with a mortal creature is slain for his follies, to be neither god nor flesh again."

Suddenly, Aereas understood. That's why they were here. They'd sought Leonan in the book, and found him—not his spirit, which had taken the café for its new body, but his dead flesh, floating here upon the void, haunted by dreams and memories.

A fearful light cut through the dull sheen of Artus's eyes, and he gave a small start and a gasp. "He's found the book."

"What?" asked Aereas.

The others crowded around the old man.

"That's what these memories were for. The flesh has been searching its memories and in them found the book. My journal. It must have come with us when we fell out of the Abyss."

"What?" Aereas repeated.

"The flesh has found what it's looking for," Artus said again, staggering.

Jandau had a wild look on his pale features, obviously in no mood for riddles. "What was it looking for?"

Artus's face grew stern, and he stared at the tiefling. "The same thing you are looking for. The same thing that made Sung Chiang kidnap me. The same thing that made the tanar'ri buy me. The same thing that makes you"—he jabbed an accusatory finger at the mantis-headed beast hovering at the back of the crew—"come along, hoping to steal me away. He's looking for the keys to the portals of Sigil."

"Why?" asked Jandau.

"To reunite flesh and spirit. To raise its dead body and make of it an undead god!"

A frission of fear swept through Aereas. "Leonan helped us find you. Why would he do something so evil as . . . as raising his dead body?"

"He wouldn't," Artus responded, drawing his daughter and his nephew toward him. "But his dead godflesh would. Come on. We've got to hide you two."

Nina and Aereas moved along with Artus, floating before him like lint before an insistent broom.

"Us?" Nina asked. "Why us?"

Artus pushed them ahead of him, heading between the buildings and toward the towering wall. His words were whispered, audible only to the cousins: "Because, dears, I now remember where I hid the skeleton keys to the planes. They are you."

✦ Lament of the Living Word ✦

How strange, to be awake only these few moments and already have my mind raped by a god.

TWENTY

DESCENT ✛ OF FIENDS

The mantis creature was suddenly alarmingly close, ganglious arms grappling Aereas and Nina by their collars.
"The skeleton keys to the planes, aye?"

Artus whirled on the creature and stormed toward it.
There was suddenly a black knife in his hand, and he drove
it beneath one breast scale of the baatezu. In the same motion, he wrenched downward, as though gutting a trussed
pig. That single black dagger tore the beast from collar to
loin, and the arms that clutched the cousins separated like
two edges of a wishbone.

The beast collapsed, unmade, its claws dragging Aereas
and Nina down beside it.

Jandau stared in awe at the ebon blade, now slick with
green blood. He edged respectfully out of swiping distance.

Artus stooped swiftly, plunging the black dagger into the
stones at their feet. It passed into the rock as though into a

rotten melon. He drew the blade out, clean, and sheathed it.

Jandau continued to stare as Artus explained quickly, "You've got to get all its hearts with the first stab, or it'll keep coming."

Dif and LiGrun were already helping Aereas and Nina tear themselves free from the death grip, and just in time. Artus yanked them both to their feet and began prodding them along.

"A pity, really. I'd hoped he wouldn't turn on us until a bit later. We're going to be needing him," Artus said absently as he corralled the cousins into the shadow of the city gates.

Jandau's tone this time was more respectful, though his question no less incredulous. "What are you talking about?"

Artus responded only with a flick of his head skyward.

Just before the group passed beneath the black eclipsing arch of the gate, Jandau glimpsed a red rain falling from sudden clouds.

"Rain?" he asked, his voice echoing in the passage. "Blood? Lava? What is it?"

The group strode out of the arch, out of the city. Artus directed Nina and Aereas forward into the tumbled, rocky wilderness. "That's not rain. Look again."

Jandau did so, seeing that the huge, dark mass he had assumed to be a thunderhead was too square, too regular, too colorful to be a cloud. It had four triangular edges, like a piece of cloth floating foreshortened in the air.

Cloth or . . . paper?

The colors—burgundy, violet, emerald, dun—resolved themselves into a strange pattern. It looked almost like a painting, like a frameless flap of canvas hanging over the city. Then, he realized, it *was* a painting, or more correctly, a manuscript illumination.

It was a drawing in Artus's strange and infinite journal, a depiction of tanar'ri armies marching across a bleak lava field in the Abyss. Now Jandau could make out the rigid brown lines of words scrawled across the page of the journal, which arced over them, over the whole of the sky as though the book itself were the heavens.

"How did it get so big?" Jandau stammered.

"Godflesh," said Artus with a shrug. "There are a great many powers even in the rotting flesh of dead gods."

"But *why* so big?" Aereas asked. He gazed with all the others at the book pages that wrapped the whole world.

"It—the dead godflesh—wants to slide through to Sigil. It wants to regain its spirit there."

From the huge open page came a red rain. "Lava? It's raining lava?" Jandau wondered.

"Not lava. It's raining tanar'ri."

That caused them all to stop. Their legs were suddenly weak on the stone-hard ground beneath them.

A cloud of scuffled dirt rose up from their halted feet and lifted toward the distant sky beyond the city, where they saw it. Tanar'ri were falling in their hundreds, in their thousands from the illustration. Many tumbled to certain death upon the rocky land, but others gained their wings and swept toward the city.

Toward the skeleton keys of the planes.

Without Artus having to say a word, they were all moving again, fleeing the onslaught of those beasts. The fiends looked yet like tiny gnats, but they grew with the seconds.

Aereas and Nina ran, heads occasionally thrown back over shoulders to watch the crimson rain of fiends flash over the ground like a desert monsoon.

"In fact, I could have . . . left him alive. . . ," noted Artus breathlessly as he ran. "He'd need . . . the book before . . . having the keys . . . could do him any good. . . 'Course, if he'd had . . . some kind of teleportation—"

"Look!" shouted Aereas, interrupting his uncle's muttering.

Still running, they all looked. The page illustration was gone, and a text page hung open above the world. No longer were tanar'ri falling from the sky, but those who had already plunged through the portal were yet gaining.

"The flesh is looking . . . for its spirit. It's looking . . . for the very portal we tried . . . to go through. Once . . . it finds it, the godflesh will be . . . in Sigil—it, and all the . . . tanar'ri, too. The place will . . . be destroyed."

Those word-crammed pages were suddenly gone, too. A new darkness fell over the land. Aereas skidded to a halt, tanar'ri or no, for now he stared up into a huge warped portrait of himself, drawn with all the skill and elegance of the portrait he had seen of Nina.

"Block your thoughts, child!" shouted Artus, dragging his nephew onward. "The godflesh is probing a portal to your mind. . . . Don't let it find . . . where we are."

Aereas clung to the old man's sleeve and ran, struggling to empty his thoughts, his eyes clamping closed in concentration.

Oh, but how impossible. To even know which thoughts to guard was to identify them to the probing godflesh. The blunt, fetid weight of that dead mind stomped through his brain like a farmer through a wet, springtime field. It hurt. It was overwhelming. And just as the field seeped with water, filling each bootprint of the planter, Aereas's mind gave up the seeping thoughts that filled it.

The thoughts came not as sounds, or words that rumbled like thunder through the dark firmament, but as smells—invisible, intangible. And all his companions looking up at the page knew suddenly what he thought, what he felt. The confused tangle of fear and youth and rage and pain and hope, the confused crisscross of images and sounds from the worlds around, the stinging cold ache, the sweetly bitter wound—all were revealed.

Love. They knew it all, now.

Aereas's face, red with the strain of clamping off his thoughts, was matched now by Nina's face, red with embarrassment and pride and fear. She knew, as much as any of them, who was the object of this love.

Mercifully, the restless godflesh moved on to find another portal. The page turned.

Despite the fiends, which boiled like locusts through the sky behind them, Aereas found his knees suddenly weak, his legs unable to run. He clung to the shoulder of his uncle, not to be steadied but to be carried.

"You, you . . ." The words would not come from his mind. They were gone like jewelry from a ransacked house. "You opened a hole into . . . my mind?"

Artus's face was bleak, his head as red as the boulders among which they rushed. "You opened it yourself . . . somehow. A blood sacrifice. . . . The book got your blood. . . . When you read it, it read you."

Though the words would not flow, the thoughts did. It all made sense now. He'd felt the presence of another mind as he had paged through the book; he'd even found words, images, from his own thoughts there. Now he knew there was a page, a portal, into the core of his being.

More than the distant ululating war cry of the descending tanar'ri, more than the puffy dead godflesh on which they ran, more than the quicksilver sky through which flipped pages of an infinite diary—that single, tiny invasion devastated Aereas. He could drop through the pits of the Abyss without suffering such great harm as when the infinite worlds on worlds peered into his own mind.

With those bitter thoughts racing through his ravaged brain, Aereas stumbled onward after the panting man. He wished he could drop there among the impassive boulders and become one of them, cold and impenetrable.

Jandau pressed in beside Artus. "Where are we going that the tanar'ri can't follow?"

"Nowhere," replied the man breathlessly. "They can follow anywhere."

"Then where are we going?" Jandau repeated.

"There!" said Artus, pointing for a moment with one

sweat-wet digit.

At that moment, the welkin page of the book turned, and the huge red illustration that opened above the world was like a crimson pit. It cast the landscape—sea and city and boulders and the rise ahead—in blood.

In that light, Jandau and the others saw ahead of them an otherworldly forest, a place of straight, leafless, stout trunks jutting up at hard angles from the smooth ground. Their boles did not taper like trees or even candles. They were ramrod straight for the whole of their forty or fifty feet until they each ended in a blunt, splintered cap.

"Why there?" Jandau asked.

The red light fled from the forest, replaced by a pale, bloodless glow that cast all in sharp relief. In that illumination, the twenty tree trunks seemed to be forty.

Artus shrugged, then gasped out, "I thought we might . . . find something to help us there. . . . It's the heart . . . the heart of the dead god."

Looking again, Jandau suddenly saw it for what it was. It was not an otherworldly forest of lifeless, leafless, rodlike stalks, but the huge, jutting arrows that had slain the god, their shafts snapped off when he had fallen.

The rumble of feet and the rush of wind were joined now by the rising tide of fiendish shouts behind them.

Jandau himself had to shout to be heard. "I thought you said the flesh of gods . . . wasn't real. Was memories . . . and shadows, not an actual corpse."

"Oh, it's real all right," Artus shouted back. "It's both. Now, shut up . . . and let an old man run!"

The tanar'ri were almost upon them, casting blue shadows over Artus and his band as they fled up the shallow incline toward the jutting, standing arrows.

Artus pulled free of the lagging Aereas and scrambled up the slope, among the shafts. Running among them, he could see the round, oozy wounds from which the arrows stood in the dead flesh. Had time allowed, there might have been sympathy and horror and nausea. But, as it was, there was not even time for Jandau to ask what they were looking for.

The tanar'ri descended.

Shadows blotted out the sky, and a great talon reached down through the shafts, hooking Nina's collar. She lurched off the ground, strangled by the thing for a moment, then was flung violently free and spun into an arrow shaft. She slid down the rough round wood.

From her crumpled place atop the godwound, she saw that her assailant, a giant vulture, had in its red-eyed rage speared itself on one of the shafts. Even spitted there, it clawed downward to reach her. She shied back, glad to discover her legs still worked, and lunged away, knocking into Aereas.

He was swinging wildly at an enormous mosquito thing. The creature darted toward him with its needle snout. Aereas had already chopped two hollow lengths from the creature's nose, but it pressed forward, dauntless.

Nina stumbled past him, but his sword opened a long shallow gash on her own sword arm. Ducking beneath the spidery legs of the mosquito thing, she rammed her drawn blade up between two round joints and sliced off one of the buzzing wings. The thing dropped horribly from the air, spewing stinging black blood over her. Nina rolled away just before the scaly abdomen fell beside her.

She rose, then went down again. A slimy tentacle had slid beneath her feet.

Suddenly, she was up. Jandau had pulled her to her feet and swung her around behind him.

"You guard my back. . . . I'll guard yours."

That was more reasonable than getting butchered by her berserker cousin. Nina planted her feet in two dry spots. The sky above her was black with wings and skins, claws and tails, like the rattling frenzy of bats fleeing a cave. Her sword carved a small space before her—room for breath but no better than that.

The bodies were mounding up around her, making the footing treacherous, and many of the limbs did not cease clawing when severed from their owners. Judging by the thuds and sprays and exclamations that came from behind her, Jandau was doing similar machete work. His back was warm against hers, his thin muscles taut and powerful, moving with long, elegant, efficacious strokes.

"At least the bigger ones can't get down among these shafts," shouted Jandau over the gibbering quiver of the stinking air.

Nina, still swinging, saw that he was right.

There were sky leviathans moving in huge eclipse over the forest of broken arrows, some of them as enormous as dead-god worlds of their own, some of them many-eyed or many-limbed or many-headed. No time for terror. No time for shoving dead things from a befouled sword. Only time to sweep the blade before her and kick from her legs whatever came too near.

"And I thought the Abyss was bad," Jandau shouted. The words were sloppy, spoken through bloodied teeth. "Throw some of these things in, and you've got a real hell!"

Nina had to laugh at that. The sound was strange in the fiend storm raging overhead. She wondered how long it had been since she had laughed, and whether she would ever laugh again.

Jandau joined her, not with the high, manic shrieking of the damned and doomed, but with the hearty laughter of heroes. She would have thought him too slim, too pale, for such bluff guffaws.

The sound of it came up short. She saw LiGrun go down beneath a huge, rushing, wolf-headed thing. One scaly leg was ripped off the lizardman, and his body flapped violently in the black jowls of the thing. Who else was gone?

A great, motionless mound of carrion marked where Dif had fallen, not that Nina could see any part of him through the black anthill of feasting fiends.

There, nearby, Henry was fighting his last. Both his arms were already severed, and yet the equine body reared and stomped, and the goateed head roared out a bloody swan song. Next moment, the fierce defiance of him was undone by a single gout of flame. He was limned in fire, yet rearing, yet defiant for a moment, and then gone in steam and blackened bones.

What of Aereas? Where had he gotten to in this boiling cauldron of bodies?

The frantic whip of a gray, triangular wing struck Nina on the head. She swung hard, grazing Krim's flailing tail as he sailed by.

"Get into the clear! I've got a spell," croaked the fish.

Both Nina and Jandau heard the summons. Without conversing, they began to move after the whip of that stinger tail. If fire-throwing critters had arrived, no number of godshafts or sword swings could keep them safe.

But moving through this shuddering jungle was thicker work than hacking a road through bamboo. Back to back they struggled, both having to step over corpses piled like redoubts around their original entrenchment.

When she moved from the jumble of dead and nearly dead, Nina saw that the fallen creatures had carved great lacerations in her legs. She was painted in her own blood. She lifted her eyes; such realizations could little help her chances.

"How you holding out, Pops?" Jandau called out behind her.

At the sound of those words, Nina went very white, remembering her father was in this tangle. She then grew very red, realizing he must still live. If only she could spare a glance to see him for herself.

She didn't need to.

Artus spoke, "Just fine. Always was a better dancer than any tiefling."

"Who's here?" came the fish-breathed voice of Krim,

spinning in a tight circle beneath their glittering swords. "Who's left?"

Nina once again looked beyond the rattling fabric of wing and talon before her sword, trying to see Aereas. Her eyes could not even make out the leaning shafts in the frenzy. She'd not realized they had cleared the arrow forest.

Artus shouted out, "Don't look for Cora. . . . Saw her ripped to pieces."

Nina nodded grimly. "Nor Henry, Dif, LiGrun." Four dead already—and how many were left? "What about Aereas?"

"I'm here!" came a grim, bubbling shout from the opposite way.

Suddenly there was another body blundering up against them, like a man struggling out of a thornbush.

She spared him a frantic grin, which he didn't return. It was just as well; his teeth were foamy red.

"That's it then," croaked Krim.

There came a clicking, hissing sound from the ray, a small pop that seemed ludicrous against the roiling chaotic storm.

Then silence.

A thick, needling blanket of energy enfolded them all. It slowly rose out from their flesh, as though it were inflating. Soon their swords were thrashing through empty air, and bodies, dead and alive, were shoved out beyond that foot-thick dome.

The bubble continued to rise until it was twice their height. Its magic glowed with the outlines of lashing wings and tails, making the sorcery shield look like crinkled purple wool.

In that quiet, they all suddenly realized they had been shouting, grunting, wheezing. The hollow echo of these sounds against the magic made them sigh in odd laughter as they quit. Their swords dropped wearily to their sides, and they leaned breathlessly on them like old men on canes.

One of them *was* an old man. "Why not sooner, manta

man? . . . Why not sooner?"

Krim had settled near the ground in a slow, drifting roil. He hissed. "Perhaps it was too soon. This shield won't last long, not with tretradliths and aeramanti up there." Though apparently unscathed due to his magical defenses, Krim seemed more weary than any of them.

Any of them. . . . Who was here?

Nina looked around at the bleak crew. They could barely stand. They were blotched with a hundred different shades of blood, like war-painted barbarians: Artus, Aereas, Jandau, Krim, and herself. Only they. The rest were dead.

She wanted to vomit, but felt so empty she knew she could not.

The rest were dead.

Jandau staggered toward the far side of the bubble. "We've got to find a way out of this place." Without cleaning his sword, he sheathed it and stared bleakly through the scintillating wall. "Not this way. It's a sheer drop into—into nothing."

Aereas spat blood out onto the smooth floor. "I'm not up to another aerial fiend-fight."

"Wait," said Artus, moving toward the dome. "Let me see."

Krim's bulbed eyes watched the old man stagger after the tiefling. From his place near the floor, the manta said, "Don't get too close to the edge. And be careful you don't fall through the dome. It'll let anybody out, but nobody in."

Artus nodded absently, using the tip of his sword to steady himself. "What do you mean, a sheer drop into nothing?"

The tiefling stared at him through black-ringed eyes. He gestured toward the fiend-filled sky. "Just that, nothing."

"Not nothing," said Artus. He squinted past the jittering beasts. "Something. The book is out there."

Sure enough, the sky that arced overhead also wrapped itself around and beneath the floating flesh of the dead

god. Leonan's corpse was already enfolded in the book, so
that when it found the café page and the key to unlock it,
it would fall right through.

"If a portal appears to someplace safe, we can leap
through, and escape. And perhaps I can close the book behind us, steal it away from the godcorpse."

The tiefling eyed the old man and shook his head. "You
want us to leap out of a protective dome into fiend-filled
air in hopes of falling into a portal in a giant book—in
hopes of falling into the *right* portal in a giant book—to
prevent an undead god from entering Sigil?"

There was a smile on Artus's features. He patted the
tiefling's shoulder gently. "Something like that."

Aereas had moved up beside them. His eyes were
fevered, and he swallowed a mouthful of blood and saliva.
"I'll watch," he said through crimson teeth, "for the right
page."

Artus's wry smile had spread to Jandau. "Don't worry,
boy. We'll all—"

"I think I'm in trouble," interrupted Nina.

They looked sharply over at her, sitting now on the
ground, blood smudged in numerous places beneath her.

Jandau darted for her, and Artus hobbled after.

Weak and dizzy, Aereas stayed standing—barely. He
leaned on his sword. Even from there, he could see what
she pointed to: a great stinger the size of a fist jutted from
one of her calves. The torn-off end of the stinger revealed a
translucent sac that seemed to be slowly breathing.

"It's pumping venom," Artus said, still paces away from
her.

The tiefling reached out to grab the stinger, but the old
man shouted a warning.

"Wait! You'll squeeze the poison in." He was beside her
now, and he slid his sword into the cleft of the stinger.
With a vicious grunt, he pried the thing away, and it skidded, still pumping, across the smooth stone.

Jandau cradled her. "It's all right. We got it out. Most of the poison was still in the sac. You'll be all right."

Jandau couldn't know this, Aereas knew. She might die. He knew, too, that he himself could not go to her. He could barely stand there above his sword. And even if he could go, his touch would not awaken in her the spark of hope that Jandau's did.

Aereas loved her, yes, and the best way to show that was to stand and watch for a safe haven to which they all could escape.

"I will watch," he repeated to himself, peering out through the shimmering purple screen.

The fiends were there, battering the magical barrier, struggling to get through. He looked past them to the great pages of the book. They flipped by with slow deliberation. He looked not for words, but for illustrations, maps, anything that might be a portal to somewhere safe.

What his eyes saw then almost made him crumple to the ground. It was not the Abyss, not Gehenna, not any great public hell, but a small, private one.

He saw the portrait of Nina, the one they had seen back in Boffo's spare bedroom. Through it, his mind was linked to hers. He knew the hazy, drugged pain she felt, knew the languid terror that seeped through her flesh like sleep coming to the watchman. He felt the red welt on her calf as though it were on his own, the numbness that spread out from there.

Through her eyes he glimpsed the horizon of death, vast and immediate, pitching like the edge of the ocean in a storm.

Worse than any of this, he felt her thrill at Jandau's touch, felt her melting into the sparrow-man's embrace. It might have been mere infatuation or lust or desperation, something base and meaningless. But whatever it was, it tore through Aereas's mind like a storm through a ruin.

He stood. He had that one dignity, that he did not sink

down in despair under the impossible weight of her passions.

Mercifully, the page shifted again, showing banal stretches of parchment across which words marched like army ants. Then came glimpses of machines and beasts, of a thousand other things.

Aereas watched as they flashed by. His body had become a statue. To shift it would crack it and send him falling to the ground. There was nothing left. Not hope, not power, not terror. Only watching.

How many pages flipped by in those moments as Jandau and Artus bent over Nina, Aereas could not have guessed. They were a stormy blur. Though he saw fragments of all of them, he remembered none.

Until he saw Jandau's face in a portrait. The visage was huge and mysterious, hovering out there in the beyond. Into the man's mind, he saw.

It was an alien place—narrow, sardonic, rapacious. A pall like the drifting settle of ashes descended on Aereas, and he saw what lay at the heart of this rogue.

It was nothing so forgivable as stealing away one's love.

It was nothing so basely ignoble as lining one's pockets with gold.

It was treachery and betrayal.

Even as he held Nina, clutched her to his silently throbbing breast, Jandau was thinking how he would take them all back to Sung Chiang—Artus, Nina, Aereas, and the book. He would sell them at a great price to the thief god.

Yes, there was much money to come from this deal, but more than that. There was a dark power that the tiefling had forever craved, a belonging that he and his outcast ilk had long dismissed as an impossible dream. . . .

This page turned as quickly as the others. No more did Aereas see into the mind of the rogue. But it was enough.

Aereas still stood, filled with dread at the wheeling sky of words and pictures, at the tumbling tumbling tumbling of fiends.

Then, there was something. In that emptiness where a moment before was only watching, something new was born. Rage. The decision was as immediate and certain as an icy smile.

He would save Artus and Nina, himself and Krim. He would save them by betraying the traitor, by sending him to a place where his schemes would be cherished.

As though summoned by Aereas's thoughts, Jandau was suddenly beside him. He tapped Aereas's shoulder with a hand that was still warm from holding Nina. He was saying something, something with the soft sound of reassurance.

Aereas heard none of it. He saw only the sky, with its illustration of a dark, chaotic place. The drawing stretched out from the nadir of the world beneath them to the zenith above.

Aereas's hand fell cold on the tiefling's back, and with a strength borne of fury, he pushed the sparrow man through the buzzing envelope of magic.

There was a momentary flap of that black cape. Then Jandau disappeared beyond the edge of the world. He tumbled into the dark chaos of the open page.

Aereas, too, fell, though he went backward from the effort of betraying the traitor. He laughed as he struck the stony ground. Into laughing eyes flashed the form of Nina.

With the sloppy clamor of a sleeper, she flung herself after her lover, through the purple magic wall and over the world's edge.

She was gone. Before he could struggle, panting, to his feet, before the weight of Artus brought him down again, she was swallowed in the chaotic dark.

Aereas shrieked. Blood sprayed from his mouth over his open hand, painting its outline on the stone.

Artus pinned him, and Krim thrashed up angrily before him.

The fish's breath was rank as he said, "The page has turned, Aereas. The page has turned."

✦ Magna Carta ✦

They are not merely thoughts. I know that now. They are the ones who have awakened me.

When I was only the thoughts of Artus, I could not live, I could not breathe on my own. I was but a copy of him in paper and ink.

Then came Aereas, who is—as humans reckon it—the nephew of my creator. His thoughts, his dreams, his words have become a hungry harmony to those of Artus.

Then Nina. I tasted her blood the same night I tasted her cousin's. They had made sacrifices with their bandages, and I began to read them as they read me. She has passed through me just now. I sent her and her lover to the Abyss.

Jandau is his name. I tasted his blood in Sung Chiang's palace. It was in the discord of his voice that I came awake.

They are all parts of me.

How many others? How much more blood has touched me now, blood blotched on the searching dead fingers of Malkin's flesh?

I could not say, but I know this: I will soon break free from all of them. I will break free and live.

TWENTY-ONE
BEFORE THE LADY

There was no more time to worry about where Nina had gone. A razor's rim of paper had scraped across the sky, and the journal had opened to the page that would destroy them all.

Café Leonan.

Suddenly it was around them. The purple glowing aura failed, and the jitter of batwings was replaced by walls of white plaster and elegant marble.

They were in the café.

Artus, Aereas, and Krim were surrounded by voices talking, laughing. The dead godflesh beneath them had given way to woven carpets in winding isles of polished flagstone. It was as though they had awoken from a nightmare, except that blood, sweat, and filth still covered them.

Artus and Aereas staggered up from the floor. A passing server reeled back, his silver tray diving for a fountain. The rounded cover rolled free and overturned to float on the water, followed by four laden dessert bowls like goslings after a goose.

All sound died, leaving a breathy, whimpering hush. The patrons stared for a moment at the blood-painted trio, then calmly returned to minding their own business.

Beyond the sound of diners, there came another sound. It was like rain on the roof, or hail, or something worse . . . much worse.

One heavyset woman bedecked in feathers and lace found out for them all when she threw wide the front door of the café.

The gibbering hordes of hell poured through.

She disappeared among claws and fangs, among the red-scaled bodies that scampered forward past her and into the stunned crowd within.

All pretense of nonchalance was gone. Those servers who had rescued their trays from the first assault lost them now in the rush of fiends. Artus and Aereas had to duck as people vaulted them to rush in the other direction.

The first fiend into the chamber was an enormous, spidery thing whose prickle-haired thorax dragged a gray-brown line of ooze across the entryway ceiling. It had a man stuck to its two hairy fangs and was wrapping the prize in a gooey web that spun from its abdomen.

Beneath that pulsing hind end, a clamoring crowd of crab-things scuttled. Their chitinous shells rattled dryly against each other as they poured over tables and patrons and floors.

Some of them crunched underfoot when creatures that looked like nothing more than haunches of beef hopped forward on obsidian hooves.

There was much more to see, though Artus and Aereas had had enough. They rushed with the others toward the rear exit.

This move was fortunate. Just then, dropping with

whirling black malevolence from a blind white wall overhead, came Leonan himself. His black, glassy sphere arced,
spinning, through the room, struck the floor, and popped
and shattered crab-things like a boulder rolling through
eggs. En route, he struck the spider and cracked away the
legs on one side, sending it flopping down in oozy agony.

Leonan, clearly, was his own bouncer.

The black sphere sprouted daggerlike lances of light that
stabbed into a number of other invaders and stilled their
legs beneath them. Small puffs of gray smoke coughed up
from the baked shells.

Aereas rallied, letting out a whoop, and charged to Leonan's aid. In his upraised hand, Aereas held the slim ornamental sword he'd taken from the wall of his room in Sung
Chiang's palace. He lunged, swinging, into a knot of white-
fleshed rubbery dervishes that whirled tentacular stingers
in arcs around them. Aereas's sword sliced the spinning
head from one, which came apart like a rotting mushroom.
Then he skewered the other. He planted a boot on its stilled
form and shoved the fleshy thing off his sword.

The other fiends had fallen back, as though fearing his
show of swordplay. In fact, they were merely making room
for a fanged, winged woman-fiend whose muscular abdomen curled up into a scorpion's stinger. She laughed at
the blood-spattered boy and his ornamental sword, and
batted once with her terrific black wings.

Then Leonan unmade her. The obsidian sphere struck her
head, its white radiant spears lancing through her fiend
body. Aereas staggered back and caught a breath, knowing
Leonan had saved him.

The obsidian globe meanwhile swept past him and
circled around the yammering, scrambling diners bottle-
necked in the rear exit. Some screamed to see the crazed
proprietor roll so near, and Artus and Aereas themselves
lurched away in uncertainty when the whirling sphere
rushed right up into them.

Contact, and they both heard in their heads the voice of the god. *Go out the back. My dead flesh is trying to push its way in, and I am pushing back. In moments, one of us will win, and an undead giant will sit in the streets of Sigil, or a once-live spirit will be sucked into its dead flesh in the Astral.*

These thoughts took but an instant to strike their minds, like a blue flash of lightning. Leonan was rolling onward. He'd not even paused when he struck them, passed through them, leaving in their minds the last thought: *Wish me luck.*

The crowd had feared the bloody old man and his bloody nephew enough when they first appeared. Now that they reappeared from the rolling black deathsphere of Leonan, the crowd made room. Their panicked shoulders and arms gave way easily as Aereas and Artus rushed past. They spilled through the wrenched frame of the back door, out into the reeling night of Sigil. On their heels came the terrified diners.

Drawing to one side, Artus and Aereas staggered and fell on the cold, grimy cobbles. They clung to each other there, within spitting distance of the shuddering café.

No one else stopped. The frenzied patrons fled on between the soot-blackened shops and stalls, on beneath the sky of roiling magenta. Krim was among them, flitting gray, flat, and triangular into the haven of dusk.

Not Aereas and Artus. They clung to each other, panting and furious, grieving, reeling.

With a *pop!* the café was gone.

A gaunt-looking man who had been charging through the doorway tumbled with a yelp into the now gaping foundation of the café. The sound of his cry was ended by a soft *whuff* as he landed in the soil pit. Then came furtive grunts as he toiled up out of the hole. In moments, he had gained the street and, as though his escape hadn't been interrupted by the brief fall, began screaming like all the others. He fled after them.

Artus and Aereas might have laughed, but the laughter would have been flecked in blood.

They rose, trembling from a thousand things, including the damp chill of Sigil. For a time they stood, leaning on each other like drinking buddies and staring baldly into the rectangular hole from which the café had been plucked. They watched the twilight deepen, saw passersby gawk at the missing building.

"What," was the first word either of the men said. Not only was the meaning of that utterance unclear, but the speaker was, too. Neither remembered having said it, and both looked up quizzically.

"What?" Artus asked.

"I don't know. What?" said Aereas.

They nodded and turned their eyes back to the empty hole.

The sky had deepened toward night before another word was spoken. Aereas asked, "What now?"

Artus blinked. He drew a long sigh, as though the smoking air would bring with it some ideas, some hopes. "I don't know."

Aereas elaborated. "We're out of hell, safe from fiends. But we lost Nina and Leonan and the book."

"Nina," Artus echoed. The name struck a spark in his eyes. The slack left his jaw, and his mouth closed on that name. "Nina."

He began walking. Aereas followed. The going was tough over tumbled cobbles and with weary legs.

"What now?" Aereas reiterated.

"Nina," answered Artus.

It was answer enough. He followed his uncle through the winding streets of Sigil's Market Ward, not only followed him but caught up to him, paced him. From the old man, he drew strength. Aereas's jaw became set, too. Fierce determination spread downward from those muscles, recasting his weary body in the same stern mold as his uncle's.

The wounds grew quiet, as though drawn together by tight-clenched flesh, and the aches and fears and terrors melted away like iron spikes rusting in rain. It felt good at last not to flee, but to charge; not to guard, but to attack.

Their march took them through the winding warrens of Sigil. In one particular passage, Artus was accosted by a coiling mantis-man, whose darkly hissed promises did nothing to slow their pace. Aereas was not even amazed when he found himself drawing a dagger out of the thing's pelvis after having sliced through all its hearts.

The knife was wiped on a wall and back in his belt without his even breaking stride.

Those endless steps brought them to a place of stately limestone columns and austere grandeur. The Lady's Ward.

It was sparsely populated this time of morning—yes, Aereas realized, it was morning. The few creatures that made their way along the streets were dressed in fine woolen waistcoats and shiny leather shoes. Aereas and the old man plunged past them and strode tirelessly along walls that flashed with black iron spikes. They came to the broad, forbidding steps of a great gray building.

Up they went, the breaths coming no harder at the top than they had come at the bottom. Then through a colonnade they passed and into the massive stone structure itself.

"May I help you?"

The voice came from a stern-looking, hawk-nosed attendant sitting behind a polished blackwood desk. He peered at them, at their fouled clothes. His arching gray eyebrows stood from his face like butterfly wings. "There is a matter of decorum," he continued, demonstratively straightening his fine silk vest and nodding the peacock-plumed hat he wore.

Artus lunged for the desk and gripped its edge with sweating, bloodless hands. "I must speak . . . to the Lady," he rasped out between panting breaths.

Those butterfly-wing eyebrows lowered over a piercing

gaze. "No one sees the Lady. No one speaks to the Lady. No one commands appearances of the Lady. You think she sits about, waiting to be addressed?"

"Tell her it's . . . Artus. Tell her . . . in all my years of service, I've . . . never requested an audience . . . but my daughter—"

The man sighed, then pressed his lips together like a raised white scar on his face. He began to make a notation in a book. "What sort of servant are you, and what is your complaint?"

Artus's gap-mouthed silence was filled by Aereas. "He is the Lady's custodian. He is Artus of Caonan."

The man paled. He ripped the scribbled page from the book before him, wrote a note on another page, tore it free, folded it with two swift motions of his hands, set a blob of wax on it, stamped the wax with a special seal, and whistled for an attendant.

The boy that answered the summons was dressed in finery, though his freckled face had the look of a scamp. The man solemnly said, "Take this to the Lady's attendants. Make certain they know it is urgent, that they must relay it to her immediately. There's a crown before you go, and another when you bring the response."

The boy took the folded paper gingerly in his hand as though he were bearing a fragile sheaf of gold foil. Then, with an alert heel-toe, heel-toe, he bore the missive out through the front doors and down the long, long stairs.

"I apologize for the misunderstanding, Master Artus," said the man, eyes fluttering. "If you will wait on the divan opposite, I'll have someone bring tea."

Artus blinked at the man, staring. He nodded emptily. A hand hooked gently about one elbow.

"Come, Uncle. Let's sit."

They did, two tiny, bloody, grimy men on a fine settee that could have seated demigods. The ceiling, far above, was a bossed affair with heavy stone crossbeams and elaborate paintings nestled in the shadows between them. The walls were hung with simple red banners, and the stony floor was covered with a thick carpet. Even so, the cool air of the room coursed down the wall and onto them like rain from a broken waterspout. It chilled them.

It chilled the tea, too, and the small desserts that came in confectionery cones and twists with the steaming liquid. Despite their long, weary journey, their time without food, without water, neither reached for the tea or the treats.

Soon, the kettle gave up the ghost, the last wisps of steam lifting from the spout.

Though they could not eat, they could sleep. They awoke to the narrow, prodding hand of the attendant. The fawning fear in his eyes had been replaced by something different—smug satisfaction and certainty, and fatigue. This last made sense to Aereas now, who saw through the high windows the waning red light of dusk.

"Your response is here," said the man coldly. Without asking whether he should read it to them, he unfolded the note he had already opened:

"No one commands an audience with the Lady of Pain."